Ralph T. H. Griffith

The Ramayan of Valmiki

Vol. II

Ralph T. H. Griffith

The Ramayan of Valmiki

Vol. II

Reprint of the original, first published in 1871.

1st Edition 2022 | ISBN: 978-3-36813-013-8

Verlag (Publisher): Outlook Verlag GmbH, Zeilweg 44, 60439 Frankfurt, Deutschland
Vertretungsberechtigt (Authorized to represent): E. Roepke, Zeilweg 44, 60439 Frankfurt, Deutschland
Druck (Print): Books on Demand GmbH, In de Tarpen 42, 22848 Norderstedt, Deutschland

THE

RÁMÁYAN OF VÁLMÍKI

TRANSLATED INTO ENGLISH VERSE

BY

RALPH T. H. GRIFFITH, M. A.,

PRINCIPAL OF THE BENARES COLLEGE.

VOL. II.

———◆———

LONDON: TRÜBNER AND CO.
BENARES: E. J. LAZARUS AND CO.

1871.

PRINTED BY E. J. LAZARUS & CO., AT THE MEDICAL HALL PRESS, BENARES.

CONTENTS

OF

THE SECOND VOLUME.

BOOK II.

THE RÁMÁYAN.

BOOK II.

CANTO XIII.

DAŚARATHA'S DISTRESS.

Unworthy of his mournful fate,
The mighty king, unfortunate,
Lay prostrate in unseemly guise,
As, banished from the blissful skies,
Yayáti, in his evil day,
His merit all exhausted, lay.[1]
The queen, triumphant in the power
Won by her beauty's fatal dower,
Still terrible and unsubdued,
Her dire demand again renewed :
' Great Monarch, 'twas thy boast till now
To love the truth and keep the vow ;
Then wherefore would thy lips refuse
The promised boon 'tis mine to choose ?'
  King Daśaratha, thus addressed,
With anger raging in his breast,
Sank for a while beneath the pain,
Then to Kaikeyí spoke again :

---

[1] Only the highest merit obtains a home in heaven for ever. Minor
degrees of merit procure only leases of heavenly mansions terminable
after periods proportioned to the fund which buys them. King Yayáti
went to heaven, and when his term expired was unceremoniously ejected, and thrown down to earth.

'Childless so long, at length I won,
With mighty toil, from Heaven a son,
Ráma, the mighty-armed; and how
Shall I desert my darling now?
A scholar wise, a hero bold,
Of patient mood, with wrath controlled,
How can I bid my Ráma fly,
My darling of the lotus eye?
In heaven itself I scarce could bear,
When asking of my Ráma there,
To hear the Gods his griefs declare,
And O, that death would take me hence
Before I wrong his innocence!'
    As thus the monarch wept and wailed,
And maddening grief his heart assailed,
The sun had sought his resting-place,
And night was closing round apace.
But yet the moon-crowned night could bring
No comfort to the wretched king,
As still he mourned with burning sighs
And fixed his gaze upon the skies:
'O Night whom starry fires adorn,
I long not for the coming morn.
Be kind and show some mercy: see,
My suppliant hands are raised to thee.
Nay, rather fly with swifter pace;
No longer would I see the face
Of Queen Kaikeyí, cruel, dread,
Who brings this woe upon mine head.'
Again with suppliant hands he tried
To move the queen, and wept and sighed:
'To me, unhappy me, inclined
To good, sweet dame, thou shouldst be kind;
Whose life is well-nigh fled, who cling

To thee for succour, me thy king.
This, only this, is all my claim:
Have mercy, O my lovely dame.
None else have I to take my part:
Have mercy: thou art good at heart.
Hear, lady of the soft black eye,
And win a name that ne'er shall die:
Let Ráma rule this glorious land,
The gift of thine imperial hand.
O lady of the dainty waist,
With eyes and lips of beauty graced,
Please Ráma, me, each saintly priest,
Bharat, and all from chief to least.'

    She heard his wild and mournful cry,
        She saw the tears his speech that broke,
    Saw her good husband's reddened eye,
        But, cruel still, no word she spoke.
    His eyes upon her face he bent,
        And sought for mercy, but in vain:
    She claimed his darling's banishment,
        He swooned upon the ground again.

CANTO XIV.

RÁMA SUMMONED.

The wicked queen her speech renewed,
When rolling on the earth she viewed
Ikshváku's son, Ayodhyá's king,
For his dear Ráma sorrowing:
' Why, by a simple promise bound,
Liest thou prostrate on the ground.
As though a grievous sin dismayed
Thy spirit ? Why so sore afraid ?
Keep still thy word.   The righteous deem
That truth, mid duties, is supreme ;
And now in truth and honour's name
I bid thee own the binding claim.
Śaivya, a king whom earth obeyed,
Once to a hawk a promise made,
Gave to the bird his flesh and bone,
And by his truth made heaven his own.[1]
Alarka, when a Bráhman famed
For Scripture lore his promise claimed,
Tore from his head his bleeding eyes
And unreluctant gave the prize.
His narrow bounds prescribed restrain
The Rivers' Lord, the mighty main,
Who, though his waters boil and rave,
Keeps faithful to the word he gave.
Truth all religion comprehends,
Through all the world its might extends :

---

[1] See *Additional Notes*, THE SUPPLIANT DOVE.

In truth alone is justice placed,
On truth the words of God are based :
A life in truth unchanging past
Will bring the highest bliss at last.
If thou the right would still pursue,
Be constant to thy word and true :
Let me thy promise fruitful see,
For bóons, O King, proceed from thee.
Now to preserve thy righteous fame,
And yielding to my earnest claim—
Thrice I repeat it—send thy child,
Thy Ráma, to the forest wild.
But if the boon thou still deny,
Before thy face, forlorn, I die.'
    Thus was the helpless monarch stung
By Queen Kaikeyí's fearless tongue,
As Bali strove in vain to loose
His limbs from Indra's fatal noose.
Dismayed in soul and pale with fear,
The monarch, like a trembling steer
Between the chariots wheel and yoke,
Again to Queen Kaikeyí spoke.
With sad eyes fixt in vacant stare,
Gathering courage from despair :
' That hand I took, thou sinful dame,
With texts, before the sacred flame,
Thee and thy son, I scorn and hate,
And all at once repudiate.
he night is fled : the dawn is near :
  n will the holy priests be here
    l me for the rite prepare
      ith my son the throne will share.
      paration made to grace
      ma in his royal place—

With this, e'en this, my darling for
My death the funeral flood shall pour.
Thou and thy son at least forbear
In offerings to my shade to share,
For by the plot thy guile has laid
His consecration will be stayed.
This very day how shall I brook
To meet each subject's altered look?
To mark each gloomy joyless brow
That was so bright and glad but now?'

   While thus the high-souled monarch spoke
To the stern queen, the morning broke,
And holy night had slowly fled,
With moon and stars engarlanded.
Yet once again the cruel queen
Spoke words in answer fierce and keen,
Still on her evil purpose bent,
Wild with her rage and eloquent:
'What speech is this? Such words as these
Seem sprung from poison-sown disease.
Quick to thy noble Ráma send
And bid him on his sire attend.
When to my son the rule is given;
When Ráma to the woods is driven;
When not a rival copes with me,
From chains of duty thou art free.'

   Thus goaded, like a generous steed
Urged by sharp spurs to double speed,
'My senses are astray,' he cried,
'And duty's bonds my hands have tied.
I long to see mine eldest son,
My virtuous, my beloved one.'

   And now the night had past away;
Out shone the Maker of the day,

Bringing the planetary hour
And moment of auspicious power.
Vaśishṭha, virtuous, far renowned,
Whose young disciples girt him round,
With sacred things without delay
Through the fair city took his way.
He traversed, where the people thronged,
And all for Ráma's coming longed,
The town as fair in festive show
As his who lays proud cities low.[1]
He reached the palace where he heard
The mingled notes of many a bird,
Where crowded thick high-honoured bands
Of guards with truncheons in their hands.
Begirt by many a sage, elate,
Vaśishṭha reached the royal gate,
And standing by the door he found
Sumantra, for his form renowned,
The king's illustrious charioteer
And noble counsellor and peer.
To him well skilled in every part
Of his hereditary art
Vaśishṭha said : 'O charioteer,
Inform the king that I am here.
Here ready by my side behold
These sacred vessels made of gold,
Which water for the rite contain
From Gangá and each distant main.
Here for installing I have brought
The seat prescribed of fig-wood wrought,
All kinds of seed and precious scent
And many a gem and ornament;
Grain, sacred grass, the garden's spoil,

---

[1] Indra, called also Puraudara, Town-destroyer.

Honey and curds and milk and oil;
Eight radiant maids, the best of all
War elephants that feed in stall;
A four-horse car, a bow and sword,
A litter, men to bear their lord;
A white umbrella bright and fair
That with the moon may well compare;
Two chouries of the whitest hair;
A golden beaker rich and rare;
A bull high-humped and fair to view,
Girt with gold bands and white of hue,
A four-toothed steed with flowing mane,
A throne which lions carved sustain;
A tiger's skin, the sacred fire,
Fresh kindled, which the rites require;
The best musicians skilled to play,
And dancing-girls in raiment gay;
Kine, Bráhmans, teachers fill the court,
And bird and beast of purest sort
From town and village, far and near,
The noblest men are gathered here,
Here merchants with their followers crowd,
And men in joyful converse loud,
And kings from many a distant land
To view the consecration stand.
The dawn is come, the lucky day;
Go bid the monarch haste away,
That now Prince Ráma may obtain
The empire, and begin his reign.'
    Soon as he heard the high behest
The driver of the chariot pressed
Within the chambers of the king,
His lord with praises honouring.
And none of all the warders checked

His entrance for their great respect
Of him well known, in place so high,
Still fain their king to gratify.
He stood beside the royal chief,
Unwitting of his deadly grief,
And with sweet words began to sing
The praises of his lord and king :
' As, when the sun begins to rise,
The sparkling sea delights our eyes,
Wake, calm with gentle soul, and thus
Give rapture, mighty King, to us.
As Mátali[1] this selfsame hour
Sang lauds of old to Indra's power,
When he the Titan hosts o'erthrew,
So hymn I thee with praises due.
The Vedas, with their kindred lore,
Brahmá their soul-born Lord adore,
With all the doctrines of the wise,
And bid him, as I bid thee, rise.
As, with the moon, the Lord of Day
Wakes with the splendour of his ray -
Prolific Earth, who neath him lies,
So, mighty King, I bid thee rise.
With blissful words, O Lord of men,
Rise, radiant in thy form, as when
The sun ascending darts his light
From Meru's everlasting height.
May Śiva, Agni, Sun, and Moon
Bestow on thee each choicest boon,
Kuvera, Varuṇ, Indra bless
Kakutstha's son with all success.
Awake, the holy night is fled,
The happy light abroad is spread ;

---

[1] Indra's charioteer.

Awake, O best of kings, and share
The glorious task that claims thy care
The holy sage Vaśishṭha waits,
With all his Bráhmans, at the gates
Give thy decree, without delay,
To consecrate thy son to-day.
As armies, by no captain led,
As flocks that feed unshepherded,
Such is the fortune of a state
Without a king and desolate'
    Such were the words the bard addressed.
With weight of sage advice impressed;
And, as he heard, the hapless king
Felt deeper yet his sorrow's sting
At length, all joy and comfort fled,
He raised his eyes with weeping red,
And, mournful for his Ráma's sake,
The good and glorious monarch spake
'Why seek with idle praise to greet
The wretch for whom no praise is meet ʼ
Thy words mine aching bosom tear,
And plunge me deeper in despair'
    Sumantra heard the sad reply,
And saw his master's tearful eye.
With reverent palm to palm applied
He drew a little space aside.
Then, as the king, with misery weak,
With vain endeavour strove to speak,
Kaikeyí, skilled in plot and plan,
To sage Sumantra thus began:
'The king, absorbed in joyful thought
For his dear son, no rest has sought:
Sleepless to him the night has past,
And now o'erwatched he sinks at last.

Then go, Sumantra, and with speed
The glorious Ráma hither lead :
Go, as I pray, nor longer wait ;
No time is this to hesitate.'
  'How can I go, O lady fair,
Unless my lord his will declare ?'
  'Fain would I see him,' cried the king,
'Quick, quick, my beauteous Ráma bring.'
  Then rose the happy thought to cheer
The bosom of the charioteer,
'The king, I ween, of pious mind,
The consecration has designed.'
Sumantra for his wisdom famed,
Delighted with the thought he framed,
From the calm chamber, like a bay
Of crowded ocean, took his way.
    He turned his face to neither side,
      But forth he hurried straight ;
    Only a little while he eyed
      The guards who kept the gate.
    He saw in front a gathered crowd
      Of men of every class,
    Who, parting as he came, allowed
      The charioteer to pass.

CANTO XV.

THE PREPARATIONS.

There slept the Bráhmans, deeply read
In Scripture, till the night had fled;
Then, with the royal chaplains, they
Took each his place in long array.
There gathered fast the chiefs of trade,
Nor peer nor captain long delayed,
Assembling all in order due
The consecrating rite to view.
The morning dawned with cloudless ray
On Pushya's high auspicious day,
And Cancer with benignant power
Looked down on Ráma's natal hour.
The twice-born chiefs, with zealous heed,
Made ready what the rite would need.
The well-wrought throne of holy wood
And golden urns in order stood.
There was the royal car whereon
A tiger's skin resplendent shone;
There water, brought for sprinkling thence
Where, in their sacred confluence,
Blend Jumná's waves with Gangá's tide,
From many a holy flood beside,
From brook and fountain far and near,
From pool and river, sea and mere.
And there were honey, curd, and oil,
Parched rice and grass, the garden's spoil,
Fresh milk, eight girls in bright attire,

An elephant with eyes of fire;
And urns of gold and silver made,
With milky branches overlaid,
All brimming from each sacred flood,
And decked with many a lotus bud.
And dancing-women fair and free,
Gay with their gems, were there to see,
Who stood in bright apparel by
With lovely brow and witching eye.
White flashed the jewelled chouri there,
And shone like moonbeams through the air;
The white umbrella overhead
A pale and moonlike lustre shed,
Wont in pure splendour to precede,
And in such rites the pomp to lead.
There stood the charger by the side
Of the great bull of snow-white hide;
There was all music soft and loud,
And bards and minstrels swelled the crowd.
For now the monarch bade combine
Each custom of his ancient line
With every rite Ayodhyá's state
Observed, her kings to consecrate.
    Then, summoned by the king's behest,
The multitudes together pressed,
And, missing still the royal sire,
Began, impatient, to inquire:
'Who to our lord will tidings bear
That all his people throng the square?
Where is the king? the sun is bright,
And all is ready for the rite.'
    As thus they spoke, Sumantra, tried
In counsel, to the chiefs replied,
Gathered from lands on every side:

'To Ráma's house I swiftly drave,
For so the king his mandate gave.
Our aged lord and Ráma too
In honour high hold all of you:
I in your words (be long your days ')
Will ask him why he thus delays.'
   Thus spoke the peer in Scripture read,
And to the ladies' bower he sped.
Quick through the gates Sumantra hied,
Which access ne'er to him denied.
Behind the curtained screen he drew,
Which veiled the chamber from the view.
In benediction loud he raised
His voice, and thus the monarch praised :
'Sun, Moon, Kuvera, Siva bless
Kakutstha's son with high success !
The Lords of air, flood, fire decree
The victory, my King, to thee !
The holy night has past away,
Auspicious shines the morning's ray.
Rise, Lord of men, thy part to take
In the great rite, awake ! awake !
Bráhmans and captains, chiefs of trade,
All wait in festive garb arrayed ;
For thee they look with eager eyes :
O Raghu's son, awake ! arise !'
   To him in holy Scripture read,
Who hailed him thus, the monarch said,
Upraising from his sleep his head :
'Go, Ráma hither lead as thou
Wast ordered by the queen but now.
Come, tell me why my mandate laid
Upon thee thus is disobeyed.
Away ! and Ráma hither bring ;

1 sleep not : make no tarrying.'
   Thus gave the king command anew :
Sumantra from his lord withdrew ;
With head in lowly reverence bent,
And filled with thoughts of joy, he went.
The royal street he traversed, where
Waved flag and pennon to the air,
And, as with joy the car he drove,
He let his eyes delighted rove.
On every side, where'er he came,
He heard glad words, their theme the same,
As in their joy the gathered folk
Of Ráma and the throning spoke.
Then saw he Ráma's palace bright
And vast as Mount Kailása's height,
That glorious in its beauty showed
As Indra's own supreme abode :
With folding doors both high and wide ;
With hundred porches beautified :
Where golden statues towering rose
O'er gemmed and coralled porticoes :
Bright like a cave in Meru's side,
Or clouds through Autumn's sky that ride :
Festooned with length of bloomy twine,
Flashing with pearls and jewels' shine,
While sandal-wood and aloe lent
The mingled riches of their scent ;
With all the odorous sweets that fill
The breezy heights of Dardar's hill.
There by the gate the Sáras screamed,
And shrill-toned peacocks' plumage gleamed.
Its floors with deftest art inlaid,
Its sculptured wolves in gold arrayed,
With its bright sheen the palace took

The mind of man and chained the look,
For like the sun and moon it glowed,
And mocked Kuvera's loved abode.
Circling the walls a crowd he viewed
Who stood in reverent attitude,
With throngs of countrymen who sought
Acceptance of the gifts they brought.
The elephant was stationed there,
Appointed Ráma's self to bear ;
Adorned with pearls, his brow and cheek
Were sandal-dyed in many a streak,
While he, in stature, bulk, and pride,
With Indra's own Airávat' vied.
Sumantra, borne by coursers fleet,
Flashing a radiance o'er the street,
   To Ráma's palace flew,
And all who lined the royal road,
Or thronged the prince's rich abode,
 · Rejoiced as near he drew.
And with delight his bosom swelled
As onward still his course he held
   Through many a sumptuous court
Like Indra's palace nobly made,
Where peacocks revelled in the shade,
   And beasts of silvan sort.
Through many a hall and chamber wide,
That with Kailása's splendour vied,
   Or mansions of the Blest,
While Ráma's friends, beloved and tried,
Before his coming stepped aside,
   Still on Sumantra pressed.
He reached the chamber door, where stood
Around his followers young and good,

_____

he elephant of Indra.

Bard, minstrel, charioteer,
Well skilled the tuneful chords to sweep,
With soothing strain to lull to sleep,
  Or laud their master dear.
Then, like a dolphin darting through
Unfathomed depths of ocean's blue
  With store of jewels decked,
Through crowded halls that rock-like rose,
Or as proud hills where clouds repose,
  Sumantra sped unchecked—
Halls like the glittering domes on high
Reared for the dwellers of the sky
  By heavenly architect.

CANTO XVI.

RÁMA SUMMONED.

So through the crowded inner door
Sumantra, skilled in ancient lore,
On to the private chambers pressed
Which stood apart from all the rest.
There youthful warriors, true and bold,
Whose ears were ringed with polished gol
All armed with trusty bows and darts,
Watched with devoted eyes and hearts.
And hoary men, a faithful train,
Whose aged hands held staves of cane,
The ladies' guard, apparelled fair
In red attire, were stationed there.
Soon as they saw Sumantra nigh,
Each longed his lord to gratify,
And from his seat beside the door
Up sprang each ancient servitor.
Then to the warders quickly cried
The skilled Sumantra, void of pride:
' Tell Ráma that the charioteer
Sumantra waits for audience here.'
The ancient men with one accord
Seeking the pleasure of their lord,
Passing with speed the chamber door
To Ráma's ear the message bore.
Forthwith the prince with duteous heed
Called in the messenger with speed,
For 'twas his sire's command, he knew,

That sent him for the interview.
Like Lord Kuvera, well arrayed,
   He pressed a couch of gold,
Wherefrom a covering of brocade
   Hung down in many a fold.
Oil and the sandal's fragrant dust
   Had tinged his body o'er
Dark as the stream the spearman's thrust
   Drains from the wounded boar.
Him Sítá watched with tender care,
   A chouri in her hand,
As Chitrá,[1] ever fond and fair,
   Beside the Moon will stand.
Him glorious with unborrowed light
A liberal lord of sunlike might,
Sumantra hailed in words like these,
Well skilled in gentle courtesies,
As, with joined hands in reverence raised,
Upon the beauteous prince he gazed
'Happy Kauśalyá! Blest is she,
The mother of a son like thee
Now rise, O Ráma, speed away
Go to thy sire without delay ;
For he and Queen Kaikeyí seek
An interview with thee to speak.'
   The lion-lord of men, the best
Of splendid heroes, thus addressed
To Sítá spake with joyful cheer :
'The king and queen, my lady dear,
Touching the throning, for my sake
Some salutary counsel take
The lady of the full black eye

---

[1] A star in the spike of Virgo hence the name of the month Chaitra
or Chait.

Would fain her husband gratify,
And, all his purpose understood,
Counsels the monarch to my good.
A happy fate is mine, I ween,
When he, consulting with his queen,
Sumantra on this charge, intent
Upon my gain and good, has sent.
An envoy of so noble sort
Well suits the splendour of the court.
The consecration rite this day
Will join me in imperial sway.
To meet the lord of earth, for so
His order bids me, I will go.
Thou, lady, here in comfort stay,
And with thy maidens rest or play'

　　Thus Ráma spake.　For meet reply
The lady of the large black eye
Attended to the door her lord,
And blessings on his head implored:
'The majesty and royal state
Which holy Bráhmans venerate,
The consecration and the rite
Which sanctifies the ruler's might,
And all imperial powers should be
Thine by thy father's high decree,
As He, the worlds who formed and planned,
The kingship gave to Indra's hand.
Then shall mine eyes my king adore
When lustral rites and fast are o'er,
And black deer's skin and roebuck's horn
Thy lordly limbs and hand adorn.
May He whose hands the thunder wield
Be in the east thy guard and shield;
May Yama's care the south befriend,

And Varuṇ's arm the west defend ;
And let Kuvera, Lord of Gold,
The north with firm protection hold.'
  Then Ráma spoke a kind farewell,
And hailed the blessings as they fell
From Sítá's gentle lips ; and then,
As a young lion from his den
Descends the mountain's stony side,
So from the hall the hero hied.
First Lakshmaṇ at the door he viewed
Who stood in reverent attitude,
Then to the central court he pressed
Where watched the friends who loved him best
To all his dear companions there
He gave kind looks and greeting fair.
On to the lofty car that glowed
Like fire the royal tiger strode.
Bright as himself its silver shone :
A tiger's skin was laid thereon.
With cloudlike thunder, as it rolled,
It flashed with gems and burnished gold,
And, like the sun's meridian blaze,
Blinded the eye that none could gaze
Like youthful elephants, tall and strong,
Fleet coursers whirled the car along :
In such a car the Thousand-eyed
Borne by swift horses loves to ride.
So like Parjạnya,¹ when he flies
Thundering through the autumn skies,
The hero from the palace sped,
As leaves the moon some cloud o'erhead.
Still close to Ráma Lakshmaṇ kept,
Behind him to the car he leapt,

¹ The Rain God.

And, watching with fraternal care,
Waved the long chouri's silver hair.
As from the palace gate he came
Up rose the tumult of acclaim,
While loud huzza and jubilant shout
Pealed from the gathered myriads out.
Then elephants, like mountains vast,
And steeds who all their kind surpassed,
Followed their lord by hundreds, nay
By thousands, led in long array.
First marched a band of warriors trained,
With sandal dust and aloe stained;
Well armed was each with sword and bow,
And every breast with hope aglow.
And ever, as they onward went,
　　Shouts from the warrior train,
And every sweet-toned instrument
　　Prolonged the minstrel strain.
On passed the tamer of his foes,
While well-clad dames, in crowded rows,
Each chamber lattice thronged to view,
And chaplets on the hero threw
Then all, of peerless face and limb,
Sang Ráma's praise for love of him,
And blent their voices, soft and sweet,
From palace high and crowded street:
'Now, sure, Kaušalyá's heart must swell
To see the son she loves so well,
Thee, Ráma, thee, her joy and pride,
Triumphant o'er the realm preside.'
Then—for they knew his bride most fair
Of all who part the soft dark hair,
His love, his life, possessed the whole
Of her young hero's heart and soul:--

' Be sure the lady's fate repays
Some mighty vow of ancient days,[1]
For blest with Ráma's love is she
As, with the Moon's, sweet Rohiṇí.'[2]
   Such were the witching words that came
From lips of many a peerless dame
Crowding the palace roofs to greet
The hero as he gained the street.

---

[1] In a former life.

[2] One of the lunar asterisms, represented as the favourite wife of the Moon. See Vol. 1. p. 9, note.

CANTO XVII.

RÁMA'S APPROACH.

As Ráma, rendering blithe and gay
His loving friends, pursued his way,
He saw on either hand a press
Of mingled people numberless.
The royal street he traversed, where
Incense of aloe filled the air,
Where rose high palaces, that vied
With paly clouds, on either side ;
With flowers of myriad colours graced,
And food for every varied taste,
Bright as the glowing path o'erhead
Which feet of Gods celestial tread.
Loud benedictions, sweet to hear,
From countless voices soothed his ear,
While he to each gave due salute
His place and dignity to suit :
' Be thou,' the joyful people cried,
' Be thou our guardian, lord, and guide
Throned and anointed king to-day,
Thy feet set forth upon the way
Wherein, each honoured as a God,
Thy fathers and forefathers trod.
Thy sire and his have graced the throne,
And loving care to us have shown :
Thus blest shall we and ours remain,
Yea still more blest in Ráma's reign.
No more of dainty fare we need,

And but one cherished object heed,
That we may see our prince to-day
Invested with imperial sway.'
  Such were the words and pleasant speech
That Ráma heard, unmoved, from each
Of the dear friends around him spread,
As onward through the street he sped
For none could turn his eye or thought
From the dear form his glances sought,
With fruitless ardour forward cast
Even when Raghu's son had past.
And he who saw not Ráma nigh,
Nor caught a look from Ráma's eye,
A mark for scorn and general blame,
Reproached himself in bitter shame.
For to each class his equal mind
With sympathy and love inclined
Most fully of the princely four,
So greatest love to him they bore.
  His circling course the hero bent
Round shrine and altar, reverent,
Round homes of Gods, where cross-roads met,
Where many a sacred tree was set.
Near to his father's house he drew
Like Indra's beautiful to view,
And with the light his glory gave
Within the royal palace drave.
Through three broad courts, where bowmen kept
Their watch and ward, his coursers swept,
Then through the two remaining went
On foot that prince preëminent.
Through all the courts the hero passed,
And gained the ladies' bower at last;
Then through the door alone withdrew,

And left without his retinue.
When thus the monarch's noble boy
  Had gone his sire to meet,
The multitude, elate with joy,
  Stood watching in the street,
And his return with eager eyes
  Expected at the gates,
As for his darling moon to rise
  The King of Rivers¹ waits.

¹ The Sea.

CANTO XVIII.

THE SENTENCE.

With hopeless eye and pallid mien
There sat the monarch with the queen.
His father's feet with reverence due
He clasped, and touched Kaikeyi's too,
The king, with eyes still brimming o'er,
Cried Rama' and could do no more.
His voice was choked, his eye was dim,
He could not speak or look on him
Then sudden fear made Ráma shake
As though his foot had roused a snake,
Soon as his eyes had seen the change
So mournful, terrible, and strange.
For there, his reason well-nigh fled,
Sighing, with soul disquieted,
　　To torturing pangs a prey,
Dismayed, despairing, and distraught,
In a fierce whirl of wildering thought
　　The hapless monarch lay.
Like Ocean wave-engarlanded
Storm-driven from his tranquil bed,
　　The Sun-God in eclipse,
Or like a holy seer, heart-stirred
With anguish, when a lying word
　　Has passed his heedless lips.
The sight of his dear father, pained
With woe and misery unexplained,
　　Filled Ráma with unrest.

As Ocean's pulses rise and swell
When the great moon he loves so well
    Shines full upon his breast.
So grieving for his father's sake,
To his own heart the hero spake:
' Why will the king my sire to-day
No kindly word of greeting say ?
At other times, though wroth he be,
 His eyes grow calm that look on me.
Then why does anguish wring his brow
To see his well-beloved now ?'
Sick and perplexed, distraught with woe,
To Queen Kaikeyí bowing low,
While pallor o'er his bright cheek spread,
With humble reverence he said :
' What have I done, unknown, amiss
To make my father wroth like this ?
Declare it, O dear Queen, and win
His pardon for my heedless sin.
Why is the sire I ever find
Filled with all love to-day unkind ?
With eyes cast down and pallid cheek
This day alone he will not speak.
Or lies he prostrate neath the blow
Of fierce disease or sudden woe ?
For all our bliss is dashed with pain,
And joy unmixt is hard to gain.
Does stroke of evil fortune smite
Dear Bharat, charming to the sight,
Or on the brave Śatrughna fall,
Or consorts, for he loves them all ?
Against his words when I rebel,
Or fail to please the monarch well;
When deeds of mine his soul offend,

That hour I pray my life may end.
How should a man to him who gave
His being and his life behave?
The sire to whom he owes his birth
Should be his deity on earth.
Hast thou, by pride and folly moved,
With bitter taunt the king reproved?
Has scorn of thine or cruel jest
To passion stirred his gentle breast?
Speak truly, Queen, that I may know
What cause has changed the monarch so'
 Thus by the high-souled prince addressed,
Of Raghu's sons the chief and best,
She cast all ruth and shame aside,
And bold with greedy words replied:
'Not wrath, O Ráma, stirs the king,
Nor misery stabs with sudden sting;
One thought that fills his soul has he,
But dares not speak for fear of thee.
Thou art so dear, his lips refrain
From words that might his darling pain
But thou, as duty bids, must still -
The promise of thy sire fulfil.
He who to me in days gone by
Vouchsafed a boon with honours high,
Dares now, a king, his word regret,
And caitiff-like disowns the debt.
The lord of men his promise gave
To grant the boon that I might crave,
And now a bridge would idly throw
When the dried stream has ceased to flow.
His faith the monarch must not break
In wrath, or e'en for thy dear sake.
From faith, as well the righteous know,

Our virtue and our merits flow.
Now, be they good or be they ill,
Do thou thy father's words fulfil:
Swear that his promise shall not fail,
And I will tell thee all the tale.
Yes, Ráma, when I hear that thou
Hast bound thee by thy father's vow,
Then, not till then, my lips shall speak,
Nor will he tell what boon I seek.'

He heard, and with a troubled breast
This answer to the queen addressed:
'Ah me, dear lady, canst thou deem
That words like these thy lips beseem?
I, at the bidding of my sire,
Would cast my body to the fire,
A deadly draught of poison drink,
Or in the waves of ocean sink:
If he command, it shall be done,—
My father and my king in one.
Then speak and let me know the thing
So longed for by my lord the king.
It shall be done: let this suffice:
Ráma ne'er makes a promise twice.'

He ended. To the princely youth
Who loved the right and spoke the truth,
Cruel, abominable came
The answer of the ruthless dame:
'When Gods and Titans fought of yore,
Transfixed with darts and bathed in gore
Two boons to me thy father gave
For the dear life 'twas mine to save.
Of him I claim the ancient debt,
That Bharat on the throne be set
And thou, O Ráma, go this day

To Daṇḍak forest far away.
Now, Ráma, if thou wilt maintain
Thy father's faith without a stain,
And thine own truth and honour clear,
Then, best of men, my bidding hear.
Do thou thy father's word obey,
Nor from the pledge he gave me stray.
Thy life in Daṇḍak forest spend
Till nine long years and five shall end.
Upon my Bharat's princely head
Let consecrating drops be shed,
With all the royal pomp for thee
Made ready by the king's decree
Seek Daṇḍak forest and resign
Rites that would make the empire thine.
For twice seven years of exile wear
The coat of bark and matted hair.
Then in thy stead let Bharat reign
Lord of his royal sire's domain,
Rich in the fairest gems that shine.
Cars, elephants, and steeds, and kine,
The monarch mourns thy altered fate
And vails his brow compassionate :
Bowed down by bitter grief he lies
And dares not lift to thine his eyes.
Obey his word : be firm and brave,
And with great truth the monarch save.'
    While thus with cruel words she spoke,
        No grief the noble youth betrayed ;
    But forth the father's anguish broke,
        At his dear Ráma's lot dismayed.

CANTO XIX.

RÁMA'S PROMISE.

Calm and unmoved by threatened woe
The noble conqueror of the foe
Answered the cruel words she spoke,
Nor quailed beneath the murderous stroke
' Yea, for my father's promise sake
I to the wood my way will take,
And dwell a lonely exile there
In hermit dress with matted hair
One thing alone I fain would learn,
Why is the king this day so stern '
Why is the scourge of foes so cold,
Nor gives me greeting as of old '
Now let not anger flush thy cheek :
Before thy face the truth I speak
In hermit's coat with matted hair
To the wild wood will I repair
How can I fail his will to do,
Friend, master, grateful sovereign too '
One only pang consumes my breast,
That his own lips have not expressed
His will, nor made his longing known
That Bharat should ascend the throne.
To Bharat I would yield my wife,
My realm and wealth, mine own dear life.
Unasked I fain would yield them all :
More gladly at my father's call,
More gladly when the gift may free

His honour and bring joy to thee.
Thus, lady, his sad heart release
From the sore shame, and give him peace.
But tell me, O, I pray thee, why
The lord of men, with downcast eye,
Lies prostrate thus, and one by one
Down his pale cheek the tear-drops run.
Let couriers to thy father speed
'On horses of the swiftest breed,
And, by the mandate of the king,
Thy Bharat to his presence bring.
My father's words I will not stay
To question, but this very day
To Daṇḍak's pathless wild will fare,
For twice seven years an exile there.'

When Ráma thus had made reply
Kaikeyí's heart with joy beat high.
She, trusting to the pledge she held,
The youth's departure thus impelled :
' 'Tis well. Be messengers despatched
On coursers ne'er for fleetness matched,
To seek my father's home and lead
My Bharat back with all their speed.
And, Ráma, as I ween that thou
Wilt scarce endure to linger now,
So surely it were wise and good
This hour to journey to the wood.
And if, with shame cast down and weak,
No word to thee the king can speak,
Forgive, and from thy mind dismiss
A trifle in an hour like this.
But till thy feet in rapid haste
Have left the city for the waste,
And to the distant forest fled,

He will not bathe nor call for bread.'
  'Woe' woe!' from the sad monarch burst,
In surging floods of grief immersed ;
Then swooning, with his wits astray.
Upon the gold-wrought couch he lay
And Ráma raised the aged king .
But the stern queen, unpitying,
Checked not her needless words, nor spared
The hero for all speed prepared,
But urged him with her bitter tongue
Like a good horse with lashes stung
She spoke her shameful speech Serene
He heard the fury of the queen,
And to her words so vile and dread
Gently, unmoved in mind, he said
 I would not in this world remain
A grovelling thrall to paltry gain,
But duty's path would fain pursue,
True as the saints themselves are true
From death itself I would not fly
My father's wish to gratify.
What deed soe'er his loving son
May do to please him, think it done
Amid all duties, Queen, I count
This duty first and paramount,
That sons, obedient, aye fulfil
Their honoured fathers' word and will
Without his word, if thou decree,
Forth to the forest will I flee,
And there shall fourteen years be spent
Mid lonely wilds in banishment
Methinks thou couldst not hope to find
One spark of virtue in my mind,
If thou, whose wish is still my lord.

Hast for this grace the king implored.
This day I go, but, ere we part,
Must cheer my Sítá's tender heart,
To my dear mother bid farewell;
Then to the woods, a while to dwell.
With thee, O Queen, the care must rest
That Bharat hear his sire's behest,
And guard the land with righteous sway,
For such the law that lives for aye.'
    In speechless woe the father heard,
Wept, with loud cries, but spoke no word.
Then Ráma touched his senseless feet,
And hers, for honour most unmeet;
Round both his circling steps he bent,
Then from the bower the hero went.
Soon as he reached the gate he found
His dear companions gathered round.
Behind him came Sumitrá's child
With weeping eyes so sad and wild.
Then saw he all that rich array
Of vases for the glorious day.
Round them with reverent steps he paced,
Nor vailed his eye, nor moved in haste.
The loss of empire could not dim
The glory that encompassed him.
So will the Lord of Cooling Rays [1]
On whom the world delights to gaze,
Through the great love of all retain
Sweet splendour in the time of wane.
Now to the exile's lot resigned
He left the rule of earth behind:
As though all worldly cares he spurned
No trouble was in him discerned.

---

[1] The Moon.

The chouries that for kings are used,
And white umbrella, he refused,
Dismissed his chariot and his men,
And every friend and citizen.
He ruled his senses, nor betrayed
The grief that on his bosom weighed,
And thus his mother's mansion sought
To tell the mournful news he brought.
Nor could the gay-clad people there
Who flocked round Ráma true and fair,
One sign of altered fortune trace
Upon the splendid hero's face
Nor had the chieftain, mighty-armed,
Lost the bright look all hearts that charmed,
As e'en from autumn moons is thrown
A splendour which is all their own
With his sweet voice the hero spoke
Saluting all the gathered folk,
Then righteous-souled and great in fame
Close to his mother's house he came.
Lakshman the brave, his brother's peer
In princely virtues, followed near,
Sore troubled, but resolved to show
No token of his secret woe.
Thus to the palace Ráma went
 Where all were gay with hope and joy ;
But well he knew the dire event
 That hope would mar, that bliss destroy.
So to his grief he would not yield
 Lest the sad change their hearts might rend,
And, the dread tidings unrevealed,
 Spared from the blow each faithful friend.

CANTO XX.

KAUŚALYÁ'S LAMENT.

But in the monarch's palace, when
Sped from the bower that lord of men,
Up from the weeping women went
A mighty wail and wild lament:
' Ah, he who ever freely did
His duty ere his sire could bid,
Our refuge and our sure defence,
This day will go an exile hence
He on Kauśalyá loves to wait
Most tender and affectionate.
And as he treats his mother, thus
From childhood has he treated us.
On themes that sting he will not speak,
And when reviled is calm and meek. '
He soothes the angry, heals offence:
He goes to-day an exile hence
Our lord the king is most unwise,
And looks on life with doting eyes,
Who in his folly casts away
The world's protection, hope, and stay.'
    Thus in their woe, like kine bereaved
Of their young calves,' the ladies grieved,

---

¹ The comparison may to a European reader seem a homely one.
But Spenser likens an infuriate woman to a cow
  ' That is berobbed of her youngling dere.' Shakspeare also makes
King Henry VI compare himself to the calf's mother that
  ' Runs lowing up and down, Looking the way her harmless young

And ever as they wept and wailed
With keen reproach the king assailed.
Their lamentation, mixed with tears,
Smote with new grief the monarch's ears,
Who, burnt with woe too great to bear,
Fell on his couch and fainted there.

Then Ráma, smitten with the pain
His heaving heart could scarce restrain,
Groaned like an elephant and strode
With Lakshman to the queen's abode
A warder there, whose hoary eld
In honour high by all was held,
Guarding the mansion, sat before
The portal, girt with many more
Swift to their feet the warders sprang,
And loud the acclamation rang,
Hail, Ráma! as to him they bent,
Of victor chiefs preëminent.
One court he passed, and in the next
Saw, masters of each Veda text,
A crowd of Bráhmans, good and sage
Dear to the king for lore and age.
To these he bowed his reverent head,
Thence to the court beyond he sped.
Old dames and tender girls, their care
To keep the doors, were stationed there.
And all, when Ráma came in view,
Delighted, to the chamber flew,
To bear to Queen Kauśalyá's ear
The tidings that she loved to hear.

---

one went.' ' Cows,' says De Quincey, 'are amongst the gentlest of breathing creatures; none show more passionate tenderness to their
young, when deprived of them, and, in short, I am not ashamed to pro-
fess a deep love for these gentle creatures.'

The queen, on rites and prayer intent,
In careful watch the night had spent,
And at the dawn, her son to aid,
To Vishnu holy offerings made.
Firm in her vows, serenely glad,
In robes of spotless linen clad,
As texts prescribe, with grace implored,
Her offerings in the fire she poured
Within her splendid bower he came,
And saw her feed the sacred flame.
There oil, and grain, and vases stood,
With wreaths, and curds, and cates, and wood,
And milk, and sesamum, and rice,
The elements of sacrifice.
She, worn and pale with many a fast
And midnight hours in vigil past,
In robes of purest white arrayed,
To Lakshmí Queen drink-offerings paid.
So long away, she flew to meet
    The darling of her soul:
So runs a mare with eager feet
    To welcome back her foal.
He with his firm support upheld
    The queen, as near she drew,
And, by maternal love impelled,
    Her arms around him threw.
Her hero son, her matchless boy
    She kissed upon the head:
She blessed him in her pride and joy
    With tender words, and said:
` Be like thy royal sires of old,
The nobly good, the lofty-souled !
Their lengthened days and fame be thine,
And virtue, as beseems thy line !

The pious king, thy father, see
True to his promise made to thee:
That truth thy sire this day will show,
And regent's power on 'thee bestow.'
   She spoke. He took the proffered seat,
And as she pressed her son to eat,
Raised reverent hands, and, touched with shame,
Made answer to the royal dame:
'Dear lady, thou hast yet to know
That danger threats, and heavy woe:
A grief that will with sore distress
On Sítá, thee, and Lakshman press.
What need of seats have such as I?
This day to Daṇḍak wood I fly
The hour is come, a time unmeet
For silken couch and gilded seat.
I must to lonely wilds repair,
Abstain from flesh, and living there
On roots, fruit, honey, hermit's food,
Pass twice seven years in solitude
To Bharat's hand the king will yield
The regent power I thought to wield,
And me, a hermit, will he send
My days in Daṇḍak wood to spend.'

   As when the woodman's axe has lopped
A Sál branch in the grove, she dropped:
So from the skies a Goddess falls
Ejected from her radiant halls.

   When Ráma saw her lying low,
Prostrate by too severe a blow,
Around her form his arms he wound
And raised her fainting from the ground,
His 'hand uphold her like a mare
Who feels her load too sore to bear.

And sinks upon the way o'ertoiled,
And all her limbs with dust are soiled.
He soothed her in her wild distress
With loving touch and soft caress.
She, meet for highest fortune, eyed
The hero watching by her side,
And thus, while Lakshman bent to hear,
Addressed her son with many a tear:
' If, Ráma, thou had ne'er been born
My child to make thy mother mourn,
Though reft of joy, a childless queen,
Such woe as this I ne'er had seen.
Though to the childless wife there clings
One sorrow armed with keenest stings,
' No child have I: no child have I,'
No second misery prompts the sigh.
When long I sought, alas, in vain,
My husband's love and bliss to gain,
In Ráma all my hopes I set
And dreamed I might be happy yet.
I, of the consorts first and best,
Must bear my rivals' taunt and jest,
And brook, though better far than they,
The soul-distressing words they say.
What woman can be doomed to pine
In misery more sore than mine,
Whose hopeless days must still be spent
In grief that ends not and lament?
They scorned me when my son was nigh;
When he is banished I must die.
Me, whom my husband never prized,
Kaikeyí's retinue despised
With boundless insolence, though she
Tops not in rank nor equals me.

And they who do me service yet,
Nor old allegiance quite forget,
Whene'er they see Kaikeyi's son,
With silent lips my glances shun.
How, O my darling, shall I brook
Each menace of Kaikeyi's look,
And listen, in my low estate,
To taunts of one so passionate?
For seventeen years since thou wast born
I sat and watched, ah me, forlorn'
Hoping some blessed day to see
Deliverance from my woes by thee.
Now comes this endless grief and wrong,
So dire I cannot bear it long,
Sinking, with age and sorrow worn,
Beneath my rivals' taunts and scorn.
How shall I pass in dark distress
My long lone days of wretchedness
Without my Ráma's face, as bright
As the full moon to cheer my sight?
Alas, my cares thy steps to train,
And fasts, and vows, and prayers are vain.
Hard, hard, I ween, must be this heart
To bear this blow nor burst apart,
As some great river bank, when first
The floods of Rain-time on it burst.
No, Fate that speeds not will not slay,
    Nor Yama's halls vouchsafe me room,
  Or, like a lion's weeping prey,
    Death now had borne me to my doom.
Hard is my heart and wrought of steel
    That breaks not with the crushing blow,
Or in the pangs this day I feel
    My lifeless frame had sunk below.

Death waits his hour, nor takes me now :
   But this sad thought augments my pain,
That prayer and largess, fast and vow,
   And Heavenward service are in vain.
Ah me, ah me ! with fruitless toil
   Of rites austere a child I sought :
Thus seed cast forth on barren soil
   Still lifeless lies and comes to naught.
If ever wretch by anguish grieved
   Before his hour to death had fled,
I mourning, like a cow bereaved,
   Had been this day among the dead.'

CANTO XXI.

KAUŚALYÁ CALMED.

While thus Kauśalyá wept and sighed,
With timely words sad Lakshman cried:
'O honoured Queen I like it ill
That, subject to a woman's will,
Ráma his royal state should quit
And to an exile's doom submit.
The aged king, fond, changed, and weak,
Will as the queen compels him speak
But why should Ráma thus be sent
To the wild woods in banishment?
No least offence I find in him,
I see no fault his fame to dim.
Not one in all the world I know,
Not outcast wretch, not secret foe,
Whose whispering lips would dare assail
His spotless life with slanderous tale
Godlike and bounteous, just, sincere,
.E'en to his very foemen dear:
Who would without a cause neglect
The right, and such a son reject?
And if a king such order gave,
In second childhood, passion's slave,
What son within his heart would lay
The senseless order, and obey?
Come, Ráma, ere this plot be known
Stand by me and secure the throne.
Stand like the King who rules below,

Stand aided by thy brother's bow:
How can the might of meaner men
Resist thy royal purpose then?
My shafts, if rebels court their fate,
Shall lay Ayodhyá desolate.
Then shall her streets with blood be dyed
Of those who stand on Bharat's side:
None shall my slaughtering hand exempt,
For gentle patience earns contempt.
If, by Kaikeyí's counsel changed,
Our father's heart be thus estranged,
No mercy must our arm restrain,
But let the foe be slain, be slain.
For should the guide, respected long,
No more discerning right and wrong,
Turn in forbidden paths to stray,
'Tis meet that force his steps should stay.
What power sufficient can he see,
What motive for the wish has he,
That to Kaikeyí would resign
The empire which is justly thine?
Can he, O conqueror of thy foes,
Thy strength and mine in war oppose?
Can he entrust, in our despite,
To Bharat's hand thy royal right?
I love this brother with the whole
Affection of my faithful soul.
Yea, Queen, by bow and truth I swear,
By sacrifice, and gift, and prayer,
If Ráma to the forest goes,
Or where the burning furnace glows,
First shall my feet the forest tread,
The flames shall first surround my head.
My might shall chase thy grief and tears,

As darkness flies when morn appears
Do thou, dear Queen, and Ráma too
Behold what power like mine can do.
My aged father I will kill,
The vassal of Kaikeyí's will,
Old, yet a child, the woman's thrall,
Infirm, and base, the scorn of all'

Thus Lakshmaṇ cried, the mighty-souled :
Down her sad cheeks the torrents rolled,
As to her son Kauśalyá spake :
' Now thou hast heard thy brother, take
His counsel if thou hold it wise,
And do the thing his words advise
Do not, my son, with tears I pray,
My rival's wicked word obey
Leave me not here consumed with woe,
Nor to the wood, an exile, go.
If thou, to virtue ever true,
Thy duty's path would still pursue,
The highest duty bids thee stay
And thus thy mother's voice obey
Thus Kaśyap's great ascetic son
A seat among the Immortals won :
In his own home, subdued, he stayed,
And honour to his mother paid.
If reverence to thy sire be due,
Thy mother claims like honour too.
And thus I charge thee, O my child,
Thou must not seek the forest wild.
Ah, what to me were life and bliss,
Condemned my darling son to miss ?
But with my Ráma near, to eat
The very grass itself were sweet.
But if thou still wilt go and leave

Thy hapless mother here to grieve,
I from that hour will food abjure,
Nor life without my son endure.
Then it will be thy fate to dwell
In depth of world-detested hell,
As Ocean in the olden time
Was guilty of an impious crime
That marked the lord of each fair flood
As one who spills a Bráhman's blood.'[1]
  Thus spake the queen, and wept, and sighed
Then righteous Ráma thus replied:
' I have no power to slight or break
Commandments which my father spake
I bend my head, dear lady, low,
Forgive me, for I needs must go
Once Kandu, mighty saint, who made
His dwelling in the forest shade,
A cow—and duty's claims he knew –
Obedient to his father, slew.
And in the line from which we spring,
When ordered by their sire the king,
Through earth the sons of Sagar clett, ·
And countless things of life bereft ˊ
So Jamadagni's son[3] obeyed
His sire, when in the wood he laid
His hand upon his axe, and smote
Through Renuká his mother's throat.
The deeds of these and more beside,
Peers of the Gods, my steps shall guide,
And resolute will I fulfil

---

[1] The commentators say that, in a former creation, Ocean grieved his mother and suffered in consequence the pains of hell.

[2] As described in Book I Canto XI.

[3] Paraśurâma

My father's word, my father's will.
Nor I, O Queen, unsanctioned tread
This righteous path, by duty led:
The road my footsteps journey o'er
Was traversed by the great of yore
This high command which all accept
Shall faithfully by me be kept,
For duty ne'er will him forsake
Who fears his sire's command to break'

   Thus to his mother wild with grief:
Then thus to Lakshman spake the chief
Of those by whom the bow is bent,
Mid all who speak, most eloquent:
'I know what love for me thou hast,
What firm devotion unsurpassed:
Thy valour and thy worth I know,
And glory that appals the foe.
Blest youth, my mother's woe is great,
It bends her neath its matchless weight:
No claims will she, with blinded eyes,
Of truth and patience recognize.
For duty is supreme in place,
And truth is duty's noblest base.
Obedient to my sire's behest
I serve the cause of duty best
For man should truly do whate'er
To mother, Bráhman, sire, he sware:
He must in duty's path remain,
Nor let his word be pledged in vain.
And, O my brother, how can I
Obedience to this charge deny?
Kaikeyí's tongue my purpose spurred,
But 'twas my sire who gave the word.
Cast these unholy thoughts aside

Which smack of war and Warriors' pride;
To duty's call, not wrath attend,
And tread the path which I commend.'
  Ráma by fond affection moved
His brothei Lakshmaṇ thus reproved ;
Then with joined hands and reveront head
Again to Queen Kauśalyá said :
   ' I needs must go—do thou consent—
To the wild wood in banishment.
O give me, by my life 1 pray,
Thy blessing ere I go away.
I, when the promised years are o'er,
Shall see Ayodhyá's town once more.
Then, mother dear, thy tears restrain,
Nor let thy heart be wrung by pain :
In time, my father's will obeyed,
Shall I return from greenwood shade.
My dear Videhan, thou, and I,
Lakshman, Sumitrá, feel this tie,
And must my father's word obey,
As duty bids that rules for aye.
Thy preparations now forgo,
And lock within thy breast thy woe,
Nor be my pious wish withstood
To go an exile to the wood.'

  Calm and unmoved the prince explained
    His duty's claim and purpose high.
  The mother life and sense regained,
    Looked on her son and made reply :
  ' If reverence be thy father's due,
    The same by right and love is mine :
  Go not, my charge I thus renew,
    Nor leave me here in woe to pine.
  What were such lonely life to me,

Rites to the shades, or deathless lot ?
More dear, my son, one hour with thee
   Than all the world where thou art not.'
As bursts to view, when brands blaze high,
   Some elephant concealed by night,
So, when he heard his mother's cry,
   Burnt Ráma's grief with fiercer might.
Thus to the queen, half senseless still,
   And Lakshman, burnt with heart-felt pain,
True to the right, with steadfast will,
   His duteous speech he spoke again ·
'Brother, I know thy loving mind,
   Thy valour and thy truth I know,
But now to claims of duty blind
   Thou and my mother swell my woe.
The fruits of deeds in human life
   Make love, gain, duty, manifest,
Dear when they meet as some fond wife
   With her sweet babes upon her breast.
But man to duty first should turn
   Whene'er the three are not combined :
For those who heed but gain we spurn,
   And those to pleasure all resigned.
Shall then the virtuous disobey
   Hests of an aged king and sire,
Though feverous joy that father sway,
   Or senseless love or causeless ire ?
I have no power, commanded thus,
   To slight his promise and decree :
The honoured sire of both of us,
   My mother's lord and life is he.
Shall she, while yet the holy king
   Is living, on the right intent,—
Shall she, like some poor widowed thing,

Go forth with me to banishment?
Now, mother, speed thy parting son,
   And let thy blessing soothe my pain,
That I may turn, mine exile done,
   Like King Yayáti, home again.
Fair glory and the fruit she gives,
   For lust of sway I ne'er will slight:
What, for the span a mortal lives,
   Were rule of earth without the right?'
He soothed her thus, firm to the last
   His counsel to his brother told:
Then round the queen in reverence passed,
   And held her in his loving hold.

CANTO XXII.

LAKSHMAN CALMED.

So Ráma kept unshaken still
His noble heart with iron will.
To his dear brother next he turned,
Whose glaring eyes with fury burned,
Indignant, panting like a snake,
And thus again his counsel spake :
'Thine anger and thy grief restrain,
And firm in duty's path remain.
Dear brother, lay thy scorn aside,
And be the right thy joy and pride.
Thy ready zeal and thoughtful care
To aid what rites should grace the heir,—
Thes· 'tis another's now to ask ;
Come, gird thee for thy noble task,
That Bharat's throning rites may be
Graced with the things prepared for me.
And with thy gentle care provide
That her fond heart, now sorely tried
With fear and longing for my sake,
With doubt and dread may never ache.
To know that thoughts of coming ill
One hour that tender bosom fill
With agony and dark despair
Is grief too great for me to bear.
I cannot, brother, call to mind
One wilful fault or undesigned,
When I have pained in anything

My mothers or my sire the king.
The right my father keeps in view,
In promise, word, and action true ;
Let him then all his fear dismiss,
Nor dread the loss of future bliss.
He fears his truth herein will fail :
Hence bitter thoughts his heart assail.
He trembles lest the rites proceed,
And at his pangs my heart should bleed.
So now this earnest wish is mine,
The consecration to resign,
And from this city turn away
To the wild wood with no delay.
My banishment to-day will free
Kaikeyí from her cares, that she,
At last contented and elate,
May Bharat's throning celebrate.
Then will the lady's trouble cease,
Then will her heart have joy and peace,
When wandering in the wood I wear
Deerskin, and bark, and matted hair.
Nor shall by me his heart be grieved
Whose choice approved, whose mind conceived
This counsel which I follow. No,
Forth to the forest will I go.
'Tis Fate, Sumitrá's son, confess,
That sends me to the wilderness.
'Tis Fate alone that gives away
To other hands the royal sway.
How could Kaikeyí's purpose bring
On me this pain and suffering,
Were not her change of heart decreed
By Fate whose will commands the deed ?
I know my filial love has been

The same throughout for every queen,
And with the same affection she
Has treated both her son and me.
Her shameful words of cruel spite
To stay the consecrating rite,
And drive me banished from the throne,-
These I ascribe to Fate alone.
How could she, born of royal race,
Whom nature decks with fairest grace,
Speak like a dame of low degree
Before the king to torture me?
But Fate, which none may comprehend,
To which all life must bow and bend,
In her and me its power has shown,
And all my hopes are overthrown.
What man, Sumitrá's darling, may
Contend with Fate's resistless sway,
Whose all-commanding power we find
Our former deeds alone can bind?
Our life and death, our joy and pain,
Anger and fear, and loss and gain,
Each thing that is, in every state,
All is the work of none but Fate.
E'en saints, inspired with rigid zeal,
When once the stroke of Fate they feel,
In sternest vows no more engage,
And fall enslaved by love and rage.
So now the sudden stroke whose weight
Descends unlooked for, comes of Fate,
And with unpitying might destroys
The promise of commencing joys.
Weigh this true counsel in thy soul:
With thy firm heart thy heart control;
Then, brother, thou wilt cease to grieve

For hindered rites which now I leave.
So cast thy needless grief away,
And strictly my commands obey.
These preparations check with speed,
Nor let my throning rites proceed.
These urns that stand prepared to shed
King-making drops upon my head,
Shall with their pure lustrations now
Inaugurate my hermit's vow.
Yet what have 1 to do with things
That touch the state and pomp of kings ?
These hands of mine shall water take
To sanctify the vow I make.
Now Lakshman, let thy heart no more
My fortune changed and lost deplore.
A forest life more joys may bring
Than those that wait upon a king.
Now though her arts successful mar
   My consecrating rite,
  Let not the youngest queen too far
   Thy jealous fear excite.
  Nor let one thought suggesting ill
   Upon our father fall,
  But let thy heart remember still
   That Fate is lord of all.'

CANTO XXIII.

LAKSHMAN'S ANGER.

Thus Ráma to his brother said ;
And Lakshman bent his drooping head.
In turns by grief and pride impelled,
A middle course of thought he held.
Then in a frown of anger, bent
His brows that chief most excellent,
And like a serpent in his hole,
Breathed fierce and fast in wrath of soul.
His threatening brows so darkly frowned,
His eyes so fiercely glanced around,
They made his glare, which none might brook,
Like some infuriate lion's look.
Like some wild elephant, full oft
He raised and shook his hand[1] aloft.
Now turned his neck to left and right,
Now bent, now raised its stately height.
Now in his rage that sword he felt
Which mangling wounds to foemen dealt.
With sidelong glance his brother eyed,
And thus in burning words replied :
'Thy rash resolve, thy eager haste,
Thy mighty fear, are all misplaced :
No room is here for duty's claim,
No cause to dread the people's blame.
Can one so brave as thou consent

---

[1] The Sanskrit word *hasta* signifies both *hand*, and the trunk of
'The beast that bears between his eyes a serpent for a hand.'

To use a coward's argument ?
The glory of the Warrior race
With craven speech his lips debase ?
Can one like thee so falsely speak,
Exalting Fate, confessed so weak ?
Canst thou, undoubting still, restrain
Suspicions of those sinful twain ?
Canst thou, most duteous, fail to know
Their hearts are set on duty's show ?
They with deceit have set their trains,
And now the fruit rewards their pains.
Had they not long ago agreed,
O Ráma, on this treacherous deed,
That promised boon, so long retained,
He erst had given and she had gained.
I cannot, O my brother, bear
To see another throned as heir
With rites which all our people hate :
Then, O, this passion tolerate.
This vaunted duty which can guide
Thy steps from wisdom's path aside,
And change the couns l of thy breast,
O lofty-hearted, I detest.
Wilt thou, when power and might are thine,
Submit to this abhorred design ?
Thy father's impious hest fulfil,
That vassal of Kaikeyí's will ?
But if thou still wilt shut thine eyes,
Nor see the guile herein that lies,
My soul is sad, I deeply mourn,
And duty seems a thing to scorn.
Canst thou one moment think to please
This pair who live for love and ease,
And 'gainst thy peace, as foes, allied,

With tenderest names their hatred hide?
Now if thy judgment still refers
To Fate this plot of his and hers,
My mind herein can ne'er agree :
And O, in this be ruled by me.
Weak, void of manly pride are they
Who bend to Fate's imputed sway :
The choicest souls, the nobly great
Disdain to bow their heads to Fate.
And he who dares his Fate control
With vigorous act and manly soul,
Though threatening Fate his hopes assail,
Unmoved through all need never quail.
This day mankind shall learn aright
The power of Fate and human might,
So shall the gulf that lies between
A man and Fate be clearly seen.
The might of Fate subdued by me
This hour the citizens shall see,
Who saw its intervention stay
Thy consecrating rites to-day.
My power shall turn this Fate aside,
That threatens, as, with furious stride,
An elephant who scorns to feel,
In rage unchecked, the driver's steel.
Not the great Lords whose sleepless might
Protects the worlds, shall stay the rite
Though earth, hell, heaven combine their powers :
And shall we fear this sire of ours?
Then if their minds are idly bent
To doom thee, King, to banishment,
Through twice seven years of exile they
Shall in the lonely forest stay.
I will consume the hopes that fire

The queen Kaikeyí and our sire,
That to her son this check will bring
Advantage, making Bharat king.
The power of Fate will ne'er withstand
The might that arms my vigorous hand ;
If danger and distress assail,
My fearless strength will still prevail.
A thousand circling years shall flee :
The forest then thy home shall be,
And thy good sons, succeeding, hold
The empire which their sire controlled.
The royal saints, of old who reigned,
For aged kings this rest ordained :
These to their sons their realm commit
That they, like sires, may cherish it.
O pious soul, if thou decline
The empire which is justly thine,
Lest, while the king distracted lies,
Disorder in the state should rise,
I,— or no mansion may I find
In worlds to hero souls assigned,—
The guardian of thy realm will be,
As the sea-bank protects the sea.
Then cast thine idle fears aside :
With prosperous rites be sanctified.
The lords of earth may strive in vain ;
My power shall all their force restrain.
My pair of arms, my warrior's bow
Are not for pride of empty show :
For no support these shafts were made ;
And binding up ill suits my blade :
To pierce the foe with deadly breach—
This is the work of all and each.
But small, methinks, the love I show

For him I count my mortal foe.
Soon as my trenchant steel is bare,
Flashing its lightning through the air,
I heed no foe, nor stand aghast
Though Indra's self the levin cast.
Then shall the ways be hard to pass,
Where chariots lie in ruinous mass ;
When elephant and man and steed
Crushed in the murderous onslaught bleed,
And legs and heads fall, heap on heap,
Beneath my sword's tremendous sweep.
Struck by my keen brand's trenchant blade,
Thine enemies shall fall dismayed,
Like towering mountains rent in twain,
Or lightning clouds that burst in rain.
When armed with brace and glove I stand,
And take my trusty bow in hand,
Who then shall vaunt his might? who dare
Count him a man to meet me there ?
Then will I loose my shafts, and strike
Man, elephant, and steed alike :
At one shall many an arrow fly,
And many a foe with one shall die.
This day the world my power shall see,
That none in arms can rival me :
My strength the monarch shall abase,
And set thee, lord, in lordliest place.
• These arms which breathe the sandal's scent,
Which golden bracelets ornament,
These hands which precious gifts bestow,
Which guard the friend and smite the foe,
A nobler service shall assay,
And fight in Ráma's cause to-day,
The robbers of thy rights to stay.

Speak, brother, tell thy foeman's name
  Whom I, in conquering strife,
May strip of followers and fame,
  Of fortune, or of life.
Say, how may all this sea-girt land
  Be brought to own thy sway :
Thy faithful servant here I stand,
  To listen and obey.'
Then strove the pride of Raghu's race
  Sad Lakshman's heart to cheer,
While slowly down the hero's face,
  Unchecked, there rolled a tear.
'The orders of my sire,' he cried,
  ' My will shall ne'er oppose :
I follow still, whate'er betide,
  The path which duty shows.'

CANTO XXIV.

KAUŚALYÁ CALMED.

But when Kauśalyá saw that he
Resolved to keep his sire's decree,
While tears and sobs her utterance broke,
Her very righteous speech she spoke:
'Can he, a stranger yet to pain,
Whose pleasant words all hearts enchain,
Son of the king and me the queen,
Live on the grain his hands may glean?
Can he, whose slaves and menials eat
The finest cakes of sifted wheat—
Can Ráma in the forest live
On roots and fruit which woodlands give?
Who will believe, who will not fear
When the sad story smites his ear,
That one so dear, so noble held,
Is by the king his sire expelled?
Now surely none may Fate resist,
Which orders all as it may list,
If, Ráma, in thy strength and grace,
The woods become thy dwelling-place.
A childless mother long I grieved,
And many a sigh for offspring heaved,
With wistful longing weak and worn
Till thou at last, my son, wast born.
Fanned by the storm of that desire
Deep in my soul I felt the fire,
Whose offerings flowed from weeping eyes,

With fuel fed of groans and sighs,
While round the flame the smoke grew hot
Of tears because thou camest not.
Now reft of thee, too fiery fierce
The flame of woe my heart will pierce,
As, when the days of spring return,
The sun's hot beams the forest burn.
The mother cow still follows near
The wanderings of her youngling dear,
So close to thine my feet shall be,
Where'er thou goest following thee.'
    Ráma, the noblest lord of men,
Heard his fond mother's speech, and then
In soothing words like these replied
To the sad queen who wept and sighed :
' Nay, by Kaikeyí's art beguiled.
When I am banished to the wild,
If thou, my mother, also fly,
The aged king will surely die.
When wedded dames their lords forsake,
Long for the crime their souls shall ache.
Thou must not e'en in thought within
Thy bosom frame so dire a sin.
Long as Kakutstha's son, who reigns
Lord of the earth, in life remains,
Thou must with love his will obey :
This duty claims, supreme for aye.
Yes, mother, thou and I must be
Submissive to my sire's decree,
King, husband, sire is he confessed,
The lord of all, the worthiest.
I in the wilds my days will spend
Till twice seven years have reached an end,
Then with great joy will come again,

And faithful to thy hests remain.'
    Kauśalyá, by her son addressed,
With love and passion sore distressed,
Afflicted, with her eyes bedewed, ·
To Ráma thus her speech renéwed :
    'Nay, Ráma, but my heart will break
If with these queens my home I make.
Lead me too with thee ; let me go
And wander like a woodland roe.'
    Then, while no tear the hero shed,
Thus to the weeping queen he said :
' Mother, while lives the husband, he
Is woman's lord and deity.
O dearest lady, thou and I
Our lord and king must ne'er deny ;
The lord of earth himself have we
Our guardian wise and friend to be.
And Bharat, true to duty's call,
Whose sweet words take the hearts of all,
Will serve thee well, and ne'er forget
The virtuous path before him set.
Be this, I pray, thine earnest care,
That the old king my father ne'er,
When I have parted hence, may know,
Grieved for his son, a pang of woe.
Let not this grief his soul distress,
To kill him with the bitterness.
With duteous care, in every thing,
Love, comfort, cheer the aged king.
Though, best of womankind, a spouse
Keeps firmly all her fasts and vows,
Not yet her husband's will obeys,
She treads in sin's forbidden ways.
She to her husband's will who bends

Goes to high bliss that never ends,
Yea, though the Gods have found in her
No reverential worshipper.
Bent on his weal, a woman still
Must seek to do her husband's will :
For Scripture, custom, law uphold
This duty Heaven revealed of old.
Honour true Bráhmans for my sake,
And constant offerings duly make,
With fire-oblations and with flowers,
To all the host of heavenly powers.
Look to the coming time, and yearn
For the glad hour of my return,
And still thy duteous course pursue,
Abstemious, humble, kind, and true.
The highest bliss shalt thou obtain
When I from exile come again,
If, best of those who keep the right,
The king my sire still see the light.'

   The queen, by Ráma thus addressed
Still with a mother's grief oppressed,
While her long eyes with tears were dim,
Began once more and answered him :
' Not by my pleading may be stayed
The firm resolve thy soul has made.
My hero, thou wilt go ; and none
The stern commands of Fate may shun.
Go forth, dear child, whom naught can bend,
And may all bliss thy steps attend.
Thou wilt return, and that dear day
Will chase mine every grief away.
Thou wilt return, thy duty done,
Thy vows discharged, high glory won ;
From filial debt wilt thou be free,

E

And sweetest joy will come on me.
My son, the will of mighty Fate
At every time must dominate,
If now it drives thee hence to stray
Heedless of me who bid thee stay.
Go, strong of arm, go forth, my boy,
Go forth, again to come with joy,
And thine expectant mother cheer
With those sweet tones she loves to hear.
O that the blessed hour were nigh
When thou shalt glad this anxious eye,
With matted hair and hermit dress
Returning from the wilderness.'

 Kauśalyá's conscious soul approved,
  As her proud glance she bent
 On Ráma constant and unmoved,
  Resolved on banishment.
 Such words, with happy omens fraught,
  To her dear son she said,
 Invoking with each eager thought
  A blessing on his head.

CANTO XXV.

KAUŚALYÁ'S BLESSING.

Her grief and woe she cast aside,
Her lips with water purified,
And thus her benison began
That mother of the noblest man :
' If thou wilt hear no words of mine,
Go forth, thou pride of Raghu's line.
Go, darling, and return with speed,
Walking where noble spirits lead.
May Virtue on thy steps attend,
And be her faithful lover's friend.
May Those to whom thy vows are paid
In temple and in holy shade,
With all the mighty saints combine
To keep that precious life of thine.
The arms wise Viśvámitra[1] gave
Thy virtuous soul from danger save.
Long be thy life : thy sure defence
Shall be thy truthful innocence,
And that obedience, naught can tire,
To me thy mother and thy sire.
May fanes where holy fires are fed,
Altars with grass and fuel spread,
Each sacrificial ground, each tree,
Rock, lake, and mountain, prosper thee.
Let old Viráj,[2] and Him who made

---

[1] See Vol. I. p. 143.

[2] The first progeny of Brahmá, or Brahmá himself.

The universe, combine to aid;
Let Indra and each guardian Lord
Who keeps the worlds, their help afford,
And be thy constant friend the Sun,
Lord Púshá, Bhaga, Aryaman.[1]
Fortnights and seasons, nights and days,
Years, months, and hours, protect thy ways.
Vrihaspati shall still be nigh,
The War-God, and the Moon on high,
And Nárad[2] and the sainted seven[3]
Shall watch thee from their starry heaven.
The mountains, and the seas which ring
The world, and Varuṇa the King,
Sky, ether, and the wind, whate'er
Moves not or moves, for thee shall care.
Each lunar mansion be benign,
With happier light the planets shine;
All Gods, each light in heaven that glows,
Protect my child where'er he goes
The twilight hours, the day and night,
Keep in the wood thy steps aright.
Watch, minute, instant, as they flee,
Shall all bring happiness to thee.
Celestials and the Titan brood
Protect thee in thy solitude,
And haunt the mighty wood to bless
The wanderer in his hermit dress
Fear not, by mightier guardians screened,
The giant or night-roving fiend;
Nor let the cruel race who tear
Man's flesh for food thy bosom scare.

---

[1] These are three names of the Sun.

[2] See Vol. I. p. 3.

[3] The saints who form the constellation of Ursa Major.

Far be the ape, the scorpion's sting,
Fly, gnat, and worm, and creeping thing.
Thee shall the hungry lion spare,
The tiger, elephant, and bear :
Safe from their furious might repose,
Safe from the horned buffaloes.
Each savage thing the forests breed,
That loves on human flesh to feed,
Shall for my child its rage abate,
When thus its wrath I deprecate.
Blest be thy ways : may sweet success
The valour of my darling bless.
To all that Fortune can bestow,
Go forth, my child, my Ráma, go.
Go forth, O happy in the love
Of all the Gods below, above ;
And in those guardian powers confide
Thy paths who keep, thy steps who guide.
May Śukra,[1] Yama, Sun, and Moon,
And He who gives each golden boon,[2]
Won by mine earnest prayers, be good
To thee, my son, in Daṇḍak wood.
Fire, wind, and smoke, each text and spell
From mouths of holy seers that fell,
Guard Ráma when his limbs he dips,
Or with the stream makes pure his lips !
May the great saints and He, the Lord
Who made the worlds, by worlds adored,
And every God in heaven beside
My banished Ráma keep and guide.'
   Thus with due praise the long-eyed dame,
Ennobled by her spotless fame,

---

[1] The regent of the planet Venus.

[2] Kuvera.

With wreaths of flowers and precious scent
Worshipped the Gods, most reverent.
A high-souled Bráhman lit the fire,
And offered, at the queen's desire,
The holy oil ordained to burn
For Ráma's weal and safe return.
Kauśalyá, best of dames, with care
Set oil, wreaths, fuel, mustard, there.
Then when the rites of fire had ceased,
For Ráma's bliss and health, the priest,
Standing without, gave what remained
In general offering,[1] as ordained.
Dealing among the twice-born train
Honey, and curds, and oil, and grain,
He bade each heart and voice unite
To bless the youthful anchorite.
Then Ráma's mother, glorious dame,
Bestowed, to meet the Bráhman's claim,
A lordly fee for duty done,
And thus again addressed her son :
    'Such blessings as the Gods o'erjoyed
Poured forth, when Vritra[2] was destroyed,
On Indra of the thousand eyes,
Attend, my child, thine enterprise !
Yea, such as Vinatá once gave
To King Suparṇa[3] swift and brave,
Who sought the drink that cheers the skies,
Attend, my child, thine enterprise'

---

[1] *Bali*, or the presentation of food to all created beings, is one of the five great sacraments of the Hindu religion it consists in throwing a small parcel of the offering, *Ghee* or rice, or the like, into the open air at the back of the house.

[2] In mythology, a demon slain by Indra

[3] Called also Garud, the King of the birds, offspring of Vinata See Vol I p. 135

Yea, such as, when the Amrit rose,
And Indra slew his Daitya foes,
The royal Aditi bestowed
On Him whose hand with slaughter glowed
Of that dire brood of monstrous size,
Attend. my child, thine enterprise !
E'en such as peerless Vishṇu graced,
When with his triple step he paced,
Outbursting from the dwarf's disguise,'
Attend, my child, thine enterprise !
Floods, isles, and seasons as they fly,
Worlds, Vedas, quarters of the sky,
Combine, O mighty-armed, to bless
Thee destined heir of happiness !'
   The long-eyed lady ceased : she shed
Pure scent and grain upon his head,
And that prized herb whose sovereign power
Preserves from dark misfortune's hour,
Upon the hero's arm she set,
To be his faithful amulet,
While holy texts she murmured low,
And spoke glad words though crushed by woe,
Concealing with obedient tongue
The pangs with which her heart was wrung.
She bent, she kissed his brow, she pressed
Her darling to her troubled breast:
'Firm in thy purpose, go,' she cried,
'Go Ráma, and may bliss betide.
Again returning safe and well,
Triumphant in Ayodhyá dwell.
Then shall my happy eyes behold
The empire by thy will controlled.

---

¹ See Vol. I. p. 199.
² See Vol. I. p. 151.

Then grief and care shall leave no trace,
Joy shall light up thy mother's face,
And I shall see my darling reign,
In moonlike glory come again.
These eyes shall fondly gaze on thee
So faithful to thy sire's decree,
When thou the forest wild shalt quit
On thine ancestral throne to sit.
Yea, thou shalt turn from exile back,
Nor choicest blessings ever lack,
Then fill with rapture ever new
My bosom and thy consort's too.
　To Śiva and the heavenly host
　　My worship has been paid,
　To mighty saint, to godlike ghost,
　　To every wandering shade.
Forth to the forest thou wilt hie,
　Therein to dwell so long:
Let all the quarters of the sky
　Protect my child from wrong.'
Her blessings thus the queen bestowed;
　Then round him fondly paced,
And often, while her eyes o'erflowed,
　Her dearest son embraced.
Kauśalyá's honoured feet he pressed,
　As round her steps she bent,
And radiant with her prayers that blessed,
　To Sítá's home he went.

CANTO XXVI.

ALONE WITH SÍTÁ.

So Ráma, to his purpose true,
To Queen Kauśalyá bade adieu,
Received the benison she gave,
And to the path of duty clave.
As through the crowded street he passed,
A radiance on the way he cast,
And each fair grace, by all approved,
The bosoms of the people moved.
  Now of the woeful change no word
The fair Videhan bride had heard,
The thought of that imperial rite
Still filled her bosom with delight.
With grateful heart and joyful thought
The Gods in worship she had sought,
And, well in royal duties learned,
Sat longing till her lord returned.
Not all unmarked by grief and shame
Within his sumptuous home he came,
And hurried through the happy crowd
With eye dejected, gloomy-browed.
Up Sítá sprang, and every limb
Trembled with fear at sight of him.
She marked that cheek where anguish fed,
Those senses care-disquieted.
For, when he looked on her, no more
Could his heart hide the load it bore,
Nor could the pious chief control

The paleness o'er his cheek that stole.
His altered cheer, his brow bedewed
With clammy drops, his grief she viewed,
And cried, consumed with fires of woe,
'What, O my lord, has changed thee so?
Vrihaspati looks down benign,
And the moon rests in Pushya's sign,
As Bráhmans sage this day declare:
Then whence, my lord, this grief and care?
Why does no canopy, like foam
For its white beauty, shade thee home,
Its hundred ribs spread wide to throw
Splendour on thy fair head below?
Where are the royal fans, to grace
The lotus beauty of thy face,
Fair as the moon or wild-swan's wing,
And waving round the new-made king?
Why do no sweet-toned bards rejoice
To hail thee with triumphant voice?
No tuneful heralds love to raise
Loud music in their monarch's praise?
Why do no Bráhmans, Scripture-read,
Pour curds and honey on thy head,
Anointed, as the laws ordain,
With holy rites, supreme to reign?
Where are the chiefs of every guild?
Where are the myriads should have filled
The streets, and followed home their king·
With merry noise and triumphing?
Why does no gold-wrought chariot lead
With four brave horses, best for speed?
No elephant precede the crowd
Like a huge hill or thunder cloud,
Marked from his birth for happy fate,

Whom signs auspicious decorate?
Why does no henchman, young and fair,
Precede thee, and delight to bear
Entrusted to his reverent hold
The burthen of thy throne of gold?
Why, if the consecrating rite
Be ready, why this mournful plight?
Why do I see this sudden change,
This altered mien so sad and strange?'
    To her, as thus she weeping cried,
Raghu's illustrious son replied:
    'Sítá, my honoured sire's decree
Commands me to the woods to flee.
O high-born lady, nobly bred
In the good paths thy footsteps tread,
Hear, Janak's daughter, while I tell
The story as it all befell.
Of old my father true and brave
Two boons to Queen Kaikeyí gave.
Through these the preparations made
For me to-day by her are stayed,
For he is bound to disallow
This promise by that earlier vow.
In Daṇḍak forest wild and vast
Must fourteen years by me be passed.
My father's will makes Bharat heir,
The kingdom and the throne to share.
Now, ere the lonely wild I seek,
I come once more with thee to speak.
In Bharat's presence, O my dame,
Ne'er speak with pride of Ráma's name:
Another's eulogy to hear
Is hateful to a monarch's ear.
Thou must with love his rule obey

To whom my father yields the sway.
With love and sweet observance learn
His grace, and more the king's, to earn.
Now, that my father may not break
The words of promise that he spake,
To the drear wood my steps are bent:
Be firm, good Sítá, and content.
Through all that time, my blameless spouse,
Keep well thy fasts and holy vows.
Rise from thy bed at break of day,
And to the Gods due worship pay.
With meek and lowly love revere
The lord of men, my father dear,
And reverence to Kauśalyá show,
My mother, worn with eld and woe:
By duty's law, O best of dames,
High worship from thy love she claims.
Nor to the other queens refuse
Observance, rendering each her dues:
By love and fond attention shown
They are my mothers like mine own.
Let Bharat and Śatrughna bear
In thy sweet love a special share:
Dear as my life, O let them be
Like brother and like son to thee.
In every word and deed refrain
From aught that Bharat's soul may pain:
He is Ayodhyá's king and mine,
The head and lord of all our line.
For those who serve and love them much
With weariless endeavour, touch
And win the gracious hearts of kings,
While wrath from disobedience springs.
Great monarchs from their presence send

Their lawful sons who still offend,
And welcome to the vacant place
Good children of an alien race.
Then, best of women, rest thou here,
And Bharat's will with love revere.
Obedient to thy king remain,
And still thy vows of truth maintain.
     To the wide wood my steps I bend :
       Make thou thy dwelling here ;
   . See that thy conduct ne'er offend,
       And keep my words, my dear.'

CANTO XXVII.

SÍTÁ'S SPEECH.

His sweetly-speaking bride, who best
Deserved her lord, he thus addressed.
Then tender love bade passion wake,
And thus the fair Videhan spake :
' What words are these that thou hast said ?
Contempt of me the thought has bred.
O best of heroes, I dismiss
With bitter scorn a speech like this :
Unworthy of a warrior's fame
It taints a monarch's son with shame,
Ne'er to be heard from those who know
The science of the sword and bow.
My lord, the mother, sire, and son
Receive their lots by merit won ;
The brother and the daughter find
The portions to their deeds assigned.
The wife alone, whate'er await,
Must share on earth her husband's fate.
So now the king's command which sends
Thee to the wild, to me extends.
The wife can find no refuge, none,
In father, mother, self, or son :
Both here, and when they vanish hence,
Her husband is her sole defence.
If, Raghu's son, thy steps are led
Where Dandak's pathless wilds are spread,
My feet before thine own shall pass
Through tangled thorn and matted grass.

Dismiss thine anger and thy doubt:
Like refuse water cast them out,
And lead me, O my hero, hence—
I know not sin—with confidence.
Whate'er his lot, 'tis far more sweet
To follow still a husband's feet
Than in rich palaces to lie,
Or roam at pleasure through the sky.
My mother and my sire have taught
What duty bids, and trained each thought,
Nor have I now mine ear to turn
The duties of a wife to learn.
I'll seek with thee the woodland dell
And pathless wild where no men dwell,
Where tribes of silvan creatures roam,
And many a tiger makes his home.
My life shall pass as pleasant there
As in my father's palace fair.
The worlds shall wake no care in me;
My only care be truth to thee.
There while thy wish I still obey,
True to my vows with thee I'll stray,
And there shall blissful hours be spent
In woods with honey redolent.
In forest shades thy mighty arm
Would keep a stranger's life from harm,
And how shall Sítá think of fear
When thou, O glorious lord, art near?
Heir of high bliss, my choice is made,
Nor can I from my will be stayed.
Doubt not. the earth will yield me roots,
These will I eat, and woodland fruits;
And as with thee I wander there
I will not bring thee grief or care.

I long, when thou, wise lord, art nigh,
All fearless, with delighted eye
To gaze upon the rocky hill,
The lake, the fountain, and the rill ;
To sport with thee, my limbs to cool,
In some pure lily-covered pool,
While the white swan's and mallard's wings
Are plashing in the water-springs.
So would a thousand seasons flee
Like one sweet day, if spent with thee.
Without my lord I would not prize
A home with Gods above the skies :
Without my lord, my life to bless.
Where could be heaven or happiness ?
   Forbid me not : with thee I go
     The tangled wood to tread.
   There will I live with thee, as though
     This roof were o'er my head.
   My will for thine shall be resigned ;
     Thy feet my steps shall guide.
   Thou, only thou, art in my mind :
     I heed not all beside.
   Thy heart shall ne'er by me be grieved ;
     Do not my prayer deny :
   Take me, dear lord ; of thee bereaved
     Thy Sítá swears to die.'
These words the duteous lady spake,
   Nor would he yet consent
His faithful wife with him to take
   To share his banishment.
He soothed her with his gentle speech ;
   To change her will he strove ;
And much he said the woes to teach
   Of those in wilds who rove.

CANTO XXVIII.

THE DANGERS OF THE WOOD.

Thus Sítá spake, and he who knew
His duty, to its orders true,
Was still reluctant as the woes
Of forest life before him rose.
He sought to soothe her grief, to dry
The torrent from each brimming eye,
And then, her firm resolve to shake,
These words the pious hero spake:
  'O daughter of a noble line,
Whose steps from virtue ne'er decline,
Remain, thy duties here pursue,
As my fond heart would have thee do.
Now hear me, Sítá, fair and weak,
And do the words that I shall speak.
Attend and hear while I explain
Each danger in the wood, each pain.
Thy lips have spoken: I condemn
The foolish words that fell from them.
This senseless plan, this wish of thine
To live a forest life, resign.
The names of trouble and distress
Suit well the tangled wilderness.
In the wild wood no joy I know,
A forest life is naught but woe.
The lion in his mountain cave
Answers the torrents as they rave,
And forth his voice of terror throws:

F

The wood, my love, is full of woes.
There mighty monsters fearless play,
And in their maddened onset slay
The hapless wretch who near them goes :
The wood, my love, is full of woes.
'Tis hard to ford each treacherous flood,
So thick with crocodiles and mud,
Where the wild elephants repose :
The wood, my love, is full of woes.
Or far from streams the wanderer strays
Through thorns and creeper-tangled ways,
While round him many a wild-cock crows :
The wood, my love, is full of woes.
On the cold ground upon a heap
Of gathered leaves condemned to sleep,
Toil-wearied, will his eyelids close :
The wood, my love, is full of woes.
Long days and nights must he content
His soul with scanty aliment,
What fruit the wind from branches blows :
The wood, my love, is full of woes.
O Sítá, while his strength may last,
The ascetic in the wood must fast,
Coil on his head his matted hair,
And bark must be his only wear.
To Gods and spirits day by day
The ordered worship he must pay,
And honour with respectful care
Each wandering guest who meets him there.
The bathing rites he ne'er must shun
At dawn, at noon, at set of sun,
Obedient to the law he knows :
The wood, my love, is full of woes.
To grace the altar must be brought

The gift of flowers his hands have sought—
The debt each pious hermit owes :
The wood, my love, is full of woes.
The devotee must be content
To live, severely abstinent,
On what the chance of fortune shows :
The wood, my love, is full of woes.
Hunger afflicts him evermore ;
The nights are black, the wild winds roar ;
And there are dangers worse than those :
The wood, my love, is full of woes.
There creeping things in every form
Infest the earth, the serpents swarm,
And each proud eye with fury glows :
The wood, my love, is full of woes.
The snakes that by the rivers hide
In sinuous course like rivers glide,
And line the path with deadly foes :
The wood, my love, is full of woes.
Scorpions, and grasshoppers, and flies
Disturb the wanderer as he lies,
And wake him from his troubled doze :
The wood, my love, is full of woes.
Trees, thorny bushes, intertwined,
Their branches' ends together bind,
And dense with grass the thicket grows :
The wood, my dear, is full of woes.
With many ills the flesh is tried,
When these and countless fears beside
Vex those who in the wood remain :
The wilds are naught but grief and pain.
Hope, anger must be cast aside,
To penance every thought applied :
No fear must be of things to fear :

Hence is the wood for ever drear.
Enough, my love: thy purpose quit:
For forest life thou art not fit.
As thus I think on all, I see
The wild wood is no place for thee.'

CANTO XXIX.

SÍTÁ'S APPEAL.

Thus Ráma spake. Her lord's address
The lady heard with deep distress,
And, as the tear bedimmed her eye,
In soft low accents made reply :
'The perils of the wood, and all
The woes thou countest to appal,
Led by my love I deem not pain ;
Each woe a charm, each loss a gain.
Tiger, and elephant, and deer,
Bull, lion, buffalo, in fear,
Soon as thy matchless form they see,
With every silvan beast will flee.
With thee, O Ráma, I must go :
My sire's command ordains it so.
Bereft of thee, my lonely heart
Must break, and life and I must part.
While thou, O mighty lord, art nigh,
Not even He who rules the sky,
Though He is strongest of the strong,
With all his might can do me wrong.
Nor can a lonely woman left
By her dear husband live bereft.
In my great love, my lord, I ween,
The truth of this thou mayst have seen.
In my sire's palace long ago
I heard the chief of those who know,
The truth-declaring Bráhmans, tell

My fortune, in the wood to dwell.
I heard their promise who divine
The future by each mark and sign,
And from that hour have longed to lead
The forest life their lips decreed.
Now, mighty Ráma, I must share
Thy father's doom which sends thee there,
In this I will not be denied,
But follow, love, where thou shalt guide.
O husband, I will go with thee,
Obedient to that high decree.
Now let the Bráhmans' words be true,
For this the time they had in view.
I know full well the wood has woes ;
But they disturb the lives of those
Who in the forest dwell, nor hold
Their rebel senses well controlled.
In my sire's halls, ere I was wed,
I heard a dame who begged her bread
Before my mother's face relate
What griefs a forest life await.
And many a time in sport I prayed
To seek with thee the greenwood shade,
For O, my heart on this is set,
To follow thee, dear anchoret.
May blessings on thy life attend :
I long with thee my steps to bend,
For with such hero as thou art
This pilgrimage enchants my heart.
Still close, my lord, to thy dear side,
My spirit will be purified :
Love from all sin my soul will free :
My husband is a God to me.
So, love, with thee shall I have bliss

And share the life that follows this.
I heard a Bráhman, dear to fame,
This ancient Scripture text proclaim :
' The woman whom on earth below
Her parents on a man bestow,
And lawfully their hands unite
With water and each holy rite,
She in this world shall be his wife,
His also in the after life.'
Then tell me, O beloved, why
Thou wilt this earnest prayer deny,
Nor take me with thee to the wood,
Thine own dear wife so true and good.
But if thou wilt not take me there
Thus grieving in my wild despair,
To fire or water I will fly,
Or to the poisoned draught, and die.'
  So thus to share his exile, she
Besought him with each earnest plea,
Nor could she yet her lord persuade
To take her to the lonely shade.
The answer of the strong-armed chief
Smote the Videhan's soul with grief,
And from her eyes the torrents came
Bathing the bosom of the dame.

CANTO XXX.

THE TRIUMPH OF LOVE.

The daughter of Videha's king,
While Ráma strove to soothe the sting
Of her deep anguish, thus began
Once more in furtherance of her plan:
And with her spirit sorely tried
By fear and anger, love and pride,
With keenly taunting words addressed
Her hero of the stately breast:
' Why did the king my sire, who reigns
O'er fair Videha's wide domains,
Hail Ráma son with joy unwise,
A woman in a man's disguise?
Now falsely would the people say,
By idle fancies led astray,
That Ráma's own are power and might,
As glorious as the Lord of Light.
Why sinkest thou in such dismay?
What fears upon thy spirit weigh,
That thou, O Ráma, fain wouldst flee
From her who thinks of naught but thee?
To thy dear will am I resigned
In heart and body, soul and mind,
As Sávitrí gave all to one,
Satyaván, Dyumatsena's son. [1]

---

[1] The story of Sávitrí, told in the Mahábhárat, has been admirably translated by Rückert, and elegantly epitomized by Mrs. Manning in *India, Ancient and Mediæval.* There is a free rendering of the story in *Idylls from the Sanskrit.*

Not e'en in fancy can I brook
To any guard save thee to look :
Let meaner wives their houses shame,
To go with thee is all my claim.
Like some low actor, deemst thou fit
Thy wife to others to commit—
Thine own, espoused in maiden youth,
Thy wife so long, unblamed for truth ?
Do thou, my lord, his will obey
For whom thou losest royal sway,
To whom thou wouldst thy wife confide—
Not me, but thee, his wish may guide.
Thou must not here thy wife forsake,
And to the wood thy journey make,
Whether stern penance, grief, and care,
Or rule or heaven await thee there.
Nor shall fatigue my limbs distress
When wandering in the wilderness :
Each path which near to thee I tread
Shall seem a soft luxurious bed.
The reeds, the bushes where I pass,
The thorny trees, the tangled grass
Shall feel, if only thou be near,   ·
Soft to my touch as skins of deer.
When the rude wind in fury blows,
And scattered dust upon me throws,
That dust, beloved lord, to me
Shall as the precious sandal be.
And what shall be more blest than I,
When gazing on the wood I lie
In some green glade upon a bed
With sacred grass beneath us spread ?
The root, the leaf, the fruit which thou
Shalt give me from the earth or bough,

Scanty or plentiful, to eat,
Shall taste to me as Amrit sweet.
As there I live on flowers and roots
And every season's kindly fruits,
I will not for my mother grieve,
My sire, my home, or all I leave.
My presence, love, shall never add
One pain to make thy heart more sad ;
I will not cause thee grief or care,
Nor be a burden hard to bear.
With thee is heaven, where'er the spot ;
Each place is hell where thou art not.
Then go with me, O Ráma ; this
Is all my hope and all my bliss.
If thou wilt leave thy wife who still
Entreats thee with undaunted will,
This very day shall poison close
The life that spurns the rule of foes.
How, after, can my soul sustain
The bitter life of endless pain,
When thy dear face, my lord, I miss ?
No, death is better far than this.
Not for an hour could I endure
The deadly grief that knows not cure,
Far less a woe I could not shun
For ten long years, and three, and one.'

While fires of woe consumed her, such
Her sad appeal, lamenting much ;
Then with a wild cry, anguish-wrung,
About her husband's neck she clung.
Like some she-elephant who bleeds
Struck by the hunter's venomed reeds,
So in her quivering heart she felt
The many wounds his speeches dealt.

Then, as the spark from wood is gained, [1]
Down rolled the tear so long restrained :
The crystal moisture, sprung from woe,
From her sweet eyes began to flow,
As runs the water from a pair
Of lotuses divinely fair.
And Sítá's face with long dark eyes,
Pure as the moon of autumn skies,
Faded with weeping, as the buds
Of lotuses when sink the floods.
Around his wife his arms he strained,
Who senseless from her woe remained,
And with sweet words, that bade her wake
To life again, the hero spake :
' I would not with thy woe, my Queen,
Buy heaven and all its blissful sheen.
Void of all fear am I as He,
The self-existent God, can be.
I knew not all thy heart till now,
Dear lady of the lovely brow,
So wished not thee in woods to dwell ;
Yet there mine arm can guard thee well.
Now surely thou, dear love, wast máde
To dwell with me in greenwood shade.
And, as a high saint's tender mind
Clings to its love for all mankind,
So I to thee will ever cling,
Sweet daughter of Videha's king.
The good, of old, O soft of frame,
Honoured this duty's sovereign claim,
And I its guidance will not shun,
True as light's Queen is to the Sun.

---

[1] Fire for sacrificial purposes is produced by the attrition of two pieces of wood.

I cannot, pride of Janak's line,
This journey to the wood decline:
My sire's behest, the oath he sware,
The claims of truth, all lead me there.
One duty, dear, the same for aye,
Is sire and mother to obey:
Should I their orders once transgress
My very life were weariness.
If glad obedience be denied
To father, mother, holy guide,
What rites, what service can be done
That stern Fate's favour may be won?
These three the triple world comprise,
O darling of the lovely eyes.
Earth has no holy thing like these
Whom with all love men seek to please.
Not truth, or gift, or bended knee,
Not honour, worship, lordly fee,
Storms heaven and wins a blessing thence
Like sonly love and reverence.
Heaven, riches, grain, and varied lore,
With sons and many a blessing more,
All these are made their own with ease
By those their elders' souls who please.
The mighty-souled, who ne'er forget,
Devoted sons, their filial debt,
Win worlds where Gods and minstrels are,
And Brahmá's sphere more glorious far.
Now as the orders of my sire,
Who keeps the way of truth, require,
So will I do, for such the way
Of duty that endures for aye.
To take thee, love, to Daṇḍak's wild
My heart at length is reconciled,

For thee such earnest thoughts impel
To follow, and with me to dwell.
O faultless form from feet to brows,
Come with me, as my will allows,
And duty there with me pursue,
Trembler, whose bright eyes thrill me through.
In all thy days, come good come ill,
Preserve unchanged such noble will,
And thou, dear love, wilt ever be
The glory of thy house and me.
Now, beauteous-armed, begin the tasks
The woodland life of hermits asks.
For me the joys of heaven above
Have charms no more without thee, love.
And now, dear Sítá, be not slow :
Food on good mendicants bestow,
And for the holy Bráhmans bring
Thy treasures and each precious thing.
Thy best attire and gems collect,
The jewels which thy beauty decked,
And every ornament and toy
Prepared for hours of sport and joy :
The beds, the cars wherein 1 ride, ˙
Among our followers, next, divide.'

 She conscious that her lord approved
Her going, with great rapture moved,
Hastened within, without delay,
Prepared to give their wealth away.

CANTO XXXI.

LAKSHMAN'S PRAYER.

When Lakshman, who had joined them there,
Had heard the converse of the pair,
His mien was changed, his eyes o'erflowed,
His breast no more could bear its load.
The son of Raghu, sore distressed,
His brother's feet with fervour pressed,
While thus to Sítá he complained,
And him by lofty vows enchained :
' If thou wilt make the woods thy home,
Where elephant and roebuck roam,
I too this day will take my bow
And in the path before thee go.
Our way will lie through forest ground
Where countless birds and beasts are found.
I heed not homes of Gods on high,
I heed not life that cannot die,
Nor would I wish, with thee away,
O'er the three worlds to stretch my sway.'
　　Thus Lakshman spake, with earnest prayer
His brother's woodland life to share.
As Ráma still his prayer denied
With soothing words, again he cried :
' When leave at first thou didst accord,
Why dost thou stay me now, my lord ?
Thou art my refuge : O, be kind,
Leave me not, dear my lord, behind.
Thou canst not, brother, if thou choose

That I still live, my wish refuse.'
   The glorious chief his speech renewed
To faithful Lakshman as he sued,
And on the eyes of Ráma gazed
Longing to lead, with hands upraised :
'Thou art a hero just and dear,
Whose steps to virtue's path adhere,
Loved as my life till life shall end,
My faithful brother and my friend.
If to the woods thou take thy way
With Sítá and with me to-day.
Who for Kaušalyá will provide,
And guard the good Sumitrá's side ?
The lord of earth, of mighty power,
Who sends good things in plenteous shower,
As Indra pours the grateful rain,
A captive lies in passion's chain.
The power imperial for her son
Has Ašvapati's daughter[1] won,
And she, proud queen, will little heed
Her miserable rivals' need.
So Bharat, ruler of the land,
By Queen Kaikeyí's side will stand,
Nor of those two will ever think,
While grieving in despair they sink.
Now, Lakshman, as thy love decrees,
Or else the monarch's heart to please,
Follow this counsel and protect
My honoured mother from neglect.
So thou, while not to me alone
Thy great affection will be shown,
To highest duty wilt adhere
By serving those thou shouldst revere.

---

[1] Kaikeyí.

Now, son of Raghu, for my sake
Obey this one request I make,
Or, of her darling son bereft,
Kauśalyá has no comfort left.'

The faithful Lakshman, thus addressed
In gentle words which love expressed,
To him in lore of language learned,
His answer, eloquent, returned :
  'Nay, through thy might each queen will share
Attentive Bharat's love and care.
Should Bharat, raised as king to sway
This noblest realm, his trust betray,
Nor for their safety well provide,
Seduced by ill-suggesting pride,
Doubt not my vengeful hand shall kill
The cruel wretch who counsels ill—
Kill him and all who lend him aid,
And the three worlds in league arrayed.
And good Kauśalyá well can fee
A thousand champions like to me.
A thousand hamlets rich in grain
The station of that queen maintain.
She may, and my dear mother too,
Live on this ample revenue.
Then let me follow thee : herein
Is naught that may resemble sin.
So shall I in my wish succeed,
And aid, perhaps, my brother's need.
My bow and quiver well supplied
With arrows hanging at my side,
My hands shall spade and basket bear,
And for thy feet the way prepare.
I'll bring thee roots and berries sweet,
And woodland fare which hermits eat.

Thou shalt with thy Videhan spouse
Recline upon the mountain's brows;
Be mine the toil, be mine to keep
Watch o'er thee waking or asleep.'
  Filled by his speech with joy and pride,
Ráma to Lakshman thus replied:
'Go then, my brother, bid adieu
To all thy friends and retinue.
And those two bows of fearful might,
Celestial, which, at that famed rite,
Lord Varun gave to Janak, king
Of fair Videha, with thee bring,
With heavenly coats of sword-proof mail,
Quivers, whose arrows never fail,
And golden-hilted swords so keen,
The rivals of the sun in sheen.
Tended with care these arms are all
Preserved in my preceptor's hall.
With speed, O Lakshman, go, produce,
And bring them hither for our use.'
So on a woodland life intent,
To see his faithful friends he went,
And brought the heavenly arms which lay
By Ráma's teacher stored away.
And Raghu's son to Ráma showed
Those wondrous arms which gleamed and glowed,
Well kept, adorned with many a wreath
Of flowers on case, and hilt, and sheath.
The prudent Ráma at the sight
Addressed his brother with delight:
'Well art thou come, my brother dear,
For much I longed to see thee here.
For with thine aid, before I go,
I would my gold and wealth bestow

G

Upon the Bráhmans sage, who school
Their lives by stern devotion's rule.
And for all those who ever dwell
Within my house and serve me well,
Devoted servants, true and good,
Will I provide a livelihood.
 Quick, go and summon to this place
  The good Vaśishṭha's son,
 Suyajna, of the Bráhman race
  The first and holiest one.
To all the Bráhmans wise and good
  Will I due reverence pay,
Then to the solitary wood
  With thee will take my way.'

CANTO XXXII.

THE GIFT OF THE TREASURES.

That speech so noble which conveyed
His friendly wish, the chief obeyed.
With steps made swift by anxious thought
The wise Suyajna's home he sought.
Him in the hall of Fire[1] he found,
And bent before him to the ground:
' O friend, to Ráma's house return,
Who now performs a task most stern.'
He, when his noonday rites were done,
Went forth with fair Sumitrá's son,
And came to Ráma's bright abode
Rich in the love which Lakshmí showed.
The son of Raghu, with his dame,
With joined hands met him as he came,
Showing to him who Scripture knew
The worship that is Agni's due.
With armlets, bracelets, collars, rings,
With costly pearls on golden strings,
With many a gem for neck and limb
The son of Raghu honoured him.
Then Ráma, at his wife's request,
The wise Suyajna thus addressed:
' Accept a necklace too to deck
With golden strings thy spouse's neck.
And Sítá here, my friend, were glad
A girdle to her gift to add.

---

[1] The chapel where the sacred fire used in worship is kept.

And many a bracelet wrought with care,
And many an armlet rich and rare,
My wife to thine is fain to give,
Departing in the wood to live.
A bed by skilful workmen made,
With gold and various gems inlaid—
This too, before she goes, would she
Present, O saintly friend, to thee.
Thine be my elephant, so famed,
My uncle's present, Victor named;
And let a thousand coins of gold,
Great Bráhman, with the gift be told.'
Thus Ráma spoke: nor he declined
The noble gifts for him designed.
On Ráma, Lakshman, Sítá he
Invoked all high felicity.

In pleasant words then Ráma gave
His hest to Lakshman prompt and brave,
As Brahmá speaks for Him to hear
Who rules the Gods' celestial sphere:
'To the two best of Bráhmans run;
Agastya bring, and Kuśik's son,
And precious gifts upon them rain,
Like fostering floods upon the grain.
O long-armed Prince of Raghu's line,
Delight them with a thousand kine,
And many a fair and costly gem,
With gold and silver, give to them.
To him, so deep in Scripture, who,
To Queen Kauśalyá ever true,
Serves her with blessing and respect,
Chief of the Taittiríya sect [1]—

---

[1] The students and teachers of the Taittiríya portion of the Yajur Veda.

To him, with women-slaves, present
A chariot rich with ornament,
And costly robes of silk beside,
Until the sage be satisfied.
On Chitrarátha, true and dear,
My tuneful bard and charioteer,
Gems, robes, and plenteous wealth confer
Mine ancient friend and minister.
And these who go with staff in hand,
Grammarians trained, a numerous band,
Who their deep study only prize,
Nor think of other exercise,
Who toil not, loving dainty fare,
Whose praises e'en the good declare—
On these be eighty cars bestowed,
And each with precious treasures load.
A thousand bulls for them suffice,
Two hundred elephants of price,
And let a thousand kine beside
The dainties of each meal provide.
The throng who sacred girdles wear,
And on Kauśalyá wait with care—
A thousand golden coins shall please,
Son of Sumitrá, each of these.
Let all, dear Lakshman, of the train
These special gifts of honour gain:
My mother will rejoice to know
Her Bráhmans have been cherished so.'
　　Then Raghu's son addressed the crowd
Who round him stood and wept aloud,
When he to all who thronged the court
Had dealt his wealth for their support:
'In Lakshman's house and mine remain,
And guard them till I come again.'

To all his people sad with grief,
In loving words thus spoke their chief,
Then bade his treasure-keeper bring
Gold, silver, and each precious thing.
Then straight the servants went and bore
Back to their chief the wealth in store.
Before the people's eyes it shone,
A glorious pile to look upon.
The prince of men with Lakshman's aid
Parted the treasures there displayed,
Gave to the poor, the young, the old,
And twice-born men, the gems and gold.

A Bráhman, long in evil case,
Named Trijat, born of Garga's race,
Earned ever toiling in a wood
With spade and plough his livelihood.
The youthful wife, his babes who bore,
Their indigence felt more and more.
Thus to the aged man she spake:
' Hear this my word: my counsel take.
Come, throw thy spade and plough away;
To virtuous Ráma go to-day,
And somewhat of his kindness pray.'

He heard the words she spoke: around
His limbs his ragged cloth he wound,
And took his journey by the road
That led to Ráma's fair abode.
To the fifth court he made his way;
Nor met the Bráhman check or stay.
Brighu, Angiras[1] could not be
Brighter with saintly light than he.
To Ráma's presence on he pressed,

----

[1] Two of the ten divine personages called *Prajápatis* and *Brahmá-díkas* who were first created by Brahmá.

And thus the noble chief addressed:
‘O Ráma, poor and weak am I,
And many children round me cry.
Scant living in the woods I earn:
On me thine eye of pity turn.’
And Ráma, bent on sport and jest,
The suppliant Bráhman thus addressed:
‘O aged man, one thousand kine,
Yet undistributed, are mine.
The cows on thee will I bestow
As far as thou thy staff canst throw.’
   The Bráhman heard. In eager haste
He bound his cloth around his waist.
Then round his head his staff he whirled,
And forth with mightiest effort hurled.
Cast from his hand it flew, and sank
To earth on Sarjú’s farther bank,
Where herds of kine in thousands fed
Near to the well-stocked bullock shed.
And all the cows that wandered o’er
The meadow, far as Sarjú’s shore,
At Ráma’s word the herdsmen drove
To Trijat’s cottage in the grove.
He drew the Bráhman to his breast,
And thus with calming words addressed:
‘Now be not angry, Sire, I pray:
This jest of mine was meant in play.
These thousand kine, but not alone,
Their herdsmen too, are all thine own.
And wealth beside I give thee: speak,
Thine shall be all thy heart can seek.’
   Thus Ráma spake. And Trijat prayed
For means his sacrifice to aid.
And Ráma gave much wealth, required
To speed his offering as desired.

CANTO XXXIII.

THE PEOPLE'S LAMENT.

———

Thus Sítá and the princes brave
Much wealth to all the Bráhmans gave.
Then to the monarch's house the three
Went forth the aged king to see.
The princes from two servants took
Those heavenly arms of glorious look,
Adorned with garland and with band
By Sítá's beantifying hand.
On each high house a mournful throng
Had gathered ere they passed along,
Who gazed in pure unselfish woe
From turret, roof, and portico.
So dense the crowd that blocked the ways,
The rest, unable there to gaze,
Were fain each terrace to ascend,
And thence their eyes on Ráma bend.
Then as the gathered multitude
On foot their well-loved Ráma viewed,
No royal shade to screen his head,
Such words, disturbed by grief, they said:
' O look, our hero, wont to ride
Leading a host in perfect pride—
Now Lakshman, sole of all his friends,
With Sítá on his steps attends.
Though he has known the sweets of power,
And poured his gifts in liberal shower,
From duty's path he will not swerve,

But still his father's truth preserve.
And she whose form so soft and fair
Was veiled from spirits of the air,
Now walks unsheltered from the day,
Seen by the crowds who throng the way.
Ah, for that gently-nurtured form !
How will it fade with sun and storm !
How will the rain, the cold, the heat
Mar fragrant breast and tinted feet !
Surely some demon has possessed
His sire, and speaks within his breast,
Or how could one that is a king
Thus send his dear son wandering ?
It were a deed unkindly done
To banish e'en a worthless son :
But what, when his pure life has gained
The hearts of all, by love enchained ?
Six sovereign virtues join to grace
Ráma the foremost of his race :
Tender and kind and pure is he,
Docile, religious, passion-free.
Hence misery strikes not him alone :
In bitterest grief the people moan;
Like creatures of the stream, when dry
In the great heat the channels lie.
The world is mournful with the grief
That falls on its beloved chief,
As, when the root is hewn away,
Tree, fruit, and flower, and bud decay.
The soul of duty, bright to see,
He is the root of you and me ;
And all of us, who share his grief,
His branches, blossom, fruit, and leaf.
Now like the faithful Lakshman, we

Will follow and be true as he;
Our wives and kinsmen call with speed,
And hasten where our lord shall lead.
Yes, we will leave each well-loved spot,
The field, the garden, and the cot,
And, sharers of his weal and woe,
Behind the pious Ráma go.
Our houses, empty of their stores,
With ruined courts and broken doors,
With all their treasures borne away,
And gear that made them bright and gay:
O'errun by rats, with dust o'erspread,
Shrines, whence the deities have fled,
Where not a hand the water pours,
Or sweeps the long-neglected floors,
No incense loads the evening air,
No Bráhmans chant the text and prayer,
No fire of sacrifice is bright,
No gift is known, no sacred rite;
With floors which broken vessels strew,
As if our woes had crushed them too—
Of these be stern Kaikeyí queen,
And rule o'er homes where we have been.
The wood where Ráma's feet may roam
Shall be our city and our home,
And this fair city we forsake,
Our flight a wilderness shall make.
Each serpent from his hole shall hie,
The birds and beasts from mountains fly,
Lions and elephants in fear
Shall quit the woods when we come near,
Yield the broad wilds for us to range,
And take our city in exchange.
With Ráma will we hence, content

If, where he is, our days be spent.'
  Such were the varied words the crowd
Of all conditions spoke aloud.
And Ráma heard their speeches, yet
Changed not his purpose firmly set.
His father's palace soon he neared,
That like Kailása's hill appeared.
Like a wild elephant he strode
Right onward to the bright abode.
Within the palace court he stepped,
Where ordered bands their station kept,
And saw Sumantra standing near
With down-cast eye and gloomy cheer.

CANTO XXXIV.

RÁMA IN THE PALACE.

The dark incomparable chief
Whose eye was like a lotus leaf,
Cried to the mournful charioteer,
'Go tell my sire that I am here.'
 Sumantra, sad and all dismayed,
The chieftain's order swift obeyed.
Within the palace doors he hied
And saw the king, who wept and sighed.
Like the great sun when wrapped in shade,
Like fire by ashes overlaid,
Or like a pool with waters dried,
So lay the world's great lord and pride.
A while the wise Sumantra gazed
On him whose senses woe had dazed,
Grieving for Ráma. Near he drew
With hands upraised in reverence due.
With blessing first his king he hailed;
Then with a voice that well-nigh failed,
In trembling accents soft and low
Addressed the monarch in his woe:
'The prince of men, thy Ráma, waits
To see thee at the palace gates.
His wealth to Bráhmans he has dealt,
And all who in his home have dwelt.
Admit thy son. His friends have heard
His kind farewell and parting word.
He longs to see thee first, and then

Will seek the wilds, O King of men.
He, with each princely virtue's blaze,
Shines as the sun engirt by rays.'
   The truthful king who loved to keep
The law, profound as Ocean's deep,
And stainless as the dark blue sky,
Thus to Sumantra made reply:
'Go then, Sumantra, go and call
My wives and ladies one and all.
Drawn round me shall they fill the place
When I behold my Ráma's face.'
   Quick to the inner rooms he sped,
And thus to all the women said,
'Come, at the summons of the king:
Come all, and make no tarrying.'
   Their husband's word, by him conveyed,
Soon as they heard, the dames obeyed,
And following his guidance all
Came thronging to the regal hall.
In number half seven hundred, they,
All lovely dames, in long array,
With their bright eyes for weeping red,
To stand round Queen Kauśalyá, sped.
They gathered, and the monarch viewed
One moment all the multitude,
Then to Sumantra spoke and said:
'Now let my son be hither led.'
   Sumantra went. Then Ráma came,
And Lakshmaṇ, and the Maithil dame,
And, as he led them on, their guide
Straight to the monarch's presence hied.
When yet far off the father saw
His son with raised palms toward him draw,
Girt by his ladies, sick with woes,

Swift from his royal seat he rose.
With all his strength the aged man
To meet his darling Ráma ran,
But trembling, wild with dark despair,
Fell on the ground and fainted there.
And Lakshmaṇ, wont in cars to ride,
And Ráma, threw them by the side
Of the poor miserable king,
Half lifeless with his sorrow's sting.
Throughout the spacious hall up went
A thousand women's wild lament:
'Ah Ráma!' thus they wailed and wept,
And anklets tinkled as they stepped.
Around his body, weeping, threw
Their loving arms the brothers two,
And then, with Sítá's gentle aid,
The king upon a couch was laid.
At length to earth's imperial lord,
When life and knowledge were restored,
Though seas of woe went o'er his head,
With suppliant hands thus Ráma said:
'Lord of us all, great King, thou art:
Bid me farewell before we part.
To Daṇḍak wood this day I go:
One blessing and one look bestow.
Let Lakshmaṇ my companion be,
And Sítá also follow me.
With truthful pleas I sought to bend
Their purpose; but no ear they lend.
Now cast this sorrow from thy heart,
And let us all, great King, depart.
As Brahmá sends his children, so
Let Lakshmaṇ, me, and Sítá go.'
    He stood unmoved, and watched intent

Until the king should grant consent.
Upon his son his eyes he cast,
And thus the monarch spake at last:
'O Ráma, by her arts enslaved,
I gave the boons Kaikeyí craved,
Unfit to reign, by her misled:
Be ruler in thy father's stead.'
   Thus by the lord of men addressed,
Ráma, of virtue's friends the best,
In lore of language duly learned,
His answer, reverent, thus returned:
'A thousand years, O King, remain
O'er this our city still to reign.
I in the woods my life will lead:
The lust of rule no more I heed.
Nine years and five I there will spend,
And when the portioned days shall end,
Will come, my vows and exile o'er,
And clasp thy feet, my King, once more.'
   A captive in the snare of truth,
Weeping, distressed with woe and ruth,
Thus spake the monarch, while the queen
Kaikeyí urged him on unseen: ·
'Go then, O Ráma, and begin
Thy course unvext by fear and sin:
Go, my beloved son, and earn
Success, and joy, and safe return.
So fast the bonds of duty bind,
O Raghu's son, thy truthful mind,
That naught can turn thee back, or guide
Thy will so strongly fortified.
But O, a little longer stay,
Nor turn thy steps this night away,
That I one little day—alas!

One only—with my son may pass.
Me and thy mother do not slight,
But stay, my son, with me to-night;
With every dainty please thy taste,
And seek to-morrow morn the waste.
Hard is thy task, O Raghu's son,
Dire is the toil thou wilt not shun,
Far to the lonely wood to flee,
And leave thy friends for love of me.
I swear it by my truth, believe,
For thee, my son, I deeply grieve,
Misguided by the traitress dame
With hidden guile like smouldering flame.
Now, by her wicked counsel stirred,
Thou fain wouldst keep my plighted word.
No marvel that my eldest born
Would hold me true when I have sworn.'
  Then Ráma having calmly heard
His wretched father speak each word,
With Lakshman standing by his side
Thus, humbly, to the king replied :
'If dainties now my taste regale,
To-morrow must those dainties fail.
This day departure I prefer
To all that wealth can minister.
O'er this fair land, no longer mine,
Which I, with all her realms, resign,
Her multitudes of men, her grain,
Her stores of wealth, let Bharat reign.
And let the promised boon which thou
Wast pleased to grant the queen ere now,
Be hers in full. Be true, O King,
Kind giver of each precious thing.
Thy spoken word I still will heed,

Obeying all thy lips decreed;
And fourteen years in woods will dwell
With those who live in glade and dell.
No hopes of power my heart can touch,
No selfish joys attract so much
As, son of Raghu, to fulfil
With heart and soul my father's will.
Dismiss, dismiss thy needless woe,
Nor let those drowning torrents flow:
The Lord of Rivers in his pride
Keeps to the banks that bar his tide.
Here in thy presence I declare;
By thy good deeds, thy truth, I swear;
Nor lordship, joy, nor lands I prize;
Life, heaven, all blessings I despise;
I wish to see thee still remain
Most true, O King, and free from stain.
It must not, Sire, it must not be:
I cannot rest one hour with thee.
Then bring this sorrow to an end,
For naught my settled will can bend.
I gave a pledge that binds me too,
And to that pledge I still am true.
Kaikeyí bade me speed away:
She prayed me, and I answered yea.
Pine not for me, and weep no more:
The wood for us has joy in store,
Filled with the wild deer's peaceful herds,
And voices of a thousand birds.
A father is the God of each,
Yea, e'en of Gods, so Scriptures teach:
And I will keep my sire's decree,
For as a God I honour thee.
O best of men, the time is nigh,

H

The fourteen years will soon pass by
And to thine eyes thy son restore:
Be comforted, and weep no more.
Thou with thy firmness shouldst support
These weeping crowds who throng the court;
Then why, O chief of high renown,
So troubled, and thy soul cast down?'

CANTO XXXV.

KAIKEYÍ REPROACHED.

Wild with the rage he could not calm,
Sumantra, grinding palm on palm,
His head in quick impatience shook,
And sighed with woe he could not brook.
He gnashed his teeth, his eyes were red,
From his changed face the colour fled.
In rage and grief that knew no law,
The temper of the king he saw.
With his word-arrows swift and keen
He shook the bosom of the queen.
With scorn, as though its lightning stroke
Would blast her body, thus he spoke:
' Thou, who, of no dread sin afraid,
Hast Daśaratha's self betrayed,
Lord of the world, whose might sustains
Each thing that moves or fixed remains,
What direr crime is left thee now ?
Death to thy lord and house art thou,
Whose cruel deeds the king distress,
Mahendra's peer in mightiness,
Firm as the mountain's rooted steep,
Enduring as the Ocean's deep.
Despise not Daśaratha, he
Is a kind lord and friend to thee.
A loving wife in worth outruns
The mother of ten million sons.
Kings, when their sires have passed away,

Succeed by birthright to the sway.
Ikshváku's son still rules the state,
Yet thou this rule wouldst violate.
Yea, let thy son, Kaikeyí, reign,
Let Bharat rule his sire's domain.
Thy will, O Queen, shall none oppose:
We all will go where Ráma goes.
No Bráhman, scorning thee, will rest
Within the realm thou governest,
But all will fly indignant hence:
So great thy trespass and offence.
I marvel, when thy crime I see,
Earth yawns not quick to swallow thee;
And that the Bráhman saints prepare
No burning scourge thy soul to scare,
With cries of shame to smite thee, bent
Upon our Ráma's banishment.
The Mango tree with axes fell,
. And tend instead the Neem tree well.
Still watered with all care the tree
Will never sweet and pleasant be.
Thy mother's faults to thee descend,
And with thy borrowed nature blend.
True is the ancient saw: the Neem
Can ne'er distil a honeyed stream.
Taught by the tale of long ago
Thy mother's hateful sin we know.
A bounteous saint, as all have heard, ·
A boon upon thy sire conferred,
And all the eloquence revealed
That fills the wood, the flood, the field.
No creature walked, or swam, or flew,
But he its varied language knew.
One morn upon his couch he heard

The chattering of a gorgeous bird,
And as he marked its close intent
He laughed aloud in merriment.
Thy mother furious with her lord,
And fain to perish by the cord,
Said to her husband : ' I would know,
O Monarch, why thou laughest so.'
The king in answer spake again :
' If I this laughter should explain,
This very hour would be my last,
For death, be sure, would follow fast.'
Again thy mother, flushed with ire,
To Kekaya spake, thy royal sire :
'Tell me the cause; then live or die :
I will not brook thy laugh, not I.'
Thus by his darling wife addressed,
The king whose might all earth confessed,
To that kind saint his story told
Who gave the wondrous gift of old.
He listened to the king's complaint,
And thus in answer spoke the saint :
' King, let her quit thy home or die,
But never with her prayer comply.'
The saint's reply his trouble stilled,
And all his heart with pleasure filled.
Thy mother from his home he sent,
And days like Lord Kuvera's spent.
So thou wouldst force the king, misled
By thee, in evil paths to tread,
And bent on evil wouldst begin,
Through folly, this career of sin.
Most true, methinks, in thee is shown,
The ancient saw so widely known :
The sons their fathers' worth declare

And girls their mothers' nature-share.
So be not thou.   For pity's sake
Accept the word the monarch spake.
Thy husband's will, O Queen, obey,
And be the people's hope and stay.
O, do not, urged by folly, draw
The king to tread on duty's law,
The lord who all the world sustains,
Bright as the God o'er Gods who reigns.
Our glorious king, by sin unstained,
Will never grant what fraud obtained ;
No shade of fault in him is seen :
Let Ráma be anointed, Queen.
Remember, Queen, undying shame
Will through the world pursue thy name,
If Ráma leave the king his sire,
And, banished, to the wood retire.
Come, from thy breast this fever fling :
Of his own realm be Ráma king.
None in this city e'er can dwell
To tend and love thee half so well.
When Ráma sits in royal place,
True to the custom of his race
Our monarch of the mighty bow
A hermit to the woods will go.' [1]

  Sumantra thus, palm joined to palm,
Poured forth his words of bane and balm,
With keen reproach, with pleading kind,

---

[1] It was the custom of the kings of the solar dynasty to resign in
their extreme old age the kingdom to the heir, and spend the remainder
of their days in holy meditation in the forest :

  'For such through ages in their life's decline
  Is the good custom of Ikshváku's line.'

Raghuvansa.

Striving to move Kaikeyí's mind.
In vain he prayed, in vain reproved,
She heard unsoftened and unmoved.
Nor could the eyes that watched her view
One yielding look, one change of hue.

CANTO XXXVI.

SIDDHÁRTH'S SPEECH.

Ikshváku's son with anguish torn
For the great oath his lips had sworn,
With tears and sighs of sharpest pain
Thus to Sumantra spake again :
' Prepare thou quick a perfect force,
Cars, elephants, and foot, and horse,
To follow Raghu's scion hence
Equipped with all magnificence.
Let traders with the wealth they sell,
And those who charming stories tell,
And dancing-women fair of face,
The prince's ample chariots grace.
On all the train who throng his courts,
And those who share his manly sports,
Great gifts of precious wealth bestow,
And bid them with their master go.
Let noble arms, and many a wain,
And townsmen swell the prince's train ;
And hunters best for woodland skill
Their places in the concourse fill.
While elephants and deer he slays,
Drinking wood honey as he strays,
And looks on streams each fairer yet,
His kingdom he may chance forget.
Let all my gold and wealth of corn
With Ráma to the wilds be borne ;
For it will soothe the exile's lot
To sacrifice in each pure spot,

Deal ample largess forth, and meet
Each hermit in his calm retreat.
The wealth shall Ráma with him bear :
Ayodhyá shall be Bharat's share.'

As thus Kakutstha's offspring spoke,
Fear in Kaikeyí's breast awoke.
The freshness of her face was dried,
Her trembling tongue was terror-tied.
Alarmed and sad, with bloodless cheek,
She turned to him and scarce could speak :
'Nay, Sire, but Bharat shall not gain
An empty realm where none remain.
My Bharat shall not rule a waste
Reft of all sweets to charm the taste—
The wine-cup's dregs, all dull and dead,
Whence the light foam and life are fled.'

Thus in her rage the long-eyed dame
Spoke her dire speech untouched by shame.
Then, answering, Daśaratha spoke :
'Why, having bowed me to the yoke,
Dost thou, most cruel, spur and goad
Me who am struggling with the load ?
Why didst thou not oppose at first ·
This hope, vile Queen, so fondly nursed ?'

Scarce could the monarch's angry speech
The ears of the fair lady reach,
When thus, with double wrath inflamed,
Kaikeyí to the king exclaimed :
'Sagar, from whom thy line is traced,
Drove forth his eldest son disgraced,
Called Asamanj, whose fate we know :
Thus should thy son to exile go.'
'Fie on thee, dame !' the monarch said ;
Each of her people bent his head,

And stood in shame and sorrow mute:
She marked not, bold and resolute.
Then great Siddhárth, inflamed with rage,
The good old councillor and sage
On whose wise rede the king relied,
To Queen Kaikeyí thus replied:
' But Asamanj the cruel laid
His hands on infants as they played,
Cast them to Sarjú's flood, and smiled
For pleasure when he drowned a child. [1]
The people saw, and, furious, sped
Straight to the king his sire and said:
' Choose us, O glory of the throne,
Choose us, or Asamanj alone.'
' Whence comes this dread?' the monarch cried;
And all the people thus replied:
' In folly, King, he loves to lay
Fierce hands upon our babes at play,
Casts them to Sarjú's flood, and joys
To murder our bewildered boys.'
With heedful ear the king of men
Heard each complaining citizen.
To please their troubled minds he strove,
And from the state his son he drove.
With wife and gear upon a car
He placed him quick, and sent him far.

---

[1] See Book I., Canto XXXIX. An Indian prince in more modern times appears to have diverted himself in a similar way.

It is still reported in Belgaum that Appay Desay was wont to amuse himself "by making several young and beautiful women stand side by side in a narrow balcony, without a parapet, overhanging the deep reservoir at the new palace in Nipani. He used then to pass along the line of trembling creatures, and suddenly thrusting one of them head-long into the water below, he used to watch her drowning, and derive pleasure from her dying agonies."—History of the Belgaum District. By H. J. Stokes, M. S. C.

And thus he gave commandment, ' He
Shall all his days an exile be.'
With basket and with plough he strayed
O'er mountain heights, through pathless shade,
Roaming all lands a weary time,
An outcast wretch defiled with crime.
Sagar, the righteous path who held,
His wicked offspring thus expelled.
But what has Ráma done to blame ?
Why should his sentence be the same ?
No sin his stainless name can dim ;
We see no fault at all in him.
Pure as the moon, no darkening blot
On his sweet life has left a spot.
'If thou canst see one fault, e'en one,
To dim the fame of Raghu's son,
That fault this hour, O lady, show,
And Ráma to the wood shall go.
To drive the guiltless to the wild,
Truth's constant lover, undefiled,
Would, by defiance of the right,
The glory e'en of Indra blight.
Then cease, O lady, and dismiss
Thy hope to ruin Ráma's bliss,
Or all thy gain, O fair of face,
Will be men's hatred, and disgrace.'

CANTO XXXVII.

THE COATS OF BÀRK.

Thus spake the virtuous sage ; and then
Ráma addressed the king of men.
In laws of meek behaviour bred,
Thus to his sire he meekly said :
   ' King, I renounce all earthly care,
And live in woods on woodland fare.
What, dead to joys, have I to do
With lordly train and retinue ?
Who gives his elephant and yet
Upon the girths his heart will set ?
How can a cord attract his eyes
Who gives away the nobler prize ?
Best of the good, with me be led
No host, my King, with banners spread.
All wealth, all lordship I resign :
The hermit's dress alone be mine.
Before I go, have here conveyed
A little basket and a spade.
With these alone I go, content,
For fourteen years of banishment.'
   With her own hands Kaikeyí took
The hermit coats of bark, and, ' Look,'
She cried with bold unblushing brow
Before the concourse, ' Dress thee now.'
That lion leader of the brave
Took from her hand the dress she gave,
Cast his fine raiment on the ground,

And round his waist the vesture bound.
Then quick the hero Lakshmian too
His garment from his shoulders threw,
And, in the presence of his sire,
Indued the ascetic's rough attire.
But Sítá, in her silks arrayed,
Threw glances, trembling and afraid,
On the bark coat she had to wear,
Like a shy doe that eyes the snare.
Ashamed and weeping for distress
From the queen's hand she took the dress.
The fair one, by her husband's side
Who matched heaven's minstrel monarch,[1] cried:
' How bind they on their woodland dress,
Those hermits of the wilderness? '

There stood the pride of Janak's race
Perplexed, with sad appealing face.
One coat the lady's fingers grasped,
One round her neck she feebly clasped,
But failed again, again, confused
By the wild garb she ne'er had used.
Then quickly hastening Ráma, pride
Of all who cherish virtue, tied
The rough bark mantle on her, o'er‑
The silken raiment that she wore.

Then the sad women when thy saw
Ráma the choice bark round her draw,
Rained water from each tender eye,
And cried aloud with bitter cry:
' O, not on her, beloved, not
On Sítá falls thy mournful lot.
If,‑faithful to thy father's will,
Thou must go forth, leave Sítá still.

---

[1] Chitraratha, King of the celestial choristers.

Let Sítá still remaining here
Our hearts with her loved presence cheer.
With Lakshman by thy side to aid
Seek thou, dear son, the lonely shade.
Unmeet, one good and fair as she
Should dwell in woods a devotee.
Let not our prayers be prayed in vain :
Let beauteous Sítá yet remain ;
For by thy love of duty tied
Thou wilt not here thyself abide.'
   Then the king's venerable guide
Vaśishṭha, when he saw each coat
Enclose the lady's waist and throat,
Her zeal with gentle words repressed,
And Queen Kaikeyí thus addressed :
'O evil-hearted sinner, shame
Of royal Kekaya's race and name ;
Who matchless in thy sin couldst cheat
Thy lord the king with vile deceit ;
Lost to all sense of duty, know
Sítá to exile shall not go.
Sítá shall guard, as 'twere her own,
The precious trust of Ráma's throne.
Those joined by wedlock's sweet control
Have but one self and common soul.
Thus Sítá shall our empress be,
For Ráma's self and soul is she.
Or if she still to Ráma cleave
And for the woods the kingdom leave :
If naught her loving heart deter,
We and this town will follow her.
The warders of the queen shall take
Their wives and go for Ráma's sake.
The nation with its stores of grain,

The city's wealth shall swell his train.
Bharat, Satrughna both will wear
Bark mantles, and his lodging share,
Still with their elder brother dwell
In the wild wood, and serve him well.
Rest here alone, and rule thy state
Unpeopled, barren, desolate ;
Be empress of the land and trees,
Thou sinner whom our sorrows please.
The land which Ráma reigns not o'er
Shall bear the kingdom's name no more :
The woods which Ráma wanders through
Shall be our home and kingdom too.
Bharat, be sure, will never deign
O'er realms his father yields, to reign.
Nay, if the king's true son he be,
He will not, sonlike, dwell with thee.
Nay, shouldst thou from the earth arise,
And send thy message from the skies,
To his forefathers' custom true
No erring course would he pursue.
So hast thou, by thy grievous fault,
Offended him thou wouldst exalt.
In all the world none draws his breath
Who loves not Ráma, true to death.
This day, O Queen, shalt thou behold
Birds, deer, and beasts from lea and fold
Turn to the woods in Ráma's train,
And naught save longing trees remain.'

CANTO XXXVIII.

CARE FOR KAUŚALYÁ.

Then when the people wroth and sad
Saw Sítá in bark vesture clad,
Though wedded, like some widowed thing,
They cried out, ' Shame upon thee, King !'
Grieved by their cry and angry look
The lord of earth at once forsook
All hope in life that still remained,
In duty, self, and fame unstained.
Ikshváku's son with burning sighs
On Queen Kaikeyí bent his eyes,
And said : ' But Sítá must not flee
In garments of a devotee.
My holy guide has spoken truth :
Unfit is she in tender youth,
So gently nurtured, soft and fair,
The hardships of the wood to share.
How has she sinned, devout and true,
　　The noblest monarch's child,
　That she should garb of bark indue
　　And journey to the wild ?
　That she should spend her youthful days
　　Amid a hermit band,
　Like some poor mendicant who strays
　　Sore troubled, through the land ?
Ah, let the child of Janak throw
　　Her dress of bark aside,

And let the royal lady go
  With royal wealth supplied.
Not such the pledge I gave before,
  Unfit to linger here :
The oath which I the sinner swore
  Is kept, and leaves her clear.
Won from her childlike love this too
  My instant death would be,
As blossoms on the old bamboo
  Destroy the parent tree. [1]
If aught amiss by Ráma done
Offend thee, O thou wicked one,
What least transgression canst thou find
In her, thou worst of womankind ?
What shade of fault in her appears,
Whose full soft eye is like the deer's ?
What canst thou blame in Janak's child,
So gentle, modest, true, and mild ?
Is not one crime complete, that sent
My Ráma forth to banishment ?
And wilt thou other sins commit,
Thou wicked one, to double it ?
This is the pledge and oath I swore,
What thou besoughtest, and no more,
Of Ráma—for I heard thee, dame—
When he for consecration came.
Now with this limit not content,
In hell should be thy punishment,
Who fain the Maithil bride wouldst press
To clothe her limbs with hermit dress.'
  Thus spake the father in his woe ;
And Ráma, still prepared to go,
To him who sat with drooping head

---

[1] It is said that the bamboo dies after flowering.

I

Spake in return these words and said :
 ‘ Just King, here stands my mother dear,
Kauśalyá, one whom all revere.
Submissive, gentle, old is she,
And keeps her lips from blame of thee.
For her, kind lord, of me bereft
A sea of whelming woe is left.
O, show her in her new distress
Still fonder love and tenderness.
Well honoured by thine honoured hand
Her grief for me let her withstand,
Who wrapt in constant thought of me
In me would live a devotee.
 Peer of Mahendra, O, to her be kind,
  And treat I pray, my gentle mother so,
 That, when I dwell afar, her life resigned,
  She may not pass to Yama's realm for woe.’

CANTO XXXIX.

COUNSEL TO SÍTÁ.

Scarce had the sire, with each dear queen,
Heard Ráma's pleading voice, and seen
His darling in his hermit dress
Ere failed his senses for distress.
Convulsed with woe, his soul that shook,
On Raghu's son he could not look ;
Or if he looked with failing eye
He could not to the chief reply.
By pangs of bitter grief assailed,
The long-armed monarch wept and wailed,
Half dead a while and sore distraught,
While Ráma filled his every thought.
'This hand of mine in days ere now
Has reft her young from many a cow,
Or living things has idly slain ;
Hence comes, I ween, this hour of pain.
Not till the hour is come to die
Can from its shell the spirit fly.
Death comes not, and Kaikeyí still
Torments the wretch she cannot kill,
Who sees his son before him quit
The fine soft robes his rank that fit,
And, glorious as the burning fire,
In hermit garb his limbs attire.
Now all the people grieve and groan
Through Queen Kaikeyí's deed alone,
Who, having dared this deed of sin,

Strives for herself the gain to win.'
  He spoke. With tears his eyes grew dim,
His senses all deserted him.
He cried, O Ráma, once, then weak
And fainting could no further speak.
Unconscious there he lay : at length
Regathering his sense and strength,
While his full eyes their torrents shed,
To wise Sumantra thus he said :
' Yoke the light car, and hither lead
Fleet coursers of the noblest breed,
And drive this heir of lofty fate
Beyond the limit of the state.
This seems the fruit that virtues bear,
The meed of worth which texts declare—
The sending of the brave and good
By sire and mother to the wood.'
  He heard the monarch, and obeyed,
With ready feet that ne'er delayed,
And brought before the palace gate
The horses and the car of state.
Then to the monarch's son he sped,
And raising hands of reverence said
That the light car which gold made fair,
With best of steeds, was standing there.
King Daśaratha called in haste
The lord o'er all his treasures placed,
And spoke, well skilled in place and time,
His will to him devoid of crime :
' Count all the years she has to live
Afar in forest wilds, and give
To Sítá robes and gems of price
As for the time may well suffice.'
Quick to the treasure-room he went,

Charged by that king most excellent,
Brought the rich stores, and gave them all
To Sítá in the monarch's hall.
The Maithil dame of high descent
Received each robe and ornament,
And tricked those limbs, whose lines foretold
High destiny, with gems and gold.
So well adorned, so fair to view,
A glory through the hall she threw:
So, when the Lord of Light upsprings,
His radiance o'er the sky he flings.
Then Queen Kaušalyá spake at last,
With loving arms about her cast,
Pressed lingering kisses on her head,
And to the high-souled lady said:
' Ah, in this faithless world below
When dark misfortune comes and woe,
Wives, loved and cherished every day,
Neglect their lords and disobey.
Yes, woman's nature still is this :—
After long days of calm and bliss
When some light grief her spirit tries,
She changes all her love, or flies.
Young wives are thankless, false in soul,
With roving hearts that spurn control,
Brooding on sin and quickly changed,
In one short hour their love estranged.
Not glorious deed or lineage fair,
Not knowledge, gift, or tender care
In chains of lasting love can bind
A woman's light inconstant mind.
But those good dames who still maintain
What right, truth, Scripture, rule ordain—
No holy thing in their pure eyes

With one beloved husband vies.
Nor let thy lord my son, condemned
To exile, be by thee contemned,
For be he poor or wealthy, he
Is as a God, dear child, to thee.'

When Sítá heard Kauśalyá's speech
Her duty and her gain to teach,
She joined her palms with reverent grace,
And gave her answer face to face:
' All will I do, forgetting naught,
Which thou, O honoured Queen, hast taught.
I know, have heard, and deep have stored
The rules of duty to my lord.
Not me, good Queen, shouldst thou include
Among the faithless multitude.
Its own sweet light the moon shall leave
Ere I to duty cease to cleave.
The stringless lute gives forth no strain,
The wheelless car is urged in vain :
No joy a lordless dame, although
Blest with a hundred sons, can know.
From father, brother, and from son
A measured share of joy is won :
Who would not honour, love, and bless
Her lord, whose gifts are measureless ?
Thus trained to think, I hold in awe
Scripture's command and duty's law.
Him can I hold in slight esteem ?
Her lord is woman's God, I deem.'
Kauśalyá heard the lady's speech,
Nor failed those words her heart to reach.
Then, pure in mind, she gave to flow
The tear that sprang of joy and woe.
Then duteous Ráma forward came

And stood before the honoured dame,
And joining reverent hands addressed
The queen in rank above the rest :
‘ O mother, from these tears refrain ;
Look on my sire and still thy pain.
To thee my days afar shall fly
As if sweet slumber closed thine eye,
And fourteen years of exile seem
To thee, dear mother, like a dream.
On me returning safe and well,
Girt by my friends, thine eyes shall dwell.’
 Thus for their deep affection’s sake
The hero to his mother spake,
Then to the half seven hundred too,
Wives of his sire, paid reverence due.
Thus Daśaratha’s son addressed
That crowd of matrons sore distressed :
‘ If from these lips, while here I dwelt,
One heedless taunt you e’er have felt,
Forgive me, pray.   And now adieu,
I bid good-bye to all of you.’
Then straight, like curlews’ cries, upwent
The voices of their wild lament,
While, as he bade farewell, the crowd
Of royal women wept aloud.
And through the ample hall’s extent,
Where erst the sound of tabour, blent
With drum and shrill-toned instrument,
 In joyous concert rose,
Now rang the sound of wailing high,
The lamentation and the cry,
The shriek, the choking sob, the sigh
 That told the ladies’ woes.

CANTO XL.

RÁMA'S DEPARTURE.

Then Ráma, Sítá, Lakshman bent
At the king's feet, and sadly went
Round him with slow steps reverent.
When Ráma of the duteous heart
Had gained his sire's consent to part,
With Sítá by his side he paid
Due reverence to the queen dismayed.
And Lakshman, with affection meet,
Bowed down and clasped his mother's feet.
Sumitrá viewed him as he pressed
Her feet, and thus her son addressed:
'Neglect not Ráma wandering there,
But tend him with thy faithful care.
In hours of wealth, in time of woe,
Him, sinless son, thy refuge know.
From this good law the just ne'er swerve,
That younger sons the eldest serve,
And to this righteous rule incline
All children of thine ancient line—
Freely to give, reward each rite,
Nor spare their bodies in the fight.
Let Ráma Daśaratha be,
Look upon Sítá as on me,
And let the cot wherein you dwell
Be thine Ayodhyá.   Fare thee well.'
Her blessing thus Sumitrá gave
To him whose soul to Ráma clave,

Exclaiming, when her speech was done,
'Go forth, O Lakshman, go, my son.
Go forth, my son, to win success,
High victory and happiness.
Go forth thy foemen to destroy,
And turn again at last with joy.'
  As Mátali his charioteer
Speaks for the Lord of Gods to hear,
Sumantra, palm to palm applied,
In reverence trained, to Ráma cried :
'O famous Prince, my car ascend,—
May blessings on thy course attend,—
And swiftly shall my horses flee
And place thee where thou biddest me.
The fourteen years thou hast to stay
Far in the wilds, begin to-day ;
For Queen Kaikeyí cries, Away.'
  Then Sítá, best of womankind,
Ascended, with a tranquil mind,
Soon as her toilet task was done,
That chariot brilliant as the sun.
Ráma and Lakshman true and bold
Sprang on the car adorned with gold.
The king those years had counted o'er,
And given Sítá robes and store
Of precious ornaments to wear
When following her husband there.
The brothers in the car found place
For nets and weapons of the chase,
There warlike arms and mail they laid,
A leathern basket and a spade.
Soon as Sumantra saw the three
Were seated in the chariot, he
Urged on each horse of noble breed,

Who matched the rushing wind in speed.
As thus the son of Raghu went
Forth for his dreary banishment,
Chill numbing grief the town assailed,
All strength grew weak, all spirit failed.
Ayodhyá through her wide extent
Was filled with tumult and lament:
Steeds neighed and shook the bells they bore,
Each elephant returned a roar.
Then all the city, young and old,
Wild with their sorrow uncontrolled,
Rushed to the car, as, from the sun
The panting herds to water run.
Before the car, behind, they clung,
And there as eagerly they hung,
With torrents streaming from their eyes,
Called loudly with repeated cries:
'Listen, Sumantra; draw thy rein;
Drive gently, and thy steeds restrain.
Once more on Ráma will we gaze,
Now to be lost for many days.
The queen his mother has, be sure,
A heart of iron, to endure
To see her godlike Ráma go,
Nor feel it shattered by the blow.
Sítá, well done! Videha's pride,
Still like his shadow by his side;
Rejoicing in thy duty still
As sunlight cleaves to Meru's hill.
Thou, Lakshman, too, hast well deserved,
Who from thy duty hast not swerved,
Tending the peer of Gods above,
Whose lips speak naught but words of love.
Thy firm resolve is nobly great,

And high success on thee shall wait.
Yea, thou shalt win a priceless meed—
Thy path with him to heaven shall lead.'
As thus they spake, they could not hold
The tears that down their faces rolled,
While still they followed for a space
Their darling of Ikshváku's race.

There stood surrounded by a ring
Of mournful wives the mournful king;
For, ' I will see once more,' he cried,
' Mine own dear son,' and forth he hied.
As he came near, there rose the sound
Of weeping, as the dames stood round.
So the she-elephants complain
When their great lord and guide is slain.
Kakutstha's son, the king of men,
The glorious sire, looked troubled then,
As the full moon is when dismayed
By dark eclipse's threatening shade.
Then Daśaratha's son, designed
For highest fate, of lofty mind,
Urged to more speed the charioteer,
' Away, away ! why linger here ?
Urge on thy horses,' Ráma cried,
And ' Stay, O stay,' the people sighed.
Sumantra, urged to speed away,
The townsmen's call must disobey.
Forth as the long-armed hero went,
The dust his chariot wheels up sent
Was laid by streams that over flowed
From their sad eyes who filled the road.
Then, sprung of woe, from eyes of all
The women drops began to fall,
As from each lotus on the lake

The darting fish the water shake.
When he, the king of high renown,
Saw that one thought held all the town,
Like some tall tree he fell and lay,
Whose root the axe has hewn away.
Then straight a mighty cry from those
Who followed Ráma's car arose,
Who saw their monarch fainting there
Beneath that grief too great to bear.
Then 'Ráma, Ráma!' with the cry
Of 'Ah, his mother!' sounded high,
As all the people wept aloud
Around the ladies' sorrowing crowd.
When Ráma backward turned his eye,
And saw the king his father lie
With troubled sense and failing limb,
And the sad queen, who followed him,
Like some young creature in the net,
That will not, in its misery, let
Its wild eyes on its mother rest,
So, by the bonds of duty pressed,
His mother's look he could not meet.
He saw them with their weary feet,
Who, used to bliss, in cars should ride,
Who ne'er by sorrow should be tried,
And, as one mournful look he cast,
'Drive on,' he cried, 'Sumantra, fast.'
As when the driver's torturing hook
Goads on an elephant, the look
Of sire and mother in despair
Was more than Ráma's heart could bear.
As mother kine to stalls return
Which hold the calves for whom they yearn,
So to the car she tried to run

As a cow seeks her little one.
Once and again the hero's eyes
Looked on his mother, as with cries
Of woe she called and gestures wild,
' O Sítá, Lakshman, O my child !'
' Stay,' cried the king, ' thy chariot stay :'
' On on,' cried Ráma, ' speed away.'
As one between two hosts, inclined
To neither was Sumantra's mind.
But Ráma spake these words again :
' A lengthened woe is bitterest pain.
On, on ; and if his wrath grow hot,
Thine answer be, ' I heard thee not.'
Sumantra, at the chief's behest,
Dismissed the crowd that toward him pressed,
And, as he bade, to swiftest speed
Urged on his way each willing steed.
The king's attendants parted thence,
And paid him heart-felt reverence :
In mind, and with the tears he wept,
Each still his place near Ráma kept.
As swift away the horses sped,
His lords to Daśaratha said :
' To follow him whom thou again
Wouldst see returning home is vain.'
    With failing limb and drooping mien
      He heard their counsel wise :
    Still on their son the king and queen
      Kept fast their lingering eyes. [1]

---

[1] ' Thirty centuries have passed since he began this memorable journey. Every step of it is known and is annually traversed by thousands : hero-worship is not extinct. What can Faith do ! How strong are the ties of religion when entwined with the legends of a country ! How many a cart creeps creaking and weary along the road from Ayodhyá to Chitrakút. It is this that gives the Rámáyan a strange interest : the story still lives.' *Calcutta Review, Vol. XXIII.*

CANTO XLI.

The lion chief with hands upraised
Was born from eyes that fondly gazed.
But then the ladies' bower was rent
With cries of weeping and lament :
' Where goes he now, our lord, the sure
Protector of the friendless poor,
In whom the wretched and the weak
Defence and aid were wont to seek ?
All words of wrath he turned aside,
And ne'er, when cursed, in ire replied.
He shared his people's woe, and stilled
The troubled breast which rage had filled.
Our chief, on lofty thoughts intent,
In glorious fame preëminent :
As on his own dear mother, thus
He ever looked on each of us.
Where goes he now ? His sire's behest,
By Queen Kaikeyí's guile distressed,
Has banished to the forest hence
Him who was all the world's defence.
Ah, senseless King, to drive away
The hope of men, their guard and stay,
To banish to the distant wood
Ráma the duteous, true, and good !'
The royal dames, like cows bereaved
Of their young calves, thus sadly grieved.
The monarch heard them as thy wailed,
And by the fire of grief assailed

For his dear son, he bowed his head,
And all his sense and memory fled.
   Then were no fires of worship fed,
Thick darkness o'er the sun was spread.
The cows their thirsty calves denied,
And elephants flung their food aside.
Triśanku,[1] Jupiter looked dread,
And Mercury and Mars the red,
In direful opposition met,
The glory of the moon beset.
The lunar stars withheld their light,
The planets were no longer bright,
But meteors with their horrid glare,
And dire Viśákhás[2] lit the air.
As troubled Ocean heaves and raves
When Doom's wild tempest sweeps the waves,
Thus all Ayodhyá reeled and bent
When Ráma to the forest went.
And chilling grief and dark despair
Fell suddenly on all men there.
Their wonted pastime all forgot,
Nor thought of food, or touched it not.
Crowds in the royal street were seen
With weeping eye and troubled mien :
No more a people gay and glad,
Each head and heart was sick and sad.
No more the cool wind softly blew,
The moon no more was fair to view.
No more the sun with genial glow
Cherished the world now plunged in woe.
Sons, brothers, husbands, wedded wives
Forgot the ties that joined their lives ;

---

[1] See Vol. I. p. 256.

[2] Four stars of the sixteenth lunar asterism.

No thought for kith and kin was spared,
But all for only Ráma cared.
And Ráma's friends who loved him best,
Their minds disordered and distressed
By the great burthen of their woes
Turned not to slumber or repose.
Like Earth with all her hills bereft
　　Of Indra's guiding care,
　Ayodhyá in her sorrow left
　　By him, the high-souled heir,
　Was bowed by fear and sorrow's force,
　　And shook with many a throe,
　While warrior, elephant, and horse
　　Sent up the cry of woe.

CANTO XLII.

DAŚARATHA'S LAMENT.

While yet the dust was seen afar
That marked the course of Ráma's car,
The glory of Ikshváku's race
Turned not away his eager face.
While yet his duteous son he saw
He could not once his gaze withdraw,
But rooted to the spot remained
With eyes that after Ráma strained.
But when that dust no more he viewed,
Fainting he fell by grief subdued.
To his right hand Kauśalyá went,
And ready aid the lady lent,
While Bharat's loving mother tried
To raise him on the other side.
The king, within whose ordered soul
Justice and virtue held control,
To Queen Kaikeyí turned and said,
With every sense disquieted :
'Touch me not, thou whose soul can plot
All sin, Kaikeyí, touch me not.
No loving wife, no friend to me,
I ne'er again would look on thee ;
Ne'er from this day have aught to do
With thee and all thy retinue ;
Thee whom no virtuous thoughts restrain,

J

Whose selfish heart seeks only gain.
The hand I laid in mine, O dame,
The steps we took around the flame, [1]
And all that links thy life to mine
Here and hereafter I resign.
If Bharat too, thy darling son,
Joy in the rule thy art has won,
Ne'er may the funeral offerings paid
By his false hand approach my shade.'
   Then while the dust upon him hung,
The monarch to Kauśalyá clung,
And she with mournful steps and slow
Turned to the palace, worn with woe.
As one whose hand has touched the fire,
Or slain a Bráhman in his ire,
He felt his heart with sorrow torn
Still thinking of his son forlorn.
Each step was torture, as the road
The traces of the chariot showed,
And as the shadowed sun grows dim
So care and anguish darkened him.
He raised a cry, by woe distraught,
As of his son again he thought,
And judging that the car had sped
Beyond the city, thus he said :
'I still behold the foot-prints made
By the good horses that conveyed
My son afar : these marks I see,
But high-souled Ráma, where is he ?
Ah me, my son ! my first and best,
On pleasant couches wont to rest,
With limbs perfumed with sandal, fanned
By many a beauty's tender hand :

---

[1] In the marriage service.

Where will he lie with log or stone
Beneath him for a pillow thrown,
To leave at morn his earthy bed,
Neglected, and with dust o'erspread,
As from the flood with sigh and pant
Comes forth the husband elephant ?
The men who make the woods their home
Shall see the long-armed hero roam
Roused from his bed, though lord of all,
In semblance of a friendless thrall.
Janak's dear child who ne'er has met
With aught save joy and comfort yet,
Will reach to-day the forest, worn
And wearied with the brakes of thorn.
Ah, gentle girl, of woods unskilled,
How will her heart with dread be filled
At the wild beasts' deep roaring there,
Whose voices lift the shuddering hair !
Kaikeyí, glory in thy gain,
And, widow queen, begin to reign :
No will, no power to live have I
When my brave son no more is nigh.'

   Thus pouring forth laments, the king
Girt by the people's crowded ring,
Entered the noble bower like one
New-bathed when funeral rites are done.
Where'er he looked naught met his gaze
But empty houses, courts, and ways.
Closed were the temples : countless feet
No longer trod the royal street,
And thinking of his son he viewed
Men weak and worn and woe-subdued.
As sinks the sun into a cloud,
So passed he on, and wept aloud,

Within that house no more to be
The dwelling of the banished three,
Brave Ráma, his Videhan bride,
And Lakshman by his brother's side:
Like broad still waters, when the king
Of all the birds that ply the wing
Has swooped from heaven and borne away
The glittering snakes that made them gay.
With choking sobs and voice half spent
The king renewed his sad lament:
With broken utterance faint and low
Scarce could he speak these words of woe:
'My steps to Ráma's mother guide,
And place me by Kauśalyá's side:
There, only there my heart may know
Some little respite from my woe.'
    The warders of the palace led
The monarch, when his words were said,
To Queen Kauśalyá's bower, and there
Laid him with reverential care.
But while he rested on the bed
Still was his soul disquieted.
In grief he tossed his arms on high
Lamenting with a piteous cry:
'O Ráma, Ráma,' thus said he,
'My son, thou hast forsaken me.
High bliss awaits those favoured men
Left living in Ayodhyá then,
Whose eyes shall see my son once more
Returning when the time is o'er.'
Then came the night, whose hated gloom
Fell on him like the night of doom.
At midnight Daśaratha cried
To Queen Kauśalyá by his side:

' I see thee not, Kauśalyá ; lay
Thy gentle hand in mine, I pray.
When Ráma left his home my sight
Went with him, nor returns to-night.'

CANTO XLIII.

KAUŚALYÂ'S LAMENT.

Kauśalyá saw the monarch lie
With drooping frame and failing eye,
And for her banished son distressed
With these sad words her lord addressed :
' Kaikeyí, cruel, false, and vile
Has cast the venom of her guile
On Ráma lord of men, and she
Will ravage like a snake set free ;
And more and more my soul alarm,
Like a dire serpent bent on harm.
For triumph crowns each dark intent,
And Ráma to the wild is sent.
Ah, were he doomed but here to stray
Begging his food from day to day,
Or do, enslaved, Kaikeyí's will,
This were a boon, a comfort still.
But she, as chose her cruel hate,
Has hurled him from his high estate,
As Bráhmans when the moon is new
Cast to the ground the demons' due.[1]
The long-armed hero, like the lord
Of Nágas, with his bow and sword
Begins, I ween, his forest life
With Lakshman and his faithful wife.
Ah, how will fare the exiles now,
Whom, moved by Queen Kaikeyí, thou

---

[1] The husks and chaff of the rice offered to the Gods.

Hast sent in forests to abide,
Bred in delights, by woe untried ?
Far banished when their lives are young,
With the fair fruit before them hung,
Deprived of all their rank that suits;
How will they live on grain and roots ?
O, that my years of woe were passed,
And the glad hour were come at last
When I shall see my children dear,
Ráma, his wife, and Lakshman here !
When shall Ayodhyá, wild with glee,
Again those mighty heroes see,
And decked with wreaths her banners wave
To welcome home the true and brave ?
When will the beautiful city view
With happy eyes the lordly two
Returning, joyful as the main
When the dear moon is full again ?
When, like some mighty bull who leads
The cow exulting through the meads,
Will Ráma through the city ride,
Strong-armed, with Sítá at his side ?
When will ten thousand thousand meet
And crowd Ayodhyá's royal street,
And grain in joyous welcome throw
Upon my sons who tame the foe ?
When with delight shall youthful bands
Of Bráhman maidens in their hands
Bear fruit and flowers in goodly show,
And circling round Ayodhyá go ?
With ripened judgment of a sage,
And godlike in his blooming age,
When shall my virtuous son appear,
Like kindly rain, our hearts to cheer ?

'Ah, in a former life, I ween,
This hand of mine, most base and mean,
Has dried the udders of the kine
And left the thirsty calves to pine,
Hence, as the lion robs the cow,
Kaikeyí makes me childless now,
Exulting from her feebler foe
To rend the son she cherished so.
I had but him, in Scripture skilled,
With every grace his soul was filled.
Now not a joy has life to give,
And robbed of him I would not live:
Yea, all my days are dark and drear
If he, my darling, be not near,
And Lakshman brave, my heart to cheer,
As for my son I mourn and yearn,
The quenchless flames of anguish burn
   And kill me with the pain,
As in the summer's noontide blaze
The glorious Day-God with his rays
   Consumes the parching plain.'

CANTO XLIV.

SUMITRÁ'S SPEECH.

Kauśalyá ceased her sad lament,
Of beauteous dames most excellent.
Sumitrá, who to duty clave,
In righteous words this answer gave :
' Dear Queen, all noble virtues grace
Thy son, of men the first in place.
Why dost thou shed these tears of woe
With bitter grief lamenting so ?
If Ráma, leaving royal sway
Has hastened to the woods away,
' Tis for his high-souled father's sake
That he his promise may not break.
He to the path of duty clings
Which lordly fruit hereafter brings—
The path to which the righteous cleave—
For him, dear Queen, thou shouldst not grieve.
And Lakshman too, the blameless-souled,
The same high course with him will hold,
And mighty bliss on him shall wait,
So tenderly compassionate.
And Sítá, bred with tender care,
Well knows what toils await her there,
But in her love she will not part
From Ráma of the virtuous heart.
Now has thy son through all the world
The banner of his fame unfurled :
True, modest, careful of his vow,

What has he left to aim at now?
The sun will mark his mighty soul,
His wisdom, sweetness, self-control,
Will spare from pain his face and limb,
And with soft radiance shine for him.
For him through forest glades shall spring
A soft auspicious breeze, and bring
Its tempered heat and cold to play
Around him ever night and day.
The pure cold moonbeams shall delight
The hero as he sleeps at night,
And soothe him with the soft caress
Of a fond parent's tenderness.
To him, the bravest of the brave,
His heavenly arms the Bráhman gave,
When fierce Suváhu dyed the plain
With his life-blood by Ráma slain.
Still trusting to his own right arm
Thy hero son will fear no harm :
As in his father's palace, he
In the wild woods will dauntless be.
Whene'er he lets his arrows fly
His stricken foemen fall and die :
And is that prince of peerless worth
Too weak to keep and sway the earth?
His sweet pure soul, his beauty's charm,
His hero heart, his warlike arm,
Will soon redeem his rightful reign
When from the woods he comes again.
The Bráhmans on the prince's head
King-making drops shall quickly shed,
And Sítá, Earth, and Fortune share
The glories which await the heir.
For him, when forth his chariot swept,

The crowd that thronged Ayodhyá wept,
With agonizing woe distressed.
With him in hermit's mantle dressed
In guise of Sítá Lakshmí went,
And none his glory may prevent.
Yea, naught to him is high or hard,
Before whose steps, to be his guard,
Lakshman, the best who draws the bow,
With spear, shaft, sword rejoiced to go.
His wanderings in the forest o'er,
Thine eyes shall see thy son once more.
Quit thy faint heart, thy grief dispel,
For this, O Queen, is truth I tell.
Thy son returning, moonlike, thence,
Shall at thy feet do reverence,
And, blest and blameless lady, thou
Shalt see his head to touch them bow.
Yea, thou shalt see thy son made king
When he returns with triumphing,
And how thy happy eyes will brim
With tears of joy to look on him !
Thou, blameless lady, shouldst the whole
Of the sad people here console :
Why in thy tender heart allow
This bitter grief to harbour now ?
As the long banks of cloud distil
Their water when they see the hill,
So shall the drops of rapture run
From thy glad eyes to see thy son
Returning, as he lowly bends
To greet thee, girt by all his friends.'

   Thus soothing, kindly eloquent,
With every hopeful argument
Kauśalyá's heart by sorrow rent,

Fair Queen Sumitrá ceased.
Kauśalyá heard each pleasant plea,
And grief began to leave her free,
As the light clouds of autumn flee,
   Their watery stores decreased.

CANTO XLV.

THE TAMASÁ.

Their tender love the people drew
To follow Ráma brave and true,
The high-souled hero, as he went
Forth from his home to banishment.
The king himself his friends obeyed;
And turned him homeward as they prayed.
But yet the people turned not back,
Still close on Ráma's chariot track.
For they who in Ayodhyá dwelt
For him such fond affection felt,
Decked with all grace and glories high,
The dear full moon of every eye.
Though much his people prayed and wept,
Kakutstha's son his purpose kept,
And still his journey would pursue
To keep the king his father true.
Deep in the hero's bosom sank
Their love, whose signs his glad eye drank.
He spoke to cheer them, as his own
Dear children, in a loving tone :
' If ye would grant my fond desire,
Give Bharat now that love entire
And reverence shown to me by all
Who dwell within Ayodhyá's wall.
For he, Kaikeyí's darling son,
His virtuous career will run,
And ever bound by duty's chain

Consult your weal and bliss and gain.
In judgment old, in years a child,
With hero virtues meek and mild, ·
A fitting lord is he to cheer
His people and remove their fear.
In him all kingly gifts abound,
More noble than in me are found :
Imperial prince, well proved and tried—
Obey him as your lord and guide.
And grant, I pray, the boon I ask :
To please the king be still your task,
That his fond heart, while I remain
Far in the woods, may feel no pain.'
  The more he showed his will to tread
The path where filial duty led,
The more the people, round him thronged,
For their dear Ráma's empire longed.
Still more attached his followers grew,
As Ráma, with his brother, drew
The people with his virtues' ties,
Lamenting all with tear-dimmed eyes.
The saintly twice-born, triply old
In glory, knowledge, seasons told,
With hoary heads that shook and bowed,
Their voices raised and spake aloud :
'O steeds, who best and noblest are,
Who whirl so swiftly Ráma's car,
Go not, return : we call on you :
Be to your master kind and true.
For speechless things are swift to hear,
And naught can match a horse's ear.
O generous steeds, return, when thus
You hear the cry of all of us.
Each vow he keeps most firm and sure,

And duty makes his spirit pure.
Back with our chief! not wood-ward hence;
Back to his royal residence!'
　　Soon as he saw the aged band,
Exclaiming in their misery, stand,
And their sad cries around him rang,
Swift from his chariot Ráma sprang.
Then, still upon his journey bent,
With Sítá and with Lakshmaṇ went
The hero by the old men's side,
Suiting to theirs his shortened stride.
He could not pass the twice-born throng
As weariedly they walked along:
With pitying heart, with tender eye,
He could not in his chariot fly.
When they the steps of Ráma viewed
That still his onward course pursued,
Woe shook the troubled heart of each,
And burnt with grief they spoke this speech:
　'With thee, O Ráma, to the wood
All Bráhmans go and Bráhmanhood:
Borne on our aged shoulders, see,
Our fires of worship go with thee.
Bright canopies that lend their shade
In Vájapeya' rites displayed,
In plenteous store are borne behind
Like cloudlets in the autumn wind.
No shelter from the sun hast thou,
And, lest his fury burn thy brow,
These sacrificial shades we bear
Shall aid thee in the noontide glare.
Our hearts, who ever loved to pore
On sacred text and Vedic lore,

---

¹ An important sacrifice at which seventeen victims were immolated

Now all to thee, beloved, turn,
And for a life in forests yearn.
Deep in our aged bosoms lies
The Vedas' lore, the wealth we prize,
There still, like wives at home, shall dwell,
Whose love and truth protect them well.
To follow thee our hearts are bent ;
We need not plan or argument.
All else in duty's law we slight,
For following thee is following right.
O noble Prince, retrace thy way :
O, hear us, Ráma, as we lay,
With many tears and many prayers,
Our aged heads and swan-white hairs
Low in the dust before thy feet ;
O, hear us, Ráma, we entreat.
Full many of these who with thee run,
Their sacred rites had just begun.
Unfinished yet those rites remain ;
But finished if thou turn again.
All rooted life and things that move
To thee their deep affection prove.
To them, when, warmed by love, they glow
And sue to thee, some favour show.
Each lowly bush, each towering tree
Would follow too for love of thee.
Bound by its root it must remain ;
But—all it can—its boughs complain,
As when the wild wind rushes by
It tells its woe in groan and sigh.
No more through air the gay birds flit,
But, foodless, melancholy sit
Together on the branch and call
To thee whose kind heart feels for all.'

As wailed the aged Bráhmans, bent
To turn him back, with wild lament,
Seemed Tamasá herself to aid,
Checking his progress, as they prayed.
Sumantra from the chariot freed
With ready hand each weary steed;
He groomed them with the utmost heed,
   Their limbs he bathed and dried,
Then led them forth to drink and feed
At pleasure in the grassy mead
   That fringed the river side.

K

CANTO XLVI.

THE HALT.

When Ráma, chief of Raghu's race,
Arrived at that delightful place,
He looked on Sítá first, and then
To Lakshman spake the lord of men :
' Now first the shades of night descend
Since to the wilds our steps we bend.
Joy to thee, brother ! do not grieve
For our dear home and all we leave.
The woods unpeopled seem to weep
Around us, as their tenants creep
Or fly to lair and den and nest,
Both bird and beast, to seek their rest.
Methinks Ayodhyá's royal town
Where dwells my sire of high renown,
With all her men and dames to-night
Will mourn us vanished from their sight.
For, by his virtues won, they cling
In fond affection to their king,
And thee and me, O brave and true,
And Bharat and Śatrughna too.
I for my sire and mother feel
Deep sorrow o'er my bosom steal,
Lest mourning us, oppressed with fears,
They blind their eyes with endless tears.
Yet Bharat's duteous love will show
Sweet comfort in their hours of woe,
And with kind words their hearts sustain,

Suggesting duty, bliss, and gain.
I mourn my parents now no more :
I count dear Bharat's virtues o'er,
And his kind love and care dispel
The doubts I had, and all is well.
And thou thy duty wouldst not shun,
And, following me, hast nobly done ;
Else, bravest, I should need a band
Around my wife as guard to stand.
On this first night, my thirst to slake,
Some water only will I take :
Thus, brother, thus my will decides,
Though varied store the wood provides.'
   Thus having said to Lakshman, he
Addressed in turn Sumantra : 'Be
Most diligent to-night, my friend,
And with due care thy horses tend.'
The sun had set : Sumantra tied
His noble horses side by side,
Gave store of grass with liberal hand,
And rested near them on the strand.
Each paid the holy evening rite,
And when around them fell the night,
The charioteer, with Lakshman's aid,
A lowly bed for Ráma laid.
To Lakshman Ráma bade adieu,
And then by Sítá's side he threw
His limbs upon the leafy bed
Their care upon the bank had spread.
When Lakshman saw the couple slept,
Still on the strand his watch he kept,
Still with Sumantra there conversed,
And, Ráma's varied gifts rehearsed.
All night he watched, nor sought repose,

Till on the earth the sun arose :
With him Sumantra stayed awake,
And still of Ráma's virtues spake.
Thus, near the river's grassy shore
Which herds unnumbered wandered o'er,
Repose, untroubled, Ráma found,
And all the people lay around.
The glorious hero left his bed,
Looked on the sleeping crowd, and said
To Lakshmaṇ, whom each lucky line
Marked out for bliss with surest sign :

  ' O brother Lakshmaṇ, look on these
Reclining at the roots of trees ;
All care of house and home resigned,
Caring for us with heart and mind,
These people of the city yearn
To see us to our home return :
To quit their lives will they consent,
But never leave their firm intent.
Come, while they all unconscious sleep,
Let us upon the chariot leap,
And swiftly on our journey speed
Where naught our progress may impede,
That these fond citizens who roam
Far from Ikshváku's ancient home,
No more may sleep 'neath bush and tree,
Following still for love of me.
A prince with tender care should heal
The self-brought woes his people feel,
And never let his subjects share
The burthen he is forced to bear.'

  Then Lakshmaṇ to the chief replied,
Who stood like Justice by his side :
' Thy rede, O sage, I well commend :

Without delay the car ascend.'
Then Ráma to Sumantra spoke:
'Thy rapid steeds, I pray thee, yoke.
Hence to the forest will I go:
Away, my lord, and be not slow.'

Sumantra, urged to utmost speed,
Yoked to the car each generous steed,
And then, with hand to hand applied,
He came before the chief and cried:
'Hail, Prince, whom mighty arms adorn,
Hail, bravest of the chariot-borne!
With Sítá and thy brother thou
Mayst mount: the car is ready now.'

The hero clomb the car with haste:
His bow and gear within were placed,
And quick the eddying flood he passed
Of Tamasá whose waves run fast.
Soon as he touched the farther side,
That strong-armed hero, glorified,
He found a road both wide and clear,
Where e'en the timid naught could fear.
Then, that the crowd might be misled,
Thus Ráma to Sumantra said:
'Speed north a while, then hasten back,
Returning in thy former track,
That so the people may not learn
The course I follow: drive and turn.'

Sumantra, at the chief's behest,
Quick to the task himself addresssed;
Then near to Ráma came, and showed
The chariot ready for the road.
With Sítá, then, the princely two,
Who o'er the line of Raghu threw
A glory ever bright and new,

Upon the chariot stood.
Sumantra fast and faster drove
His horses, who in fleetness strove,
Still onward to the distant grove,
   The hermit-haunted wood.

CANTO XLVII.

THE CITIZENS' RETURN.

The people, when the morn shone fair,
Arose to find no Ráma there.
Then fear and numbing grief subdued
The senses of the multitude.
The woe-born tears were running fast
As all around their eyes they cast,
And sadly looked, but found no trace
Of Ráma, searching every place.
Bereft of Ráma good and wise,
With drooping cheer and weeping eyes,
Each woe-distracted sage gave vent
To sorrow in his wild lament:
' Woe worth the sleep that stole our sense
With its beguiling influence,
That now we look in vain for him
Of the broad chest and stalwart limb!
How could the strong-armed hero, thus
Deceiving all, abandon us?
His people so devoted see,
Yet to the woods, a hermit, flee?
How can he, wont our hearts to cheer,
As a fond sire his children dear.—
How can the pride of Raghu's race
Fly from us to some desert place?
Here let us all for death prepare,
Or on the last great journey fare;'

---

[1] The great pilgrimage to the Himálayas, in order to die there.

Of Ráma our dear lord bereft,
What profit in our lives is left ?
Huge trunks of trees around us lie,
With roots and branches sere and dry,
Come let us set these logs on fire
And throw our bodies on the pyre.
What shall we speak ? How can we say
We followed Ráma on his way,
The mighty chief whose arm is strong,
Who sweetly speaks, who thinks no wrong ?
Ayodhyá's town, with sorrow dumb,
Without our lord will see us come,
And hopeless misery will strike
Elder, and child, and dame alike.
Forth with that p erless chief we came,
Whose mighty heart is aye the same .
How, reft of him we love, shall we
Returning dare that town to see ? '
    Complaining thus with varied cry
They tossed their aged arms on high,
And their sad hearts with grief were wrung,
Like cows who sorrow for their young.
A while they followed on the road
Which traces of his chariot showed,
But when at length those traces failed,
A deep despair their hearts assailed.
The chariot marks no more discerned,
The hopeless sages backward turned :
' Ah, what is this? What can we more ?
Fate stops the way, and all is o'er.'
With wearied hearts, in grief and shame
They took the road by which they came,
And reached Ayodhyá's city, where
From side to side was naught but care.

With troubled spirits quite cast down
They looked upon the royal town,
And from their eyes, oppressed with woe,
Their tears again began to flow.
Of Ráma reft, the city wore
No look of beauty as before.
Like a dull river or a lake
By Garuḍ robbed of every snake.
Dark, dismal as the moonless sky,
Or as a sea whose bed is dry,
So sad, to every pleasure dead,
They saw the town, disquieted.
On to their houses, high and vast,
Where stores of precious wealth were massed,
The melancholy Bráhmans passed,
    Their hearts with anguish cleft :
Aloof from all, they came not near
To stranger or to kinsman dear,
Showing in faces blank and drear
    That not one joy was left.

CANTO XLVIII.

THE WOMEN'S LAMENT.

When those who forth with Ráma went
Back to the town their steps had bent,
It seemed that death had touched and chilled
Those hearts which piercing sorrow filled.
Each to his several mansion came,
And girt by children and his dame,
From his sad eyes the water shed
That o'er his cheek in torrents spread.
All joy was fled : oppressed with cares
No bustling trader showed his wares.
Each shop had lost its brilliant look,
Each householder forbore to cook.
No hand with joy its earnings told,
None cared to win a wealth of gold,
And scarce the youthful mother smiled
To see her first, her new-born child.
In every house a woman wailed,
And her returning lord assailed
With keen taunt piercing like the steel
That bids the tusked monster kneel :
' What now to them is wedded dame,
What house and home and dearest aim,
Or son, or bliss, or gathered store,
Whose eyes on Ráma look no more ?
There is but one in all the earth,
One man alone of real worth,
Lakshman, who follows, true and good,

Ráma, with Sítá, through the wood.
Made holy for all time we deem
Each pool and fountain, lake and stream,
If great Kakutstha's son shall choose
Their water for his bath to use.
Each forest, dark with lovely trees,
Shall yearn Kakutstha's son to please ;
Each mountain peak and woody hill,
Each mighty flood and mazy rill,
Each rocky height, each shady grove
Where the blest feet of Ráma rove,
Shall gladly welcome with the best
Of all they have their honoured guest.
The trees that clustering blossoms bear,
And bright-hued buds to gem their hair,
The heart of Ráma shall delight,
And cheer him on the breezy height.
For him the upland slopes will show
The fairest roots and fruit that grow,
And all their wealth before him fling
Ere the due hour of ripening.
For him each earth-upholding hill
Its crystal water shall distil,
And all its floods shall be displayed
In many a thousand-hued cascade.
Where Ráma stands is naught to fear,
No danger comes if he be near ;
For all who live on him depend,
The world's support, and lord, and friend.
Ere in too distant wilds he stray,
Let us to Ráma speed away,
For rich reward on those will wait '
Who serve a prince of soul so great.
We will attend on Sítá there ;

Be Raghu's son your special care.'
The city dames, with grief distressed,
Thus once again their lords addressed :
'Ráma shall be your guard and guide,
And Sítá will for us provide.
For who would care to linger here,
Where all is sad and dark and drear?
Who, mid the mourners, hope for bliss
In a poor soulless town like this?
If Queen Kaikeyí's treacherous sin,
Our lord expelled, the kingdom win,
We heed not sons or golden store,
Our life itself we prize no more.
If she, seduced by lust of sway,
Her lord and son could cast away,
Whom would she leave unharmed, the base
Defiler of her royal race?
We swear it by our children dear,
We will not dwell as servants here ;
If Queen Kaikeyí live to reign,
We will not in her realm remain.
Bowed down by her oppressive hand,
The helpless, lordless, godless land,
Cursed for Kaikeyí's guilt will fall,
And swift destruction seize it all.
For, Ráma forced from home to fly,
The king his sire will surely die,
And when the king has breathed his last
Ruin will doubtless follow fast.
Sad, robbed of merits, drug the cup
And drink the poisoned mixture up,
Or share the exiled Ráma's lot,
Or seek some land that knows her not.
No reason, but a false pretence

Drove Ráma, Sítá, Lakshmaṇ hence,
And we to Bharat have been given
Like cattle to the shambles driven.'

  While in each house the women, pained
At loss of Ráma, still complained,
Sank to his rest the Lord of Day,
And night through all the sky held sway.
The fires of worship all were cold,
No text was hummed, no tale was told,
And shades of midnight gloom came down
Enveloping the mournful town.
Still, sick at heart, the women shed,
As for a son or husband fled,
For Ráma tears, disquieted :
  No child was loved as he.
And all Ayodhyá, where the feast,
Music, and song, and dance had ceased,
  And merriment and glee,
Where every merchant's store was closed
That erst its glittering wares exposed,
  Was like a dried up sea.

CANTO XLIX.

THE CROSSING OF THE RIVERS.

Now Ráma, ere the night was fled,
O'er many a league of road had sped,
Till, as his course he onward held,
The morn the shades of night dispelled.
The rites of holy dawn he paid,
And all the country round surveyed.
He saw, as still he hurried through
With steeds which swift as arrows flew,
Hamlets and groves with blossoms fair,
And fields which showed the tillers' care,
While from the clustered dwellings near
The words of peasants reached his ear:
'Fie on our lord the king, whose soul
Is yielded up to love's control!
Fie on the vile Kaikeyí! Shame
On that malicious sinful dame,
Who, keenly bent on cruel deeds,
No bounds of right and virtue heeds,
But with her wicked art has sent
So good a prince to banishment,
Wise, tender-hearted, ruling well
His senses, in the woods to dwell.
Ah cruel king! his heart of steel
For his own son no love could feel,
Who with the sinless Ráma parts,
The darling of the people's hearts.'
These words he heard the peasants say,
Who dwelt in hamlets by the way,
And, lord of all the realm by right,

Through Kośala pursued his flight.
Through the auspicious flood, at last,
Of Vedaśruti's stream he passed,
And onward to the place he sped
By Saint Agastya tenanted.
Still on for many an hour he hied,
And crossed the stream whose cooling tide
Rolls onward till she meets the sea,
The herd-frequented Gomatí.[1]
Borne by his rapid horses o'er,
He reached that river's farther shore,
And Syandiká's, whose swan-loved stream
Resounded with the peacock's scream.
Then as he journeyed on his road
To his Videhan bride he showed
The populous land which Manu old
To King Ikshváku gave to hold.
The glorious prince, the lord of men
Looked on the charioteer, and then
Voiced like a wild swan, loud and clear,
He spake these words and bade him hear:
'When shall I, with returning feet
My father and my mother meet?
When shall I lead the hunt once more
In bloomy woods on Sarjú's shore?
Most eagerly I long to ride
Urging the chase on Sarjú's side,
For royal saints have seen no blame
In this, the monarch's matchless game.'
  Thus speeding on,—no rest or stay,—
Ikshváku's son pursued his way.
Oft his sweet voice the silence broke,
And thus on varied themes he spoke.

---

[1] Known to Europeans as the Goomtee.

CANTO L.

THE HALT UNDER THE INGUDÍ.[1]

So through the wide and fair extent
Of Kosala the hero went.
Then toward Ayodhyá back he gazed,
And cried, with suppliant hands upraised :
' Farewell, dear city, first in place,
Protected by Kakutstha's race !
And Gods, who in thy temples dwell,
And keep thine ancient citadel !
I from his debt my sire will free,
Thy well-loved towers again will see.
And, coming from my wild retreat,
My mother and my father meet.'
Then burning grief inflamed his eye,
As his right arm he raised on high,
And, while hot tears his cheek bedewed.
Addressed the mournful multitude :
' By love and tender pity moved,
Your love for me you well have proved ,
Now turn again with joy, and win
Success in all your hands begin.'
Before the high-souled chief they bent,
With circling steps around him went,
And then with bitter wailing, they
Departed each his several way.
Like the great sun engulfed by night,
The hero sped beyond their sight,

---

[1] A tree, commonly called *Ingua.*

While still the people mourned his fate
And wept aloud disconsolate.
The car-borne chieftain passed the bound
Of Kośala's delightful ground,
Where grain and riches bless the land,
And people give with liberal hand:
A lovely realm unvexed by fear,
Where countless shrines and stakes[1] appear:
Where mango-groves and gardens grow,
And streams of pleasant water flow:
Where dwells content a well-fed race,
And countless kine the meadows grace:
Filled with the voice of praise and prayer:
Each hamlet worth a monarch's care.
Before him three-pathed Gangá rolled
Her heavenly waters bright and cold;
O'er her pure breast no weeds were spread,
Her banks were hermit-visited.
The car-borne hero saw the tide
That ran with eddies multiplied,
And thus the charioteer addressed:
'Here on the bank to-day we rest.
Not distant from the river, see!
There grows a lofty Ingudí
With blossoms thick on every spray:
There rest we, charioteer, to-day.
I on the queen of floods will gaze,
Whose holy stream has highest praise,
Where deer, and bird, and glittering snake,
God, Daitya, bard their pastime take.'

Sumantra, Lakshman gave assent,
And with the steeds they thither went.

---

[1] Sacrificial posts to which the victims were tied.

L

When Ráma reached the lovely tree,
With Sítá and with Lakshman, he
Alighted from the car: with speed
Sumantra loosed each weary steed,
And, hand to hand in reverence laid,
Stood near to Ráma in the shade.
Ráma's dear friend, renowned by fame,
Who of Nisháda lineage came,
Guha, the mighty chief, adored
Through all the land as sovereign lord,
Soon as he heard that prince renowned
Was resting on Nisháda ground,
Begirt by counsellor and peer
And many an honoured friend drew near.
Soon as the monarch came in view,
Ráma and Lakshman toward him flew.
Then Guha, at the sight distressed,
His arms around the hero pressed,
Laid both his hands upon his head,
Bowed to those lotus feet, and said:
'O Ráma, make thy wishes known,
And be this kingdom as thine own.
Who, mighty-armed, will ever see
A guest so dear as thou to me?'

He placed before him dainty fare
Of every flavour, rich and rare,
Brought forth the gift for honoured guest,
And thus again the chief addressed:
'Welcome, dear Prince, whose arms are strong;
These lands and all to thee belong.
Thy servants we, our lord art thou;
Begin, good King, thine empire now.
See, various food before thee placed,
And cups to drink and sweets to taste.

For thee soft beds are hither borne,
And for thy horses grass and corn.'
   To Guha as he pressed and prayed,
Thus Raghu's son his answer made :
''Twas aye thy care my heart to please
With honour, love, and courtesies,
And friendship brings thee now to greet
Thy guest thus humbly on thy feet.'
   Again the hero spake, as round
The king his shapely arms he wound :
'Guha, I see that all is well
With thee and those who with thee dwell ;
That health and bliss and wealth attend
Thy realm, thyself, and every friend.
But all these friendly gifts of thine,
Bound to refuse, I must decline.
Grass, bark, and hide my only wear,
And woodland roots and fruit my fare,
On duty all my heart is set ;
I seek the woods, an anchoret.
A little grass and corn to feed
The horses--this is all I need.
So by this favour, King, alone
Shall honour due to me be shown.
For these good steeds who brought me here
Are to my sire supremely dear ;
And kind attention paid to these
Will honour me and highly please.'
   Then Guha quickly bade his train
Give water to the steeds, and grain.
And Ráma, ere the night grew dark,
Paid evening rites in dress of bark,
And tasted water, on the strand,
Drawn from the stream by Lakshmaṇ's hand.

And Lakshman with observance meet
Bathed his beloved brother's feet,
Who rested with his Maithil spouse ;
Then sat him down 'neath distant boughs.
And Guha with his bow sat near
To Lakshman and the charioteer,
And with the prince conversing kept
His faithful watch while Ráma slept.
As Daśaratha's glorious heir,
Of lofty soul and wisdom rare,
Reclining with his Sítá there
   Beside the river lay—
He who no troubles e'er had seen,
Whose life a life of bliss had been—
That night beneath the branches green
   Passed pleasantly away.

CANTO LI.

LAKSHMAN'S LAMENT.

As Lakshman still his vigil held
By unaffected love impelled,
Guha, whose heart the sight distressed,
With words like these the prince addressed
'Beloved youth, this pleasant bed
Was brought for thee, for thee is spread ;
On this, my Prince, thine eyelids close,
And heal fatigue with sweet repose.
My men are all to labour trained,
But hardship thou hast ne'er sustained.
All we this night our watch will keep
And guard Kakutstha's son asleep.
In all the world there breathes not one
More dear to me than Raghu's son.
The words I speak, heroic youth,
Are true : I swear it by my truth.
Through his dear grace supreme renown
Will, so I trust, my wishes crown.
So shall my life rich store obtain
Of merit, blest with joy and gain.
While Raghu's son and Sítá lie
Entranced in happy slumber, I
Will, with my trusty bow in hand,
Guard my dear friend with all my band.
To me, who oft these forests range,
Is naught therein or new or strange.
We could with equal might oppose

A four-fold army led by foes.'
   Then royal Lakshman made reply :
' With' thee to stand as guardian nigh,
Whose faithful soul regards the right,
Fearless we well might rest to-night.
But how, when Ráma lays his head
With Sítá on his lowly bed,—
How can I sleep? how can I care
For life, or aught that's bright and fair ?
Behold the conquering chief, whose might
Is match for Gods and fiends in fight ;
With Sítá now he rests his head
Asleep on grass beneath him spread.
Won by devotion, text, and prayer,
And many a rite performed with care,
Chief of our father's sons he shines
Well marked, like him, with favouring signs.
Brief, brief the monarch's life will be
Now his dear son is forced to flee ;
And quickly will the widowed state
Mourn for her lord disconsolate.
Each mourner there has wept her fill ;
The cries of anguish now are still :
In the king's hall each dame, o'ercome
With weariness of woe is dumb.
This first sad night of grief, I ween,
Will do to death each sorrowing queen :
Scarce is Kauśalyá left alive ;
My mother, too, can scarce survive.
If when her heart is fain to break,
She lingers for Śatrughna's sake,
Kauśalyá, mother of the chief,
Must sink beneath the chilling grief.
That town which countless thousands fill,

Whose hearts with love of Ráma thrill,—
The world's delight, so rich and fair,—
Grieved for the king, his death will share.
The hopes he fondly cherished, crossed,
Ayodhyá's throne to Ráma lost,—
With mournful cries, Too late, too late!
The king my sire will meet his fate.
And when my sire has passed away,
Most happy in their lot are they,
Allowed, with every pious care,
Part in his funeral rites to bear.
And O, may we with joy at last,—
These years of forest exile past,—
Turn to Ayodhyá's town to dwell
With him who keeps his promise well!'
　　While thus the hero mighty-souled,
In wild lament his sorrow told,
Faint with the load that on him lay,
The hours of darkness passed away.
As thus the prince, impelled by zeal
For his loved brother, prompt to feel
Strong yearnings for the people's weal,
　　His words of truth outspake,　．
King Guha, grieved to see his woe,.
Heart-stricken, gave his tears to flow,.
Tormented by the common blow,
　　Sad, as a wounded snake.

CANTO LII.

THE CROSSING OF GANGÁ.

Soon as the shades of night had fled,
Uprising from his lowly bed,
Ráma the famous, broad of chest,
His brother Lakshmaṇ thus addressed :
'Now swift upsprings the Lord of Light,
And fled is venerable night.
That dark-winged bird the Kuíl now
Is calling from the topmost bough,
And sounding from the thicket nigh
Is heard the peacock's early cry.
Come, cross the flood that seeks the sea,
The swiftly flowing Jáhnaví.'[1]
     King Guha heard his speech, agreed,
And called his minister with speed :
'A boat,' he cried,' swift, strong, and fair,
With rudder, oars, and men, prepare,
And place it ready by the shore
To bear the pilgrims quickly o'er.'
Thus Guha spake : his followers all
Bestirred them at their master's call ;
Then told the king that ready manned
A gay boat waited near the strand.
Then Guha, hand to hand applied,
With reverence thus to Ráma cried :
'The boat is ready by the shore :
How, tell me, can I aid thee more ?

---

[1] Daughter of Jahnu, a name of the Ganges. See Vol. I. p. 196.

O lord of men, it waits for thee
To cross the flood that seeks the sea.
O godlike keeper of thy vow,
Embark : the boat is ready now.'
   Then Ráma, lord of glory high,
Thus to King Guha made reply :
' Thanks for thy gracious care, my lord :
Now let the gear be placed on board.'
Each bow-armed chief, in mail encased,
Bound sword and quiver to his waist,
And then with Sítá near them hied
Down the broad river's shelving side.
Then with raised palms the charioteer,
In lowly reverence drawing near,
Cried thus to Ráma good and true :
' Now what remains for me to do ?'
   With his right hand, while answering,
     The hero touched his friend :
   ' Go back,' he said,' and on the king
     With watchful care attend.
Thus far, Sumantra, thou wast guide ;
Now to Ayodhyá turn,' he cried :
' Hence seek we, leaving steeds and car,
On foot the wood that stretches far.'

   Sumantra, when, with grieving heart,
He heard the hero bid him part,
Thus to the bravest of the brave,
Ikshváku's son, his answer gave :
' In all the world men tell of naught,
To match thy deed, by heroes wrought—
Thus with thy brother and thy wife
Thrall-like to lead a forest life.
No meet reward of fruit repays
Thy holy lore, thy saintlike days,

Thy tender soul, thy love of truth,
If woe like this afflicts thy youth.
Thou, roaming under forest boughs
With thy dear brother and thy spouse,
Shalt richer meed of glory gain
Than if three worlds confessed thy reign.
Sad is our fate, O Ráma; we,
Abandoned and repelled by thee,
Must serve as thralls Kaikeyí's will,
Imperious, wicked, born to ill.'
　　Thus cried the faithful charioteer,
As Raghu's son, in rede his peer,
Was fast departing on his road,—
And long his tears of anguish flowed.
But Ráma, when those tears were dried,
His lips with water purified,
And in soft accents, sweet and clear,
Again addressed the charioteer:
'I find no heart, my friend, like thine,
So faithful to Ikshváku's line.
Still first in view this object keep,
That ne'er for me my sire may weep.
For he, the world's far-ruling king,
Is old, and wild with sorrow's sting;
With love's great burthen worn and weak:
Deem this the cause that thus I speak.
Whate'er the high-souled king decrees
His loved Kaikeyí's heart to please,
Yea, be his order what it may,
Without demur thou must obey.
For this alone great monarchs reign,
That ne'er a wish be formed in vain.
Then, O Sumantra, well provide
That by no check the king be tried;

Nor let his heart in sorrow pine :
This care, my faithful friend, be thine.
The honoured king my father greet,
And thus for me my words repeat
To him whose senses are controlled,
Untried till now by grief, and old :
' I, Sítá, Lakshman sorrow not,
O Monarch, for our altered lot :
The same to us, if here we roam,
Or if Ayodhyá be our home.
The fourteen years will quickly fly,
The happy hour will soon be nigh
When thou, my lord, again shalt see
Lakshman, the Maithil dame, and me.'
Thus having soothed, O charioteer,
My father and my mother dear,
Let all the queens my message learn,
But to Kaikeyí chiefly turn.
With loving blessings from the three,
From Lakshman, Sítá, and from me,
My mother, Queen Kausalyá, greet
With reverence to her sacred feet.
And add this prayer of mine : ' O King,
Send quickly forth and Bharat bring,
And set him on the royal throne
Which thy decree has made his own.
When he upon the throne is placed,
When thy fond arms are round him laced,
Thine aged heart will cease to ache
With bitter pangs for Ráma's sake.'
And say to Bharat : ' See thou treat
The queens with all observance meet :
What care the king receives, the same
Show thou alike to every dame.

Obedience to thy father's will
Who chooses thee the throne to fill,
Will earn for thee a store of bliss
Both in the world to come and this.'

　Thus Ráma bade Sumantra go
With thoughtful care instructed so.
Sumantra all his message heard,
And spake again, by passion stirred:
'O, should deep feeling mar in aught
The speech by fond devotion taught,
Forgive whate'er I wildly speak:
My love is strong, my tongue is weak
How shall I, if deprived of thee,
Return that mournful town to see?
Where sick at heart the people are
Because their Rama roams afar.
Woe will be theirs too deep to brook
When on the empty car they look,
As when from hosts, whose chiefs are slain,
One charioteer comes home again.
This very day, I ween, is food
Forsworn by all the multitude,
Thinking that thou, with hosts to aid,
Art dwelling in the wild wood's shade.
The great despair, the shriek of woe
They uttered when they saw thee go,
Will, when I come with none beside,
A hundred-fold be multiplied.
How to Kauśalyá can I say:
'O Queen, I took thy son away,
And with thy brother left him well:
Weep not for him; thy woe dispel'?
So false a tale I cannot frame,
Yet how speak truth and grieve the dame?

How shall these horses, fleet and bold,
Whom not a hand but mine can hold,
Bear others, wont to whirl the car
Wherein Ikshváku's children are?
Without thee, Prince, I cannot, no,
I cannot to Ayodhyá go.
Then deign, O Ráma, to relent,
And let me share thy banishment.
But if no prayers can move thy heart,
If thou wilt quit me and depart,
The flames shall end my car and me,
Deserted thus and reft of thee.
In the wild wood when foes are near,
When dangers check thy vows austere,
Borne in my car will I attend, ·
All danger and all care to end.
For thy dear sake I love the skill
That guides the steed and curbs his will
And soon a forest life will be
As pleasant, for my love of thee.
And if these horses near thee dwell,
And serve thee in the forest well,
They, for their service, will not miss
The due reward of highest bliss.
Thine orders, as with thee I stray,
Will I with heart and head obey,
Prepared, for thee, without a sigh,
To lose Ayodhyá or the sky.
As one defiled with hideous sin,
I never more can pass within
Ayodhyá, city of our king,
Unless beside me thee I bring.
One wish is mine, I ask no more,
That, when thy banishment is o'er,

I in my car may bear my lord,
Triumphant, to his home restored.
The fourteen years, if spent with thee,
Will swift as light-winged moments flee ;
But the same years, without thee told,
Were magnified a hundred-fold.
Do not, kind lord, thy servant leave,
Who to his master's son would cleave,
And the same path with him pursue,
Devoted, tender, just, and true.'
  Again, again Sumantra made
His varied plaint, and wept and prayed.
Him Raghu's son, whose tender breast
Felt for his servants, thus addressed :
' O faithful servant, well my heart
Knows how attached and true thou art.
Hear thou the words I speak, and know
Why to the town I bid thee go.
Soon as Kaikeyí, youngest queen,
Thy coming to the town has seen,
No doubt will then her mind oppress
That Ráma roams the wilderness.
And so the dame, her heart content
With proof of Ráma's banishment,
Will doubt the virtuous king no more
As faithless to the oath he swore.
Chief of my cares is this, that she,
Youngest amid the queens, may see
Bharat her son securely reign
O'er rich Ayodhyá's wide domain.
For mine and for the monarch's sake
Do thou thy journey homeward take,
And, as I bade, repeat each word
That from my lips thou here hast heard.'

Thus spake the prince, and strove to cheer
The sad heart of the charioteer,
And then to royal Guha said
These words most wise and spirited :
' Guha, dear friend, it is not meet
'I'let people throng my calm retreat :
Ther must live a strict recluse,
_And mould my life by hermits' use.
I now the ancient rule accept
By good ascetics gladly kept.
I go : bring fig-tree juice that I
In matted coils my hair may tie.'
  , Quick Guha hastened to produce,
To thie king's son, that sacred juice.
Wher Ráma of his long locks made,
And Lakshman's too, the hermit braid.
And the two royal brothers there
With coats of bark and matted hair,
Transformed in lovely likeness stood
To hermit saints who love the wood.
So Ráma, with his brother bold,
A pious anchorite enrolled,
Obeyed the vow which hermits take,
And to his friend, King Guha, spake :
' May people, treasure, army share,
And fenced forts, thy constant care :
Attend to all : supremely haid
The sovereign's task, to watch and guard.'
  Ikshváku's son, the good and brave,
This last farewell to Guha gave.
And then, with Lakshman and his bride,
Determined, on his way he hied.
Soon as he viewed, upon the shore,
The bark prepared to waft them o'er

Impetuous Gangá's rolling tide,
To Lakshman thus the chieftain cried:
' Brother, embark ; thy hand extend,
Thy gentle aid to Sítá lend ;
With care her trembling footsteps guide,
And place the lady by thy side.'
When Lakshman heard, prepared to aid,
His brother's words he swift obeyed.
Within the bark he placed the dame, '
Then to her side the hero came.
Next Lakshman's elder brother, lord
Of brightest glory, went on board,
Breathing a prayer for blessings, meet
For priest or warrior to repeat.
Then he and car-borne Lakshman bent,
Well-pleased, their heads, most reverent,
Their hands, with Sítá, having dipped,
As Scripture bids, and water sipped,
Farewell to wise Sumantra said,
And Guha, with the train he led.
So Ráma took, on board, his stand,
And urged the vessel from the land.
Then swift by vigorous arms impelled
Her onward course the vessel held,
And guided by the helmsman through
The dashing waves of Gangá flew,
Half way across the flood they came,
When Sítá, free from spot and blame,
Her reverent hands together pressed,
The Goddess of the stream addressed:
' May the great chieftain here who springs
From Daśaratha, best of kings,
Protected by thy care, fulfil
His prudent father's royal will.

When in the forest he has spent
His fourteen years of banishment,
With his dear brother and with me
His home again my lord shall see.
Returning on that blissful day,
I will to thee mine offerings pay,
Dear Queen, whose waters gently flow,
Who canst all blessed gifts bestow.
For, three-pathed Queen, though wandering here,
Thy waves descend from Brahmá's sphere,
Spouse of the God o'er floods supreme,
Though rolling here thy glorious stream.
To thee, fair Queen, my head shall bend,
To thee shall hymns of praise ascend,
When my brave lord shall turn again,
And, joyful, o'er his kingdom reign.
To win thy grace, O Queen divine,
A hundred thousand fairest kine,
And precious robes and finest meal
Among the Bráhmans will I deal.
A hundred jars of wine shall flow,
When to my home, O Queen, I go ;
With these, and flesh, and corn, and rice,
Will I, delighted, sacrifice.
Each hallowed spot, each holy shrine
That stands on these fair shores of thine,
Each fane and altar on thy banks
Shall share my offerings and thanks.
With me and Lakshman, free from harm,
May he the blameless, strong of arm,
Rescek Ayodhyá from the wild,
O blameless Lady undefiled !'
   As, praying for her husband's sake,
The faultless dame to Gangá spake,

                 M

To the right bank the vessel flew
With her whose heart was right and true.
Soon as the bark had crossed the wave,
The lion leader of the brave,
Leaving the vessel on the strand,
With wife and brother leapt to land.
Then Ráma thus the piince addressed
Who filled with joy Sumitrá's breast:
' Be thiue alike to guard and aid
In peopled spot, in lonely shade.
Do thou, Sumitrá's son, precede:
Let Sítá walk where thou shalt lead.
Behind you both my place shall be,
To guard the Maithil dame and thee.
For she, to woe a stranger yet,
No toil or grief till now has met ;
The fair Videhan will assay
The pains of forest life to-day.
To-day her tender feet must tread
Rough rocky wilds around her spread :
No tilth is there, no gardens grow,
No crowding people come and go.'
 The hero ceased : and Lakshmaṇ led
Obedient to the words he said :
And Sítá followed him, and then
Came Raghu's pride, the lord of men.
With Sítá walking o'er the sand
They sought the forest, bow in hand,
But still their lingering glances threw
Where yet Sumantra stood in view.
Sumantra, when his watchful eye
The royal youths no more could spy,
Turned from the spot whereon he stood
Homeward with Guha from the wood.

Still on the brothers forced their way
Where sweet birds sang on every spray,
Though scarce the eye a path could find
Mid flowering trees where creepers twined.
Far on the princely brothers pressed,
And stayed their feet at length to rest
Beneath a fig-tree's mighty shade
With countless pendent shoots displayed.
Reclining there a while at ease,
They saw, not far, beneath fair trees
A lake with many a lotus bright
That bore the name of Lovely Sight.
Ráma his wife's attention drew,
And Lakshmaṇ's, to the charming view :
' Look, brother, look how fair the flood
Glows with the lotus, flower and bud !'
     They drank the water fresh and clear,
And with their shafts they slew a deer.
A fire of boughs they made in haste,
And in the flame the meat they placed.
So Raghu's sons with Sítá shared
The hunter's meal their hands prepared,
Then counselled that the spreading tree
Their shelter and their home should be.

CANTO LIII.

— ◦◦ —

RÁMA'S LAMENT.

———•———

When evening rites were duly paid,
Reclined beneath the leafy shade,
To Lakshman thus spake Rám , best
Of those who glad a people's breast :
'Now the first night has closed the day
That saw us from our country stray,
And parted from the charioteer ;
Yet grieve not thou, my brother dear
Henceforth by night, when others sleep,
Must we our careful vigil keep,
Watching for Sítá's welfare thus,
For her dear life depends on us.
Bring me the leaves that lie around,
And spread them here upon the ground,
That we on lowly beds may lie,
And let in talk the night go by.'

So on the ground with leaves o'erspread,
He who should press a royal bed,
Ráma with Lakshman thus conversed,
And many a pleasant tale rehearsed :
'This night the king,' he cried, 'alas !
In broken sleep will sadly pass.
Kaikeyí now content should be,
For mistress of her wish is she.
So fiercely she for empire yearns,
That when her Bharat home returns,
She in her greed, may even bring

Destruction on our lord the king.
What can he do, in feeble eld,
Reft of all aid and me expelled,
His soul enslaved by love, a thrall
Obedient to Kaikeyí's call?
As thus I muse upon his woe
And all his wisdom's overthrow,
Love is, methinks, of greater might
To stir the heart than gain and right.
For who, in wisdom's lore untaught,
Could by a beauty's prayer be bought
To quit his own obedient son,
Who loves him, as my sire has done?
Bharat, Kaikeyí's child, alone
Will, with his wife, enjoy the throne,
And blissfully his rule maintain
O'er happy Kośala's domain.
To Bharat's single lot will fall
The kingdom and the power and all,
When fails the king from length of days,
And Ráma in the forest strays.
Whoe'er, neglecting right and gain,
Lets conquering love his soul enchain,
To him, like Daśaratha's lot,
Comes woe with feet that tarry not.
Methinks at last the royal dame,
Dear Lakshman, has secured her aim,
To see at once her husband dead,
Her son enthroned, and Ráma fled.
Ah me! I fear, lest borne away
By frenzy of success, she slay
Kauśalyá, through her wicked hate
Of me, bereft, disconsolate;
Or her who aye for me has striven,

Sumitrá, to devotion given.
Hence, Lakshman, to Ayodhyá speed,
Returning in the hour of need.
With Sítá I my steps will bend
Where Dandak's mighty woods extend.
No guardian has Kauśalyá now:
O, be her friend and guardian thou.
Strong hate may vile Kaikeyí lead
To many a base unrighteous deed,
Treading my mother 'neath her feet
When Bharat holds the royal seat.
Sure in some antenatal time
Were children, by Kauśalyá's crime,
Torn from their mothers' arms away,
And hence she mourns this evil day.
She for her child no toil would spare,
Tending me long with pain and care;
Now in the hour of fruitage she
Has lost that son, ah, woe is me.
O Lakshman, may no matron e'er
A son so doomed to sorrow bear
As I, my mother's heart who rend
With anguish that can never end.
The Sáriká,¹ methinks, possessed
More love than glows in Ráma's breast,
Who, as the tale is told to us,
Addressed the stricken parrot thus:
'Parrot, the capturer's talons tear,
While yet alone thou flutterest there,
Before his mouth has closed on me':
So cried the bird, herself to free.
Reft of her son, in childless woe,

---

¹ The *Mainá* or Gracula religiosa, a favourite cage-bird, easily taught
to talk.

My mother's tears for ever flow :
Ill-fated, doomed with grief to strive,
What aid can she from me derive ?
Pressed down by care, she cannot rise
From sorrow's flood wherein she lies.
In righteous wrath my single arm
Could, with my bow, protect from harm
Ayodhyá's town and all the earth:
But what is hero prowess worth ?
Lest breaking duty's law I sin,
And lose the heaven I strive to win,
The forest life to-day I choose,
And kingly state and power refuse.'
　　Thus mourning in that lonely spot
The troubled chief bewailed his lot,
And filled with tears, his eyes ran o'er ;
Then silent sat, and spake no more.
To him, when ceased his loud lament,
Like fire whose brilliant might is spent,
Or the great sea when sleeps the wave,
Thus Lakshman consolation gave :
' Chief of the brave who bear the bow,
E'en now Ayodhyá, sunk in woe,
By thy departure reft of light
Is gloomy as the moonless night.
Unfit it seems that thou, O chief,
Shouldst so afflict thy soul with grief :
So wilt thou Sítá's heart consign
To deep despair as well as mine.
Not I, O Raghu's son, nor she
Could live one hour deprived of thee :
We were, without thine arm to save,
Like fish deserted by the wave.
Although my mother dear to meet,

Śatrughna, and the king, were sweet,
On them, or heaven, to feed mine eye
Were nothing, if thou wert not by.'
   Sitting at ease, their glances fell
Upon the beds, constructed well,
And there the sons of virtue laid
Their limbs beneath the fig-tree's shade.

CANTO LIV.

BHARADVÁJA'S HERMITAGE.

So there that night the heroes spent
Under the boughs that o'er them bent,
And when the sun his glory spread,
Upstarting, from the place they sped.
On to that spot they made their way,
Through the dense wood that round them lay,
Where Yamuná's[1] swift waters glide
To blend with Gangá's holy tide.
Charmed with the prospect ever new
The glorious heroes wandered through
Full many a spot of pleasant ground,
Rejoicing as they gazed around,
With eager eye and heart at ease.
On countless sorts of flowery trees.
And now the day was half-way sped
When thus to Lakshman Ráma said :
'There, there, dear brother, turn thine eyes ;
See near Prayág[2] that smoke arise :
The banner of our Lord of Flames
The dwelling of some saint proclaims.
Near to the place our steps we bend
Where Yamuná and Gangá blend.
I hear and mark the deafening roar
When chafing floods together pour.
See, near us on the ground are left

---

[1] The Jumna.
[2] The Hindu name of Allahabad.

Dry logs, by labouring woodmen cleft,
And the tall trees, that blossom near
Saint Bharadvája's home, appear.'
    The bow-armed princes onward passed,
And as the sun was sinking fast
They reached the hermit's dwelling, set
Near where the rushing waters met.
The presence of the warrior scared
The deer and birds as on he fared,
And struck them with unwonted awe:
Then Bharadvája's cot they saw.
The high-souled hermit soon they found
Girt by his dear disciples round:
Calm saint, whose vows had well been wrought,
Whose fervent rites keen sight had bought.
Duly had flames of worship blazed
When Ráma on the hermit gazed;
His suppliant hands the hero raised,
Drew nearer to the holy man
With his companions, and began,
Declaring both his name and race
And why they sought that distant place:
'Saint, Daśaratha's children we,
Ráma and Lakshman, come to thee.
This my good wife from Janak springs,
The best of fair Videha's kings;
Through lonely wilds, a faultless dame,
To this pure grove with me she came.
My younger brother follows still
Me banished by my father's will:
Sumitrá's son, bound by a vow,—
He roams the wood beside me now.
Sent by my father forth to rove,
We seek, O Saint, some holy grove,

Where lives of hermits we may lead,
And upon fruits and berries feed.'
  When Bharadvája, prudent-souled,
Had heard the prince his tale unfold,
Water he bade them bring, a bull,
And honour-gifts in dishes full,
And drink and food of varied taste,
Berries and roots, before him placed,
And then the great ascetic showed
A cottage for the guests' abode.
The saint these honours gladly paid
To Ráma who had thither strayed,
Then compassed sat by birds and deer
And many a hermit resting near.
The prince received the service kind,
And sat him down rejoiced in mind.
Then Bharadvája silence broke,
And thus the words of duty spoke :
' Kakutstha's royal son, that thou
Hadst sought this grove I knew ere now.
Mine ears have heard thy story, sent
Without a sin to banishment.
Behold, O Prince, this ample space
Near where the mingling floods embrace,
Holy, and beautiful, and clear :
Dwell with us, and be happy here.'
  By Bharadvája thus addressed,
Ráma whose kind and tender breast
All living things would bless and save,
In gracious words his answer gave :
  ' My honoured lord, this tranquil spot,
Fair home of hermits, suits me not :
For all the neighbouring people here
Will seek us when they know me near :

With eager wish to look on me,
And the Videhan dame to see,
A crowd of rustics will intrude
Upon the holy solitude.
Provide, O gracious lord, I pray,
Some quiet home that lies away,
Where my Videhan spouse may dwell
Tasting the bliss deserved so well.'
　The hermit heard the prayer he made :
A while in earnest thought he stayed,
And then in words like these expressed
His answer to the chief's request :
'Ten leagues away there stands a hill
Where thou mayst live, if such thy will :
A holy mount, exceeding fair ;
Great saints have made their dwelling there :
There great Langúrs [1] in thousands play,
And bears amid the thickets stray ;
Wide-known by Chitrakúṭa's name,
It rivals Gandhamádan's [2] fame.
Long as the man that hill who seeks
Gazes upon its sacred peaks,
To holy things his soul he gives
And pure from thought of evil lives
There, while a hundred autumns fled,
Has many a saint with hoary head
Spent his pure life, and won the prize,
By deep devotion, in the skies :
Best home, I ween, if such retreat,
Far from the ways of men, be sweet :
Or let thy years of exile flee
Here in this hermitage with me.'

---

[1] The Langúr is a large monkey.

[2] A mountain said to lie to the east of Meru

Thus Bharadvája spake, and trained
In lore of duty, entertained
The princes and the dame, and pressed
His friendly gifts on every guest.
    Thus to Prayág the hero went,
Thus saw the saint preëminent,
And varied speeches heard and said :
Then holy night o'er heaven was spread.
And Ráma took, by toil oppressed,
With Sítá and his brother, rest ;
And so the night, with sweet content,
In Bharadvája's grove was spent.
But when the dawn dispelled the night,
Ráma approached the anchorite,
And thus addressed the holy sire
Whose glory shone like kindled fire :
' Well have we spent, O truthful Sage,
The night within thy hermitage :
Now let my lord his guests permit
For their new home his grove to quit.'
    Then, as he saw the morning break,
In answer Bharadvája spake :
' Go forth to Chitrakúṭa's hill,
Where berries grow, and sweets distil :
Full well, I deem, that home will suit
Thee, Ráma, strong and resolute.
Go forth, and Chitrakúṭa seek,
Famed mountain of the Varied Peak.
In the wild woods that gird him round
All creatures of the chase are found :
Thou in the glades shalt see appear
Vast herds of elephants and deer.
With Sítá there shalt thou delight
To gaze upon the woody height ;

There with expanding heart to look
On river, table-land, and brook,
And see the foaming torrent rave
Impetuous from the mountain cave.
Auspicious hill ! where all day long
The lapwing's cry, the Koïl's song
   Make all who listen gay :
Where all is fresh and fair to see,
Where elephants and deer roam free,
    There, as a hermit, stay.'

CANTO LV.

THE PASSAGE OF YAMUNÁ.

The princely tamers of their foes
Thus passed the night in calm repose,
Then to the hermit having bent
With reverence, on their way they went.
High favour Bharadvája showed,
And blessed them ready for the road,
With such fond looks as fathers throw
On their own sons before they go.
Then spake the saint with glory bright
To Ráma peerless in his might :
' First, lords of men, direct your feet
Where Yamuná and Gangá meet ;
Then to the swift Kálindí [1] go,
Whose westward waves to Gangá flow.
When thou shalt see her lovely shore
Worn by their feet who hasten o'er,.
Then, Raghu's son, a raft prepare,
And cross the Sun-born river there.
Upon her farther bank a tree,
Near to the landing, wilt thou see.
The blessed source of varied gifts,
There her green boughs that Fig-tree lifts :
A tree where countless birds abide,
By Śyáma's name known far and wide.
Sítá, revere that holy shade :
There be thy prayers for blessing prayed.

---

[1] Another name of the Jumna, daughter of the Sun.

Thence for a league your way pursue,
And a dark wood shall meet your view,
Where tall bamboos their foliage show,
The Gum-tree and the Jujube grow.
To Chitrakúṭa have I oft
Trodden that path so smooth and soft,
Where burning woods no traveller scare,
But all is pleasant, green, and fair.'
   When thus the guests their road had learned,
Back to his cot the hermit turned,
And Ráma, Lakshman, Sítá paid
Their reverent thanks for courteous aid.
Thus Ráma spake to Lakshman, when
The saint had left the lords of men :
'Great store of bliss in sooth is ours
On whom his love the hermit showers.'
As each to other wisely talked,
The lion lords together walked
On to Kálindí's woody shore ;
And gentle Sítá went before.
They reached that flood, whose waters flee
With rapid current to the sea ;
Their minds a while to thought they gave,
And counselled how to cross the wave.
At length, with logs together laid,
A mighty raft the brothers made.
Then dry bamboos across were tied,
And grass was spread from side to side.
And the great hero Lakshman brought
Cane and Rose-Apple boughs, and wrought,
Trimming the branches smooth and neat,
For Sítá's use a pleasant seat.
And Ráma placed thereon his dame
Touched with a momentary shame,

Resembling in her glorious mien
All-thought-surpassing Fortune's Queen.
Then Ráma hastened to dispose,
Each in its place, the skins and bows,
And by the fair Videhan laid
The coats, the ornaments, and spade.
When Sítá thus was set on board,
And all their gear was duly stored,
The heroes, each with vigorous hand,
Pushed off the raft and left the land.
When half its way the raft had made,
Thus Sítá to Kálindí prayed:
' Goddess, whose flood I traverse now,
Grant that my lord may keep his vow.
My gift shall be a thousand kine,
A hundred jars shall pour their wine,
When Ráma sees that town again
Where old Ikshváku's children reign.'
  Thus to Kálindí's stream she sued
And prayed in suppliant attitude.
Then to the river's bank the dame,
Fervent in supplication, came.
They left the raft that brought them o'er,
And the thick wood that clothed the shore,
And to the Fig-tree Śyáma made
Their way, so cool with verdant shade.
Then Sítá viewed that best of trees,
And reverent spake in words like these:
'Hail, hail, O mighty tree ! Allow
My husband to complete his vow ;
Let us returning, I entreat,
Kauśalyá and Sumitrá meet.'
Then with her hands together placed
Around the tree she duly paced.

N

When Ráma saw his blameless spouse
A suppliant under holy boughs,
The gentle darling of his heart,
He thus to Lakshman spake apart :
'Brother, by thee our way be led ;
Let Sítá close behind thee tread :
I, best of men, will grasp my bow,
And hindmost of the three will go.
What fruits soe'er her fancy take,
Or flowers half hidden in the brake,
For Janak's child forget not thou
To gather from the brake or bough.'

Thus on they fared. The tender dame
Asked Ráma, as they walked, the name
Of every shrub that blossoms bore,
Creeper, and tree unseen before :
And Lakshman fetched, at Sítá's prayer,
Boughs of each tree with clusters fair.
Then Janak's daughter joyed to see
The sand-discoloured river flee,
Where the glad cry of many a bird,
The sáras and the swan, was heard.
A league the brothers travelled through
The forest : noble game they slew :
Beneath the trees their meal they dressed,
And sat them down to eat and rest.
A while in that delightful shade
Where elephants unnumbered strayed,
Where peacocks screamed and monkeys played
  They wandered with delight.
Then by the river's side they found
A pleasant spot of level ground,
Where all was smooth and fair around,
  Their lodging for the night.

CANTO LVI.

CHITRAKÚṬA

Then Ráma, when the morning rose,
Called Lakshmaṇ gently from repose :
' Awake, the pleasant voices hear
Of forest birds that warble near.
Scourge of thy foes, no longer stay ;
The hour is come to speed away.'
　　The slumbering prince unclosed his eyes
When thus his brother bade him rise,
Compelling, at the timely cry,
Fatigue, and sleep, and rest to fly.
The brothers rose and Sítá too ;
Pure water from the stream they drew,
Paid morning rites, then followed still
The road to Chitrakúṭa's hill.
Then Ráma as he took the road
With Lakshmaṇ, while the morning glowed,
To the Videhan lady cried,
Sítá the fair, the lotus-eyed :
' Look round thee, dear ; each flowery tree
Touched with the fire of morning see :
The Kinśuk, now the Frosts are fled,—
How glorious with his wreaths of red !
The Bel-trees see, so loved of men,
Hanging their boughs in every glen,
O'erburthened with their fruit and flowers :
A plenteous store of food is ours.

See, Lakshmaṇ, in the leafy trees,
　　Where'er they make their home,
Down hangs, the work of labouring bees,
　　The ponderous honeycomb.
In the fair wood before us spread
　　The startled wild-cock cries:
Hark, where the flowers are soft to tread,
　　The peacock's voice replies.
Where elephants are roaming free,
　　And sweet birds' songs are loud,
The glorious Chitrakúṭa see:
　　His peaks are in the cloud.
On fair smooth ground he stands displayed,
　　Begirt by many a tree:
O brother, in that holy shade
　　How happy shall we be!'[1]
Then Ráma, Lakshmaṇ, Sítá, each
Spoke raising suppliant hands this speech
To him, in woodland dwelling met,
Válmíki, ancient anchoret:
'O Saint, this mountain takes the mind,
With creepers, trees of every kind,
With fruit and roots abounding thus,
A pleasant life it offers us:
Here for a while we fain would stay,
And pass a season blithe and gay.'
　　Them the great saint, in duty trained,
With honour gladly entertained:

---

[1] ' We have often looked on that green hill: it is the holiest spot of that sect of the Hindu faith who devote themselves to this incarnation of Vishṇu. The whole neighbourhood is Ráma's country. Every head-land has some legend, every cavern is connected with his name; some of the wild fruits are still called *Sítáphal,* being the reputed food of the exiles. Thousands and thousands annually visit the spot, and round the hill is a raised foot-path, on which the devotee, with naked feet, reads full of pious awe.' *Calcutta Review.* Vol. XXIII.

He gave his guests a welcome fair,
And bade them sit and rest them there.
Ráma of mighty arm and chest
His faithful Lakshman then addressed :
‘ Brother, bring hither from the wood
Selected timber strong and good,
And build therewith a little cot :
My heart rejoices in the spot
That lies beneath the mountain’s side,
Remote, with water well supplied.’
    Sumitrá’s son his words obeyed,
Brought many a tree, and deftly made,
With branches in the forest cut,
As Ráma bade, a leafy hut.
Then Ráma, when the cottage stood
Fair, firmly built, and walled with wood,
To Lakshman spake, whose eager mind
To do his brother’s will inclined :
‘ Now, Lakshman, as our cot is made,
Must sacrifice be duly paid
By us, for lengthened life who hope,
With venison of the antelope.
Away, O bright-eyed Lakshman, speed :
Struck by thy bow a deer must bleed :
As Scripture bids, we must not slight
The duty that commands the rite.’
    Lakshman, the chief whose arrows laid
His foemen low, his word obeyed ;
And Ráma thus again addressed
The swift performer of his hest :
‘ Prepare the venison thou hast shot,
To sacrifice for this our cot.
Haste, brother dear, for this the hour,
And this the day of certain power.’

Then glorious Lakshman took the buck
His arrow in the wood had struck;
Bearing his mighty load he came,
And laid it in the kindled flame.
Soon as he saw the meat was done,
And that the juices ceased to run
. From the broiled carcass, Lakshman then
Spoke thus to Ráma best of men :
'The carcass of the buck, entire,
Is ready dressed upon the fire.
Now be the sacred rites begun
To please the Gods, thou godlike one.'

Ráma the good, in ritual trained,
Pure from the bath, with thoughts restrained,
Hasted those verses to repeat
Which make the sacrifice complete.
The hosts celestial came in view,
And Ráma to the cot withdrew,
While a sweet sense of rapture stole
Through the unequalled hero's soul.
He paid the Viśvedevas'[1] due,
And Rudra's right, and Vishnu's too,
Nor wonted blessings, to protect
Their new-built home, did he neglect.
With voice repressed he breathed the prayer,
Bathed duly in the river fair,
And gave good offerings that remove
The stain of sin, as texts approve.
And many an altar there he made,
And shrines, to suit the holy shade,
All decked with woodland chaplets sweet,

---

[1] Deities of a particular class in which five or ten are enumerated. They are worshipped particularly at the funeral obsequies in honour of deceased progenitors.

And fruit and roots and roasted meat,
With muttered prayer, as texts require,
Water, and grass and wood and fire.
So Ráma, Lakshman, Sítá paid
Their offerings to each God and shade,
And entered then their pleasant cot
That bore fair signs of happy lot.
They entered, the illustrious three,
The well-set cottage, fair to see,
Roofed with the leaves of many a tree,
  And fenced from wind and rain :
So, at their Father Brahmá's call,
The Gods of heaven, assembling all,
To their own glorious council hall
  Advance in shining train.
So, resting on that lovely hill,
Near the fair lily-covered rill,
  The happy prince forgot,
Surrounded by the birds and deer,
The woe, the longing, and the fear
  That gloom the exile's lot.

CANTO LVII.

SUMANTRA'S RETURN.

When Ráma reached the southern bank,
King Guha's heart with sorrow sank:
He with Sumantra talked, and spent
With his deep sorrow, homeward went.
Sumantra, as the king decreed,
Yoked to the car each noble steed,
And to Ayodhyá's city sped
With his sad heart disquieted.
On lake and brook and scented grove
His glances fell, as on he drove:
City and village came in view
As o'er the road his coursers flew.
On the third day the charioteer,
When now the hour of night was near,
Came to Ayodhyá's gate, and found
The city all in sorrow drowned.
To him, in spirit quite cast down,
Forsaken seemed the silent town,
And by the rush of grief oppressed
He pondered in his mournful breast:
' Is all Ayodhyá burnt with grief,
Steed, elephant, and man, and chief?
Does her loved Ráma's exile so
Afflict her with the fires of woe?'
Thus as he mused, his steeds flew fast,
And swiftly through the gate he passed.
On drove the charioteer, and then

In hundreds, yea in thousands, men
Ran to the car from every side,
And, 'Ráma, where is Ráma?' cried.
Sumantra said : 'My chariot bore
The duteous prince to Gangá's shore ;
I left him there at his behest,
And homeward to Ayodhyá pressed.'
Soon as the anxious people knew
That he was o'er the flood, they drew
Deep sighs, and crying, Ráma ! all
Wailed, and big tears began to fall.
He heard the mournful words prolonged,
As here and there the people thronged :
' Woe, woe for us, forlorn, undone,
No more to look on Raghu's son!
His like again we ne'er shall see,
Of heart so true, of hand so free,
In gifts, in gatherings for debate,
When marriage pomps we celebrate.
What should we do ?   What earthly thing
Can rest, or hope, or pleasure bring ?'
   Thus the sad town, which Ráma kept
As a kind father, wailed and wept.
Each mansion, as the car went by,
Sent forth a loud and bitter cry,
As to the window every dame,
Mourning for banished Ráma, came.
As his sad eyes with tears o'erflowed,
He sped along the royal road
To Daśaratha's high abode.
There leaping down his car he stayed ;
Within the gates his way he made ;
Through seven broad courts he onward hied, .
Where people thronged on every side.

From each high terrace, wild with woe,
The royal ladies flocked below :
He heard them talk in gentle tone,
As each for Ráma made her moan :
' What will the charioteer reply
To Queen Kauśalyá's eager cry ?
With Ráma from the gates he went ;
Homeward alone, his steps are bent.
Hard is a life with woe distressed,
But difficult to win is rest,
If, when her son is banished, still
She lives beneath her load of ill.'
   Such was the speech Sumantra heard
From them whom grief unfeigned had stirred.
As fires of anguish burnt him through,
Swift to the monarch's hall he drew,
Past the eighth court : there met his sight
The sovereign in his palace bright,
Still weeping for his son, forlorn,
Pale, faint, and all with sorrow worn.
As there he sat, Sumantra bent
And did obeisance reverent,
And to the king repeated o'er
The message he from Ráma bore.
   The monarch heard, and well-nigh brake
His heart, but yet no word he spake :
Fainting to earth he fell, and dumb,
By grief for Ráma overcome.
Rang through the hall a startling cry,
And women's arms were tossed on high,
When, with his senses all astray,
Upon the ground the monarch lay.
Kauśalyá, with Sumitrá's aid,
Raised from the ground her lord dismayed :

'Sire, of high fate,' she cried, 'O, why
Dost thou no single word reply
To Ráma's messenger who brings
News of his painful wanderings?
The great injustice done, art thou
Shame-stricken for thy conduct now?
Rise up, and do thy part: bestow
Comfort and help in this our woe.
Speak freely, King; dismiss thy fear,
For Queen Kaikeyí stands not near,
Afraid of whom thou wouldst not seek
Tidings of Ráma: freely speak.'
  When the sad queen had ended so,
She sank, insatiate in her woe,
And prostrate lay upon the ground,
While her faint voice by sobs was drowned.
When all the ladies in despair
Saw Queen Kaúsalyá wailing there,
And the poor king oppressed with pain,
They flocked around and wept again.

CANTO LVIII.

RÁMA'S MESSAGE.

The king a while had senseless lain,
When care brought memory back again.
Then straight he called, the news to hear
Of Ráma, for the charioteer.
With reverent hand to hand applied
He waited by the old man's side,
Whose mind with anguish was distraught
Like a great elephant newly caught.
The king with bitter pain distressed
The faithful charioteer addressed,
Who, sad of mien, with flooded eye,
And dust upon his limbs, stood by :
' Where will be Ráma's dwelling now
At some tree's foot, beneath the bough ?
Ah, what will be the exile's food,
Bred up with kind solicitude ?
Can he, long lapped in pleasant rest,
Unmeet for pain, by pain oppressed,
Son of earth's king, his sad night spend
Earth-couched, as one that has no friend ?
Behind him, when abroad he sped,
Cars, elephant, and foot were led :
Then how shall Ráma dwell afar
In the wild woods where no men are ?
How, tell me, did the princes there,
With Sítá good and soft and fair,
Alighting from the chariot, tread

The forest wilds around them spread ?
A happy lot is thine, I ween,
Whose eyes my two dear sons have seen
Seeking on foot the forest shade,
Like the bright Twins to view displayed,
The heavenly Aśvins, when they seek
The woods that hang 'neath Mandar's peak.
What words, Sumantra, quickly tell,
From Ráma, Lakshman, Sítá, fell ?
How in the wood did Ráma eat ?
What was his bed, and what his seat ?
Full answer to my questions give,
For I on thy replies shall live,
As with the saints Yayáti held
Sweet converse, from the skies expelled.'

Urged by the lord of men to speak,
Whose sobbing voice came faint and weak,
Thus he, while tears his utterance broke,
In answer to the monarch spoke :
' Hear then the words that Ráma said,
Resolved in duty's path to tread.
Joining his hands, his head he bent,
And gave this message, reverent :
'Sumantra, to my father go,
Whose lofty mind all people know :
Bow down before him, as is meet,
And in my stead salute his feet.
Then to the queen my mother bend,
And give the greeting that I send :
Ne'er may her steps from duty err,
And may it still be well with her.
And add this word : ' O Queen, pursue
Thy vows with faithful heart and true ;
And ever at due season turn

Where holy fires of worship burn.
And, lady, on our lord bestow
Such honour as to Gods we owe.
Be kind to every queen : let pride
And thought of self be cast aside.
In the king's fond opinion raise
Kaikeyí, by respect and praise.
Let the young Bharat ever be
Loved, honoured as the king by thee :
Thy king-ward duty ne'er forget :
High over all are monarchs set.'
    And Bharat, too, for me address :
Pray that all health his life may bless.
Let every royal lady share,
As justice bids, his love and care.
Say to the strong-armed chief who brings
Joy to Ikshváku's line of kings :
' As ruling prince thy care be shown
Of him, our sire, who holls the throne.
Stricken in years he feels their weight ;
But leave him in his royal state.
As regent heir content thee still,
Submissive to thy father's will.'
Ráma again his charge renewed,
As the hot flood his cheek bedewed :
' Hold as thine own my mother dear
Who drops for me the longing tear.'
Then Lakshmaṇ, with his soul on fire,
Spake breathing fast these words of ire :
' Say, for what sin, for what offence
Was royal Ráma banished thence ?
He is the cause, the king ; poor slave
To the light charge Kaikeyí gave.
Let right or wrong the motive be,

The author of our woe is he.
Whether the exile were decreed
Through foolish faith or guilty greed,
For promises or empire, still
The king has wrought a grievous ill.
Grant that the Lord of all saw fit
To prompt the deed and sanction it,
In Ráma's life no cause I see
For which the king should bid him flee.
His blinded eyes refused to scan
The guilt and folly of the plan,
And from the weakness of the king
Here and hereafter woe shall spring.
No more my sire : the ties that used
To bind me to the king are loosed.
My brother Ráma, Raghu's son,
To me is lord, friend, sire in one.
The love of men how can he win,
Deserting, by this cruel sin,
Their joy, whose heart is swift to feel
A pleasure in the people's weal ?
Shall he whose mandate could expel
The virtuous Ráma, loved so well,
To whom his subjects' fond hearts cling—
Shall he in spite of them be king ?'
    But Janak's child, my lord, stood by,
And oft the votaress heaved a sigh.
She seemed with dull and wandering sense,
Beneath a spirit's influence.
The noble princess, pained with woe
Which till that hour she ne'er could know,
Tears in her heavy trouble shed,
But not a word to me she said.
She raised her face which grief had dried,

And tenderly her husband eyed,
Gazed on him as he turned to go,
While tear chased tear in rapid flow.'

CANTO LIX.

DAŚARATHA'S LAMENT.

As thus Sumantra, best of peers,
Told his sad tale with many tears,
The monarch cried, 'I pray thee, tell
At length again what there befell.'
Sumantra, at the king's behest,
Striving with sobs he scarce repressed,
His trembling voice at last controlled,
And thus his further tidings told :
'Their locks in votive coils they wound,
Their coats of bark upon them bound,
To Gangá's farther shore they went,
Thence to Prayág their steps were bent.
I saw that Lakshman walked ahead
To guard the path the two should tread.
So far I saw, no more could learn,
Forced by the hero to return.
Retracing slow my homeward course,
Scarce could I move each stubborn horse :
Shedding hot tears of grief he stood
When Ráma turned him to the wood. [1]

---

[1] 'So in Homer the horses of Achilles lamented with many bitter
tears the death of Patroclus slain by Hector:

Ἵπποι δ' Αἰακίδαο, μάχης ἀπάνευθεν ἐόντες,
Κλᾶιον, ἐπειδὴ πρῶτα πυθέσθην ἡνιόχοιο
Ἐν κονίῃσι πεσόντας ὑφ' Ἕκτορος ἀνδροφόνοιο.
ILIAD. XVII. 426.

Ancient poesy frequently associated nature with the joys and sorrows
of man.' GORRESIO.

O

As the two princes parted thence
I raised my hands in reverence,
Mounted my ready car, and bore
The grief that stung me to the core,
With Guha all that day I stayed,
Still by the earnest hope delayed
That Ráma, ere the time should end,
Some message from the wood might send.
Thy realms, great Monarch, mourn the blow,
And sympathize with Ráma's woe.
Each withering tree hangs low his head,
And shoot, and bud, and flower are dead.
Dried are the floods that wont to fill
The lake, the river, and the rill.
Drear is each grove and garden now,
Dry every blossom on the bough.
Each beast is still, no serpents crawl :
A lethargy of woe on all.
The very wood is silent ; crushed
With grief for Ráma, all is hushed.
Fair blossoms from the water born,
Gay garlands that the earth adorn,
And every fruit that gleams like gold,
Have lost the scent that charmed of old.
Empty is every grove I see,
Or birds sit pensive on the tree.
Where'er I look, its beauty o'er,
The pleasance charms not as before.
I drove through fair Ayodhyá's street ;
None flew with joy the car to meet,
They saw that Ráma was not there,
And turned them sighing in despair.
The people in the royal way
Wept tears of bitter grief, when they

Beheld me coming, from afar,
No Ráma with me in the car.
From palace roof and turret high
Each woman bent her eager eye;
She looked for Ráma, but in vain;
Gazed on the car and shrieked for pain.
Their long clear eyes with sorrow drowned,
They, when this common grief was found,
Looked each on other, friend and foe,
In sympathy of levelling woe:
No shade of difference between
Foe, friend, or neutral, there was seen.
Without a joy, her bosom rent
With grief for Ráma's banishment,
Ayodhyá like the queen appears
Who mourns her son with many tears.'

   He ended: and the king, distressed,
With sobbing voice that lord addressed:
'Ah me, by false Kaikeyí led,
Of evil race, to evil bred,
I took no counsel of the sage,
Nor sought advice from skill and age.
I asked no lord his aid to lend,
I called no citizen or friend.
Rash was my deed, bereft of sense,
Slave to a woman's influence.
Surely, my lord, a woe so great
Falls on us by the will of Fate:
It lays the house of Raghu low,
For Destiny will have it so.
I pray thee, if I e'er have done
An act to please thee, yea, but one,
Fly, fly, and Ráma homeward lead:
My life, departing, counsels speed.

Fly, ere the power to bid I lack,
Fly to the wood : bring Ráma back.
I cannot live for even one
Short hour bereaved of my son.
But ah, the prince, whose arms are strong,
Has journeyed far : the way is long :
Me, me upon the chariot place,
And let me look on Ráma's face.
Ah me, my son, mine eldest-born,
Where roams he in the wood forlorn,
The wielder of the mighty bow,
Whose shoulders like the lion's show ?
O, ere the light of life be dim,
Take me to Sítá and to him.
O Ráma, Lakshmaṇ, and O thou
Dear Sítá, constant to thy vow,
Beloved ones, you cannot know
That I am dying of my woe.'

  ' The king to bitter grief a prey,
That drove each wandering sense away,
Sunk in affliction's sea, too wide
To traverse, in his anguish cried :
' Hard, hard to pass, my Queen, this sea
Of sorrow raging over me :
No Ráma near to soothe mine eye,
Plunged in its lowest deeps I lie.
Sorrow for Ráma swells the tide,
And Sítá's absence makes it wide :
My tears its foamy flood distain,
Made billowy by my sighs of pain :
My cries its roar, the arms I throw
About me are the fish below.
Kaikeyí is the fire that feeds
Beneath : my hair the tangled weeds ;

Its source the tears for Ráma shed :
The hump-back's words its monsters dread
The boon I gave the wretch its shore,
Till Ráma's banishment be o'er. [1]
  Ah me, that I should long to set
      My eager eyes to-day
  On Raghu's son, and he be yet
      With Lakshman far away!'
  Thus he of lofty glory wailed,
      And sank upon the bed.
  Beneath the woe his spirit failed,
      And all his senses fled.

[1] The lines containing this heap of forced metaphors are marked as spurious by Schlegel.

CANTO LX.

KAUŚALYÁ CONSOLED.

As Queen Kauśalyá, trembling much,
As blighted by a goblin's touch,
Still lying prostrate, half awoke
To consciousness, 'twas thus she spoke:
' Bear me away, Sumantra, far,
Where Ráma, Sítá, Lakshman are.
Bereft of them I have no power
To linger on a single hour.
Again, I pray, thy steps retrace,
And me in Daṇḍak forest place.
For after them I needs must go,
Or sink to Yama's realms below.'

His utterance choked by tears that rolled
Down from their fountains uncontrolled,
With suppliant hands the charioteer
Thus spake, the lady's heart to cheer:
' Dismiss thy grief, despair, and dread
That fills thy soul, of sorrow bred,
For pain and anguish thrown aside,
Will Ráma in the wood abide.
And Lakshmaṇ, with unfailing care
Will guard the feet of Ráma there,
Earning, with governed sense, the prize
That waits on duty in the skies.
And Sítá in the wild as well
As in her own dear home will dwell;
To Ráma all her heart she gives,

And free from doubt and terror lives.
No faintest sign of care or woe
The features of the lady show :
Methinks Videha's pride was made
For exile in the forest shade.
E'en as of old she used to rove
Delighted in the city's grove,
Thus, even thus she joys to tread
The woodlands uninhabited.
Like a young child, her face as fair
As the young moon, she wanders there.
What though in lonely woods she stray
Still Ráma is her joy and stay :
All his the heart no sorrow bends,
Her very life on him depends.
For, if her lord she might not see,
Ayodhyá like the wood would be.
She bids him, as she roams, declare
The names of towns and hamlets there,
Marks various trees that meet her eye,
And many a brook that hurries by.
And Janak's daughter seems to roam
One little league away from home
When Ráma or his brother speaks
And gives the answer that she seeks.
This, Lady, I remember well ;
Nor angry words have I to tell :
Reproaches at Kaikeyí shot,
Such, Queen, my mind remembers not.'
The speech when Sítá's wrath was high,
Sumantra passed in silence by,
That so his pleasant words might cheer
With sweet report Kauśalyá's ear.
' Her moonlike beauty suffers not

Though winds be rude and suns be hot :
The way, the danger, and the toil
Her gentle lustre may not soil.
Like the red lily's leafy crown
Or as the fair full moon looks down,
So the Videhan lady's face
Still shines with undiminished grace.
What if the borrowed colours throw
O'er her fine feet no rosy glow,
Still with their natural tints they spread
A lotus glory where they tread.
In sportive grace she walks the ground,
And sweet her chiming anklets sound.
No jewels clasp the faultless limb :
She leaves them all for love of him.
If in the woods her gentle eye
A lion sees, or tiger nigh,
Or elephant, she fears no ill,
For Ráma's arm supports her still.
No longer be their fate deplored,
Nor thine, nor that of Kośal's lord,
For conduct such as theirs shall buy
Wide glory that can never die.
For casting grief and care away,
Delighting in the forest, they
With joyful spirits, blithe and gay,
Set forward on the ancient way
    Where mighty saints have led ;
Their highest aim, their dearest care
To keep their father's honour fair,
Observing still the oath he sware,
    They roam, on wild fruit fed.'
Thus with persuasive art he tried
To turn her from her grief aside,

  By soothing fancies won.
But still she gave her sorrow vent :
' Au ¡ima !,' was her shrill lament,
  ' My love, my son, my son !'

CANTO LXI.

KAUŚALYÁ'S LAMENT.

When, best of all who give delight,
Her Ráma wandered far from sight,
Kauśalyá weeping, sore distresed,
The king her husband thus addresed :
' Thy name, O Monarch, far and wide
Through the three worlds is glorified :
Yet Ráma's is the pitying mind,
His speech is true, his heart is kind.
How will thy sons, good lord, sustain
With Sítá all their care and pain ?
How in the wild endure distress,
Nursed in the lap of tenderness ?
How will the dear Videhan bear
The heat and cold when wandering there,
Bred in the bliss of princely state,
So young and fair and delicate ?
The large-eyed lady, wont to eat
The best of finely seasoned meat—
How will she now her life sustain
With woodland fare of self-sown grain ?
Will she, with joys encompassed long,
Who loved the music and the song,
In the wild wood endure to hear
The ravening lion's voice of fear ?
Where sleeps my strong-armed hero, where,
Like Lord Mahendra's standard, fair ?
Where is, by Lakshman's side, his bed,

His club-like arm beneath his head ?
When shall I see his flower-like eyes,
And face that with the lotus vies,
Feel his sweet lily breath, and view
His glorious hair and lotus hue ?
The heart within my breast, I feel,
Is adamant or hardest steel,
Or, in a thousand fragments split,
The loss of him had shattered it,
When those I love, who should be blest,
Are wandering in the wood distressed,
Condemned their wretched lives to lead
In exile, by thy ruthless deed.
If, when the fourteen years are past,
Ráma reseeks his home at last,
I think not Bharat will consent
To yield the wealth and government.
At funeral feasts some mourners deal
To kith and kin the solemn meal,
And having duly fed them all
Some Bráhmans to the banquet call.
The best of Bráhmans, good and wise,
The tardy summoning despise,
And, equal to the Gods, disdain
Cups, e'en of Amrit, thus to drain.
Nay e'en when Bráhmans first have fed,
They loathe the meal for others spread,
And from the leavings turn with scorn,
As bulls avoid a fractured horn.
So Ráma, sovereign lord of men,
Will spurn the sullied kingship then :
He, born the eldest and the best,
His younger's leavings will detest,
Turning from tasted food away,

As tigers scorn another's prey.
The sacred post is used not twice,
Nor elements, in sacrifice.
But once the sacred grass is spread,
But once with oil the flame is fed:
So Ráma's pride will ne'er receive
The royal power which others leave,
Like wine when tasteless dregs are left,
Or rites of Soma juice bereft.
Be sure the pride of Raghu's race
Will never stoop to such disgrace:
The lordly lion will not bear
That man should beard him in his lair.
Were all the worlds against him ranged
His dauntless soul were still unchanged:
He, dutiful, in duty strong,
Would purge the impious world from wrong.
Could not the hero, brave and bold,
The archer, with his shafts of gold,
Burn up the very seas, as doom
Will in the end all life consume ?
Of lion's might, eyed like a bull,
A prince so brave and beautiful,
Thou hast with wicked hate pursued,
Like sea-born tribes who eat their brood.
If thou, O Monarch, hadst but known
The duty all the Twice-born own,
If the good laws had touched thy mind,
Which sages in the Scriptures find,
Thou ne'er hadst driven forth to pine
This brave, this duteous son of thine.
First on her lord the wife depends,
Next on her son and last on friends:
These three supports in life has she,

And not a fourth for her may be.
Thy heart, O King, I have not won ;
In wild woods roams my banished son ;
Far are my friends : ah, hapless me,
Quite ruined and destroyed by thee.'.

CANTO LXII.

DAŚARATHA CONSOLED.

The queen's stern speech the monarch heard,
As rage and grief her bosom stirred,
And by his anguish sore oppressed
Reflected in his secret breast.
Fainting and sad, with woe distraught,
He wandered in a maze ot thought;
At length the queller of the foe
Grew conscious, rallying from his woe.
When consciousness returned anew
Long burning sighs the monarch drew.
Again immersed in thought he eyed
Kauśalyá standing by his side.
Back to his pondering soul was brought
The direful deed his hand had wrought,
When, guiltless of the wrong intent,
His arrow at a sound was sent.
Distracted by his memory's sting,
And mourning for his son, the king
To two consuming griefs a prey,
A miserable victim lay.
The double woe devoured him fast,
As on the ground his eyes he cast,
Joined suppliant hands, her heart to touch,
And spake in answer, trembling much:
'Kauśalyá, for thy grace I sue,
Joining these hands as suppliants do.
Thou e'en to foes hast ever been

A gentle, good, and loving queen.
Her lord, with noble virtues graced,
Her lord, by lack of all debased,
Is still a God in woman's eyes,
If duty's low she hold and prize.
Thou, who the right hast aye pursued,
Life's changes and its chances viewed,
Shouldst never launch, though sorrow-stirred,
At me distressed, one bitter word.'

She listened, as with sorrow faint
He murmured forth his sad complaint:
Her brimming eyes with tears ran o'er,
As spouts the new-fallen water pour,
His suppliant hands, with fear dismayed
She gently clasped in hers, and laid,
Like a fair lotus, on her head,
And faltering in her trouble said:
'Forgive me; at thy feet I lie,
With low bent head to thee I cry.
By thee besought, thy guilty dame
Pardon from thee can scarcely claim.
She merits not the name of wife
Who cherishes perpetual strife
With her own husband good and wise,
Her lord both here and in the skies.
I know the claims of duty well,
I know thy lips the truth must tell.
All the wild words I rashly spoke,
Forth from my heart, through anguish, broke;
For sorrow bonds the stoutest soul,
And cancels Scripture's high control.
Yea, sorrow's might all else o'erthrows,
The strongest and the worst of foes.
'Tis thus with all . we keenly feel,

Yet bear the blows our foemen deal,
But when a slender woe assails
The manliest spirit bends and quails.
The fifth long night has now begun
Since the wild woods have lodged my son
To me whose joy is drowned in tears,
Each day a dreary year appears.
While all my thoughts on him are set
Grief at my heart swells wilder yet:
With doubled might thus Ocean raves
When rushing floods increase his waves.'

   As from Kauśalyá reasoning well
The gentle words of wisdom fell,
The sun went down with dying flame,
And darkness o'er the landscape came.
His lady's soothing words in part
Relieved the monarch's aching heart,
Who, wearied out by all his woes,
Yielded to sleep and took repose.

CANTO LXIII.

THE HERMIT'S SON.

But soon by rankling grief oppressed
The king awoke from troubled rest,
And his sad heart was tried again
With anxious thought where all was pain.
Ráma and Lakshman's mournful fate
On Daśaratha, good and great
As Indra, pressed with crushing weight,
As when the demon's might assails
The Sun-God, and his glory pales.
Ere yet the sixth long night was spent,
Since Ráma to the woods was sent,
The king at midnight sadly thought
Of the old crime his hand had wrought,
And thus to Queen Kauśalyá cried
Who still for Ráma moaned and sighed :
' If thou art waking, give, I pray,
Attention to the words I say.
Whate'er the conduct men pursue,
Be good or ill the acts they do,
Be sure, dear Queen, they find the meed
Of wicked or of virtuous deed.
A heedless child we call the man
Whose feeble judgment fails to scan
The weight of what his hands may do,
Its lightness, fault, and merit too.
One lays the Mango garden low,
And bids the gay Paláśas grow :

P

Longing for fruit their bloom he sees,
But grieves when fruit should bend the trees.
Cut by my hand, my fruit-trees fell,
Paláśa trees I watered well.
My hopes this foolish heart deceive,
And for my banished son I grieve.
Kauśalyá, in my youthful prime
Armed with my bow I wrought the crime,
Proud of my skill, my name renowned,
An archer prince who shoots by sound.
The deed this hand unwitting wrought
This misery on my soul has brought,
As children seize the deadly cup
And blindly drink the poison up.
As the unreasoning man may be
Charmed with the gay Paláśa tree,
I unaware have reaped the fruit
Of joying at a sound to shoot.
As regent prince I shared the throne,
Thou wast a maid to me unknown.
The early Rain-time duly came,
And strengthened love's delicious flame.
The sun had drained the earth that lay
All glowing neath the summer day,
And to the gloomy clime had fled
Where dwell the spirits of the dead.[1]
The fervent heat that moment ceased,
The darkening clouds each hour increased,
And frogs and deer and peacocks all
Rejoiced to see the torrents fall.
Their bright wings heavy from the shower,
The birds, new-bathed, had scarce the power

---

[1] The southern region is the abode of Yama the Indian Pluto, and of departed spirits.

To reach the branches of the trees
Whose high tops swayed beneath the breeze.
The fallen rain, and falling still,
Hung like a sheet on every hill,
Till, with glad deer, each flooded steep
Showed glorious as the mighty deep.
The torrents down its wooded side
Poured, some unstained, while others dyed
Gold, ashy, silver, ochre, bore
The tints of every mountain ore.
In that sweet time, when all are pleased,
My arrows and my bow I seized;
Keen for the chase, in field or grove,
Down Sarjú's bank my car I drove.
I longed with all my lawless will
Some elephant by night to kill,
Some buffalo that came to drink,
Or tiger, at the river's brink.
When all around was dark and still,
I heard a pitcher slowly fill,
And thought, obscured in deepest shade,
An elephant the sound had made. .
I drew a shaft that glittered bright,
Fell as a serpent's venomed bite;
I longed to lay the monster dead,
And to the mark my arrow sped.
Then in the calm of morning, clear
A hermit's wailing smote my ear:
' Ah me, ah me,' he cried, and sank,
Pierced by my arrow, on the bank.
E'en as the weapon smote his side,
I heard a human voice that cried :
' Why lights this shaft on one like me,
A poor and harmless devotee?

I came by night to fill my jar
From this lone stream where no men are.
Ah, who this deadly shaft has shot?
Whom have I wronged, and knew it not?
Why should a boy so harmless feel
The vengeance of the winged steel?
Or who should slay the guiltless son
Of hermit sire who injures none,
Who dwells retired in woods, and there
Supports his life on woodland fare?
Ah me, ah me, why am I slain,
What booty will the murderer gain?
In hermit coils I bind my hair,
Coats made of skin and bark I wear.
Ah, who the cruel deed can praise
Whose idle toil no fruit repays,
As impious as the wretch's crime
Who dares his master's bed to climb?
Nor does my parting spirit grieve
But for the life which thus I leave:
Alas, my mother and my sire,—
I mourn for them when I expire.
Ah me, that aged, helpless pair,
Long cherished by my watchful care,
How will it be with them this day
When to the Five[1] I pass away?
Pierced by the self-same dart we die,
Mine aged mother, sire, and I.
Whose mighty hand, whose lawless mind
Has all the three to death consigned?'

　　When I, by love of duty stirred,
That touching lamentation heard,

---

[1] The five elements of which the body consists, and to which returns.

Pierced to the heart by sudden woe,
I threw to earth my shafts and bow.
My heart was full of grief and dread
As swiftly to the place I sped,
Where, by my arrow wounded sore,
A hermit lay on Sarjú's shore.
His matted hair was all unbound,
His pitcher empty on the ground,
And by the fatal arrow pained,
He lay with dust and gore distained.
I stood confounded and amazed:
His dying eyes to mine he raised,
And spoke this speech in accents stern,
As though his light my soul would burn:
' How have I wronged thee, King, that I
Struck by thy mortal arrow die?
The wood my home, this jar I brought,
And water for my parents sought.
This one keen shaft that strikes me through
Slays sire and aged mother too.
Feeble and blind, in helpless pain,
They wait for me and thirst in vain.
They with parched lips their pangs must bear,
And hope will end in blank despair.
Ah me, there seems no fruit in store
For holy zeal or Scripture lore,
Or else ere now my sire would know
That his dear son is lying low.
Yet, if my mournful fate he knew,
What could his arm so feeble do?
The tree, firm-rooted, ne'er may be
The guardian of a stricken tree.
Haste to my father, and relate
While time allows, my sudden fate,

Lest he consume thee, as the fire
Burns up the forest, in his ire.
This little path, O King, pursue:
My father's cot thou soon wilt view.
There sue for pardon to the sage
Lest he should curse thee in his rage.
First from the wound extract the dart
That kills me with its deadly smart,
E'en as the flushed impetuous tide
Eats through the river's yielding side.'
    I feared to draw the arrow out,
And pondered thus in painful doubt:
'Now tortured by the shaft he lies,
But if I draw it forth he dies.'
Helpless I stood, faint, sorely grieved:
The hermit's son my thought perceived;
As one o'ercome by direst pain
He scarce had strength to speak again,
With writhing limb and struggling breath,
Nearer and ever nearer death:
'My senses undisturbed remain,
And fortitude has conquered pain:
Now from one fear thy soul be freed,
Thy hand has made no Bráhman bleed.
Let not this pang thy bosom wring:
No twice-born youth am I, O King,
For of a Vaiśya sire I came,
Who wedded with a Śúdrá dame.'
    These words the boy could scarcely say,
As tortured by the shaft he lay,
Twisting his helpless body round,
Then trembling senseless on the ground.
Then from his bleeding side I drew
The rankling shaft that pierced him through.

With death's last fear my face he eyed,
And, rich in store of penance, died.'

CANTO LXIV.

DAŚARATHA'S DEATH.

The son of Raghu to his queen
Thus far described the unequalled scene,
And, as the hermit's death he rued,
The mournful story thus renewed :
'The deed my heedless hand had wrought
Perplexed me with remorseful thought,
And all alone I pondered still
How kindly deed might salve the ill.
The pitcher from the ground I took,
And filled it from that fairest brook,
Then, by the path the hermit showed,
I reached his sainted sire's abode.
I came, I saw : the aged pair,
Feeble and blind, were sitting there,
Like birds with clipped wings, side by side,
With none their helpless steps to guide.
Their idle hours the twain beguiled
With talk of their returning child,
And still the cheering hope enjoyed,
The hope, alas, by me destroyed.
Then spoke the sage, as drawing near
The sound of footsteps reached his ear :
'Dear son, the water quickly bring ;
Why hast thou made this tarrying ?
Thy mother thirsts, and thou hast played,
And bathing in the brook delayed.
She weeps because thou camest not ;

Haste, O my son, within the cot.
If she or I have ever done
A thing to pain thee, dearest son,
Dismiss the memory from thy mind :
A hermit thou, be good and kind.
On thee our lives, our all, depend :
Thou art thy friendless parents' friend.
The eyeless couple's eye art thou :
Then why so cold and silent now ?'

 With sobbing voice and bosom wrung
I scarce could move my faltering tongue,
And with my spirit filled with dread
I looked upon the sage, and said,
While mind, and sense, and nerve I strung
To fortify my trembling tongue,
And let the aged hermit know
His son's sad fate, my fear and woe :
' High-minded Saint, not I thy child,
A warrior, Daśaratha styled.
I bear a grievous sorrow's weight
Born of a deed which good men hate.
My lord, I came to Sarjú's shore,
And in my hand my bow I bore
For elephant or beast of chase
That seeks by night his drinking place.
There from the stream a sound I heard
As if a jar the water stirred.
An elephant, I thought, was nigh :
I aimed, and let an arrow fly.
Swift to the place I made my way,
And there a wounded hermit lay
Gasping for breath : the deadly dart
Stood quivering in his youthful heart.
I hastened near with pain oppressed :

He faltered out his last behest,
And quickly, as he bade me do,
From his pierced side the shaft I drew.
I drew the arrow from the rent,
And up to heaven the hermit went,
Lamenting, as from earth he passed,
His aged parents to the last.
Thus, unaware, the deed was done:
My hand, unwitting, killed thy son.
For what remains, O, let me win
Thy pardon for my heedless sin.'

As the sad tale of sin I told,
The hermit's grief was uncontrolled;
With flooded eyes, and sorrow-faint,
Thus spake the venerable saint:
I stood with hand to hand applied,
And listened as he spoke and sighed:
'If thou, O King, hadst left unsaid
By thine own tongue this tale of dread,
Thy head for hideous guilt accursed
Had in a thousand pieces burst.
A hermit's blood by warrior spilt,
In such a case, with purposed guilt,
Down from his high estate would bring
Even the thunder's mighty King.
And he a dart who conscious sends
Against the devotee who spends
His pure life by the law of Heaven—
That sinner's head will split in seven.
Thou livest, for thy heedless hand
Has wrought a deed thou hast not planned,
Else thou and all of Raghu's line
Had perished by this act of thine.
Now guide us,' thus the hermit said,

' Forth to the spot where he lies dead.
Guide us, this day, O Monarch, we
For the last time our son would see:
The hermit dress of skin he wore
Rent from his limbs distained with gore;
His senseless body lying slain,
His soul in Yama's dark domain.'
  Alone the mourning pair I led,
Their souls with woe disquieted,
And let the dame and hermit lay
Their hands upon the breathless clay.
The father touched his son, and pressed
The body to his aged breast;
Then falling by the dead boy's side,
He lifted up his voice, and cried:
' Hast thou no word, my child, to say?
No greeting for thy sire to-day?
Why art thou angry, darling? why
Wilt thou upon the cold earth lie?
If thou, my son, art wroth with me,
Here, duteous child, thy mother see.
What! no embrace for me, my son?
No word of tender love—not one?
Whose gentle voice, so soft and clear,
Soothing my spirit, shall I hear
When evening comes, with accents sweet
Scripture or ancient lore repeat?
Who, having fed the sacred fire,
And duly bathed, as texts require,
Will cheer, when evening rites are done,
The father mourning for his son?
Who will the daily meal provide
For the poor wretch who lacks a guide,
Feeding the helpless with the best

Berries and roots, like some dear guest?
How can these hands subsistence find
For thy poor mother, old and blind?
The wretched votaress how sustain,
.Who mourns her child in ceaseless pain?
Stay yet a while, my darling, stay,
Nor fly to Yama's realm to-day.
To-morrow I thy sire and she
Who bare thee, child, will go with thee. [1]
Then when I look on Yama, I
To great Vivasvat's son will cry:
'Hear, King of justice, and restore
Our child to feed us, I implore. .
Lord of the world, of mighty fame,
Faithful and just, admit my claim,
And grant this single boon, to free
My soul from fear, to one like me.'
Because, my son, untouched by stain,
By sinful hands thou fallest slain,
Win, through thy truth, the sphere where those
Who die by hostile darts repose.
Seek the blest home prepared for all
The valiant who in battle fall,
Who face the foe and scorn to yield,
In glory dying on the field.
Rise to the heaven where Dhundhumár
And Nahush, mighty heroes, are,
Where Janamejay and the blest
Dilípa, Sagar, Saivya, rest:
Home of all virtuous spirits, earned

---

[1] So dying York cries over the body of Suffolk:
  'Tarry, dear cousin Suffolk!
My soul shall thine keep company to heaven:
Tarry, sweet soul, for mine, then fly abreast.'

                    King Henry V. Act. IV. 6.

By fervent rites and Scripture learned :
By those whose sacred fires have glowed,
Whose liberal hands have fields bestowed :
By givers of a thousand cows,
By lovers of one faithful spouse :
By those who serve their masters well,
And cast away this earthy shell.
None of my race can ever know
The bitter pain of lasting woe.
But doomed to that dire fate is he
Whose guilty hand has slaughtered thee.'

    Thus with wild tears the aged saint
Made many a time his piteous plaint,
Then with his wife began to shed
The funeral water for the dead.
But in a shape celestial clad,
Won by the merits of the lad,
The spirit from the body brake
And to the mourning parents spake :
' A glorious home in realms above
Rewards my care and filial love.
You, honoured parents, soon shall be
Partakers of that home with me.'

    He spake, and swiftly mounting high,
With Indra near him, to the sky
On a bright car, with flame that glowed,
Sublime the duteous hermit rode.

    The father, with his consort's aid,
The funeral rites with water paid,
And thus his speech to me renewed
Who stood in suppliant attitude :
'Slay me this day, O, slay me, King,
For death no longer has a sting.
Childless am I : thy dart has done

To death my dear, my only son.
Because the boy I loved so well
Slain by thy heedless arrow fell,
My curse upon thy soul shall press
With bitter woe and heaviness.
I mourn a slaughtered child, and thou
Shalt feel the pangs that kill me now.
Bereft and suffering e'en as I,
So shalt thou mourn thy son, and die.
Thy hand unwitting dealt the blow
That laid a holy hermit low,
And distant, therefore, is the time
When thou shalt suffer for the crime.
The hour shall come when, crushed by woes
Like these I feel, thy life shall close:
A debt to pay in after days
Like his the priestly fee who pays.'
    This curse on me the hermit laid,
Nor yet his tears and groans were stayed.
Then on the pyre their bodies cast
The pair; and straight to heaven they passed.
As in sad thought I pondered long
Back to my memory came the wrong
Done in wild youth, O lady dear,
When 'twas my boast to shoot by ear.
The deed has borne the fruit, which now
Hangs ripe upon the bending bough:
Thus dainty meats the palate please,
And lure the weak to swift disease.
Now on my soul return with dread
The words that noble hermit said,
That I for a dear son should grieve,
And of the woe my life should leave.'

    Thus spake the king with many a tear;

Then to his wife he cried in fear:
'I cannot see thee, love ; but lay
Thy gentle hand in mine, I pray.
Ah me, if Ráma touched me thus,
If once, returning home to us,
He bade me wealth and lordship give,
Then, so I think, my soul would live.
Unlike myself, unjust and mean
Have been my ways with him, my Queen,
But like himself is all that he,
My noble son, has done to me.
His son, though far from right he stray,
What prudent sire would cast away ?
What banished son would check his ire,
Nor speak reproaches of his sire ?
I see thee not : these eyes grow blind,
And memory quits my troubled mind.
Angels of Death are round me : they
Summon my soul with speed away.
What woe more grievous can there be,
That, when from light and life I flee,
I may not, ere I part, behold
My virtuous Ráma, true and bold ?
Grief for my son, the brave and true,
Whose joy it was my will to do,
Dries up my breath, as summer dries
The last drop in the pool that lies.
Not men, but blessed Gods, are they
Whose eyes shall see his face that day ;
See him, when fourteen years are past,
With earrings decked return at last.
My fainting mind forgets to think :
Low and more low my spirits sink.
Each from its seat, my senses steal :

I cannot hear, or taste, or feel.
This lethargy of soul o'ercomes
Each organ, and its function numbs:
So when the oil begins to fail,
The torch's rays grow faint and pale.
This flood of woe caused by this hand
Destroys me helpless and unmanned,
Resistless as the floods that bore
A passage through the river shore.
Ah Raghu's son, ah mighty-armed,
By whom my cares were soothed and charmed,
My son in whom I took delight,
Now vanished from thy father's sight!
Kauśalyá, ah, I cannot see;
Sumitrá, gentle devotee!
Alas, Kaikeyí, cruel dame,
My bitter foe, thy father's shame!'

 Kauśalyá and Sumitrá kept
Their watch beside him as he wept.
And Daśaratha moaned and sighed,
And grieving for his darling died.

CANTO LXV.

THE WOMEN'S LAMENT.

And now the night had past away,
And brightly dawned another day ;
The minstrels, trained to play and sing,
Flocked to the chamber of the king :
Bards, who their gayest raiment wore,
And heralds famed for ancient lore :
And singers, with their songs of praise,
Made music in their several ways
There as they poured their blessings choice,
And hailed their king with hand and voice,
Their praises with a swelling roar
Echoed through court and corridor.
Then as the bards his glory sang,
From beaten palms loud answer rang,
As glad applauders clapped their hands,
And told his deeds in distant lands.
The swelling conceit woke a throng
Of sleeping birds to life and song :
Some in the branches of the trees,
Some caged in halls and galleries.
Nor was the soft string music mute ;
The gentle whisper of the lute,
And blessings sung by singers skilled
The palace of the monarch filled.
Eunuchs and dames of life unstained,
Each in the arts of waiting trained,
Drew near attentive as before,

Q

And crowded to the chamber door :
These skilful when and how to shed
The lustral stream o'er limb and head,
Others with golden ewers stood
Of water stained with sandal wood.
And many a maid, pure, young, and fair,
Her load of early offerings bare,
Cups of the flood which all revere,
And sacred things, and toilet gear.
Each several thing was duly brought
As rule of old observance taught,
And lucky signs on each impressed
Stamped it the fairest and the best.
There anxious, in their long array,
All waited till the shine of day :
But when the king nor rose nor spoke,
Doubt and alarm within them woke.
Forthwith the dames, by duty led,
Attendants on the monarch's bed,
Within the royal chamber pressed
To wake their master from his rest.
Skilled in the lore of dreaming, they
First touched the bed on which he lay.
But none replied : no sound was heard,
Nor hand, nor head, nor body stirred.
They trembled, and their dread increased,
Fearing his breath of life had ceased,
And bending low their heads, they shook
Like the tall reeds that fringe the brook.
In doubt and terror down they knelt,
Looked on his face, his cold hand felt,
And then the gloomy truth appeared
Of all their hearts had darkly feared.
Kauśalyá and Sumitrá, worn

With weeping for their sons, forlorn,
Woke not, but lay in slumber deep
And still as death's unending sleep.
Bowed down by grief, her colour fled,
Her wonted lustre dull and dead,
Kauśalyá shone not, like a star
Obscured behind a cloudy bar.
Beside the king's her couch was spread,
And next was Queen Sumitrá's bed,
Who shone no more with beauty's glow,
Her face bedewed with tears of woe.
There lapped in sleep each wearied queen,.
There as in sleep, the king was seen ;
And swift the troubling thought came o'er
Their spirits that he breathed no more.
At once with wailing loud and high
The matrons shrieked a bitter cry,
As widowed elephants bewail
Their dead lord in the woody vale.
At the loud shriek that round them rang,
Kauśalyá and Sumitrá sprang
Awakened from their beds, with eyes
Wide open in their first surprise.
Quick to the monarch's side they came,
And saw and touched his lifeless frame ;
One cry, O husband ! forth they sent,
And prostrate to the ground they went.
The king of Kośal's daughter¹ there
Writhed, with the dust on limb and hair,.
Lustreless,. as a star might lie
Hurled downward from the glorious sky.
When the king's voice in death was stilled,
The women who the chamber filled,

¹ Kauśalyá, daughter of the king of another Kośal.

Saw, like a widow elephant slain,
Kauśalyá prostrate in her pain.
Then all the monarch's ladies led
By Queen Kaikeyí at their head,
Poured forth their tears, and, weeping so,
Sank on the ground, consumed by woe.
The cry of grief so long and loud
Went up from all the royal crowd,
That, doubled by the matron train,
It made the palace ring again.
Filled with dark fear and eager eyes,
Anxiety and wild surmise ;
Echoing with the cries of grief
Of sorrowing friends who mourned their chief,
Dejected, pale with deep distress,
Hurled from their height of happiness :
Such was the look the palace wore
Where lay the king who breathed no more.

CANTO LXVI.

THE EMBALMING.

Kauśalyá's eyes with tears o'erflowed,
Weighed down by varied sorrows' load ;
On her dead lord her gaze she bent,
Who lay like fire whose might is spent,
Like the great deep with waters dry,
Or like the clouded sun on high.
Then on her lap she laid his head,
And on Kaikeyí looked and said :
' Triumphant now enjoy thy reign
Without a thorn thy side to pain.
Thou hast pursued thy single aim,
And killed the king, O wicked dame.
Far from my sight my Ráma flies,
My perished lord has sought the skies.
No friend, no hope my life to cheer,
I cannot tread the dark path here.
Who would forsake her husband, who
That God to whom her love is due,
And wish to live one hour, but she
Whose heart no duty owns, like thee ?
The ravenous sees no fault : his greed
Will e'en on poison blindly feed.
Kaikeyí, through a hump-back maid,
This royal house in death has laid.
King Janak, with his queen, will hear
Heart-rent like me the tidings drear
Of Ráma banished by the king,

Urged by her impious counselling.
No son has he, his age is great,
And sinking with the double weight,
He for his darling child will pine,
And pierced with woe his life resign.
Sprung from Videha's monarch, she
A sad and lovely devotee,
Roaming the wood, unmeet for woe,
Will toil and trouble undergo.
She in the gloomy night with fear
The cries of beast and bird will hear,
And trembling in her wild alarm
Will cling to Ráma's sheltering arm.
Ah, little knows my duteous son
That I am widowed and undone—
My Ráma of the lotus eye,
Gone hence, gone hence, alas, to die.
Now, as a loving wife and true,
I, e'en this day, will perish too:
Around his form these arms will throw,
And to the fire with him will go.'

Clasping her husband's lifeless clay
A while the weeping votaress lay,
Till chamberlains removed her thence
O'ercome by sorrow's violence.
Then in a cask of oil they laid
Him who in life the world had swayed,
And finished, as the lords desired,
All rites for parted souls required.
The lords, all-wise, refused to burn
The monarch ere his son's return;
So for a while the corpse they set
Embalmed in oil, and waited yet.
The women heard : no doubt remained,

And wildly for the king they plained.
With gushing tears that drowned each eye
Wildly they waved their arms on high,
And each her mangling nails impressed
Deep in her head and knee and breast :
' Of Ráma reft,—who ever spake
The sweetest words the heart to take,
Who firmly to the truth would cling,—
Why dost thou leave us, mighty King ?
How can the consorts thou hast left
Widowed, of Raghu's son bereft,
Live with our foe Kaikeyí near,
The wicked queen we hate and fear ?
She threw away the king, her spite
Drove Ráma forth and Lakshmaṇ's might,
And gentle Sítá : how will she
Spare any, whosoe'er it be ? '
    Oppressed with sorrow, tear-distained,
The royal women thus complained.
Like night when not a star appears,
Like a sad widow drowned in tears,
Ayodhyá's city, dark and dim,
Reft of her lord was sad for him.
When thus for woe the king to heaven had fled,
    And still on earth his lovely wives remained,
With dying light the sún to rest had sped,
    And night triumphant o'er the landscape reigned.

CANTO LXVII.

THE PRAISE OF KINGS.

That night of sorrow passed away,
And rose again the God of Day.
Then all the twice-born peers of state
Together met for high debate.
Jáváli, lord of mighty fame,
And Gautam, and Kátyáyan came,
And Márkandeya's reverend age,
And Vámadeva, glorious sage:
Sprung from Mudgalya's seed the one,
The other ancient Kaśyap's son.
With lesser lords these Bráhmans each
Spoke in his turn his several speech,
And turning to Vaśishtha, best
Of household priests, him thus addressed:
' The night of bitter woe has past,
Which seemed a hundred years to last,
Our king, in sorrow for his son,
Reunion with the Five has won.
His soul is where the Blessed are,
While Ráma roams in woods afar,
And Lakshman, bright in glorious deeds,
Goes where his well-loved brother leads.
And Bharat and Śatrughna, they
Who smite their foes in battle fray,
Far in the realm of Kekaya stay,
Where their maternal grandsire's care
Keeps Rájagriha's city fair.

Let one of old Ikshváku's race
Obtain this day the sovereign's place,
Or havoc and destruction straight
Our kingless land will devastate.
In kingless lands no thunder's voice,
No lightning wreaths the heart rejoice,
Nor does Parjanya's heavenly rain
Descend upon the burning plain.
Where none is king, the sower's hand
Casts not the seed upon the land ;
The son against the father strives,
And husbands fail to rule their wives.
In kingless realms no princes call
Their friends to meet in crowded hall ;
No joyful citizens resort
To garden trim or sacred court.
In kingless realms no Twice-born care
To sacrifice with text and prayer,
Nor Bráhmans, who their vows maintain,
The great solemnities ordain.
The joys of happier days have ceased :
No gathering, festival, or feast
Together calls the merry throng
Delighted with the play and song.
In kingless lands it ne'er is well
With sons of trade who buy and sell :
No men who pleasant tales repeat
Delight the crowd with stories sweet.
In kingless realms we ne'er behold
Young maidens decked with gems and gold,
Flock to the gardens blithe and gay
To spend their evening hours in play.
No lover in the flying car
Rides with his love to woods afar.

In kingless lands no wealthy swain
Who keeps the herd and reaps the grain,
Lies sleeping, blest with ample store,
Securely near his open door.
Upon the royal roads we see
No tusked elephant roaming free,
Of three-score years, whose head and neck
Sweet tinkling bells of silver deck.
We hear no more the glad applause
When his strong bow each rival draws,
No clap of hands, no eager cries
That cheer each martial exercise.
In kingless realms no merchant bands
Who travel forth to distant lands,
With precious wares their wagons load,
And fear no danger on the road.
No sage secure in self-control,
Brooding on God with mind and soul,
In lonely wanderings finds his home
Where'er at eve his feet may roam.
In kingless realms no man is sure
He holds his life and wealth secure.
In kingless lands no warriors smite
The foeman's host in glorious fight.
In kingless lands the wise no more,
Well trained in Scripture's holy lore,
In shady groves and gardens meet
To argue in their calm retreat.
No longer, in religious fear,
Do they who pious vows revere,
Bring dainty cates and wreaths of flowers
As offerings to the heavenly powers.
No longer, bright as trees in spring,
Shine forth the children of the king

Resplendent in the people's eyes
With aloe wood and sandal dyes.
A brook where water once has been,
A grove where grass no more is green,
Kine with no herdsman's guiding hand—
So wretched is a kingless land.
The car its waving banner rears,
Banner of fire the smoke appears:
Our king, the banner of our pride,
A God with Gods is glorified.
In kingless lands no law is known,
And none may call his wealth his own,
Each preys on each from hour to hour,
As fish the weaker fish devour.
Then, fearless, atheists overleap
The bounds of right the godly keep,
And when no royal powers restrain,
Preëminence and lordship gain.
As in the frame of man the eye
Keeps watch and ward, a careful spy,
The monarch in his wide domains
Protects the truth, the right maintains.
He is the right, the truth is he,
Their hopes in him the well-born see.
On him his people's lives depend,
Mother is he, and sire, and friend.
The world were veiled in blinding night,
And none could see or know aright,
Ruled there no king in any state
The good and ill to separate.
We will obey thy word and will
As if our king were living still:
As keeps his bounds the faithful sea,
So we observe thy high decree.

O best of Bráhmans, first in place,
  Our kingless land lies desolate :
Some scion of Ikshváku's race
  Do thou as monarch consecrate.'

CANTO LXVIII.

THE ENVOYS.

Vaśishṭha heard their speech and prayer,
And thus addressed the concourse there,
Friends, Bráhmans, counsellors, and all
Assembled in the palace hall:
'Ye know that Bharat, free from care,
Still lives in Rájagriha[1] where
The father of his mother reigns:
Śatrughna by his side remains.
Let active envoys, good at need,
Thither on fleetest horses speed,
To bring the hero youths away:
Why waste the time in dull delay?'
 Quick came from all the glad reply:
'Vaśishṭha, let the envoys fly.'
He heard their speech, and thus rěnewed
His charge before the multitude:
'Nandan, Aśok, Siddhárth, attend,
Your ears, Jayanta, Vijay, lend:
Be yours, what need requires, to do:
I speak these words to all of you.
With coursers of the fleetest breed
To Rájagriha's city speed.
Then rid your bosoms of distress,
And Bharat thus from me address:
'The household priest and peers by us

Send health to thee and greet thee thus :
'Come to thy father's home with haste :
Thine absent time no longer waste.'
But speak no word of Ráma fled,
Tell not the prince his sire is dead,
Nor to the royal youth the fate
That ruins Raghu's race relate.
Go quickly hence, and with you bear
Fine silken vestures rich and rare,
And gems and many a precious thing
As gifts to Bharat and the king.'

With ample stores of food supplied,
Each to his home the envoys hied,
Prepared, with steeds of swiftest race,
To Kekaya's land[1] their way to trace.
They made all due provision there,
And every need arranged with care,
Then ordered by Vasishtha, they
Went forth with speed upon their way.
Then northward of Pralamba, west
Of Apartála, on they pressed,
Crossing the Málini that flowed
With gentle stream athwart the road.
They traversed Gangá's holy waves
Where she Hástinapura[2] laves,
Thence to Panchála[3] westward fast
Through Kurujángal's land[4] they passed.

---

[1] The Kekayas or Kaikayas in the Punjab appear amongst the chief nations in the war of the Mahábhárata ; their king being a kinsman of Krishna.

[2] Hástinapura was the capital of the kingdom of Kuru, near the modern Delhi.

[3] The Panchálas occupied the upper part of the Doab.

[4] 'Kurujángala and its inhabitants are frequently mentioned in the *Mahúbhárata*, as in the *Ádi-parv.* 3789, 4337, *et al.*' WILSON's *Vishṇu Puráṇa.* Vol, II. P. 176. DR. HALL's Note.

On, on their course the envoys held
By urgency of task impelled,
Quick glancing at each lucid flood
And sweet lake gay with flower and bud.
Beyond, they passed unwearied o'er,
Where glad birds fill the flood and shore
Of Śaradaṇḍá racing fleet
With heavenly waters clear and sweet.
Thereby a tree celestial grows
Which every boon on prayer bestows:
To its blest shade they humbly bent,
Then to Kulingá's town they went.
Then, having passed the Warrior's Wood,
In Abhikála next they stood,
O'er sacred Ikshumatí[1] came,
Their ancient kings' ancestral claim.
They saw the learned Bráhmans stand,
Each drinking from his hollowed hand,
And through Báhíka[2] journeying still
They reached at length Sudáman's hill:
There Vishṇu's footstep turned to see,
Vipáśá[3] viewed, and Śálmalí,
And many a lake and river met,
Tank, pool, and pond, and rivulet.
And lions saw, and tigers near,
And elephants and herds of deer,
And still, by prompt obedience led,
Along the ample road they sped.

---

[1] 'The Ὀξύματις of Arrian. See *As. Res.* Vol. XV., p. 420, 421,
also *Indische Alterthumskunde*, Vol. I. p. 602, first foot-note.' WILSON'S
Vishṇu Purána. Vol. I. p. 421. DR. HALL's edition. The Ikshumatí
was a river in Kurukshetra.

[2] 'The Báhíkas are described in the Mahábhárata, Karṇa Parvan,
with some detail, and comprehend the different nations of the Punjab
from the Sutlej to the Indus.' WILSON'S *Vishṇu Purána*. Vol. I. p. 167.

[3] The Beas, Hyphasis or, Bibasis.

Then when their course so swift and long,
Had worn their steeds though fleet and strong,
To Girivraja's splendid town
They came by night, and lighted down.
To please their master, and to guard
  The royal race, the lineal right,
  The envoys, spent with riding hard,
    To that fair city came by night.[1]

.[1] It would be lost labour to attempt to verify all the towns and streams
mentioned in Cantos LXVIII and LXXII. Professor Wilson observes
(*Vishnu Purana*, p. 139 Dr Hall's Edition) 'States, and tribes, and
cities have disappeared, even from recollection; and some of the natural
features of the country, especially the rivers, have undergone a total
alteration . . . .
Notwithstanding these impediments, however, we should be able to
identify at least mountains and rivers, to a much greater extent than
is now practicable, if our maps were not so miserably defective in
their nomenclature. None of our surveyors or geographers have been
oriental scholars. It may be doubted if any of them have been
conversant with the spoken language of the country. They have,
consequently put down names at random, according to their own
inaccurate appreciation of sounds carelessly, vulgarly, and corruptly
uttered; and their maps of India are crowded with appellations which
bear no similitude whatever either to past or present denominations.
We need not wonder that we cannot discover Sanskrit names in Eng-
lish maps, when, in the immediate vicinity of Calcutta, Barnagore
represents Barahanagar, Dakshineswar is metamorphosed into Duckin-
sore, and Ulubaria into Willoughbury .. . . . . There is scarcely
a name in our Indian maps that does not afford proof of extreme in-
difference to accuracy in nomenclature, and of an incorrectness in
estimating sounds. which is, in some degree, perhaps, a national defect.'

For further information regarding the road from Ayodhyá to Rájagriha, see *Additional Notes.*

CANTO LXIX.

BHARAT'S DREAM.

The night those messengers of state
Had past within the city's gate,
In dreams the slumbering Bharat saw
A sight that chilled his soul with awe.
The dream that dire events foretold
Left Bharat's heart with horror cold,
And with consuming woes distraught,
Upon his aged sire he thought.
His dear companions, swift to trace
The signs of anguish on his face,
Drew near, his sorrow to expel,
And pleasant tales began to tell.
Some woke sweet music's cheering sound,
And others danced in lively round.
With joke and jest they strove to raise
His spirits, quoting ancient plays ;
But Bharat still, the lofty-souled,
Deaf to sweet tales his fellows told,
Unmoved by music, dance, and jest,
Sat silent, by his woe oppressed.
To him, begirt by comrades near,
Thus spoke the friend he held most dear :
' Why ringed around by friends, art thou
So silent and so mournful now ?'
' Hear thou,' thus Bharat made reply,
' What chills my heart and dims mine eye.
I dreamt I saw the king my sire

R

Sink headlong in a lake of mire
Down from a mountain high in air,
His body soiled, and loose his hair.
Upon the miry lake he seemed
To lie and welter, as I dreamed;
With hollowed hands full many a draught
Of oil he took, and loudly laughed.
With head cast down I saw him make
A meal on sesamum and cake;
The oil from every member dripped,
And in its clammy flood he dipped.
The ocean's bed was bare and dry,
The moon had fallen from the sky,
And all the world lay still and dead,
With whelming darkness overspread.
The earth was rent and opened wide,
The leafy trees were scorched, and died;
I saw the seated mountains split,
And wreaths of rising smoke emit.
The stately beast the monarch rode
His long tusks rent and splintered showed;
And flames that quenched and cold had lain
Blazed forth with kindled light again.
I looked, and many a handsome dame,
Arrayed in brown and sable came,
And bore about the monarch, dressed,
On iron stool, in sable vest
And then the king, of virtuous mind,
A blood-red wreath around him twined,
Forth on an ass-drawn chariot sped,
As southward still he bent his head.
Then, crimson-clad, a dame appeared
Who at the monarch laughed and jeered;
And a she-monster, dire to view,

Her hand upon his body threw.
Such is the dream I dreamt by night,
Which chills me yet with wild affright:
Either the king or Ráma, I
Or Lakshmaṇ now must surely die.
For when an ass-drawn chariot seems
To bear away a man in dreams,
Be sure above his funeral pyre
The smoke soon rears its cloudy spire.
This makes my spirit low and weak,
My tongue is slow and loth to speak:
My lips and throat are dry for dread,
And all my soul disquieted.
My lips, relaxed, can hardly speak,
And chilling dread has changed my cheek.
I blame myself in aimless fears,
And still no cause of blame appears.
I dwell upon this dream of ill
    Whose changing scenes I viewed,
  And on the startling horror still
    My troubled thoughts will brood.
  Still to my soul these terrors cling,
    Reluctant to depart,
  And the strange vision of the king
    Still weighs upon my heart.'

CANTO LXX.

BHARAT'S DEPARTURE.

While thus he spoke, the envoys borne
On horses faint and travel-worn
Had gained the city fenced around
With a deep moat's protecting bound.
An audience of the king they gained,
And honours from the prince obtained ;
The monarch's feet they humbly pressed,
To Bharat next these words addressed :
' The household priest and peers by us
Send health to thee and greet thee thus :
' Come to thy father's house with haste :
Thine absent time no longer waste.
Receive these vestures rich and rare,
These costly gems and jewels fair,
And to thy uncle here present
Each precious robe and ornament.
These for the king and him suffice—
Two hundred millions is their price—
These, worth a hundred millions, be
Reserved, O large-eyed Prince, for thee.'

Loving his friends with heart and soul,
The joyful prince received the whole,
Due honour to the envoys paid,
And thus in turn his answer made :
' Of Daśaratha tidings tell :
Is the old king my father well ?
Is Ráma, and is Lakshman, he

Of the high-soul, from sickness free ?
And she who walks where duty leads,
Kauśalyá, known for gracious deeds,
Mother of Ráma, loving spouse,
Bound to her lord by well kept vows ?
And Lakshman's mother too, the dame
Sumitrá skilled in duty's claim,
Who brave Śatrughna also bare,
Second in age,—her health declare.
And she, in self-conceit most sage,
With selfish heart most prone to rage,
My mother, fares she well ? has she
Sent message or command to me ?'

    Thus Bharat spake, the mighty-souled,
And they in brief their tidings told :
'All they of whom thou askest dwell,
O lion lord, secure and well :
Thine all the smiles of fortune are :
Make ready : let them yoke the car.'

    Thus by the royal envoys pressed,
Bharat again the band addressed :
'I go with you : no long delay,
A single hour I bid you stay.'
Thus Bharat, son of him who swayed
Ayodhyá's realm, his answer made,
And then bespoke, his heart to please,
His mother's sire in words like these :
'I go to see my father, King,
Urged by the envoys' summoning ;
And when thy soul desires to see
Thy grandson, will return to thee.'

    The king his grandsire kissed his head,
And in reply to Bharat said :
'Go forth, dear child ; how blest is she,

The mother of a son like thee!
Greet well thy sire, thy mother greet,
O thou whose arms the foe defeat;
The household priest, and all the rest
Amid the Twice-born chief and best;
And Ráma and brave Lakshman, who
Shoot the long shaft with aim so true.'

To him the king high honour showed,
And store of wealth and gifts bestowed,
The choicest elephants to ride,
And skins and blankets deftly dyed,
A thousand strings of golden beads,
And sixteen hundred mettled steeds;
And boundless wealth before him piled
Gave Kekaya to Kaikeyí's child.
And men of counsel, good and tried,
On whose firm truth he aye relied,
King Aśvapati gave with speed
Prince Bharat on his way to lead.
And noble elephants, strong and young,
From sires of Indraśira sprung,
And others tall and fair to view
Of great Airávat's lineage true:
And well yoked asses fleet of limb
The prince his uncle gave to him.
And dogs within the palace bred,
Of body vast and massive head,
With mighty fangs for battle, brave,
The tiger's match in strength, he gave.
Yet Bharat's bosom hardly glowed
To see the wealth the king bestowed;
For he would speed that hour away,
Such care upon his bosom lay:
Those eager envoys urged him thence,

And that sad vision's influence.
He left his court-yard, crowded then
With elephants and steeds and men,
And, peerless in immortal fame,
To the great royal street he came.
He saw, as farther still he went,
The inner rooms most excellent,
And passed the doors, to him unclosed,
Where check nor bar his way opposed.
There Bharat stayed to bid adieu
To grandsire and to uncle too,
Then, with Śatrughna by his side,
Mounting his car, away he hied.
The strong-wheeled cars were yoked, and they,
More than a hundred, rolled away :
Servants, with horses, asses, kine,
Followed their lord in endless line.
So, guarded by his own right hand,
   Forth high-souled Bharat hied,
Surrounded by a lordly band
   On whom the king relied.
Beside him sat Śatrughna dear,
   The scourge of trembling foes :
Thus from the light of Indra's sphere
   A saint made perfect goes.

CANTO LXXI.

BHARAT'S RETURN.

Then Bharat's face was eastward bent
As from the royal town he went.
He reached Sudámá's farther side,
And glorious, gazed upon the tide;
Passed Hládiní, and saw her toss
Her westering billows hard to cross.
Then old Ikshváku's famous son
O'er Śatadrú[1] his passage won,
Near Ailadhána on the strand,
And came to Aparparyaṭ's land.
O'er Śilá's flood he hurried fast,
Akurvatí's fair stream he passed,
Crossed o'er Ágneya's rapid rill,
And Śalyakartan onward still.
Śilávahá's swift stream he eyed,
True to his vows and purified,
Then crossed the lofty hills, and stood
In Chaitraratha's mighty wood.
He reached the confluence where meet
Sarasvatí[2] and Gangá fleet,
And through Bhárunda forest, spread
Northward of Víramatsya, sped.
He sought Kalinda's child, who fills

---

[1] 'The Śatadrú, 'the hundred-channelled' – the Zaradrus of Ptolemy,
Hesydrus of Pliny –is the Sutlej.' WILSON's *Vishṇu Puráṇa.* Vol. II.
p. 130.

[2] The Sarasvatí or Sursooty is a tributary of the Caggar or Guggur
in Sirhind.

The soul with joy, begirt by hills,
Reached Yamuná, and passing o'er,
Rested his army on the shore:
He gave his horses food and rest,
Bathed reeking limb and drooping crest.
They drank their fill and bathed them there,
And water for their journey bare.
Thence through a mighty wood he sped
All wild and uninhabited,
As in fair chariot through the skies,
Most fair in shape a Storm-God flies.
At Anśudhána Gangá, hard
To cross, his onward journey barred,
So turning quickly thence he came
To Prágvaṭ's city dear to fame.
There having gained the farther side
To Kuṭikoshtiká he hied:
The stream he crossed, and onward then
To Dharmavardhan brought his men.
Thence, leaving Toraṇ on the north,
To Jambuprastha journeyed forth.
Then onward to a pleasant grove.
By fair Varútha's town he drove,
And when a while he there had stayed,
Went eastward from the friendly shade.
Eastward of Ujjiháná, where
The Priyak trees are tall and fair,
He passed, and rested there each steed
Exhausted with the journey's speed.
There orders to his men addressed,
With quickened pace he onward pressed,
A while at Sarvatírtha spent,
Then o'er Uttániká he went.
O'er many a stream beside he sped

With coursers on the mountains bred,
And passing Hastiprishṭhak, took
The road o'er Kuṭiká's fair brook.
Then, at Lohitya's village, he
Crossed o'er the swift Kapívatí,
Then passed, where Ekaśála stands,
The Sthánumatí's flood and sands,
And Gomatí of fair renown
By Vinata's delightful town.
When to Kalinga near he drew,
A wood of Sál trees charmed the view;
That passed, the sun began to rise,
And Bharat saw with happy eyes,
Ayodhyá's city, built and planned
By ancient Manu's royal hand.
Seven nights upon the road had passed,
And when he saw the town at last
Before him in her beauty spread,
Thus Bharat to the driver said:
'This glorious city from afar,
Wherein pure groves and gardens are,
Seems to my eager eyes to-day
A lifeless pile of yellow clay.
Through all her streets where erst a throng
Of men and women streamed along,
Uprose the multitudinous roar:
To-day I hear that sound no more.
No longer do mine eyes behold
The leading people, as of old,
On elephants, cars, horses, go
Abroad and homeward, to and fro.
The brilliant gardens where we heard
The wild note of each rapturous bird,
Where men and women loved to meet,

In pleasant shades, for pastime sweet,—
These to my eyes this day appear
Joyless, and desolate, and drear:
Each tree that graced the garden grieves,
And every path is spread with leaves.
The merry cry of bird and beast,
That spake aloud their joy, has ceased:
Still is the long melodious note
That charmed us from each warbling throat.
Why blows the blessed air no more,
The incense-breathing air that bore
Its sweet incomparable scent
Of sandal and of aloe blent?
Why are the drum and tabour mute?
Why is the music of the lute
That woke responsive to the quill,
Loved by the happy, hushed and still?
My boding spirit gathers hence
Dire sins of awful consequence,
And omens, crowding on my sight,
Weigh down my soul with wild affright.
Scarce shall I find my friends who dwell
Here in Ayodhyá safe and well:
For surely not without a cause
This crushing dread my soul o'erawes.'
  Heart-sick, dejected, every sense
Confused by terror's influence,
On to the town he quickly swept
Which King Ikshváku's children kept.
He passed through Vaijayanta's gate,
With weary steeds, disconsolate,
And all who near their station held,
His escort, crying Victory, swelled.
With heart distracted still he bowed

Farewell to all the following crowd,
Turned to the driver and began
To question thus the weary man :
'Why was I brought, O free from blame,
So fast, unknown for what I came ?
Yet fear of ill my heart appals,
And all my wonted courage falls.
For I have heard in days gone by
The changes seen when monarchs die ;
And all those signs, O charioteer,
I see to-day surround me here :
Each kinsman's house looks dark and grim,
No hand delights to keep it trim :
The beauty vanished, and the pride,
The doors, unkept, stand open wide.
No morning rites are offered there,
No grateful incense loads the air,
And all therein, with brows o'ercast,
Sit joyless on the ground and fast.
Their lovely chaplets dry and dead,
Their courts unswept, with dust o'erspread,
The temples of the Gods to-day
No more look beautiful and gay.
Neglected stands each holy shrine,
Each image of a Lord divine.
No shop where flowery wreaths are sold
Is bright and busy as of old.
The women and the men I mark
Absorbed in fancies dull and dark,
Their gloomy eyes with tears bedewed,
A poor afflicted multitude.'

His mind oppressed with woe and dread,
Thus Bharat to his driver said,
Viewed the dire signs Ayodhyá showed,
And onward to the palace rode.

CANTO LXXII.

BHARAT'S INQUIRY.

He entered in, he looked around,
Nor in the house his father found ;
Then to his mother's dwelling, bent
To see her face, he quickly went.
She saw her son, so long away,
Returning after many a day,
And from her golden seat in joy
Sprang forward to her darling boy.
Within the bower, no longer bright,
Came Bharat lover of the right,
And bending with observance sweet
Clasped his dear mother's lovely feet.
Long kisses on his brow she pressed,
And held her hero to her breast,
Then fondly drew him to her knees,
And questioned him in words like these :
' How many nights have fled, since thou
Leftest thy grandsire's home, till now ?
By flying steeds so swiftly borne,
Art thou not weak and travel-worn ?
How fares the king my father, tell ;
Is Yudhájit thine uncle well ?
And now, my son, at length declare
The pleasures of thy visit there.'

Thus to the offspring of the king
She spake with tender questioning,
And to his mother made reply

Young Bharat of the lotus eye:
'The seventh night has come and fled
Since from my grandsire's home I sped:
My mother's sire is well, and he,
Yudhájit, from all trouble free.
The gold and every precious thing
Presented by the conqueror king,
The slower guards behind convey:
I left them weary on the way.
Urged by the men my father sent,
My hasty course I hither bent:
Now, I implore, an answer deign,
And all I wish to know, explain.
Unoccupied I now behold
This couch of thine adorned with gold,
And each of King Ikshváku's race
Appears with dark and gloomy face.
The king is aye, my mother dear,
Most constant in his visits here.
To meet my sire I sought this spot:
How is it that I find him not?
I long to clasp my father's feet:
Say where he lingers, I entreat.
Perchance the monarch may be seen
Where dwells Kauśalyá, eldest queen.'

His father's fate, from him concealed,
Kaikeyí to her son revealed:
Told as glad news the story sad,
For lust of sway had made her mad:
'Thy father, O my darling, know,
Has gone the way all life must go:
Devout and famed, of lofty thought,
In whom the good their refuge sought.'
　. When Bharat pious, pure, and true,

Heard the sad words which pierced him through,
Grieved for the sire he loved so well.
Prostrate upon the ground he fell:
Down fell the strong-armed hero, high
Tossing his arms, and a sad cry,
'Ah, woe is me, unhappy, slain!'
Burst from his lips again, again.
Afflicted for his father's fate
By grief's intolerable weight,
With every sense amazed and cowed
The splendid hero wailed aloud:
'Ah me, my royal father's bed
Of old a gentle radiance shed,
Like the pure sky when clouds are past,
And the moon's light is o'er it cast:
Ah, of its wisest lord bereft,
It shows to-day faint radiance left,
As when the moon has left the sky,
Or mighty Ocean's depths are dry.'
   With choking sobs, with many a tear,
Pierced to the heart with grief sincere,
The best of conquerors poured his sighs,
And with his robe veiled face and eyes.
Kaikeyí saw him fallen there,
Godlike, afflicted, in despair,
Used every art to move him thence,
And tried him thus with eloquence:
'Arise, arise, my dearest; why
Wilt thou, famed Prince, so lowly lie?
Not by such grief as this are moved
Good men like thee, by all approved.
The earth thy father nobly swayed,
And rites to Heaven he duly paid.
At length his race of life was run:

Thou shouldst not mourn for him, my son.'
  Long on the ground he wept, and rolled
From side to side, still unconsoled,
And then, with bitter grief oppressed,
His mother with these words addressed :
'This joyful hope my bosom fed
When from my grandsire's halls I sped—
'The king will throne his eldest son,
And sacrifice, as should be done.'
But all is changed, my hope was vain,
And this sad heart is rent in twain,
For my dear father's face I miss,
Who ever sought his loved ones' bliss.
But in my absence, mother, say,
What sickness took my sire away?
Ah, happy Ráma, happy they
Allowed his funeral rites to pay !
The glorious monarch has not learned
That I his darling have returned,
Or quickly had he hither sped,
And pressed his kisses on my head.
Where is that hand whose gentle touch,
Most soft and kind I loved so much,
The hand that loved to brush away
The dust that on his darling lay?
Quick, bear the news to Ráma's ear;
Tell the great chief that I am here:
Brother, and sire and friend, and all
Is he, and I his trusty thrall.
For noble hearts, to virtue true,
Their sires in elder brothers view.
To clasp his feet I fain would bow:
He is my hope and refuge now.
What said my glorious sire, who knew

Virtue and vice, so brave and true?
Firm in his vows, dear lady, say,
What said he ere he passed away?
What was his rede to me? I crave
To hear the last advice he gave.'

   Thus closely questioned by the youth,
Kaikeyí spoke the mournful truth:
'The high-souled monarch wept and sighed,
For Ráma, Sítá, Lakshman, cried,
Then, best of all who go to bliss,
Passed to the world which follows this.
'Ah, blessed are the people who
Shall Ráma and his Sítá view,
And Lakshman of the mighty arm,
Returning free from scathe and harm.'
Such were the words, the last of all,
Thy father, ere he died, let fall,
By Fate and Death's dread coils enwound,
As some great elephant is bound.'

   He heard, yet deeper in despair,
Her lips this double woe declare,
And with sad brow that showed his pain
Questioned his mother thus again:
'But where is he, of virtue tried,
Who fills Kauśalyá's heart with pride,
Where is the noble Ráma? where
Is Lakshman brave, and Sítá fair?'

   Thus pressed, the queen began to tell
The story as each thing befell,
And gave her son in words like these,
The mournful news she meant to please:
'The prince is gone in hermit dress
To Dandak's mighty wilderness,
And Lakshman brave and Sítá share

S

The wanderings of the exile there.'
 Then Bharat's soul with fear was stirred
Lest Ráma from the right had erred,
And jealous for ancestral fame,
He put this question to the dame:
'Has Ráma grasped with lawless hold
A Bráhman's house, or land, or gold?
Has Ráma harmed with ill intent
Some poor or wealthy innocent?
Was Ráma, faithless to his vows,
Enamoured of another's spouse?
Why was he sent to Daṇḍak's wild,
Like one who kills an unborn child?'
 He questioned thus: and she began
To tell her deeds and crafty plan,
Deceitful-hearted, fond, and blind
As is the way of womankind:
'No Bráhman's wealth has Ráma seized,
No dame his wandering fancy pleased:
His very eyes he ne'er allows
To gaze upon a neighbour's spouse.
But when I heard the monarch planned
To give the realm to Ráma's hand,
I prayed that Ráma hence might flee,
And claimed the throne, my son, for thee.
The king maintained the name he bare,
And did according to my prayer,
And Ráma, with his brother, sent,
And Sítá, forth to banishment.
When his dear son was seen no more,
The lord of earth was troubled sore:
Too feeble with his grief to strive,
He joined the elemental Five.
Up then, most dutiful! maintain

Thy royal state, arise, and reign.
For thee, my darling son, for theè
All this was planned and wrought by me.
Come, cast thy grief and pain aside,
With manly courage fortified.
This town and realm are all thine own,
And fear and grief are here unknown.
Come, with Vaśishṭha's guiding aid,
   And priests in ritual skilled
Let the king's funeral dues be paid,
   And every claim fulfilled.
Perform his obsequies with all
   That suits his rank and worth,
Then give the mandate to install
   Thyself as lord of earth.'

CANTO LXXIII.

KAIKEYÍ REPROACHED.

But when he heard the queen relate
His brothers' doom, his father's fate,
Thus Bharat to his mother said
With burning grief disquieted :
' Alas, what boots it now to reign,
Struck down by grief and well-nigh slain ?
Ah, both are gone, my sire, and he
Who was a second sire to me.
Grief upon grief thy hand has made,
And salt upon my gashes laid :
For my dear sire has died through thee,
And Ráma roams a devotee.
Thou camest like the night of Fate
This royal house to devastate.
Unwitting ill, my hapless sire
Placed in his bosom coals of fire,
And through thy crimes his death he met,
O thou whose heart on sin is set.
Shame of thy house ! thy senseless deed
Has reft all joy from Raghu's seed
The truthful monarch, dear to fame,
Received thee as his wedded dame,
And by thy act to misery doomed
Has died by flames of grief consumed.
Kauśalyá and Sumitrá too
The coming of my mother rue,
And if they live oppressed by woe,

For their dear sons their sad tears flow.
Was he not ever good and kind,—
That hero of the duteous mind?
Skilled in all filial duties, he
As a dear mother treated thee.
Kauśalyá too, the eldest queen,
Who far foresees with insight keen,
Did she not ever show thee all
A sister's love at duty's call?
And hast thou from the kingdom chased
Her son, with bark around his waist,
To 'he wild wood, to dwell therein,
And dost not sorrow for thy sin?
The love I bare to Raghu's son
Thou knewest not, ambitious one,
If thou hast wrought this impious deed
For royal sway, in lawless greed.
With him and Lakshman far away,
What power have I the realm to sway?
What hope will fire my bosom, when
I see no more those lords of men?
The holy king who loved the right
Relied on Ráma's power and might,
His guardian and his glory : so
Joys Meru in his woods below.
How can I bear, a steer untrained,
The load his mightier strength sustained?
What power have I to brook alone
This weight on feeble shoulders thrown?
But if the needful power were bought
By strength of mind and brooding thought,
No triumph shall attend the dame
Who dooms her son to lasting shame.
Now should no doubt that son prevent

From quitting thee on evil bent,
But Ráma's love o'erpowers my will,
Who holds thee as his mother still.
Whence did the thought, O thou whose eyes
Are turned to sinful deeds, arise—
A plan our ancient sires would hate,
O fallen from thy virtuous state?
For in the line from which we spring
The eldest is anointed king:
No monarchs from the rule decline,
And, least of all, Ikshváku's line.
Our holy sires, to virtue true,
Upon our race a lustre threw,
But with subversive frenzy thou
Hast marred our lineal honour now.
Of lofty birth, a noble line
Of previous kings is also thine:
Then whence this hated folly? whence
This sudden change that steals thy sense?
Thou shalt not gain thine impious will,
O thou whose thoughts are bent on ill,
Thou from whose guilty hand descend
These sinful blows my life to end.
Now to the forest will I go,
Thy cherished plans to overthrow,
And bring my brother, free from stain,
His people's darling, home again.
And Ráma, when again he turns,
Whose glory like a beacon burns,
In me a faithful slave shall find
To serve him with contented mind.'

CANTO LXXIV.

BHARAT'S LAMENT.

When Bharat's anger-sharpened tongue
Reproaches on the queen had flung,
Again, with mighty rage possessed,
The guilty dame he thus addressed :
' Flee, cruel, wicked sinner, flee,
Let not this kingdom harbour thee.
Thou who hast thrown all right aside,
Weep thou for me when I have died.
Canst thou one charge against the king,
Or the most duteous Ráma, bring ?
The one thy sin to death has sent,
The other chased to banishment.
Our line's destroyer, sin-defiled
Like one who kills an unborn child,
Ne'er with thy lord in heaven to dwell,
Thy portion shall be down in hell.
Because thy hand, that stayed for naught,
This awful wickedness has wrought,
And ruined him whom all held dear,
My bosom too is stirred with fear.
My father by thy sin is dead,
And Ráma to the wood is fled ;
And of thy deed I bear the stain,
And fameless in the world remain.
Ambitious, evil-souled, in show
My mother, yet my direst foe,
My throning ne'er thine eyes shall bless,

Thy husband's wicked murderess.
Thou art not Aśvapati's child,
That righteous king, most sage and mild,
But thou wast born a fiend, a foe
My father's house to overthrow.
Thou who hast made Kauśalyá, pure,
Gentle, affectionate, endure
The loss of him who was her bliss,—
What worlds await thee, Queen, for this?
Was it not patent to thy sense
That Ráma was his friends' defence,
Kauśalyá's own true child most dear,
The eldest and his father's peer?
Men in the son not only trace
The father's figure, form, and face,
But in his heart they also find
The offspring of the father's mind;
And hence, though dear their kinsmen are,
To mothers sons are dearer far.
There goes an ancient legend how
Good Surabhi, the God-loved cow,
Saw two of her dear children strain,
Drawing a plough and faint with pain.
She saw them on the earth outworn,
Toiling till noon from early morn,
And as she viewed her children's woe,
A flood of tears began to flow.
As through the air beneath her swept
The Lord of Gods, the drops she wept,
Fine, laden with delicious smell,
Upon his heavenly body fell.
And Indra lifted up his eyes
And saw her standing in the skies,
Afflicted with her sorrow's weight,

Sad, weeping, all disconsolate.
The Lord of Gods in anxious mood
Thus spoke in suppliant attitude :
'No fear disturbs our rest, and how
Comes this great dread upon thee now ?
Whence can this woe upon thee fall,
Say, gentle one who lovest all ?'
   Thus spake the God who rules the skies,
Indra, the Lord supremely wise ;
And gentle Surabhi, well learned
In eloquence, this speech returned :
'Not thine the fault, great God, not thine,
And guiltless are the Lords divine :
I mourn two children faint with toil,
Labouring hard in stubborn soil.
Wasted and sad I see them now,
While the sun beats on neck and brow,
Still goaded by the cruel hind,—
No pity in his savage mind.
O Indra, from this body sprang
These children, worn with many a pang.
For this sad sight I mourn, for none
Is to the mother like her son.'
   He saw her weep whose offspring feed
In thousands over hill and mead,
And knew that in a mother's eye
Naught with a son, for love, can vie.
He deemed her, when the tears that came
From her sad eyes bedewed his frame,
Laden with their celestial scent,
Of living things most excellent.
If she these tears of sorrow shed
Who many a thousand children bred,
Think what a life of woe is left

Kauśalyá, of her Ráma reft.
An only son was hers, and she
Is rendered childless now by thee.
Here and hereafter, for thy crime,
Woe is thy lot through endless time.
And now, O Queen, without delay,
With all due honour will I pay
Both to my brother and my sire
The rites their several fates require.
Back to Ayodhyá will I bring
The long-armed chief, her lord and king,
And to the wood myself betake
Where hermit saints their dwelling make.
For, sinner both in deed and thought!
This hideous crime which thou hast wrought
I cannot bear, or live to see
The people's sad eyes bent on me.
Begone, to Daṇḍak wood retire,
Or cast thy body to the fire,
Or bind around thy neck the rope:
No other refuge mayst thou hope.
When Ráma, lord of valour true,
Has gained the earth, his right and due,
Then, free from duty's binding debt,
My vanished sin shall I forget.'
    Thus like an elephant forced to brook
The goading of the driver's hook,
Quick panting like a serpent maimed,
He fell to earth with rage inflamed.

CANTO LXXV.

THE ABJURATION.

A while he lay : he rose at length,
And slowly gathering sense and strength,
With angry eyes which tears bedewed,
The miserable queen he viewed,
And spake with keen reproach to her
Before each lord and minister :
‘ No lust have I for kingly sway,
My mother I no more obey :
Naught of this consecration knew
Which Daśaratha kept in view.
I with Śatrughna all the time
Was dwelling in a distant clime :
I knew of Ráma's exile naught,
That hero of the noble thought :
I knew not how fair Sítá went,
And Lakshman, forth to banishment.’
   Thus high-souled Bharat, mid the crowd,
Lifted his voice and cried aloud.
Kauśalyá heard, she raised her head,
And quickly to Sumitrá said :
‘ Bharat, Kaikeyí's son, is here,—
Hers whose fell deeds I loathe and fear :
That youth of foresight keen I fain
Would meet and see his face again.’
Thus to Sumitrá spake the dame,
And straight to Bharat's presence came
With altered mien, neglected dress,

Trembling and faint with sore distress.
Bharat, Śatrughna by his side,
To meet her, toward her palace hied.
And when the royal dame they viewed
Distressed with dire solicitude,
Sad, fallen senseless on the ground,
About her neck their arms they wound.
The noble matron prostrate there,
Embraced, with tears, the weeping pair,
And with her load of grief oppressed,
To Bharat then these words addressed :
' Now all is thine, without a foe,
This realm for which thou longest so.
Ah, soon Kaikeyí's ruthless hand
Has won the empire of the land,
And made my guiltless Ráma flee
Dressed like some lonely devotee.
Herein what profit has the queen,
Whose eye delights in havoc, seen ?
Me also, me 'twere surely good
To banish to the distant wood,
To dwell amid the shades that hold
My famous son with limbs like gold.
Nay, with the sacred fire to guide,
Will I, Sumitrá by my side,
Myself to the drear wood repair
And seek the son of Raghu there.
This land which rice and golden corn
And wealth of every kind adorn,
Car, elephant, and steed, and gem,—
She makes thee lord of it and them.'

    With taunts like these her bitter tongue
The heart of blameless Bharat wrung,
And direr pangs his bosom tore

Than when the lancet probes a sore.
With troubled senses all astray
Prone at her feet he fell and lay.
With loud lament a while he plained,
And slowly strength and sense regained.
With suppliant hand to hand applied
He turned to her who wept and sighed,
And thus bespake the queen, whose breast
With sundry woes was sore distressed :
' Why these reproaches, noble dame ?
I, knowing naught, am free from blame.
Thou knowest well what love was mine
For Ráma, chief of Raghu's line.
O, never be his darkened mind
To Scripture's guiding lore inclined,
By whose consent the prince who led
The good, the truthful hero, fled.
May he obey the vilest lord,
Offend the sun with act abhorred, [1]
And strike a sleeping cow, who lent
His voice to Ráma's banishment.
May the good king who all befriends,
And, like his sons, the people tends,
Be wronged by him who gave consent
To noble Ráma's banishment.
On him that king's injustice fall,
Who takes, as lord, a sixth of all,
Nor guards, neglectful of his trust,
His people, as a ruler must.
The crime of those who swear to fee,
At holy rites, some devotee,
And then the promised gift deny,

---

[1] *Súryamcha pratimehatu*, adversus solem mingat. An offence expressly forbidden by the Laws of Manu.

Be his who willed the prince should fly.
When weapons clash and heroes bleed,
With elephant and harnessed steed,
Ne'er, like the good, be his to fight
Whose heart allowed the prince's flight.
'Though taught with care by one expert
May he the Veda's text pervert,
With impious mind or evil bent,
Whose voice approved the banishment.
May he with traitor lips reveal
Whate'er he promised to conceal,
And bruit abroad his friend's offence,
Betrayed by generous confidence.
No wife of equal lineage born
The wretch's joyless home adorn :
Ne'er may he do one virtuous deed,
And dying see no child succeed.
When in the battle's awful day
Fierce warriors stand in dread array,
Let the base coward turn and fly,
And smitten by the foeman, die.
Long may he wander, rags his wear,
Doomed in his hand a skull to bear,
And like an idiot beg his bread,
Who gave consent when Ráma fled.
His sin who holy rites forgets,
Asleep when shows the sun and sets,
A load upon his soul shall lie
Whose will allowed the prince to fly.
His sin who loves his Master's dame,
His, kindler of destructive flame,
His who betrays his trusting friend
Shall, mingled all, on him descend.
By him no reverence due be paid

To blessed God or parted shade :
May sire and mother's sacred name
In vain from him obedience claim.
Ne'er may he go where dwell the good,
Nor win their fame and neighbourhood,
But lose all hopes of bliss to-day,
Who willed the prince should flee away.
May he deceive the poor and weak
Who look to him and comfort seek,
Betray the suppliants who complain,
And make the hopeful hope in vain.
Long may his wife his kiss expect,
And pine away in cold neglect.
May he his lawful love despise,
And turn on other dames his eyes,
Fool, on forbidden joys intent.
Whose will allowed the banishment.
His sin who deadly poison throws
To spoil the water as it flows,
Lay on the wretch its burden dread
Who gave consent when Ráma fled.'[1]

Thus with his words he undeceived
Kauśalyá's troubled heart, who grieved
For son and husband reft away ;
Then prostrate on the ground he lay.
Him as he lay half-senseless there,
Freed by the mighty oaths he sware,
Kauśalyá, by her woe distressed,
With melancholy words addressed :
'Anew, my son, this sorrow springs
To rend my heart with keener stings ;
These awful oaths which thou hast sworn

---

[1] Bharat does not intend these curses for any particular person : he merely wishes to prove his own innocence by invoking them on his own head if he had any share in banishing Ráma.

My breast with double grief have torn.
Thy soul, and faithful Lakshman's too,
Are still, thank Heaven! to virtue true.
True to thy promise, thou shalt gain
The mansions which the good obtain.'

　　Then to her breast that youth she drew,
Whose sweet fraternal love she knew,
And there in strict embraces held
The hero, as her tears outwelled.
And Bharat's heart grew sick and faint
With grief and oft-renewed complaint,
And all his senses were distraught
By the great woe that in him wrought.

　　Thus as he lay and still bewailed
　　　With sighs and loud lament
　　Till all his strength and reason failed,
　　　The hours of night were spent.

CANTO LXXVI.

THE FUNERAL.

The saint Vaśishṭha, best of all
Whose words with moving wisdom fall,
Bharat, Kaikeyí's son, addressed,
Whom burning fires of grief distressed:
'O Prince, whose fame is widely spread,
Enough of grief: be comforted.
The time is come: arise, and lay
Upon the pyre the monarch's clay.'
  He heard the words Vaśishṭha spoke,
And slumbering resolution woke.
Then skilled in all the laws declare,
He bade his friends the rites prepare.
They raised the body from the oil,
And placed it, dripping, on the soil;
Then laid it on a bed, whereon
Wrought gold and precious jewels shone.
There, pallor o'er his features spread,
The monarch, as in sleep, lay dead.
Then Bharat sought his father's side,
And lifted up his voice and cried:
'O King, and has thy heart designed
To part and leave thy son behind?
Make Ráma flee, who loves the right,
And Lakshmaṇ of the arm of might?
Whither, great Monarch, wilt thou go,
And leave this people in their woe,
Mourning their hero, wild with grief,

Of Ráma reft, their lion chief ?
Ah, who will guard the people well
Who in Ayodhyá's city dwell,
When thou, my sire, hast sought the sky,
And Ráma has been forced to fly ?
In widowed woe, bereft of thee,
The land no more is fair to see :
The city, to my aching sight,
Is gloomy as a moonless night.'

   Thus, with o'erwhelming sorrow pained,
Sad Bharat by the bed complained :
And thus Vaśishṭha, holy sage,
Spoke his deep anguish to assuage :
' O Lord of men, no longer stay ;
The last remaining duties pay :
Haste, mighty-armed, as I advise,
The funeral rites to solemnize.'
   And Bharat heard Vaśishṭha's rede
With due attention, and agreed.
He summoned straight from every side
Chaplain, and priest, and holy guide.
The sacred fires he bade them bring
Forth from the chapel of the king,
Wherein the priests in order due,
And ministers, the offerings threw.
Distraught in mind, with sob and tear,
They laid the body on a bier,
And servants, while their eyes brimmed o'er,
The monarch from the palace bore.
Another band of mourners led
The long procession of the dead :
Rich garments in the way they cast,
And gold and silver, as they passed.
Then other hands the corse bedewed

With fragrant juices that exude
From sandal, cedar, aloe, pine,
And every perfume rare and fine,
Then priestly hands the mighty dead
Upon the pyre deposited.
The sacred fires they tended next,
And muttered low each funeral text ;
And priestly singers who rehearse
The Sáman[1] sang their holy verse.
Forth from the town in litters came,
Or chariots, many a royal dame,
And honoured so the funeral ground,
With aged followers ringed around.
With steps in inverse order bent,[2]
The priests in sad procession went
Around the monarch's burning pyre
Who well had nursed each sacred fire :
With Queen Kauśalyá and the rest,
Their tender hearts with woe distressed.
The voice of women, shrill and clear
As screaming curlews, smote the ear,
As from a thousand voices rose
The shriek that tells of woman's woes.
Then weeping, faint, with loud lament,
Down Sarjú's shelving bank they went.
  There standing on the river side
    With Bharat, priest, and peer,
  Their lips the women purified
    With water fresh and clear.
  Returning to the royal town,
    Their eyes with tear-drops filled,
  Ten days on earth they laid them down,
    And wept till grief was stilled.

---

[1] The Sáma-veda, the hymns of which are chanted aloud.
[2] Walking from right to left.

CANTO LXXVII.

THE GATHERING OF THE ASHES.

The tenth day passed : the prince again
Was free from every legal stain.
He bade them on the twelfth the great
Remaining honour celebrate.
Much gold he gave, and gems, and food,
To all the Bráhman multitude,
And goats whose hair was white and fine,
And many a thousand head of kine :
Slaves, men and damsels, he bestowed,
And many a cu and fair abode :
Such gifts he gave the Bráhman race,
His father's obsequies to grace.
Then when the morning's earliest ray
Appeared upon the thirteenth day,
Again the hero wept and sighed
Distraught and sorrow-stupefied ;
Drew, sobbing in his anguish, near,
The last remaining debt to clear,
And at the bottom of the pyre,
He thus bespake his royal sire :
' O father, hast thou left me so,
Deserted in my friendless woe,
When he to whom the charge was given
To keep me, to the wood is driven ?
Her only son is forced away
Who was his helpless mother's stay :
Ah, whither, father, art thou fled,

Leaving the queen uncomforted ?'

He looked upon the pile where lay
The bones half-burnt and ashes grey,
And uttering a piteous moan,
Gave way, by anguish overthrown.
Then as his tears began to well,
Prostrate to earth the hero fell ;
So from its seat the staff they drag,
And cast to earth some glorious flag.
The ministers approached again
The prince whom rites had freed from stain :
So when Yayáti fell, each seer,
In pity for his fate, drew near.
Śatrughna saw him lying low
O'erwhelmed beneath the rush of woe,
And as upon the king he thought,
He fell upon the earth distraught.
When to his loving memory came
Those noble gifts, that kingly frame,
He sorrowed, by his woe distressed,
As one by frenzied rage possessed :
' Ah me, this surging sea of woe .
Has drowned us with its overflow :
The source is Manthará, dire and dark,
Kaikeyí is the ravening shark :
And the great boons the monarch gave
Lend conquering might to every wave.
Ah, whither wilt thou go, and leave
Thy Bharat in his woe to grieve,
Whom ever 'twas thy greatest joy
To fondle as a tender boy ?
Didst thou not give with thoughtful care
Our food, our drink, our robes to wear ?
Whose love will now for us provide,

When thou, our king and sire, hast died?
At such a time bereft, forlorn,
Why is not earth in sunder torn,
Missing her monarch's firm control,
His love of right, his lofty soul?
Ah me, for Ráma roams afar,
My sire is where the Blessed are:
How can I live deserted? I
Will pass into the fire and die.
Abandoned thus, I will not brook
Upon Ayodhyá's town to look,
Once guarded by Ikshváku's race:
The wood shall be my dwelling-place.'

Then when the princes' mournful train
Heard the sad brothers thus complain,
And saw their misery, at the view
Their grief burst wilder out anew.
Faint with lamenting, sad and worn,
Each like a bull with broken horn,
The brothers in their wild despair
Lay rolling, mad with misery, there.
Then old Vaśishṭha good and true,
Their father's priest, all lore who knew,
Raised weeping Bharat on his feet,
And thus bespake with counsel meet:
' Twelve days, my lord, have past away
Since flames consumed thy father's clay:
Delay no more: as rules ordain,
Gather what bones may yet remain.
Three constant pairs are ever found
To hem all mortal creatures round: [1]
Then mourn not thus, O Prince, for none
Their close companionship may shun.'

---

[1] Birth and death, pleasure and pain, loss and gain.

Sumantra bade Śatrughna rise,
And soothed his soul with counsel wise,
And skilled in truth, his hearer taught
How all things are and come to naught.
When rose each hero from the ground,
A lion lord of men, renowned,
He showed like Indra's flag,[1] whereon
Fierce rains have dashed and suns have shone.
They wiped their red and weeping eyes,
And gently made their sad replies ;
Then, urged to haste, the royal pair
Performed the rites that claimed their care.

---

[1] Erected upon a tree or high staff in honour of Indra.

CANTO LXXVIII.

MANTHARÁ PUNISHED.

Śatrughna thus to Bharat spake
Who longed the forest road to take :
' He who in woe was wont to give
Strength to himself and all that live—
Dear Ráma, true and pure in heart,
Is banished by a woman's art.
Yet here was Lakshman, brave and strong,
Could not his might prevent the wrong ?
Could not his arm the king restrain,
Or make the banished free again ?
One loving right and fearing crime
Had checked the monarch's sin in time,
When, vassal of a woman's will,
His feet approached the path of ill.'

    While Lakshman's younger brother, dread
Śatrughna, thus to Bharat said,
Came to the fronting door, arrayed
In glittering robes, the hump-back maid.
There she, with sandal-oil besmeared,
In garments meet for queens appeared :
And lustre to her form was lent
By many a gem and ornament.
She gird'ed with her broidered zone,
And many a chain about her thrown,
Showed like a female monkey round
Whose body many a string is bound.
When on that cause of evil fell

The quick eye of the sentinel,
He grasped her in his ruthless hold,
And hastening in, Śatrughna told :
' Here is the wicked pest,' he cried,
' Through whom the king thy father died,
And Ráma wanders in the wood :
Do with her as thou deemest good.'
The warder spoke : and every word
Śatrughna's breast to fury stirred :
He called the servants, all and each,
And spake in wrath his hasty speech :
'This is the wretch my sire who slew,
And misery on my brothers drew :
Let her this day obtain the meed,
Vile sinner, of her cruel deed.'
He spake ; and moved by fury laid
His mighty hand upon the maid;
Who as her fellows ringed her round,
Made with her cries the hall resound.
Soon as the gathered women viewed
Śatrughna in his angry mood,
Their hearts disturbed by sudden dread,
They turned and from his presence fled.
' His rage,' they cried, ' on us will fall,
And ruthless, he will slay us all.
Come, to Kauśalyá let us flee :
Our hope, our sure defence is she,
Approved by all, of virtuous mind,
Compassionate, and good, and kind.'

His eyes with burning wrath aglow,
Śatrughna, shatterer of the foe,
Dragged on the ground the hump-back maid
Who shrieked aloud and screamed for aid.
This way and that with no remorse

He dragged her with resistless force,
And chains and glittering trinkets burst
Lay here and there with gems dispersed,
Till like the sky of Antumn shone
The palace floor they sparkled on.
The lord of men, supremely strong,
Haled in his rage the wretch along :
Where Queen Kaikeyí dwelt he came,
And sternly then addressed the dame.
Deep in her heart Kaikeyí felt
The stabs his keen reproaches dealt,
And of Satrughna's ire afraid,
To Bharat flew and cried for aid.
He looked and saw the prince inflamed
With burning rage, and thus exclaimed :
' Forgive ! thine angry arm restrain :
A woman never may be slain.
My hand Kaikeyí's blood would spill,
The sinner ever bent on ill,
But Ráma, long in duty tried,
Would hate the impious matricide :
And if he knew thy vengeful blade
Had slaughtered e'en this hump back maid,
Never again, be sure, would he
Speak friendly word to thee or me.'
When Bharat's speech Satrughna heard,
He calmed the rage his breast that stirred,
Releasing from her dire constraint
The trembling wretch with terror faint.
Then to Kaikeyí's feet she crept,
And prostrate in her misery wept.
Kaikeyí on the hump-back gazed,
And saw her weep and gasp,
Still quivering, with her senses dazed,

From fierce Śatrughna's grasp.
With gentle words of pity she
  Assuaged her wild despair,
E'en as a tender hand might free
  A curlew from the snare.

CANTO LXXIX.

BHARAT'S COMMANDS.

Now when the sun's returning ray
Had ushered in the fourteenth day,
The gathered peers of state addressed
To Bharat's ear their new request:
'Our lord to heaven has parted hence,
Long served with deepest reverence;
Ráma, the eldest, far from home,
And Lakshman, in the forest roam.
O Prince, of mighty fame, be thou
Our guardian and our monarch now,
Lest secret plot or foeman's hate
Assail our unprotected state.
With longing eyes, O Lord of men,
To thee look friend and citizen,
And ready is each sacred thing
To consecrate our chosen king.
Come, Bharat, and accept thine own
Ancient hereditary throne.
Thee let the priests this day install
As monarch to preserve us all.'
   Around the sacred gear he bent
His circling footsteps reverent,
And, firm to vows he would not break,
Thus to the gathered people spake:
'The eldest son is ever king:
So rules the house from which we spring
Nor should ye, Lords, like men unwise,

With words like these to wrong advise.
Ráma is eldest born, and he
The ruler of the land shall be.
Now to the woods will I repair,
Five years and nine to lodge me there.
Assemble straight a mighty force,
Cars, elephants, and foot and horse,
For I will follow on his track
And bring my eldest brother back.
Whate'er the rites of throning need
Placed on a car the way shall lead :
The sacred vessels I will take
To the wild wood for Ráma's sake.
I o'er the lion prince's head
The sanctifying balm will shed,
And bring him, as the fire they bring
Forth from the shrine, with triumphing.
Nor will I let my mother's greed
In this her cherished aim succeed :
In pathless wilds will I remain,
And Ráma here as king shall reign.
To make the rough ways smooth and clear
Send workman out and pioneer :
Let skilful men attend beside
Our way through pathless spots to guide.'
    As thus the royal Bharat spake,
Ordaining all for Ráma's sake,
The audience gave with one accord
Auspicious answer to their lord :
' Be royal Fortune aye benign
To thee for this good speech of thine,
Who wishest still thine elder's hand
To rule with kingly sway the land.'
    Their glorious speech, their favouring cries

Made his proud bosom swell ;
And from the prince's noble eyes
The tears of rapture fell. [1]

---

[1] I follow in this stanza the Bombay edition in preference to Schlegel's which gives the tears of joy to the courtiers.

CANTO LXXX.

THE WAY PREPARED.

All they who knew the joiner's art,
Or distant ground in every part;
Each busied in his several trade,
To work machines or ply the spade;
Deft workmen skilled to frame the wheel,
Or with the ponderous engine deal;
Guides of the way, and craftsmen skilled
To sink the well, make bricks, and build;
And those whose hands the tree could hew,
And work with slips of cut bamboo,
Went forward, and to guide them, they
Whose eyes before had seen the way.
Then onward in triumphant mood
Went all the mighty multitude,
Like the great sea whose waves leap high
When the full moon is in the sky.
Then, in his proper duty skilled,
Each joined him to his several guild,
And onward in advance they went
With every tool and implement.
Where bush and tangled creeper lay
With trenchant steel they made the way;
They felled each stump, removed each stone,
And many a tree was overthrown.
In other spots, on desert lands,
Tall trees were reared by busy hands.
Where'er the line of road they took,

They plied the hatchet, axe, and hook.
Others, with all their strength applied,
Cast vigorous plants and shrubs aside,
In shelving valleys rooted deep,
And levelled every dale and steep.
Each pit and hole that stopped the way
They filled with stones, and mud, and clay,
And all the ground that rose and fell
With busy care was levelled well.
They bridged ravines with ceaseless toil,
And pounded fine the flinty soil.
Now here, now there, to right and left,
A passage through the ground they cleft,
And soon the rushing flood was led
Abundant through the new-cut bed,
Which by the running stream supplied
With ocean's boundless waters vied.
In dry and thirsty spots they sank
Full many a well and ample tank,
And altars round about them placed
To deck the station in the waste.
With well-wrought plaster smoothly spread,
With bloomy trees that rose o'erhead,
With banners waving in the air,
And wild birds singing here and there,
With fragrant sandal-water wet,
With many a flower beside it set,
Like the Gods' heavenly pathway showed
That mighty host's imperial road.
Deft workmen, chosen for their skill
To do the high-souled Bharat's will,
In every pleasant spot where grew
Trees of sweet fruit and fair to view,
As he commanded, toiled to grace

With all delights his camping-place.
And they who read the stars, and well
Each lucky sign and hour could tell,
Raised carefully the tented shade
Wherein high-minded Bharat stayed.
With ample space of level ground,
With broad deep moat encompassed round ;
Like Mandar in his towering pride,
With streets that ran from side to side ;
Enwreathed with many a palace tall
Surrounded by its noble wall ;
With roads by skilful workmen made,
Where many a glorious banner played ;
With stately mansions, where the dove
Sat nestling in her cote above,
Rising aloft supremely fair
Like heavenly cars that float in air,
Each camp in beauty and in bliss
Matched Indra's own metropolis.

As shines the heaven on some fair night,
    With moon and constellations filled,
The prince's royal road was bright,
    Adorned by art of workmen skilled.

CANTO LXXXI.

THE ASSEMBLY.

Ere yet the dawn had ushered in
The day should see the march begin,
Herald and bard who rightly knew
Each nice degree of honour due,
Their loud auspicious voices raised,
And royal Bharat blessed and praised.
With sticks of gold the drum they smote,
Which thundered out its deafening note,
Blew loud the sounding shell, and blent
Each high and low-toned instrument.
The mingled sound of drum and horn
Through all the air was quickly borne,
And as in Bharat's ear it rang,
Gave the sad prince another pang.
    Then Bharat, starting from repose,
Stilled the glad sounds that round him rose,
'I am not king: no more mistake:'
Then to Śatrughna thus he spake :
'O see what general wrongs succeed
Sprung from Kaikeyí's evil deed !
The king my sire has died and thrown
Fresh miseries on me alone.
The royal bliss, on duty based,
Which our just high-souled father graced,
Wanders in doubt and sore distress
Like a tossed vessel rudderless.
And he who was our lordly stay

Roams in the forest far away,
Expelled by this my mother, who
To duty's law is most untrue.'
　As royal Bharat thus gave vent
To bitter grief in wild lament,
Gazing upon his face the crowd
Of pitying women wept aloud.
His lamentation scarce was o'er,
When Saint Vaśishṭha, skilled in lore
Of royal duty, dear to fame,
To join the great assembly came.
Girt by disciples ever true
Still nearer to that hall he drew,
Resplendent, heavenly to behold,
Adorned with wealth of gems and gold:
E'en so a man in duty tried
Draws near to meet his virtuous bride.
He reached his golden seat o'erlaid
With coverlet of rich brocade,
There sat, in all the Vedas read,
And called the messengers, and said:
'Go forth, let Bráhman, Warrior, peer,
And every captain gather here:
Let all attentive hither throng:
Go, hasten: we delay too long.
Śatrughna, glorious Bharat bring,
The noble children of the king, [1]
Yudhájit [2] and Sumantra, all
The truthful and the virtuous call.'
　He ended: soon a mighty sound
Of thickening tumult rose around,

---

[1] The commentator says 'Śatrughna accompanied by the other sons of the king.'

[2] Not Bharat's uncle, but some councillor.

As to the hall they bent their course
With car, and elephant, and horse.
The people all with glad acclaim
Welcomed Prince Bharat as he came :
E'en as they loved their king to greet,
Or as the Gods Lord Indra [1] meet.
 The vast assembly shone as fair
  With Bharat's kingly face
 As Daśaratha's self were there
  To glorify the place.
 It gleamed like some unruffled lake
  Where monsters huge of mould
 With many a snake their pastime take
  O'er shells, sand, gems, and gold.

---

[1] *Śatakratu,* Lord of a hundred sacrifices, the performance of a hundred *Aśvamedhas* or sacrifices of a horse entitling the sacrificer to this exalted dignity.

CANTO LXXXII.

THE DEPARTURE.

The prudent prince the assembly viewed
Thronged with its noble multitude,
Resplendent as a cloudless night
When the full moon is in his height :
While robes of every varied hue
A glory o'er the synod threw.
The priest in lore of duty skilled
Looked on the crowd the hall that filled,
And then in accents soft and grave
To Bharat thus his counsel gave :
'The king, dear son, so good and wise,
Has gone from earth and gained the skies,
Leaving to thee, her rightful lord,
This rich wide land with foison stored.
And still has faithful Ráma stood ⁔
Firm to the duty of the good,
And kept his father's hest aright,
As the moon keeps its own dear light.
Thus sire and brother yield to thee
This realm from all annoyance free :
Rejoice thy lords : enjoy thine own :
Anointed king, ascend the throne.
Let vassal princes hasten forth
From distant lands west, south, and north,
From Kerala,[1] from every sea,
And bring ten million gems to thee.'

---

[1] The modern Malabar.

As thus the sage Vaśishṭha spoke,
A storm of grief o'er Bharat broke,
And longing to be just and true,
His thoughts to duteous Ráma flew.
With sobs and sighs and broken tones,
E'en as a wounded mallard moans,
He mourned with deepest sorrow moved,
And thus the holy priest reproved :
'O, how can such as Bharat dare
The power and sway from him to tear,
Wise, and devout, and true, and chaste,
With Scripture lore and virtue graced ?
Can one of Daśaratha's seed
Be guilty of so vile a deed ?
The realm and I are Ráma's : thou
Shouldst speak the words of justice now.
For he, to claims of virtue true,
Is eldest born and noblest too :
Nahush, Dilípa could not be
More famous in their lives than he.
As Daśaratha ruled of right,
So Ráma's is the power and right.
If I should do this sinful deed,
And forfeit hope of heavenly meed,
My guilty act would dim the shine
Of old Ikshváku's glorious line.
Nay, as the sin my mother wrought
Is grievous to my inmost thought,
I here, my hands together laid,
Will greet him in the pathless shade.
To Ráma shall my steps be bent,
My king, of men most excellent,
Raghu's illustrious son, whose sway
Might hell, and earth, and heaven obey.'

That righteous speech, whose every word
Bore virtue's stamp, the audience heard ;
On Ráma every thought was set,
And with glad tears each eye was wet.
'Then, if the power I still should lack
To bring my noble brother back,
I in the wood will dwell, and share
His banishment with Lakshman there.
By every art persuasive I
To bring him from the wood will try,
And show him to your loving eyes,
O Bráhmans noble, good, and wise.
E'en now, the road to make and clear,
Each labourer pressed, and pioneer
Have I sent forward to precede
The army I resolve to lead.'

Thus, by fraternal love possessed,
His firm resolve the prince expressed,
Then to Sumantra, deeply read
In holy texts, he turned and said :
'Sumantra, rise without delay,
And as I bid my words obey.   ·
Give orders for the march with speed,
And all the army hither lead.'

The wise Sumantra, thus addressed,
Obeyed the high-souled chief's behest.
He hurried forth with joy inspired
And gave the orders he desired.
Delight each soldier's bosom filled,
And through each chief and captain thrilled,
To hear that march proclaimed, to bring
Dear Ráma back from wandering.
From house to house the tidings flew :
Each soldier's wife the order knew,

And as she listened blithe and gay
Her husband urged to speed away.
Captain and soldier soon declared
The host equipped and all prepared
With chariots matching thought for speed,
And wagons drawn by ox and steed.
When Bharat by Vaśishṭha's side
His ready host of warriors eyed,
Thus in Sumantra's ear he spoke:
'My car and horses quickly yoke.'
Sumantra hastened to fulfil
With ready joy his master's will,
And quickly with the chariot sped
Drawn by fleet horses nobly bred.
Then glorious Bharat, true, devout,
Whose genuine valour none could doubt,
Gave in fit words his order out;
　　For he would seek the shade
Of the great distant wood, and there
Win his dear brother with his prayer:
'Sumantra, haste! my will declare
　　The host be all arrayed.
I to the wood my way will take,
To Ráma supplication make,
And for the world's advantage sake
　　Will lead him home again.'
Then, ordered thus, the charioteer
Who listened with delighted ear,
Went forth and gave his orders clear
　　To captains of the train.
He gave the popular chiefs the word,
And with the news his friends he stirred,
And not a single man deferred
　　Preparing for the road.

Then Bráhman, Warrior, Merchant, thrall,
Obedient to Sumantra's call,
Each in his house arose, and all
Yoked elephant or camel tall,
Or ass or noble steed in stall,
    And full appointed showed.

CANTO LXXXIII.

THE JOURNEY BEGUN.

Then Bharat rose at early morn,
And in his noble chariot borne
Drove forward at a rapid pace
Eager to look on Ráma's face.
The priests and lords, a fair array,
In sun-bright chariots led the way.
Behind, a well appointed throng,
Nine thousand elephants streamed along.
Then sixty thousand cars, and then,
With various arms, came fighting men.
A hundred thousand archers showed
In lengthened line the steeds they rode—
A mighty host, the march to grace
Of Bharat, pride of Raghu's race.
Kaikeyí and Sumitrá came,
And good Kauśalyá, dear to fame:
By hopes of Ráma's coming cheered
They in a radiant car appeared.
On fared the noble host to see
Ráma and Lakshmaṇ, wild with glee,
And still each other's ear to please,
Of Ráma spoke in words like these:
'When shall our happy eyes behold
Our hero true, and pure, and bold,
So lustrous dark, so strong of arm,
Who keeps the world from woe and harm?
The tears that now our eyeballs dim

Will vanish at the sight of him,
As the whole world's black shadows fly
When the bright sun ascends the sky.'
  Conversing thus their way pursued
The city's joyous multitude,
And each in mutual rapture pressed
A friend or neighbour to his breast.
Thus every man of high renown,
And every merchant of the town,
And leading subjects, joyous went
Toward Ráma in his banishment.
And those who worked the potter's wheel,
And artists skilled in gems to deal ;
And masters of the weaver's art,
And those who shaped the sword and dart ;
And they who golden trinkets made,
And those who plied the fuller's trade ;
And servants trained the bath to heat,
And they who dealt in incense sweet ;
Physicians in their business skilled,
And those who wine and mead distilled ;
And workmen deft in glass who wrought,
And those whose snares the peacock caught ;
With them who bored the ear for rings,
Or sawed, or fashioned ivory things ;
And those who knew to mix cement,
Or lived by sale of precious scent ;
And men who washed, and men who sewed,
And thralls who mid the herds abode ;
And fishers of the flood, and they
Who played and sang, and women gay ;
And virtuous Bráhmans, Scripture-wise,
Of life approved in all men's eyes ;
These swelled the prince's lengthened train,

Borne each in car or bullock wain.
Fair were the robes they wore upon
Their limbs where red-hued unguents shone.
These all in various modes conveyed
Their journey after Bharat made ;
The soldiers' hearts with rapture glowed,
Following Bharat on his road,
Their chief whose tender love would fain
Bring his dear brother home again.
With elephant, and horse, and car,
The vast procession travelled far,
And came where Gangá's waves below
The town of Sringavora [1] flow.
There, with his friends and kinsmen nigh,
Dwelt Guha, Ráma's dear ally,
Heroic guardian of the land
With dauntless heart and ready hand.
There for a while the mighty force
That followed Bharat stayed its course,
Gazing on Gangá's bosom stirred
By many a graceful water-bird.
When Bharat viewed his followers there,
And Gangá's water, blest and fair,
The prince, who lore of words possessed,
His councillors and lords addressed :
' The captains of the army call :
Proclaim this day a halt for all,
That so to-morrow, rested, we
May cross this flood that seeks the sea.
Meanwhile, descending to the shore,
The funeral stream I fain would pour
From Gangá's fair auspicious tide
To him, my father glorified.'

---

[1] Now Sungroor, in the Allahabad district.

Thus Bharat spoke : each peer and lord
Approved his words with one accord,
And bade the weary troops repose
In separate spots where'er they chose.
There by the mighty stream that day,
Most glorious in its vast array
The prince's wearied army lay
 In various groups reclined.
There Bharat's hours of night were spent,
While every eager thought he bent
On bringing home from banishment
 His brother, great of mind.

CANTO LXXXIV.

GUHA'S ANGER.

King Guha saw the host spread o'er
The wide expanse of Gangá's shore,
With waving flag and pennon graced,
And to his followers spoke in haste :
'A mighty army meets my eyes,
That rivals Ocean's self in size :
Where'er I look my very mind
No limit to the host can find.
Sure Bharat with some evil thought
His army to our land has brought.
See, huge of form, his flag he rears,
That like an Ebony-tree appears.
He comes with bonds to take and chain,
Or triumph o'er our people slain :
And after, Ráma will he slay,—
Him whom his father drove away :
The power complete he longs to gain,
And—task too hard—usurp the reign.
So Bharat comes with wicked will
His brother Ráma's blood to spill.
But Ráma's slave and friend am I ;
He is my lord and dear ally.
Keep here your watch in arms arrayed
Near Gangá's flood to lend him aid,
And let my gathered servants stand
And line with troops the river strand.
Here let the river keepers meet,

Who flesh and roots and berries eat ;
A hundred fishers man each boat
Of the five hundred here afloat,
And let the youthful and the strong
Assemble in defensive throng.
But yet, if, free from guilty thought
'Gainst Ráma, he this land have sought,
The prince's happy host to-day
Across the flood shall make its way.'

He spoke : then bearing in a dish
A gift of honey, meat, and fish,
The king of the Nishádas drew
Toward Bharat for an interview.
When Bharat's noble charioteer
Observed the monarch hastening near,
He duly, skilled in courteous lore,
The tidings to his master bore :
'This aged prince who hither bends
His footsteps with a thousand friends,
Knows, firm ally of Ráma, all
That may in Daṇḍak wood befall :
Therefore, Kakutstha's son, admit .
The monarch, as is right and fit :
For doubtless he can clearly tell
Where Ráma now and Lakshmaṇ dwell.'
When Bharat heard Sumantra's rede,
To his fair words the prince agreed :
'Go quickly forth,' he cried, 'and bring
Before my face the aged king.'
King Guha, with his kinsmen near,
Rejoiced the summoning to hear :
He nearer drew, bowed low his head,
And thus to royal Bharat said :
'No mansions can our country boast,

And unexpected comes thy host :
But what we have I give thee all :
Rest in the lodging of thy thrall.
See, the Nishádas here have brought
The fruit and roots their hands have sought :
And we have woodland fare beside,
And store of meat both fresh and dried.
To rest their weary limbs, I pray
This night at least thy host may stay :
Then cheered with all we can bestow
To-morrow thou with it mayst go.'

CANTO LXXXV.

GUHA AND BHARAT.

Thus the Nishádas' king besought :
The prince with spirit wisdom-fraught
Replied in seemly words that blent
Deep matter with the argument :
'Thou, friend of him whom I revere,
With honours high hast met me here,
For thou alone wouldst entertain
And feed to-day so vast a train.'
In such fair words the prince replied,
Then, pointing to the path he cried :
'Which way aright will lead my feet
To Bharadvája's calm retreat ;
For all this land near Gangá's streams
Pathless and hard to traverse seems ?'
   Thus spoke the prince : King Guha heard
Delighted every prudent word,
And gazing on that forest wide,
Raised suppliant hands, and thus replied :
'My servants, all the ground who know,
O glorious Prince, with thee shall go
With constant care thy way to guide,
And I will journey by thy side.
But this thy host so wide dispread
Wakes in my heart one doubt and dread,
Lest, threatening Ráma good and great,
Ill thoughts thy journey stimulate.'
   But when King Guha, ill at ease,

Declared his fear in words like these,
As pure as is the cloudless sky
With soft voice Bharat made reply :
‹Suspect me not : ne'er come the time
For me to plot so foul a crime !
He is my eldest brother, he
Is like a father dear to me.
I go to lead my brother thence
Who makes the wood his residence.
No thought but this thy heart should frame :
This simple truth my lips proclaim.'
     Then with glad cheer King Guha cried,
With Bharat's answer gratified :
‘Blessed art thou : on earth I see
None who may vie, O Prince, with thee,
Who canst of thy free will resign
The kingdom which unsought is thine.
For this, a name that ne'er shall die,
Thy glory through the worlds shall fly,
Who fain wouldst balm thy brother's pain
And lead the exile home again.'
     As Guha thus, and Bharat, each
To other spoke in friendly speech,
The Day-God sank with glory dead,
And night o'er all the sky was spread.
Soon as King Guha's thoughtful care
Had quartered all the army there,
Well honoured, Bharat laid his head
Beside Sátrughna on a bed.
But grief for Ráma yet oppressed
High-minded Bharat's faithful breast—
Such torment little was deserved
By him who ne'er from duty swerved.
The fever raged through every vein

And burnt him with its inward pain :
So when in woods the flames leap free
The fire within consumes the tree.
From heat of burning anguish sprung
The sweat upon his body hung,
As when the sun with fervid glow
On high Himálaya melts the snow.
As, banished from the herd, a bull
Wanders alone and sorrowful,
   Thus sighing and distressed,
In misery and bitter grief,
With fevered heart that mocked relief,
Distracted in his mind, the chief
   Still mourned and found no rest.

CANTO LXXXVI.

GUHA'S SPEECH.

Guha the king, acquainted well
With all that in the wood befell,
To Bharat the unequalled told
The tale of Lakshmaṇ mighty-souled :
' With many an earnest word I spake
To Lakshmaṇ as he stayed awake,
And with his bow and shaft in hand
To guard his brother kept his stand :
' Now sleep a little, Lakshmaṇ, see
This pleasant bed is strewn for thee :
Hereon thy weary body lay,
And strengthen thee with rest, I pray.
Inured to toil are men like these,
But thou hast aye been nursed in ease.
Rest, duteous-minded ! I will keep
My watch while Ráma lies asleep :
For in the whole wide world is none
Dearer to me than Raghu's son.
Harbour no doubt or jealous fear :
I speak the truth with heart sincere :
For from the grace which he has shown
Will glory on my name be thrown :
Great store of merit shall I gain,
And duteous, form no wish in vain.
Let me enforced by many a row
Of followers, armed with shaft and bow,
For well-loved Ráma's weal provide

Who lies asleep by Sítá's side.
For through this wood I often go,
And all its shades conceal, I know:
And we with conquering arms can meet
A four-fold host arrayed complete.'
' With words like these I spoke, designed
To move the high-souled Bharat's mind,
But he upon his duty bent,
Plied his persuasive argument:
' O, how can slumber close mine eyes
When lowly couched with Sítá lies
The royal Ráma? can I give
My heart to joy, or even live?
He whom no mighty demon, no,
Nor heavenly God can overthrow,
See, Guha, how he lies, alas,
With Sítá couched on gathered grass.
By varied labours, long, severe,
By many a prayer and rite austere,
He, Daśaratha's cherished son,
By Fortune stamped, from Heaven was won.
Now as his son is forced to fly,
The king ere long will surely die:
Reft of his guardian hand, forlorn
In widowed grief this land will mourn.
E'en now perhaps, with toil o'erspent,
The women cease their loud lament,
And cries of woe no longer ring
Throughout the palace of the king.
But ah for sad Kauśalyá! how
Fare she and mine own mother now?
How fares the king? this night, I think,
Some of the three in death will sink.
With hopes upon Satrughna set

My mother may survive as yet,
But the sad queen will die who bore
The hero, for her grief is sore.
His cherished wish that would have made
Dear Ráma king, so long delayed,
'Too late! too late!' the king will cry,
And conquered by his misery die.
When Fate has brought the mournful day
Which sees my father pass away,
How happy in their lives are they
Allowed his funeral rites to pay.
Our exile o'er, with him who ne'er
Turns from the oath his lips may swear,
May we returning safe and well
Again in fair Ayodhyá dwell.'
'Thus Bharat stood with many a sigh
Lamenting, and the night went by.
Soon as the morning light shone fair
In votive coils both bound their hair.
And then I sent them safely o'er
And left them on the farther shore.
With Sítá then they onward passed,
Their coats of bark about them cast,
    Their locks like hermits' bound,
The mighty tamers of the foe,
Each with his arrows and his bow,
    Went o'er the rugged ground,
Proud in their strength and undeterred
Like elephants that lead the herd,
    And gazing oft around.

CANTO LXXXVII.

GUHA'S STORY.

That speech of Guha Bharat heard
With grief and tender pity stirred,
And as his ears the story drank,
Deep in his thoughtful heart it sank.
His large full eyes in anguish rolled,
His trembling limbs grew stiff and cold ;
Then fell he, like a tree uptorn,
In woe too grievous to be borne.
When Guha saw the long-armed chief
Whose eye was like a lotus leaf,
With lion shoulders strong and fair,
High-mettled, prostrate in despair,—
Pale, bitterly afflicted, he
Reeled as in earthquake reels a tree.
But when Śatrughna standing nigh
Saw his dear brother helpless lie,
Distraught with woe his head he bowed,
Embraced him oft and wept aloud.
Then Bharat's mothers came, forlorn
Of their dear king, with fasting worn,
And stood with weeping eyes around
The hero prostrate on the ground.
Kauśalyá, by her woe oppressed,
The senseless Bharat's limbs caressed,
As a fond cow in love and fear
Caresses oft her youngling dear :
Then yielding to her woe she said,

Weeping and sore disquieted :
'What torments, O my son, are these
Of sudden pain or swift disease ?
The lives of us and all the line
Depend, dear child, on only thine.
Ráma and Lakshman forced to flee,
I live by naught but seeing thee :
For as the king has past away
Thou art my only help to-day.
Hast thou, perchance, heard evil news
Of Lakshman, which thy soul subdues,
Or Ráma dwelling with his spouse—
My all is he—neath forest boughs ?'

Then slowly gathering sense and strength
The weeping hero rose at length,
And words like these to Guha spake,
That bade Kauśalyá comfort take :
'Where lodged the prince that night ? and where
Lakshman the brave, and Sítá fair ?
Show me the couch whereon he lay,
Tell me the food he ate, I pray.'
Then Guha the Nishádas' king
Replied to Bharat's questioning :
'Of all I had I brought the best
To serve my good and honoured guest :
Food of each varied kind I chose,
And every fairest fruit that grows.
Ráma the hero truly brave
Declined the gift I humbly gave :
His Warrior part he ne'er forgot,
And what I brought accepted not :
'No gifts, my friend, may we accept :
Our law is, Give, and must be kept.'
'The high-souled chief, O Monarch, thus

With gracious words persuaded us.
Then calm and still, absorbed in thought,
He drank the water Lakshman brought,
And then, obedient to his vows,
He fasted with his gentle spouse.
So Lakshman too from food abstained,
And sipped the water that remained ;
Then with ruled lips, devoutly staid,
The three¹ their evening worship paid.
Then Lakshman with unwearied care
Brought heaps of sacred grass, and there
With his own hands he quickly spread,
For Ráma's rest, a pleasant bed,
And faithful Sítá's too, where they
Reclining each by other lay.
Then Lakshman bathed their feet, and drew
A little distance from the two.
Here stands the tree which lent them shade,
Here is the grass beneath it laid,
Where Ráma and his consort spent
The night together ere they went.
Lakshman, whose arms the foeman quell,
Watched all the night as sentinel,
    And kept his great bow strung :
His hand was gloved, his arm was braced,
Two well-filled quivers at his waist,
    With deadly arrows, hung.
I took my shafts and trusty bow,
And with that tamer of the foe
    Stood ever wakeful near,
And with my followers, bow in hand,
Behind me ranged, a ready band,
    Kept watch o'er Indra's peer.'

---

¹ Ráma, Lakshman, and Sumantra.

CANTO LXXXVIII.

THE INGUDÍ TREE.

When Bharat with each friend and peer
Had heard that tale so full and clear,
They went together to the tree
The bed which Ráma pressed to see.
Then Bharat to his mothers said :
' Behold the high-souled hero's bed :
These tumbled heaps of grass betray
Where he that night with Sítá lay :
Unmeet, the heir of fortune high
Thus on the cold bare earth should lie,
The monarch's son, in counsel sage,
Of old imperial lineage.
That lion-lord whose noble bed
With finest skins of deer was spread,—
How can he now endure to press
The bare earth, cold and comfortless ?
This sudden fall from bliss to grief
Appears untrue, beyond belief :
My senses are distraught : I seem
To view the fancies of a dream.
There is no deity so great,
No power in heaven can master Fate,
If Ráma, Daśaratha's heir,
Lay on the ground and slumbered there ;
And lovely Sítá, she who springs
From fair Videha's ancient kings,
Ráma's dear wife, by all adored,

Lay on the earth beside her lord.
Here was his couch, upon this heap
He tossed and turned in restless sleep:
On the hard soil each manly limb
Has stamped the grass with signs of him.
That night, it seems, fair Sítá spent
Arrayed in every ornament,
For here and there my eyes behold
Small particles of glistering gold.
She laid her outer garment here,
For still some silken threads appear.
How dear in her devoted eyes
Must be the bed where Ráma lies,
Where she so tender could repose
And by his side forget her woes.
Alas, unhappy, guilty me!
For whom the prince was forced to flee,
And chief of Raghu's sons and best,
A bed like this with Sítá pressed.
Son of a royal sire whose hand
Ruled paramount o'er every land,
Could he who every joy bestows,
Whose body like the lotus shows,
The friend of all, who charms the sight,
Whose flashing eyes are darkly bright,
Leave the dear kingdom, his by right,
Unmeet for woe, the heir of bliss,
And lie upon a bed like this?
Great joy and happy fate are thine,
O Lakshman, marked with each fair sign,
Whose faithful footsteps follow still
Thy brother in his hour of ill.
And blest is Sítá, nobly good,
Who dwells with Ráma in the wood.

Ours is, alas, a doubtful fate
Of Ráma reft and desolate.
My royal sire has gained the skies,
In woods the high-souled hero lies ;
The state is wrecked and tempest-tossed,
A vessel with her rudder lost.
Yet none in secret thought has planned
With hostile might to seize the land :
Though forced in distant wilds to dwell,
The hero's arm protects it well.
Unguarded, with deserted wall,
No elephant or steed in stall,
My father's royal city shows
Her portals open to her foes,
Of bold protectors reft and bare,
Defenceless in her dark despair :
But still her foes the wish restrain,
As men from poisoned cates refrain.
I from this hour my nights will pass
Couched on the earth or gathered grass,
Eat only fruit and roots, and wear
A coat of bark, and matted hair.
I in the woods will pass, content,
For him the term of banishment ;
So shall I still unbroken save
The promise which the hero gave.
While I remain for Ráma there,
Śatrughna will my exile share,
And Ráma in his home again,
With Lakshman, o'er Ayodhyá reign,
For him, to rule and guard the state,
The twice-born men shall consecrate.
O, may the Gods I serve incline
To grant this earnest wish of mine !

If when I bow before his feet
And with all moving arts entreat,
   He still deny my prayer,
Then with my brother will I live:
He must, he must permission give,
   Roaming in forests there.'

CANTO LXXXIX.

THE PASSAGE OF GANGÁ.

That night the son of Raghu lay
On Gangá's bank till break of day :
Then with the earliest light he woke
And thus to brave Satrughna spoke :
'Rise up, Satrughna, from thy bed :
Why sleepest thou ? the night is fled.
See how the sun who chases night
Wakes every lotus with his light.
Arise, arise, and first of all
The lord of Sringavera call,
For he his friendly aid will lend
Our army o'er the flood to send.'
   Thus urged, Satrughna answered . 'I,
Remembering Ráma, sleepless lie.'
As thus the brothers, each to each,
The lion-mettled, ended speech,
Came Guha, the Nishádas' king,
And spoke with kindly questioning :
'Hast thou in comfort passed,' he cried,
'The night upon the river side ?
With thee how fares it ? and are these,
Thy soldiers, healthy and at ease ?'
Thus the Nishádas' lord inquired
In gentle words which love inspired,
And Bharat, Ráma's faithful slave,
'Thus to the king his answer gave :
'The night has sweetly passed, and we

Are highly honoured, King, by thee.
Now let thy servants boats prepare,
Our army o'er the stream to bear.'

. The speech of Bharat Guha heard,
And swift to do his bidding stirred.
Within the town the monarch sped
And to his ready kinsmen said:
'Awake, each kinsman, rise, each friend!
May every joy your lives attend.
Gather each boat upon the shore
And ferry all the army o'er.'
Thus Guha spoke: nor they delayed,
But, rising quick, their lord obeyed,
And soon, from every side secured,
Five hundred boats were ready moored.
Some reared aloft the mystic sign, [1]
And mighty bells were hung in line:
Of firmest build, gay flags they bore,
And sailors for the helm and oar.
One such King Guha chose, whereon,
Of fair white cloth, an awning shone,
And sweet musicians charmed the ear,—
And bade his servants urge it near.
Then Bharat swiftly sprang on board,
And then Śatrughna, famous lord,
To whom, with many a royal dame,
Kauśalyá and Sumitrá came.
The household priest went first in place,
The elders, and the Bráhman race,
And after them the monarch's train
Of women borne in many a wain.
Then high to heaven the shouts of those

---

[1] The *svastika*, a little cross with a transverse line at each extremity.

Who fired the army's huts, [1] arose,
With theirs who bathed along the shore,
Or to the boats the baggage bore.
Full freighted with that mighty force
The boats sped swiftly on their course,
By royal Guha's servants manned,
And gentle gales the banners fanned.
Some boats a crowd of dames conveyed,
In others noble coursers neighed ;
Some chariots and their cattle bore,
Some precious wealth and golden store.
Across the stream each boat was rowed,
There duly disembarked its load,
And then returning on its way,
Sped here and there in merry play.
Then swimming elephants appeared
With flying pennons high upreared,
And as the drivers urged them o'er,
The look of winged mountains wore.
Some men in barges reached the strand,
Others on rafts came safe to land :
Some buoyed with pitchers crossed the tide,
And others on their arms relied.
Thus with the help the monarch gave
The army crossed pure Gangá's wave :
Then in auspicious hour it stood
Within Prayága's famous wood.
The prince with cheering words addressed
His weary men, and bade them rest
  Where'er they chose : and he,
With priest and deacon by his side,
To Bharadvája's dwelling hied
  That best of saints to see.

---

[1] When an army marched it was customary to burn the huts in which it had spent the night.

CANTO XC.

THE HERMITAGE.

The prince of men a league away
Saw where the hermit's dwelling lay,
Then with his lords his path pursued,
And left his warrior multitude.
On foot, as duty taught his mind,
He left his warlike gear behind :
Two robes of linen cloth he wore,
And bade Vaśishṭha walk before.
Then Bharat from his lords withdrew
When Bharadvája came in view,
And toward the holy hermit went
Behind Vaśishṭha, reverent.
When Bharadvája, saint austere,
Saw good Vaśishṭha drawing near,
He cried, upspringing from his seat,
'The grace-gift bring, my friend to greet.'
When Saint Vaśishṭha near him drew,
And Bharat paid the reverence due,
The glorious hermit was aware
That Daśaratha's son was there.
The grace-gift, water for their feet
He gave, and offered fruit to eat ;
Then, duty-skilled, with friendly speech
In seemly order questioned each :
' How fares it in Ayodhyá now
With treasury and army ? how
With kith and kin and friends most dear,

W

With councillor, and prince, and peer?'
But, for he knew the king was dead,
Of Daśaratha naught he said.
Vaśishṭha and the prince in turn
Would of the hermit's welfare learn:
Of holy fires they fain would hear,
Of pupils, trees, and birds, and deer.
The glorious saint his answer made
That all was well in holy shade:
Then love of Ráma moved his breast,
And thus he questioned of his guest:
'Why art thou here, O Prince, whose hand
With kingly sway protects the land?
Declare the cause, explain the whole,
For yet some doubt disturbs my soul.
He whom Kauśalyá bare, whose might
The foemen slays, his line's delight,
He who with wife and brother sent
Afar, now roams in banishment,
Famed prince, to whom his father spake
This order for a woman's sake:
'Away! and in the forest spend
Thy life till fourteen years shall end'—
Hast thou the wish to harm him, bent
On sin against the innocent?
Wouldst thou thine elder's realm enjoy
Without a thorn that can annoy?'
  'With sobbing voice and tearful eye
Thus Bharat sadly made reply:
'Ah, lost am I, if thou, O Saint,
Canst thus in thought my heart attaint:
No warning charge from thee I need;
Ne'er could such crime from me proceed.
The words my guilty mother spake .

When fondly jealous for my sake
Think not that I, to triumph moved,
Those words approve or e'er approved.
O Hermit, I have sought this place
To win the lordly hero's grace,
To throw me at my brother's feet
And lead him to his royal seat.
To this, my journey's aim and end,
Thou shouldst, O Saint, thy favour lend:
Where is the lord of earth? do thou,
Most holy, say, where roams he now?'

 Then, by the saint Vaśishṭha pressed,
  And all the gathered priests beside,
 To Bharat's dutiful request
  The hermit graciously replied:
'Worthy of thee, O Prince, this deed,
True son of Raghu's ancient seed.
I know thee reverent, well-controlled,
The glory of the good of old.
I grant thy prayer: in this pursuit
I know thy heart is resolute.
'Tis for thy sake those words I said
That wider still thy fame may spread.
I know where Ráma, duty-tried,
His brother, and his wife abide.
Where Chitrakúṭa's heights arise
Thy brother Ráma's dwelling lies.
Go thither with the morning's light,
And stay with all thy lords to-night:
For I would show thee honour high,
And do not thou my wish deny.'

CANTO XCI.

BHARADVÁJA'S FEAST.

Soon as he saw the prince's mind
To rest that day was well inclined,
He sought Kaikeyí's son to please
With hospitable courtesies.
Then Bharat to the saint replied :
' Our wants are more than satisfied.
The gifts which honoured strangers greet,
And water for our weary feet
Hast thou bestowed with friendly care,
And every choice of woodland fare.'
  Then Bharadvája spoke, a smile
Playing upon his lips the while :
' I know, dear Prince, thy friendly mind
Will any fare sufficient find,
But gladly would I entertain
And banquet all thine armed train :
Such is my earnest wish : do thou
This longing of my heart allow.
Why hast thou hither bent thy way,
And made thy troops behind thee stay ?
Why unattended ? couldst thou not
With friends and army seek this spot ? '
  Bharat, with reverent hands raised high,
To that great hermit made reply :
' My troops, for awe of thee, O Sage,
I brought not to thy hermitage :
Troops of a king or monarch's son

A hermit's home should ever shun.
Behind me comes a mighty train
Wide spreading o'er the ample plain,
Where every chief and captain leads
Men, elephants, and mettled steeds.
I feared, O reverend Sage, lest these
Might harm the holy ground and trees,
Springs might be marred and cots o'erthrown,
So with the priests I came alone.'

   'Bring all thy host,' the hermit cried,
And Bharat, to his joy, complied.
Then to the chapel went the sire,
Where ever burnt the sacred fire,
And first, in order due, with sips
Of water purified his lips:
To Viśvakarmá then he prayed,
His hospitable feast to aid:
'Let Viśvakarmá hear my call,
The God who forms and fashions all:
A mighty banquet I provide,
Be all my wants this day supplied.
Lord Indra at their head, the three[1]
Who guard the worlds I call to me:
A mighty host this day I feed,
Be now supplied my every need.
Let all the streams that eastward go,
And those whose waters westering flow,
Both on the earth and in the sky,
Flow hither and my wants supply.
Be some with ardent liquor filled,
And some with wine from flowers distilled,
While some their fresh cool streams retain
Sweet as the juice of sugar-cane.

---

[1] Yama, Varuṇa, and Kuvera.

I call the Gods, I call the band
Of minstrels that around them stand:
I call the Háhá and Huhú,
I call the sweet Viśvávasu.
I call the heavenly wives of these
With all the bright Apsarases,
Alambushá of beauty rare,
The charmer of the tangled hair,
Ghritáchí and Viśváchí fair,
Hemá and Bhímá sweet to view,
And lovely Nágadantá too,
And all the sweetest nymphs who stand
By Indra or by Brahmá's hand—
I summon these with all their train
And Tumburu to lead the strain.
Here let Kuvera's garden rise
Which far in Northern Kuru [1] lies:
For leaves let cloth and gems entwine,
And let its fruit be nymphs divine.
Let Soma [2] give the noblest food
To feed the mighty multitude,
Of every kind, for tooth and lip,
To chew, to lick, to suck, and sip.
Let wreaths, where fairest flowers abound,
Spring from the trees that bloom around.
Each sort of wine to woo the taste,
And meats of every kind be placed.'

---

[1] A happy land in the remote north where 'the inhabitants enjoy a natural perfection attended with complete happiness obtained without exertion. There is there no vicissitude, nor decrepitude, nor death, nor fear ; no distinction of virtue and vice, none of the inequalities denoted by the words best, worst, and intermediate, nor any change resulting from the succession of the four Yugas.' See MUIR'S *Sanskrit Texts*, Vol. I. p. 492.

[2] The Moon.

Thus spake the hermit self-restrained,
With proper tone by rules ordained,
On deepest meditation bent,
In holy might preëminent.
Then as with hands in reverence raised
Absorbed in thought he eastward gazed,
The deities he thus addressed
Came each in semblance manifest.
Delicious gales that cooled the frame
From Malaya and Dardar came,
That kissed those scented hills and threw
Auspicious fragrance where they blew.
Then falling fast in sweetest showers
Came from the sky immortal flowers,
And all the airy region round
With heavenly drums was made to sound.
Then breathed a soft celestial breeze,
Then danced the bright Apsarases,
The minstrels and the Gods advanced,
And warbling lutes the soul entranced.
The earth and sky that music filled,
And through each ear it softly thrilled,
As from the heavenly quills it fell
With time and tune attempered well.
Soon as the minstrels ceased to play
And airs celestial died away,
The troops of Bharat saw amazed
What Viśvakarmá's art had raised.
On every side, five leagues around,
All smooth and level lay the ground,
With fresh green grass that charmed the sight
Like sapphires blent with lazulite.
There the Wood-apple hung its load,
The Mango and the Citron glowed,

The Bel and scented Jak were there,
And Aonlá with fruitage fair.
There, brought from Northern Kuru, stood,
Rich in delights, the glorious wood,
And many a stream was seen to glide
With flowering trees along its side.
There mansions rose with four wide halls,
And elephants and chargers' stalls,
And many a house of royal state,
Triumphal arc and bannered gate
With noble doorways, sought the sky,
Like a pale cloud, a palace high,
Which far and wide rare fragrance shed,
With wreaths of white engarlanded.
Square was its shape, its halls were wide,
With many a seat and couch supplied,
Drink of all kinds, and every meat
Such as celestial Gods might eat.
Then at the bidding of the seer
Kaikeyí's strong-armed son drew near,
And passed within that fair abode
Which with the noblest jewels glowed.
Then, as Vaśishṭha led the way,
The councillors, in due array,
Followed delighted and amazed
And on the glorious structure gazed.
Then Bharat, Raghu's son, drew near
The kingly throne, with prince and peer,
Whereby the chouri in the shade
Of the white canopy was laid.
Before the throne he humbly bent
And honoured Ráma, reverent,
Then in his hand the chouri bore,
And sat where sits a councillor.

His ministers and household priest
Sat by degrees from chief to least,
Then sat the captain of the host
And all the men he honoured most.
Then when the saint his order gave,
Each river with enchanted wave
Rolled milk and curds divinely sweet
Before the princely Bharat's feet ;
And dwellings fair on either side,
With gay white plaster beautified,
Their heavenly roofs were seen to lift,
The Bráhman Bharadvája's gift.
Then straight by Lord Kuvera sent,
Gay with celestial ornament
Of bright attire and jewels' shine,
Came twenty thousand nymphs divine :
The man on whom those beauties glanced
That moment felt his soul entranced.
With them from Nandan's blissful shades
Came twenty thousand heavenly maids.
Tumburu, Nárad, Gopa came,
And Sutanu, like radiant flame,   .
The kings of the Gandharva throng,
And ravished Bharat with their song.
Then spoke the saint, and swift obeyed
Alambushá, the fairest maid,
And Miśrakeśí bright to view,
Ramaṇá, Puṇḍaríká too,   .
And danced to him with graceful ease
The dances of Apsarases.
All chaplets that by Gods are worn,
Or Chaitraratha's groves adorn,
Bloomed by the saint's command arrayed
On branches in Prayága's shade.

When at the saint's command the breeze
Made music with the Vilva trees,
To wave in rhythmic beat began
The boughs of each Myrobolan,
And holy fig-trees wore the look
Of dancers, as their leaflets shook.
The fair Tamála, palm, and pine,
With trees that tower and plants that twine,
The sweetly varying forms displayed
Of stately dame or bending maid.
Here men the foaming winecup quaffed,
Here drank of milk full many a draught,
And tasted meats of every kind,
Well dressed, whatever pleased their mind.
Then beauteous women, seven or eight,
Stood ready by each man to wait :
Beside the stream his limbs they stripped
And in the cooling water dipped.
And then the fair ones, sparkling-eyed,
With soft hands rubbed his limbs and dried,
And sitting on the lovely bank
Held up the winecup as he drank.
Nor did the grooms'forget to feed
Camel and mule and ox and steed,
For there were stores of roasted grain,
Of honey and of sugar-cane.
So fast the wild excitement spread
Among the warriors Bharat led,
That all the mighty army through
The groom no more his charger knew,
And he who drove might seek in vain
To tell his elephant again.
With every joy and rapture fired,
Entranced with all the heart desired,

The myriads of the host that night
Revelled delirious with delight.
Urged by the damsels at their side
In wild delight the warriors cried :
'Ne'er will we seek Ayodhyá, no,
Nor yet to Daṇḍak forest go :
Here will we stay : may happy fate
On Bharat and on Ráma wait.'
Thus cried the army gay and free
Exulting in their lawless glee,
Both infantry and those who rode
On elephants, or steeds bestrode,
Ten thousand voices shouting, 'This
Is heaven indeed for perfect bliss.'
With garlands decked they idly strayed,
And danced and laughed and sang and played.
At length as every soldier eyed,
With food like Amrit satisfied,
Each dainty cate and tempting meat,
No longer had he care to eat.
Thus soldier, servant, dame, and slave
Received whate'er the wish might crave,
As each in new-wrought clothes arrayed
Enjoyed the feast before him laid.
Each man was seen in white attire
Unstained by spot or speck of mire :
None was athirst or hungry there,
And none had dust upon his hair.
On every side in woody dells
Was milky food in bubbling wells,
And there were all-supplying cows
And honey dropping from the boughs.
Nor wanted lakes of flower-made drink
With piles of meat upon the brink,

Boiled, stewed, and roasted, varied cheer,
Peachick and jungle-fowl and deer,
There was the flesh of kid and boar,
And dainty sauce in endless store,
With juice of flowers concocted well,
And soup that charmed the taste and smell,
And pounded fruits of bitter taste,
And many a bath was ready placed.
Down by each river's shelving side
There stood great basins well supplied,
And laid therein, of dazzling sheen,
White brushes for the teeth were seen,
And many a covered box wherein
Was sandal powdered for the skin.
And mirrors bright with constant care,
And piles of new attire were there,
And store of sandals and of shoes,
Thousands of pairs, for all to choose :
Eye-unguents, combs for hair and beard,
Umbrellas fair and bows appeared.
Lakes gleamed, that lent digestive aid, [1]
And some for pleasant bathing made,
With waters fair, and smooth incline
For camels, horses, mules, and kine.
There saw they barley heaped on high
The countless cattle to supply :
The golden grain shone fair and bright
As sapphires or the lazulite.
To all the gathered host it seemed
As if that magic scene they dreamed,
And wonder, as they gazed, increased
At Bharadvája's glorious feast.

　　Thus in the hermit's grove they spent

---

[1] The poet does not tell us what these lakes contained.

That night in joy and merriment,
Blest as the Gods who take their ease
Under the shade of Nandan's trees.
Each minstrel bade the saint adieu,
And to his blissful mansion flew,
And every stream and heavenly dame
Returned as swiftly as she came.

CANTO XCII.

BHARAT'S FAREWELL.

So Bharat with his army spent
The watches of the night content,
And gladly, with the morning's light
Drew near his host the anchorite.
When Bharadvája saw him stand
With hand in reverence joined to hand,
When fires of worship had been fed,
He looked upon the prince and said :
' O blameless son, I pray thee tell,
Did the past night content thee well ?
Say if the feast my care supplied
Thy host of followers gratified.'
His hands he joined, his head he bent
And spoke in answer reverent
To the most high and radiant sage
Who issued from his hermitage :
' Well have I passed the night : thy feast
Gave joy to every man and beast ;
And I, great lord, and every peer
Were satisfied with sumptuous cheer.
Thy banquet has delighted all
From highest chief to meanest thrall,
And rich attire and drink and meat
Banished the thought of toil and heat.
And now, O Hermit good and great,
A boon of thee I supplicate.
To Ráma's side my steps I bend :

Do thou with friendly eye commend.
O tell me how to guide my feet
To virtuous Ráma's lone retreat :
Great Hermit, I entreat thee, say
How far from here and which the way.'
  Thus by fraternal love inspired
The chieftain of the saint inquired :
Then thus replied the glorious seer
Of matchless might, of vows austere :
' Ere the fourth league from here be passed,
Amid a forest wild and vast,
Stands Chitrakúṭa's mountain tall,
Lovely with wood and waterfall.
North of the mountain thou wilt see
The beauteous stream Mandákiní,
Where swarm the waterfowl below,
And gay trees on the margin grow.
Then will a leafy cot between
The river and the hill be seen :
' Tis Ráma's, and the princely pair
Of brothers live for certain there.
Hence to the south thine army lead,
And then more southward still proceed,
So shalt thou find his lone retreat,
And there the son of Raghu meet.'
  Soon as the ordered march they knew,
The widows of the monarch flew,
Leaving their cars, most meet to ride,
And flocked to Bharadvája's side.
There with the good Sumitrá Queen
Kauśalyá, sad and worn, was seen,
Caressing, still with sorrow faint,
The feet of that illustrious saint.
Kaikeyí too, her longings crossed,

Reproached of all, her object lost,
Before the famous hermit came,
And clasped his feet, o'erwhelmed with shame.
With circling steps she humbly went
Around the saint preëminent,
And stood not far from Bharat's side
With heart oppressed, and heavy-eyed.
Then the great seer, who never broke
One holy vow, to Bharat spoke:
'Speak, Raghu's son: I fain would learn
The story of each queen in turn.'
    Obedient to the high request
By Bharadvája thus addressed,
His reverent hands together laid,
He, skilled in speech, his answer made:
'She whom, O Saint, thou seest here
A Goddess in her form appear,
Was the chief consort of the king,
Now worn with fast and sorrowing.
As Aditi in days of yore
The all-preserving Vishṇu bore,
Kauśalyá bore with happy fate
Lord Ráma of the lion's gait.
She who, transfixed with torturing pangs,
On her left arm so fondly hangs,
As when her withering leaves decay
Droops by the wood the Cassia spray,
Sumitrá, pained with woe, is she,
The consort second of the three:
Two princely sons the lady bare,
Fair as the Gods in heaven are fair.
And she, the wicked dame through whom
My brothers' lives are wrapped in gloom,
And mourning for his offspring dear,

The king has sought his heavenly sphere,—
Proud, foolish-hearted, swift to ire,
Self-fancied darling of my sire,
Kaikeyí, most ambitious queen,
Unlovely with her lovely mien,
My mother she, whose impious will
Is ever bent on deeds of ill,
In whom the root and spring I see
Of all this woe which crushes me.'
    Quick breathing like a furious snake,
With tears and sobs the hero spake,
With reddened eyes aglow with rage.
And Bharadvája, mighty sage,
Supreme in wisdom, calm and grave,
In words like these good counsel gave :
'O Bharat, hear the words I say ;
On her the fault thou must not lay :
For many a blessing yet will spring
From banished Ráma's wandering.'
And Bharat, with that promise cheered,
Went circling round that saint revered,
He humbly bade farewell, and then
Gave orders to collect his men.
Prompt at the summons thousands flew
To cars which noble coursers drew,
Bright-gleaming, glorious to behold,
Adorned with wealth of burnished gold.
Then female elephants and male,
Gold-girthed, with flags that wooed the gale,
Marched with their bright bells' tinkling chime
Like clouds when ends the summer time :
Some cars were huge and some were light,
For heavy draught or rapid flight,
Of costly price, of every kind,

X

With clouds of infantry behind.
The dames, Kauśalyá at their head,
Were in the noblest chariots led,
And every gentle bosom beat
With hope the banished prince to meet.
The royal Bharat, glory-crowned,
With all his retinue around,
Borne in a beauteous litter rode,
Like the young moon and sun that glowed.
The army as it streamed along,
Cars, elephants, in endless throng,
Showed, marching on its southward way,
Like autumn clouds in long array.

CANTO XCIII.

CHITRAKÚṬA IN SIGHT.

As through the woods its way pursued
That mighty bannered multitude,
Wild elephants in terror fled
With all the startled herds they led,
And bears and deer were seen on hill,
In forest glade, by every rill.
Wide as the sea from coast to coast,
The high-souled Bharat's mighty host
Covered the earth as cloudy trains
Obscure the sky when fall the rains.
The stately elephants he led,
And countless steeds the land o'erspread,
So closely crowded that between
Their serried ranks no ground was seen.
Then when the host had travelled far,
And steeds were worn who drew the car,
The glorious Bharat thus addressed
Vaśishṭha, of his lords the best :
'The spot, methinks, we now behold
Of which the holy hermit told,
For, as his words described, I trace
Each several feature of the place :
Before us Chitrakúṭa shows,
Mandákiní beside us flows :
Afar umbrageous woods arise
Like darksome clouds that veil the skies.
Now tread these mountain-beasts of mine

On Chitrakúṭa's fair incline.
The trees their rain of blossoms shed
On table-lands beneath them spread,
As from black clouds the floods descend
When the hot days of summer end.
Śatrughna, look, the mountain see
Where heavenly minstrels wander free,
And horses browse beneath the steep,
Countless as monsters in the deep.
Scared by my host the mountain deer
Starting with tempest speed appear
Like the long lines of cloud that fly
In autumn through the windy sky.
See, every warrior shows his head
With fragrant blooms engarlanded;
All look like southern soldiers who
Lift up their shields of azure hue.
This lonely wood beneath the hill,
That was so dark and drear and still,
Covered with men in endless streams
Now like Ayodhyá's city seems.
The dust which countless hoofs excite
Obscures the sky and veils the light;
But see, swift winds those clouds dispel
As if they strove to please me well.
See, guided in their swift career
By many a skilful charioteer,
Those cars by fleetest coursers drawn
Race onward over glade and lawn.
Look, startled as the host comes near
The lovely peacocks fly in fear,
Gorgeous as if the fairest blooms
Of earth had glorified their plumes.
Look where the sheltering covert shows

The trooping deer, both bucks and does,
That occupy in countless herds
This mountain populous with birds.
Most lovely to my mind appears
This place which every charm endears :
Fair as the road where tread the Blest :
Here holy hermits take their rest.
Then let the army onward press
And duly search each green recess
For the two lion-lords, till we
Ráma once more and Lakshman see.'

Thus Bharat spoke : and hero bands
Of men with weapons in their hands
Entered the tangled forest : then
A spire of smoke appeared in ken.
Soon as they saw the rising smoke
To Bharat they returned and spoke :
'No fire where men are not : 'tis clear
That Raghu's sons are dwelling here.
Or if not here those heroes dwell
Whose mighty arms their foeman quell,
Still other hermits here must be .
Like Ráma, true and good as he.'

His ears attentive Bharat lent
To their resistless argument,
Then to his troops the chief who broke
His foe's embattled armies spoke :
'Here let the troops in silence stay :
One step beyond they must not stray.
Come Dhrishṭi and Sumantra, you
With me alone the path pursue.'
Their leader's speech the warriors heard,
And from his place no soldier stirred.
And Bharat bent his eager eyes

Where curling smoke was seen to rise.
     The host his order well obeyed,
And halting there in silence stayed
Watching where from the thicket's shade
    They saw the smoke appear.
And joy through all the army ran,
'Soon shall we meet,' thought every man,
    'The prince we hold so dear.'

CANTO XCIV.

CHITRAKÚTA.

There long the son of Rághu dwelt
And love for hill and wood he felt.
Then his Videhan spouse to please
And his own heart of woe to ease,
Like some Immortal—Indra so
Might Swarga's charms to Sachí show—
Drew her sweet eyes to each delight
Of Chitrakúṭa's lovely height:
'Though reft of power and kingly sway,
Though friends and home are far away,
I cannot mourn my altered lot,
Enamoured of this charming spot.
Look, darling, on this noble hill
Which sweet birds with their music fill.
Bright with a thousand metal dyes
His lofty summits cleave the skies.
See, there a silvery sheen is spread,
And there like blood the rocks are red.
There shows a streak of emerald green,
And pink and yellow glow between.
There where the higher peaks ascend,
Crystal and flowers and topaz blend,
And others flash their light afar
Like mercury or some fair star:
With such a store of metals dyed
The king of hills is glorified.
There through the wild birds' populous home

The harmless bear and tiger roam :
Hyænas range the woody slopes
With herds of deer and antelopes.
See, love, the trees that clothe his side
All lovely in their summer pride,
In richest wealth of leaves arrayed,
With flower and fruit and light and shade.
Look where the young Rose-apple glows ;
What loaded boughs the Mango shows ;
See, waving in the western wind
The light leaves of the Tamarind ;
And mark that giant Peepul through
The feathery clump of tall bamboo. [1]
Look, on the level lands above,
Delighting in successful love
In sweet enjoyment many a pair
Of heavenly minstrels revels there,
While overhanging boughs support
Their swords and mantles as they sport :
Then see that pleasant shelter where
Play the bright Daughters of the Air. [2]
The mountain seems with bright cascade

---

[1] These ten lines are a substitution for, and not a translation of the text which Carey and Marshman thus render : ' This mountain adorned with mango,[1] jumboo [2] *asuna*,[3] lodhra,[4] piala,[5] *punnae*,[6] dhava,[7] unkotha,[8] bhavya,[9] tinisha,[10] vilwa,[11] tindooka,[12] bamboo,[13] kashmaree,[14] *arista*,[15] *varuna*,[16] *madhooka*,[17] tilaka,[18] vaduree [19] amluka,[20] nipa,[21] vetra,[22] dhanwana,[23] veejaka,[24] and other trees, affording flowers, and fruits, and the most delightful shade, how charming does it appear !'

[1] Mangifera Indica. [2] Eugenia Jambolifera. [3] Terminalia alata tomentosa. [4] This tree is not ascertained. [5] Chironjia Sapida. [6] Artocarpus integrifolia. [7] Grislea tomentosa. [8] Allangium hexapetalum. [9] Averrhoa carimbola. [10] Dalbergia Oujeinensis. [11] Ægle marmelos [12] Diospyrus melanoxylon. [13] Well known. [14] Gmelina Arborea. [15] Sapindus Saponaria. [16] Cratoeva tapia. [17] Bassia latifolia. [18] Not yet ascertained. [19] Zizyphus jujuba. [20] Phyllanthus emblica. [21] Nauclea Orientalis. [22] Calamus rotang. [23] Echites antidysenterica. [24] The citron tree.'

[2] *Vidyádharis*, Spirits of Air, sylphs.

And sweet rill bursting from the shade,
Like some majestic elephant o'er
Whose burning head the torrents pour.
Where breathes the man who would not feel
Delicious languor o'er him steal,
As the young morning breeze that springs
From the cool cave with balmy wings,
Breathes round him laden with the scent
Of bud and blossom dew-besprent?
If many autumns here I spent
With thee, my darling innocent,
And Lakshmaṇ, I should never know
The torture of the fires of woe,
This varied scene so charms my sight,
This mount so fills me with delight,
Where flowers in wild profusion spring,
And ripe fruits glow and sweet birds sing.
My beauteous one, a double good
Springs from my dwelling in the wood:
Loosed is the bond my sire that tied,
And Bharat too is gratified.
My darling, dost thou feel with me
Delight from every charm we see,
Of which the mind and every sense
Feel the enchanting influence?
My fathers who have passed away,
The royal saints, were wont to say
That life in woodland shades like this
Secures a king immortal bliss.
See, round the hill at random thrown,
Huge masses lie of rugged stone
Of every shape and many a hue,
Yellow and white and red and blue.
But all is fairer still by night:

Each rock reflects a softer light,
When the whole mount from foot to crest
In robes of lambent flame is dressed ;
When from a million herbs a blaze
Of their own luminous glory plays,
And clothed in fire each deep ravine,
Each pinnacle and crag is seen.
Some parts the look of mansions wear,
And others are as gardens fair,
While others seem a massive block
Of solid undivided rock.
Behold those pleasant beds o'erlaid
With lotus leaves, for lovers made,
Where mountain birch and costus throw
Cool shadows on the pair below.
See where the lovers in their play
Have cast their flowery wreaths away,
And fruit and lotus buds that crowned
Their brows lie trodden on the ground.
North Kuru's realm is fair to see,
Vasvaukasárá,[1] Naliní,[2]
But rich in fruit and blossom still
More fair is Chitrakúṭa's hill.
Here shall the years appointed glide
With thee, my beauty, by my side,
      And Lakshmaṇ ever near ;
Here shall I live in all delight,
Make my ancestral fame more bright,
Tread in their path who walk aright,
      And to my oath adhere.'

---

[1] A lake attached either to Amarávatí the residence of Indra, or Alaká that of Kuvera.

[2] The Ganges of heaven.

CANTO XCV.

MANDÁKINÍ.

Then Ráma, like the lotus eyed,
Descended from the mountain side,
And to the Maithil lady showed
The lovely stream that softly flowed.
And thus Ayodhyá's lord addressed
His bride, of dames the loveliest,
Child of Videha's king, her face
Bright with the fair moon's tender grace.
'How sweetly glides, O darling, look,
Mandákiní's delightful brook,
Adorned with islets, blossoms gay,
And sárases and swans at play!
The trees with which her banks are lined
Show flowers and fruit of every kind:
The match in radiant sheen is she
Of King Kuvera's Naliní.[1]
My heart exults with pleasure new
The shelving bank and ford to view,
Where gathering herds of thirsty deer
Disturb the wave that ran so clear.
Now look, those holy hermits mark
In skins of deer and coats of bark;
With twisted coils of matted hair,
The reverend men are bathing there,
And as they lift their arms on high
The Lord of Day they glorify:

---

[1] Naliní, as here, may be the name of any lake covered with lotuses.

These best of saints, my large-eyed spouse,
Are constant to their sacred vows.
The mountain dances while the trees
Bend their proud summits to the breeze,
And scatter many a flower and bud
From branches that o'erhang the flood.
There flows the stream like lucid pearl,
Round islets here the currents whirl,
And perfect saints from middle air
Are flocking to the waters there.
See, there lie flowers in many a heap
From boughs the whistling breezes sweep,
And others wafted by the gale
Down the swift current dance and sail.
Now see that pair of wild-fowl rise,
Exulting with their joyful cries:
Hark, darling, wafted from afar
How soft their pleasant voices are.
To gaze on Chitrakúṭa's hill,
To look upon this lovely rill,
To bend mine eyes on thee, dear wife,
Is sweeter than my city life.
Come, bathe we in the pleasant rill
Whose dancing waves are never still,
Stirred by those beings pure from sin,
The sanctities who bathe therein:
Come, dearest, to the stream descend,
Approach her as a darling friend,
And dip thee in the silver flood
Which lotuses and lilies stud.
Let this fair hill Ayodhyá seem,
Its silvan things her people deem,
And let these waters as they flow
Our own beloved Sarjú show.

How blest, mine own dear love, am I ;
Thou, fond and true, art ever nigh,
And duteous, faithful Lakshmaṇ stays
Beside me, and my word obeys.
Here every day I bathe me thrice,
Fruit, honey, roots for food suffice,
And ne'er my thoughts with longing stray
To distant home or royal sway.
For who this charming brook can see
Where herds of roedeer wander free,
And on the flowery-wooded brink
Apes, elephants, and lions drink,
　　Nor feel all sorrow fly ?'
Thus eloquently spoke the pride
Of Raghu's children to his bride,
And wandered happy by her side
Where Chitrakúṭa azure-dyed
　　Uprears his peaks on high.

CANTO XCVI.[1]

THE MAGIC SHAFT.

Thus Ráma showed to Janak's child
The varied beauties of the wild,
The hill, the brook and each fair spot,
Then turned to seek their leafy cot.
North of the mountain Ráma found
A cavern in the sloping ground,
Charming to view, its floor was strown
With many a mass of ore and stone,
In secret shadow far retired
Where gay birds sang with joy inspired,
And trees their graceful branches swayed
With loads of blossom downward weighed.
Soon as he saw the cave which took
Each living·heart and chained the look,
Thus Ráma spoke to Síta who
Gazed wondering on the silvan view:
'Does this fair cave beneath the height,
Videhan lady, charm thy sight?
Then let us resting here a while
The languor of the way beguile.
That block of stone so smooth and square
Was set for thee to rest on there,
And like a thriving Keśar tree
This flowery shrub o'ershadows thee.'
Thus Ráma spoke, and Janak's child,

---

[1] This canto is allowed, by Indian commentators, to be an interpolation. It cannot be the work of Válmíki.

By nature ever soft and mild,
In tender words which love betrayed
Her answer to the hero made:
'O pride of Raghu's children, still
My pleasure is to do thy will.
Enough for me thy wish to know:
Far hast thou wandered to and fro.'
    Thus Sítá spake in gentle tone,
And went obedient to the stone,
Of perfect face and faultless limb
Prepared to rest a while with him.
And Ráma, as she thus replied,
Turned to his spouse again and cried:
'Thou seest, love, this flowery shade
For silvan creatures' pleasure made.
How the gum streams from trees and plants
Torn by the tusks of elephants!
Through all the forest clear and high
Resounds the shrill cicala's cry
Hark how the kite above us moans,
And calls her young in piteous tones;
So may my hapless mother be   ·
Still mourning in her home for me.
There mounted on that lofty Sál
The loud Bhringráj ¹ repeats his call:
How sweetly now he tunes his throat
Responsive to the Koïl's note.
Or else the bird that now has sung
May be himself the Koïl's young,
Linked with such winning sweetness are
The notes he pours irregular.
See, round the blooming Mango clings
That creeper with her tender rings,

---

¹ A fine bird with a strong, sweet note, and great imitative powers.

So in thy love, when none is near,
Thine arms are thrown round me, my dear.'
   Thus in his joy he cried ; and she,
Sweet speaker, on her lover's knee,
Of faultless limb and perfect face,
Grew closer to her lord's embrace.
Reclining in her husband's arms,
A goddess in her wealth of charms,
She filled his loving breast anew
With mighty joy that thrilled him through.
His finger on the rock he laid,
Which veins of sanguine ore displayed,
And painted o'er his darling's eyes
The holy sign in mineral dyes.
Bright on her brow the metal lay
Like the young sun's first gleaming ray,
And showed her in her beauty fair
As the soft light of morning's air.
Then from the Keśar's laden tree
He picked fair blossoms in his glee,
And as he decked each lovely tress,
His heart o'erflowed with happiness.
So resting on that rocky seat
A while they spent in pastime sweet,
Then onward neath the shady boughs
Went Ráma with his Maithil spouse.
She roaming in the forest shade
Where every kind of creature strayed
Observed a monkey wandering near,
And clung to Ráma's arm in fear.
The hero Ráma fondly laced
His mighty arms around her waist,
Consoled his beauty in her dread,
And scared the monkey till he fled.

That holy mark of sanguine ore
That gleamed on Sítá's brow before,
Shone by that close embrace impressed
Upon the hero's ample chest.
Then Sítá, when the beast who led
The monkey troop, afar had fled,
Laughed loudly in light-hearted glee
That mark on Ráma's chest to see.
A clump of bright Aśokas fired
The forest in their bloom attired :
The restless blossoms as they gleamed
A host of threatening monkeys seemed.
Then Sítá thus to Ráma cried,
As longingly the flowers she eyed :
' Pride of thy race, now let us go
Where those Aśoka blossoms grow.'
He on his darling's pleasure bent
With his fair goddess thither went
And roamed delighted through the wood
Where blossoming Aśokas stood,
As Śiva with Queen Umá roves
Through Himaván's majestic groves.
Bright with purpureal glow the pair
Of happy lovers sported there,
And each upon the other set
A flower-inwoven coronet.
There many a crown and chain they wove
Of blooms from that Aśoka grove,
And in their graceful sport the two
Fresh beauty o'er the mountain threw.
The lover let his love survey
Each pleasant spot that round them lay,
Then turned they to their green retreat
Where all was garnished, gay, and neat.

Y

By brotherly affection led,
Sumitrá's son to meet them sped,
And showed the labours of the day
Done while his brother was away.
There lay ten black-deer duly slain
With arrows pure of poison stain,
Piled in a mighty heap to dry,
With many another carcass nigh.
And Lakshman's brother saw, o'erjoved,
The work that had his hands employed,
Then to his consort thus he cried:
' Now be the general gifts supplied.'
Then Sítá, fairest beauty, placed
The food for living things to taste,
And set before the brothers meat
And honey that the pair might eat.
They ate the meal her hands supplied,
Their lips with water purified:
Then Janak's daughter sat at last
And duly made her own repast.
The other venison, to be dried,
Piled up in heaps was set aside,
And Ráma told his wife to stay
And drive the flocking crows away.
Her husband saw her much distressed
By one more bold than all the rest,
Whose wings where'er he chose could fly,
Now pierce the earth, now roam the sky.
Then Ráma laughed to see her stirred
To anger by the plaguing bird:
Proud of his love the beauteous dame
With burning rage was all aflame.
Now here, now there, again, again
She chased the crow, but all in vain,

Enraging her, so quick to strike
With beak and wing and claw alike :
Then how the proud lip quivered, how
The dark frown marked her angry brow !
When Ráma saw her cheek aglow
With passion, he rebuked the crow.
But bold in impudence the bird,
With no respect for Ráma's word,
Fearless again at Sítá flew :
Then Ráma's wrath to fury grew.
The hero of the mighty arm
Spoke o'er a shaft the mystic charm,
Laid the dire weapon on his bow
And launched it at the shameless crow.
The bird, empowered by Gods to spring
Through earth itself on rapid wing,
Through the three worlds in terror fled
Still followed by that arrow dread.
Where'er he flew, now here now there,
A cloud of weapons filled the air.
Back to the high-souled prince he fled
And bent at Ráma's feet his head,
And then, as Sítá looked, began
His speech in accents of a man :
' O pardon, and for pity's sake
Spare, Ráma, spare my life to take !
Where'er I turn, where'er I flee,
No shelter from this shaft I see.'

The chieftain heard the crow entreat
Helpless and prostrate at his feet,
And while soft pity moved his breast,
With wisest speech the bird addressed :
' I took the troubled Sítá's part,
And furious anger filled my heart.

Then on the string my arrow lay
Charmed with a spell thy life to slay.
Thou seekest now my feet, to crave
Forgiveness and thy life to save.
So shall thy prayer have due respect :
The suppliant I must still protect.
But ne'er iu vain this dart may flee :
Yield for thy life a part of thee.
What portion of thy body, say,
Shall this mine arrow rend away ?
Thus far, O bird, thus far alone
On thee my pity may be shown.
Forfeit a part thy life to buy :
'Tis better so to live than die.'

Thus Ráma spoke : the bird of air
Pondered his speech with anxious care,
And wisely deemed it good to give
One of his eyes that he might live.
To Raghu's son he made reply :
'O Ráma, I will yield an eye.
So let me in thy grace confide
And live hereafter single-eyed.'
Then Ráma charged the shaft, and lo,
Full in the eye it smote the crow.
And the Videhan lady gazed
Upon the ruined eye amazed.
The crow to Ráma humbly bent,
Then where his fancy led he went.
Ráma with Lakshmaṇ by his side
With needful work was occupied.

CANTO XCVII.

LAKSHMAN'S ANGER.

Thus Ráma showed his love the rill
Whose waters ran beneath the hill,
Then resting on his mountain seat
Refreshed her with the choicest meat,
So there reposed the happy two :
Then Bharat's army nearer drew :
Rose to the skies a dusty cloud,
The sound of trampling feet was loud.
The swelling roar of marching men
Drove the roused tiger from his den,
And scared amain the serpent race
Flying to hole and hiding-place.
The herds of deer in terror fled,
The air was filled with birds o'erhead,
The bear began to leave his tree,
The monkey to the cave to flee.
Wild elephants were all amazed
As though the wood around them blazed.
The lion oped his ponderous jaw,
The buffalo looked round in awe.
The prince, who heard the deafening sound,
And saw the silvan creatures round
Fly wildly startled from their rest,
The glorious Lakshman thus addressed :
' Sumitrá's noble son most dear,
Hark, Lakshman, what a roar I hear,
The tumult of a coming crowd,

Appalling, deafening, deep, and loud !
The din that yet more fearful grows
Scares elephants and buffaloes,
Or frightened by the lions, deer
Are flying through the wood in fear.
I fain would know who seeks this place :
Comes prince or monarch for the chase ?
Or does some mighty beast of prey
Frighten the silvan herds away ?
'Tis hard to reach this mountain height,
Yea, e'en for birds in airy flight.
Then fain, O Lakshman, would I know
What cause disturbs the forest so.'

Lakshman in haste, the wood to view,
Climbed a high Sál that near him grew,
The forest all around he eyed,
First gazing on the eastern side.
Then northward when his eyes he bent
He saw a mighty armament
Of elephants, and cars, and horse,
And men on foot, a mingled force,
And banners waving in the breeze,
And spoke to Ráma words like these :
'Quick, quick. my lord, put out the fire,
Let Sítá to the cave retire.
Thy coat of mail around thee throw,
Prepare thine arrows and thy bow.'

In eager haste thus Lakshman cried,
And Ráma, lion lord, replied :
'Still closer be the army scanned,
And say who leads the warlike band.'
Lakshman his answer thus returned,
As furious rage within him burned,
Exciting him like kindled fire

To scorch the army in his ire :
' 'Tis Bharat : he has made the throne
By consecrating rites his own :
To gain the whole dominion thus
He comes in arms to slaughter us.
I mark tree-high upon his car
His flagstaff of the Kovidár, [1]
I see his glittering banner glance,
I see his chivalry advance :
I see his eager warriors shine
On elephants in lengthened line.
Now grasp we each the shafts and bow,
And higher up the mountain go,
Or in this place, O hero, stand
With weapons in each ready hand.
Perhaps beneath our might may fall
This leader of the standard tall,
And Bharat I this day may see
Who brought this mighty woe on thee,
Sítá, and me, who drove away
My brother from the royal sway.
Bharat our foe at length is nigh;
And by this hand shall surely die :
Brother, I see no sin at all
If Bharat by my weapon fall.
No fault is his who slays the foe
Whose hand was first to strike the blow :
With Bharat now the crime begins
Who against thee and duty sins.
The queen athirst for royal sway
Will see her darling son to-day
Fall by this hand, like some fair tree
Struck by an elephant, slain by me.

---

[1] Bauhinea variegata, a species of ebony.

Kaikeyí's self shall perish too
With kith and kin and retinue,
And earth by my avenging deed
Shall from this mass of sin be freed.
This day my wrath, too long restrained,
Shall fall upon the foe, unchained,
Mad as the kindled flame that speeds
Destroying through the grass and reeds.
This day mine arrows keen and fierce
The bodies of the foe shall pierce :
The woods on Chitrakúṭa's side
Shall run with torrents crimson-dyed.
The wandering beasts of prey shall feed
On heart-cleft elephant and steed,
And drag to mountain caves away
The bodies that my arrows slay.
Doubt not that Bharat and his train
Shall in this mighty wood be slain :
So shall I pay the debt my bow
And these my deadly arrows owe.'

CANTO XCVIII.

LAKSHMAN CALMED.

Then Ráma nobly calm allayed
The wrath that Lakshman's bosom swayed
' What need have we the sword to wield,
To bend the bow or lift the shield,
If Bharat brave, and wise, and good,
Himself has sought this sheltering wood ?
I sware my father's will to do,
And if I now my brother slew
What gain in kingship should I find,
Despised and scorned by all mankind ?
Believe me, e'en as I would shrink
From poisoned meat or deadly drink,
No power or treasure would I win
By fall of friend or kith or kin.
Brother, believe the words I speak :
For your dear sakes alone I seek
Duty and pleasure, wealth and gain,
A holy life, a happy reign.
If royal sway my heart desires,
My brothers' weal the wish inspires :
Their bliss and safety is my care,
By this uplifted bow I swear.
' Twere not so hard for me to gain
This broad land girdled by the main,
But even Indra's royal might
Should ne'er be mine in duty's spite.
If any bliss my soul can see

Deprived of dear Satrughna, thee,
And Bharat, may the flame destroy
With ashy gloom the selfish joy.
Far dearer than this life of mine,
Knowing the custom of our line,
His heart with fond affection fraught,
Bharat Ayodhyá's town resought,
And hearing when he came that I,
With thee and Sítá, forced to fly,
With matted hair and hermit dress
Am wandering in the wilderness,
While grief his troubled senses storms,
And tender love his bosom warms,
From every thought of evil clear,
Is come to meet his brother here.
Some grievous words perchance he spoke
Kaikeyí's anger to provoke,
Then won the king, and comes to lay
Before my feet the royal sway.
Hither, methinks, in season due
Comes Bharat for an interview,
Nor in his secret heart has he
One evil thought 'gainst thee or me.
What has he done ere now, reflect !
How failed in love or due respect
To make thee doubt his faith and lay
This evil to his charge to-day ?
Thou shouldst not join with Bharat's name
So harsh a speech and idle blame.
The blows thy tongue at Bharat deals,
My sympathizing bosom feels.
How, urged by stress of any ill,
Should sons their father's life-blood spill,
Or brother slay in impious strife

A brother dearer than his life?
If thou these cruel words hast said
By strong desire of empire led,
My brother Bharat will I pray
To give to thee the kingly sway.
' Give him the realm', my speech shall be,
And Bharat will, methinks, agree.'
    Thus spoke the prince whose chief delight
Was duty, and to aid the right:
And Lakshman keenly felt the blame,
And shrank within himself for shame:
And then his answer thus returned,
With downcast eye and cheek that burned:
' Brother, I ween, to see thy face
Our sire himself has sought this place.'
Thus Lakshman spoke and stood ashamed,
And Ráma saw and thus exclaimed:
' It is the strong-armed monarch: he
Is come, methinks, his sons to see,
To bid us both the forest quit
For joys for which he deems us fit:
He thinks on all our care and pain,
And now would lead us home again.
My glorious father hence will bear
Sítá who claims all tender care.
I see two coursers fleet as storms,
Of noble breed and lovely forms.
I see the beast of mountain size
Who bears the king our father wise,
The aged Victor, march this way
In front of all the armed array.
But doubt and fear within me rise,
For when I look with eager eyes
I see no white umbrella spread,

World-famous, o'er the royal head.
Now, Lakshman, from the tree descend,
And to my words attention lend.'

   Thus spoke the pious prince : and he
Descended from the lofty tree,
And reverent hand to hand applied,
Stood humbly by his brother's side.

   The host, compelled by Bharat's care,
The wood from trampling feet to spare,
Dense crowding half a league each way
Encamped around the mountain lay.
Below the tall hill's shelving side
Gleamed the bright army far and wide

   Spread o'er the ample space,
By Bharat led who firmly true
In duty from his bosom threw
All pride, and near his brother drew

   To win the hero's grace.

CANTO XCIX.

BHARAT'S APPROACH.

Soon as the warriors took their rest
Obeying Bharat's high behest,
Thus Bharat to Śatrughna spake :
' A band of soldiers with thee take,
And with these hunters o'er and o'er
The thickets of the wood explore.
With bow, sword, arrows in their hands
Let Guha with his kindred bands
Within this grove remaining trace
The children of Kakutstha's race.
And I meanwhile on foot will through
This neighbouring wood my way pursue,
With elders and the twice-born men,
And every lord and citizen.
There is, I feel, no rest for me
Till Ráma's face again I see,
Lakshman, in arms and glory great,
And Sítá born to happy fate :
No rest, until his cheek as bright
As the fair moon rejoice my sight,
No rest until I see the eye
With which the lotus petals vie ;
Till on my head those dear feet rest
With signs of royal rank impressed ;
None, till my kingly brother gain
His old hereditary reign,
Till o'er his limbs and noble head

The consecrating drops be shed.
How blest is Janak's daughter, true
To every wifely duty, who
Cleaves faithful to her husband's side
Whose realm is girt by Ocean's tide!
This mountain too above the rest
E'en as the King of Hills is blest,—
Whose shades Kakutstha's scion hold
As Nandan charms the Lord of Gold.
Yea, happy is this tangled grove
Where savage beasts unnumbered rove,
Where, glory of the Warrior race,
King Ráma finds a dwelling-place.'

Thus Bharat, strong-armed hero, spake,
And walked within the pathless brake.
O'er plains where gay trees bloomed he went,
Through boughs in tangled net-work bent,
And then from Ráma's cot appeared
The banner which the flame upreared.
And Bharat joyed with every friend
To mark those smoky wreaths ascend :
'Here Ráma dwells,' he thought ; 'at last
The ocean of our toil is passed.'

Then sure that Ráma's hermit cot
  Was on the mountain's side,
He stayed his army on the spot,
  And on with Guha hied.

CANTO C.

THE MEETING.

Then Bharat to Śatrughna showed
The spot, and eager onward strode,
First bidding Saint Vaśishṭha bring
The widowed consorts of the king.
As by fraternal love impelled
His onward course the hero held,
Sumantra followed close behind
Śatrughna with an anxious mind :
Not Bharat's self more fain could be
To look on Ráma's face than he.
As, speeding on, the spot he neared,
Amid the hermits' homes appeared
His brother's cot with leaves o'erspread,
And by its side a lowly shed.
Before the shed great heaps were left
Of gathered flowers and billets cleft,
And on the trees hung grass and bark
Ráma and Lakshmaṇ's path to mark :
And heaps of fuel to provide
Against the cold stood ready dried.
The long-armed chief, as on he went
In glory's light preëminent,
With joyous words like these addressed
The brave Śatrughna and the rest :
' This is the place, I little doubt,
Which Bharadvája pointed out,
Not far from where we stand must be
The woodland stream, Mandákiní.

Here on the mountain's woody side
Roam elephants in tusked piide,
And ever with a roar and cry
Each other, as they meet, defy.
And see those smoke-wreaths thick and dark:
The presence of the flame they mark,
Which hermits in the forest strive
By every art to keep alive.
O happy me! my task is done,
And I shall look on Raghu's son,
Like some great saint, who loves to treat
His elders with all reverence meet'

    Thus Bharat reached that forest rill,
Thus roamed on Chitrakúta's hill;
Then pity in his breast awoke,
And to his friends the hero spoke:
'Woe, woe upon my life and birth!
The prince of men, the lord of earth
Has sought the lonely wood to dwell
Sequestered in a hermit's cell.
Through me, through me these sorrows fall
On him the splendid lord of all:
Through me resigning earthly bliss
He hides him in a home like this.
Now will I, by the world abhorred,
Fall at the dear feet of my lord,
And at fair Sítá's too, to win
His pardon for my heinous sin.'

    As thus he sadly mourned and sighed,
The son of Daśaratha spied
A bower of leafy branches made,
Sacred and lovely in the shade,
Of fair proportions large and tall,
Well roofed with boughs of palm and Sál,

Arranged in order due o'erhead
Like grass upon an altar spread.
Two glorious bows were gleaming there,
Like Indra's [1] in the rainy air,
Terror of foemen, backed with gold,
Meet for the mightiest hand to hold :
And quivered arrows cast a blaze
Bright gleaming like the Day-God's rays :
Thus serpents with their eyes aglow
Adorn their capital below.[2]
Great swords adorned the cottage, laid
Each in a case of gold brocade ;
There hung the trusty shields, whereon
With purest gold the bosses shone.
The brace to bind the bowman's arm,
The glove to shield his hand from harm,
A lustre to the cottage lent
From many a golden ornament :
Safe was the cot from fear of men
As from wild beasts the lion's den.
The fire upon the altar burned,
That to the north and east was turned.
Bharat his eager glances bent
And gazed within the cot intent ;
In deerskin dress, with matted hair,
Ráma his chief was sitting there :
With lion-shoulders broad and strong,
With lotus eyes, arms thick and long,
The righteous sovereign, who should be
Lord paramount from sea to sea,
High-minded, born to lofty fate,
Like Brahmá's self supremely great ;

---

[1] The rainbow is called the bow of Indra.
[2] Bhogavatí, the abode of the Nágas or Serpent race.

With Lakshman by his side, and her,
Fair Sítá, for his minister.
And Bharat gazing, overcome
By sorrow for a while was dumb,
Then, yielding to his woe, he ran
To Ráma and with sobs began:
' He who a royal seat should fill
With subjects round to do his will,
My elder brother,—see him here,
With silvan creatures waiting near.
The high-souled hero, wont to wear
The costliest robes exceeding fair,
Now banished, in a deerskin dress,
Here keeps the path of righteousness.
How brooks the son of Raghu now
The matted locks which load his brow,
Around whose princely head were twined
Sweet blossoms of the rarest kind?
The prince whose merits grew, acquired
By rites performed as he desired,
Would now a store of merit gain
Bought by his body's toil and pain.
Those limbs to which pure sandal lent
The freshness of its fragrant scent,
Exposed to sun, and dust, and rain,
Are now defiled with many a stain.
And I the wretched cause why this
Falls on the prince whose right is bliss!
Ah me, that ever I was born
To be the people's hate and scorn!'

　　Thus Bharat cried: of anguish sprung,
Great drops upon his forehead hung.
He fell o'erpowered—his grief was such—
Ere he his brother's feet could touch.

As on the glorious prince he gazed
In vain his broken voice he raised :
' Dear lord'—through tears and sobbing came,
The only words his lips could frame.
And brave Śatrughna wept aloud,
As low at Ráma's feet he bowed.
Then Ráma, while his tears ran fast,
His arms around his brothers cast.
Guha, Sumantra came to meet
The princes in their wild retreat.

    Vrihaspati and Śukra bright
        Their greeting thus rejoice to pay
    To the dear Lord who brings the night,
        And the great God who rules the day.
    Then wept the dwellers of the shade,
        Whose eyes the princes, meet to ride
    On mighty elephants, surveyed ;
        And cast all thought of joy aside.

CANTO CI.

BHARAT QUESTIONED.

Then Ráma gazed, and scarcely knew
Bharat so worn and changed in hue.
He raised him, kissed him on the head,
Embraced him, and thus kindly said:
' Where was thy father, brother dear,
That thou art come to seek me here?
Unmeet, if he be living yet,
Thy feet within the wood to set.
I pray thee now the cause declare
Why thou hast left the kingdom there,
With matted locks and deerskin dress
To roam the distant wilderness.'
　　Thus questioned by the prince, at length
Kaikeyí's son regained his strength,
And hand to hand in reverence laid,
To Ráma thus his answer made:
' The great-armed monarch, O my lord,
Has dared to do a thing abhorred,
Left us, and grieving for his son,
A home among the Gods has won.
My mother Queen Kaikeyí gave
The order to the king her slave,
And at the bidding of the dame
He wrought the sin which mars his fame.
Athirst for sway, her hopes are crossed,
She mourns her son, her husband lost,
And through her impious crime will go

For punishment to hell below.
Now O my lord, forgive me all ;
Be gracious to thy lowly thrall :
Anointed king, accept to-day
Like Indra's self, the royal sway.
Be gracious, Prince, to lord and peer,
And widowed queens who seek thee here.
Accept the kingdom thine by right,
And so thy faithful friends delight.
Let the broad land no longer be
All widowed and forlorn of thee :
Let the full moon of autumn reign
Triumphant o'er the night again.
These lords and I before thee bend :
O Ráma, to our prayer attend.
O do not thou this grace deny :
Thy brother, pupil, slave am I.
Look on this venerable ring,
Advisers of our sire the king,
From age to age so honoured : thou
Shouldst grant their supplication now.'
    As weeping thus the hero prayed,
His head at Ráma's feet he laid.
Like a mad elephant he sighed :
And Ráma gazed and thus replied :
' How, brother, can a man of worth,
True to his vows, of noble birth—
A man like me, commit a sin
The lordship of the land to win ?
No slightest shade of fault I see,
O tamer of thy foes, in thee.
But ne'er shouldst thou in childish thought
The queen thy mother blame in aught.
O brother wise and sinless, know

The sacred laws would have it so,
That from good wife and son require
Obedience to their lord and sire.
And we are all the king's, for thus
The virtuous ever reckon us:
Yea brother, be it known to thee,
His wives, and sons, and pupils we.
His is the right, if he deem fit,
To bid me, throned as monarch, sit,
Or in a coat of bark expel,
And deerskin, in the wood to dwell.
And O remember, best of all
Who act as claims of duty call,
As to a virtuous sire is due,
Such honour claims a mother too.
So they whose lives have ever been
By duty led, the king and queen,
Said, ' Ráma, seek the forest shade':
And I (what could I else?) obeyed.
Thou must the royal power retain,
And o'er the famed Ayodhyá reign:
I dressed in bark my days will spend
Where Daṇḍak's forest wilds extend.
So Daśaratha spoke, our king,
His share to each apportioning
Before his honoured servants' eyes:
Then, heir of bliss, he sought the skies.
The righteous monarch's honoured will,
Whom all revered, must guide thee still,
And thou must still enjoy the share
Assigned thee by our father's care.
So I till twice seven years are spent
Will roam this wood in banishment,
Contented with the lot which he,

My high-souled sire, has given me.
The charge the monarch gave, endeared
To all mankind, by all revered,
  Peer of the Lord Supreme,
Far better, richer far in gain
Of every blessing than to reign
  O'er all the worlds, I deem.'

CANTO CII.

BHARAT'S TIDINGS.

He spoke : and Bharat thus replied :
' If, false to every claim beside,
I ne'er in kingly duties fail,
What will my royal life avail ?
Still should the custom be observed,
From which our line has never swerved,
Which to the younger son ne'er gives
The kingdom while the elder lives.
Now to Ayodhyá rich and fair
With me, O Raghu's son, repair,
And to protect and gladden all
Our house, thyself as king install.
A king the world's opinion deems
A man : to me a God he seems,
Whose life in virtuous thoughts and deeds
The lives of other men exceeds.
When I in distant Kekaya stayed,
And thou hadst sought the forest shade,
Our father died, the saints' delight,
So constant in each holy rite.
Scarce with thy wife and Lakshman thou
Hadst journeyed forth to keep thy vow,
When mourning for his son, forspent,
To heavenly rest the monarch went.
Then up, O lord of men, away !
His funeral rites of water pay :
I and Satrughna, ere we came,

Neglected not the sacred claim.
But in the spirit-world, they say,
That gift alone is fresh for aye
Which best beloved hands have poured ;
And thou his dearest art, my lord.
 For thee he longed, for thee he grieved, ·
  His every thought on thee was bent,
  And crushed by woe, of thee bereaved,
   He thought of thee as hence he went.'

CANTO CIII.

THE FUNERAL LIBATION.

When Ráma heard from Bharat each
Dark sorrow of his mournful speech,
And tidings of his father dead,
His spirits fell, his senses fled.
For the sad words his brother spoke
Struck on him like a thunder stroke,
Fierce as the bolt which Indra throws,
The victor of his Daitya foes.
Raising his arms in anguish, he,
As when the woodman hews a tree
With its fair flowery branches crowned,
Fainted and fell upon the ground.
Lord of the earth to earth he sank,
Helpless, as when a towering bank
With sudden ruin buries deep
An elephant who lay asleep.
Then swift his wife and brothers flew,
And water, weeping, o'er him threw.
As slowly sense and strength he gained,
Fast from his eyes the tears he rained,
And then in accents sad and weak
Kakutstha's son began to speak,
And mourning for the monarch dead,
With righteous words to Bharat said :
'What calls me home, when he, alas,
Has gone the way which all must pass ?
Of him, the best of kings, bereft

What guardian has Ayodhyá left?
How may I please his spirit? how
Delight the high-souled monarch now,
Who wept for me and went above
By me ungraced with mourning love?
Ah, happy brothers! you have paid
Due offerings to his parting shade.
E'en when my banishment is o'er,
Back to my home I go no more,
To look upon the widowed state
Reft of her king, disconsolate.
E'en then, O tamer of the foe,
If to Ayodhyá's town I go,
Who will direct me as of old,
Now other worlds our father hold?
From whom, my brother, shall I hear
Those words which ever charmed mine ear
And filled my bosom with delight
Whene'er he saw me act aright?'
    Thus Ráma spoke: then nearer came
And looking on his moonbright dame,
'Sítá, the king is gone,' he said:.
'And Lakshmaṇ, know thy sire is dead,
And with the Gods on high enrolled:
This mournful news has Bharat told.'
He spoke: the noble youths with sighs
Rained down the torrents from their eyes.
And then the brothers of the chief
With words of comfort soothed his grief:
'Now to the king our sire who swayed
The earth be due libations paid.'
Soon as the monarch's fate she knew,
Sharp pangs of grief smote Sítá through:
Nor could she look upon her lord

With eyes from which the torrents poured.
And Ráma strove with tender care
To soothe the weeping dame's despair,
And then, with piercing woe distressed,
The mournful Lakshman thus addressed :
' Brother, I pray thee bring for me
The pressed fruit of the Ingudí,
And a bark mantle fresh and new,
That I may pay this offering due.
First of the three shall Sítá go,
Next thou, and I the last : for so
Moves the funereal pomp of woe.' [1]

Sumantra of the noble mind,
Gentle and modest, meek and kind,
Who, follower of each princely youth,
To Ráma clung with constant truth,
Now with the royal brothers' aid
The grief of Ráma soothed and stayed,
And lent his arm his lord to guide
Down to the river's holy side.
That lovely stream the heroes found,
With woods that ever blossomed crowned,
And there in bitter sorrow bent
Their footsteps down the fair descent.
Then where the stream that swiftly flowed
A pure pellucid shallow showed,
The funeral drops they duly shed,
And 'Father, this be thine,' they said.
But he, the lord who ruled the land,

---

[1] 'The order of the procession on these occasions is that the children precede according to age, then the women and after that the men according to age, the youngest first and the eldest last : when they descend into the water this is reversed, and resumed when they come out of it.'

CAREY AND MARSHMAN.

Filled from the stream his hollowed hand,
And turning to the southern side
Stretched out his arm and weeping cried :
' This sacred water clear and pure,
An offering which shall aye endure,
To thee, O lord of kings, I give :
Accept it where the spirits live !'

Then, when the solemn rite was o'er,
Came Ráma to the river shore,
And offered, with his brothers' aid,
Fresh tribute to his father's shade.
With jujube fruit he mixed the seed
Of Ingudís from moisture freed,
And placed it on a spot o'erspread
With sacred grass, and weeping said :
' Enjoy, great King, the cake which we
Thy children eat and offer thee !
For ne'er do blessed Gods refuse
To share the food which mortals use.'

Then Ráma turned him to retrace
The path that brought him to the place,
And up the mountain's pleasant side
Where lovely lawns lay fair, he hied.
Soon as his cottage door he gained,
His brothers to his breast he strained.
From them and Sítá in their woes
So loud the cry of weeping rose,
That like the roar of lions round
The mountain rolled the echoing sound.
And Bharat's army shook with fear
The weeping of the chiefs to hear.
' Bharat', the soldiers cried, ''tis plain,
His brother Ráma meets again,
And with these cries that round us ring

They sorrow for their sire the king.'
Then leaving car and wain behind,
One eager thought in every mind,
Swift toward the weeping, every man,
As each could find a passage, ran.
Some thither bent their eager course
With car, and elephant, and horse,
And youthful captains on their feet
With longing sped their lord to meet,
As though the new-come prince had been
An exile for long years unseen.
Earth beaten in their frantic zeal
By clattering hoof and rumbling wheel,
Sent forth a deafening noise as loud
As heaven when black with many a cloud.
Then, with their consorts gathered near,
Wild elephants in sudden fear
Rushed to a distant wood, and shed
An odour round them as they fled.
And every silvan thing that dwelt
Within those shades the terror felt,
Deer, lion, tiger, boar, and roe,
Bison, wild-cow, and buffalo.
And when the tumult wild they heard,
With trembling pinions flew each bird,
From tree, from thicket, and from lake,
Swan, koïl, curlew, crane, and drake.
With men the ground was overspread,
With startled birds the sky o'erhead.
Then on his sacrificial ground
The sinless, glorious chief was found.
Loading with curses deep and loud
The hump-back and the queen, the crowd.
Whose cheeks were wet, whose eyes were dim,

In fond affection ran to him.
While the big tears their eyes bedewed,
He looked upon the multitude,
And then as sire and mother do,
His arms about his loved ones threw.
  Some to his feet with reverence pressed,
    Some in his arms he strained :
  Each friend, with kindly words addressed,
    . Due share of honour gained.
  Then, by their mighty woe o'ercome,
    The weeping heroes' cry
  Filled, like the roar of many a drum,
    Hill, cavern, earth, and sky.

CANTO CIV.

THE MEETING WITH THE QUEENS.

Vaśishṭha with his soul athirst
To look again on Ráma, first
In line the royal widows placed,
And then the way behind them traced.
The ladies moving, faint and slow,
Saw the fair stream before them flow,
And by the bank their steps were led
Which the two brothers visited.
Kauśalyá with her faded cheek
And weeping eyes began to speak,
And thus in mournful tones addressed
The queen Sumitrá and the rest:
'See, in the wood the bank's descent,
Which the two orphan youths frequent,
Whose noble spirits never fall,
Though woes surround them, reft of all.
Thy son with love that never tires
Draws water hence which mine requires.
This day, for lowly toil unfit,
His pious task thy son should quit.'

As on the long-eyed lady strayed,
On holy grass, whose points were laid
Directed to the southern sky,
The funeral offering met her eye.
When Ráma's humble gift she spied
Thus to the queens Kauśalyá cried:
'The gift of Ráma's hand behold,

His tribute to the king high-souled,
Offered to him, as texts require,
Lord of Ikshváku's line, his sire !
Not such I deem the funeral food
Of kings with godlike might endued.
Can he who knew all pleasures, he
Who ruled the earth from sea to sea,
The mighty lord of monarchs, feed
On Ingudí's extracted seed ?
In all the world there cannot be
A woe, I ween, more sad to see,
Than that my glorious son should make
His funeral gift of such a cake.
The ancient text I oft have heard
This day is true in every word :
' Ne'er do the blessed Gods refuse
To eat the food their children use.'
  The ladies soothed the weeping dame :
To Ráma's hermitage they came,
And there the hero met their eyes
Like a God fallen from the skies.
Him joyless, reft of all, they viewed,
And tears their mournful eyes bedewed.
The truthful hero left his seat,
And clasped the ladies' lotus feet,
And they with soft hands brushed away
The dust that on his shoulders lay.
Then Lakshman, when he saw each queen
With weeping eyes and troubled mien,
Near to the royal ladies drew
And paid them gentle reverence too.
He, Daśaratha's offspring, signed
The heir of bliss by Fortune kind,
Received from every dame no less

Each mark of love and tenderness.
And Sítá came and bent before
The widows, while her eyes ran o'er,
And pressed their feet with many a tear.
They when they saw the lady dear
Pale, worn with dwelling in the wild,
Embraced her as a darling child :
' Daughter of royal Janak, bride
Of Daśaratha's son,' they cried,
' How couldst thou, offspring of a king,
Endure this woe and suffering
In the wild forest ? When I trace
Each sign of trouble on thy face—
That lotus which the sun has dried,
That lily by the tempest tried,
That gold whereon the dust is spread,
That moon whence all the light is fled—
Sorrow assails my heart, alas !
As fire consumes the wood and grass.'

Then Ráma, as she spoke distressed,
The feet of Saint Vaśishṭha pressed,
  Touched them with reverential love,
    Then near him took his seat:
Thus Indra clasps in realms above
    The Heavenly Teacher's [1] feet.
Then with each counsellor and peer,
    Bharat of duteous mind,
With citizens and captains near,
    Sat humbly down behind.
When with his hands to him upraised,
    In devotee's attire,
Bharat upon his brother gazed
    Whose glory shone like fire,

---

[1] Vrihaspati, the preceptor of the Gods.

As when the pure Mahendra bends
　To the great Lord of Life,　·
Among his noble crowd of friends
　This anxious thought was rife :
' What words to Raghu's son to-day
　Will royal Bharat speak,
Whose heart has been so prompt to pay
　Obeisance fond and meek ?'
Then steadfast Ráma, Lakshmaṇ wise,
　Bharat for truth renowned,
Shone like three fires that heavenward rise
　With holy priests around.

CANTO CV.

RÁMA'S SPEECH.

A while they sat, each lip compressed,
Then Bharat thus his chief addressed:
' My mother here was made content;
To me was given the government.
This now, my lord, I yield to thee:
Enjoy it, from all trouble free.
Like a great bridge the floods have rent,
Impetuous in their wild descent,
All other hands but thine in vain
Would strive the burthen to maintain.
In vain the ass with steeds would vie,
With Tárkshya,[1] birds that wing the sky;
So, lord of men, my power is slight
To rival thine imperial might.
Great joys his happy days attend
On whom the hopes of men depend,
But wretched is the life he leads
Who still the aid of others needs.
And if the seed a man has sown,
With care and kindly nurture grown,
Rear its huge trunk and spring in time
Too bulky for a dwarf to climb,
Yet, with perpetual blossom gay,
No fruit upon its boughs display,
Ne'er can that tree, thus nursed in vain,
Approval of the virtuous gain.

---

[1] Garud, the king of birds.

The simile is meant to be
Applied, O mighty-armed, to thee,
Because, our lord and leader, thou
Protectest not thy people now.
O, be the longing wish fulfilled
Of every chief of house and guild,
To see again their sun-bright lord
Victorious to his realm restored!
As thou returnest through the crowd
Let roars of elephants be loud,
And each fair woman lift her voice
And in her new-found king rejoice.'

  The people all with longing moved,
The words that Bharat spoke approved,
And crowding near to Ráma pressed
The hero with the same request.
The steadfast Ráma, when he viewed
His glorious brother's mournful mood,
With each ambitious thought controlled,
Thus the lamenting prince consoled:
'I cannot do the things I will,
For Ráma is but mortal still.
Fate with supreme, resistless law-
This way and that its slave will draw.
All gathered heaps must waste away,
All lofty lore and powers decay.
Death is the end of life, and all,
Now firmly joined, apart must fall.
One fear the ripened fruit must know,
To fall upon the earth below;
So every man who draws his breath
Must fear inevitable death.
The pillared mansion, high, compact,
Must fall by Time's strong hand attacked;

So mortal men, the gradual prey
Of eld and ruthless death, decay.
The night that flies no more returns:
Yamuná for the Ocean yearns;
Swift her impetuous waters flee,
But roll not backward from the sea.
The days and nights pass swiftly by
And steal our moments as they fly,
E'en as the sun's unpitying rays
Drink up the floods in summer blaze.
Then for thyself lament and leave
For death of other men to grieve,
For if thou go or if thou stay,
Thy life is shorter day by day.
Death travels with us: death attends
Our steps until our journey ends,
Death, when the traveller wins the goal,
Returns with the returning soul.
The flowing hair grows white and thin,
And wrinkles mark the altered skin.
The ills of age man's strength assail:
Ah, what can mortal power avail?
Men joy to see the sun arise,
They watch him set with joyful eyes:
But ne'er reflect, too blind to see,
How fast their own brief moments flee.
With lovely change for ever new
The seasons' sweet return they view, ·
Nor think with heedless hearts the while
That lives decay as seasons smile.
As haply on the boundless main
Meet drifting logs and part again,
So wives and children, friends and gold,
Ours for a little time we hold:

Soon by resistless laws of fate
To meet no more we separate.
In all this changing world not one
The common lot of all can shun :
Then why with useless tears deplore
The dead whom tears can bring no more ?
As one might stand upon the way
And to a troop of travellers say :
'If ye allow it, sirs, I too
Will travel on the road with you' :
So why should mortal man lament
When on that path his feet are bent
Which all men living needs must tread,
Where sire and ancestors have led ?
Life flies as torrents downward fall
Speeding away without recall,
So virtue should our thoughts engage,
For bliss' is mortals' heritage.
By ceaseless care and earnest zeal
For servants and for people's weal,
By gifts, by duty nobly done,
Our glorious sire the skies has won.
Our lord the king, o'er earth who reigned,
A blissful home in heaven has gained
By wealth in ample largess spent,
And many a rite magnificent ;
With constant joy from first to last
A long and noble life he passed,
Praised by the good, no tears should dim
Our eyes, O brother dear, for him.
His human body, worn and tried
By length of days, he cast aside,
And gained the godlike bliss to stray

---

¹ To be won by virtue.

In Brahma's heavenly home for aye.
For such the wise as we are, deep
In Veda lore, should never weep.
Those who are firm and ever wise
Spurn vain lament and idle sighs.
Be self-possessed : thy grief restrain :
Go, in that city dwell again.
Return, O best of men, and be
Obedient to our sire's decree,
While I with every care fulfil
Our holy father's righteous will,
Observing in the lonely wood
His charge approved by all the good.'

  Thus Ráma of the lofty mind
    To Bharat spoke his righteous speech,
By every argument designed
    Obedience to his sire to teach.

CANTO CVI.

BHARAT'S SPEECH.

Good Bharat, by the river side,
To virtuous Ráma's speech replied,
And thus with varied lore addressed
The prince, while nobles round him pressed
'In all this world whom e'er can we
Find equal, scourge of foes, to thee?
No ill upon thy bosom weighs,
No thoughts of joy thy spirit raise.
Approved art thou of sages old,
To whom thy doubts are ever told.
Alike in death and life, to thee
The same to be and not to be.
The man who such a soul can gain
Can ne'er be crushed by woe or pain.
Pure as the Gods, high-minded, wise,
Concealed from thee no secret lies.
Such glorious gifts are all thine own,
And birth and death to thee are known,
That ill can ne'er thy soul depress
With all-subduing bitterness.
O let my prayer, dear brother, win
Thy pardon for my mother's sin,
Wrought for my sake who willed it not
When absent in a distant spot.
Duty alone with binding chains
The vengeance due to crime restrains,
Or on the sinner I should lift

My hand in retribution swift.
Can I who know the right, and spring
From Daśaratha, purest king—
Can I commit a heinous crime,
Abhorred by all through endless time ?
The aged king I dare not blame,
Who died so rich in holy fame,
My honoured sire, my parted lord,
E'en as a present God adored.
Yet who in lore of duty skilled
So foul a crime has ever willed,
And dared defy both gain and right
To gratify a woman's spite ?
When death draws near, so people say,
The sense of creatures dies away ;
And he has proved the ancient saw
By acting thus in spite of law.
But O my honoured lord, be kind,
Dismiss the trespass from thy mind,
The sin the king committed, led
By haste, his consort's wrath, and dread.
For he who veils his sire's offence
With tender care and reverence—
His sons approved by all shall live :
Not so their fate who ne'er forgive.
Be thou, my lord, the noble son,
And the vile deed my sire has done,
Abhorred by all the virtuous, ne'er
Resent, lest thou the guilt too share.
Preserve us, for on thee we call,
Our sire, Kaikeyí, me, and all
Thy citizens, thy kith and kin ;
Preserve us and reverse the sin.
To live in woods a devotee

Can scarce with royal tasks agree,
Nor can the hermit's matted hair
Suit fitly with a ruler's care.
Do not, my brother, do not still
Pursue this life that suits thee ill.
Mid duties of a king we count
His consecration paramount,
That he with ready heart and hand
May keep his people and his land.
What Warrior born to royal sway
From certain good would turn away,
A doubtful duty to pursue,
That mocks him with the distant view?
Thou wouldst to duty cleave, and gain
The meed that follows toil and pain.
In thy great task no labour spare :
Rule the four castes with justest care.
Mid all the four, the wise prefer
The order of the householder :[1]
Canst thou, whose thoughts to duty cleave,
The best of all the orders leave?
My better thou in lore divine,
My birth, my sense must yield to thine :
While thou, my lord, art here to reign,
How shall my hands the rule maintain?
O faithful lover of the right,
Take with thy friends the royal might,
Let thy sires' realm, from trouble free,
Obey her rightful king in thee.
Here let the priests and lords of state
Our monarch duly consecrate,
With prayer and holy verses blessed

---

[1] The four religious orders, referable to different times of life are,
that of the student, that of the householder, that of the anchorite,
and that of the mendicant.

By Saint Vaśishṭha and the rest.
Anointed king by us, again
Seek fair Ayodhyá, there to reign,
And like imperial Indra girt
By Gods of Storm, thy might assert.
From the three debts¹ acquittance earn,
And with thy wrath the wicked burn,
O'er all of us thy rule extend,
And cheer with boons each faithful friend.
Let thine enthronement, lord, this day
Make all thy lovers glad and gay,
And let all those who hate thee flee
To the ten winds for fear of thee.
Dear lord, my mother's words of hate
With thy sweet virtues expiate,
And from the stain of folly clear
The father whom we both revere.
Brother, to me compassion show,
I pray thee with my head bent·low,
And to these friends who on thee call,—
As the Great Father pities all.
But if my tears and prayers be vain,
And thou in woods wilt still remain,
I will with thee my path pursue
And make my home in forests too.'
  Thus Bharat strove to bend his will
  With suppliant head, but he,
Earth's lord, inexorable still
  Would keep his sire's decree.
The firmness of the noble chief
  The wondering people moved,
And rapture mingling with their grief,
  All wept and all approved.

¹ To Gods, men, and Manes.

‘ How firm his steadfast will, ‘ they cried,
  · Who keeps his promise thus !
Ah, to Ayodhyá's town,’ they sighed,
  ‘ He comes not back with us.’
The holy priests, the swains who tilled
  The earth, the sons of trade,
And e'en the mournful queens, were filled
  With joy as Bharat prayed,
And bent their heads, their weeping stilled
  A while, his prayers to aid.

CANTO CVII.

RÁMA'S SPEECH.

Thus, by his friends encompassed round,
He spoke, and Ráma far renowned
To his dear brother thus replied,
Whom holy rites had purified :
'O thou whom Queen Kaikeyí bare
The best of kings, thy words are fair.
Our royal father, when of yore
He wed her, to her father swore
The best of kingdoms to confer,
A noble dowry meet for her ;
Then, grateful, on the deadly day
Of heavenly Gods' and demons' fray,
A future boon on her bestowed
To whose sweet care his life he owed.
She to his mind that promise brought,
And then the best of kings besought
To bid me to the forest flee,
And give the rule, O Prince, to thee.
Thus bound by oath, the king our lord
Gave her those boons of free accord,
And bade me, O thou chief of men,
Live in the woods four years and ten.
I to this lonely wood have hied
With faithful Lakshman by my side,
And Sítá by no fears deterred,
Resolved to keep my father's word.
And thou, my noble brother, too

Shouldst keep our father's promise true :
Anointed ruler of the state
Maintain his word inviolate.
From his great debt, dear brother, free
Our lord the king for love of me,
Thy mother's breast with joy inspire,
And from all woe preserve thy sire.
' Tis said, near Gayá's holy town [1]
Gaya, great saint of high renown,
This text recited when he paid
Due rites to each ancestral shade :
  ' A son is born his sire to free
   From Put's infernal pains :
  Hence, saviour of his father, he
   The name of Puttra gains.' [2]
Thus numerous sons are sought by prayer,
In Scripture trained, with graces fair,
That of the number one some day
May funeral rites at Gayá pay.
The mighty saints who lived of old
This holy doctrine ever hold.
Then, best of men, our sire release
From pains of hell, and give him peace.
Now Bharat, to Ayodhyá speed,
The brave Satrughna with thee lead,
Take with thee all the twice-born men,
And please each lord and citizen.
I now, O King, without delay

---

[1] Gayá is a very holy city in Behar. Every good Hindu ought once in his life to make funeral offerings in Gayá in honour of his ancestors.

[2] *Put* is the name of that region of hell to which men are doomed who leave no son to perform the funeral rites which are necessary to assure the happiness of the departed *Putra*, the common word for a son, is said by the highest authority to be derived from *Put* and *tra* deliverer.

To Daṇḍak wood will bend my way,
And Lakshmaṇ and the Maithil dame
Will follow still, our path the same.
    Now, Bharat, lord of men be thou,
        And o'er Ayodhyá reign :
    The silvan world to me shall bow,
        King of the wild domain.
    Yea, let thy joyful steps be bent
        To that fair town to-day,
    And I as happy and content,
        To Daṇḍak wood will stray.
    The white umbrella o'er thy brow
        Its cooling shade shall throw :
    I to the shadow of the bough
        And leafy trees will go.
    Śatrughna, for wise plans renowned,
        Shall still on thee attend ;
    And Lakshmaṇ, ever faithful found,
        Be my familiar friend.
    Let us his sons, O brother dear,
        The path of right pursue,
    And keep the king we all revere
        Still to his promise true.'

CANTO CVIII.

JÁVÁLI'S SPEECH.

Thus Ráma soothed his brother's grief :
Then virtuous Jáváli, chief
Of twice-born sages, thus replied
In words that virtue's law defied :
' Hail, Raghu's princely son, dismiss
A thought so weak and vain as this.
Canst thou, with lofty heart endowed,
Think with the dull ignoble crowd ?
For what are ties of kindred ? can
One profit by a brother man ?
Alone the babe first opes his eyes,
And all alone at last he dies.
The man, I ween, has little sense
Who looks with foolish reverence
On father's or on mother's name :
In others, none a right may claim.
E'en as a man may leave his home
And to a distant village roam,
Then from his lodging turn away
And journey on the following day,
Such brief possession mortals hold
In sire and mother, house and gold,
And never will the good and wise
The brief uncertain lodging prize.
Nor, best of men, shouldst thou disown
Thy sire's hereditary throne,
And tread the rough and stony ground

B b

Where hardship, danger, woes abound.
Come, let Ayodhyá rich and bright
See thee enthroned with every rite :
Her tresses bound in single braid [1]
She waits thy coming long delayed.
O come, thou royal Prince, and share
The kingly joys that wait thee there,
And live in bliss transcending price
As Indra lives in Paradise.
The parted king is naught to thee,
Nor right in living man has he :
The king is one, thou, Prince of men,
Another art : be counselled then.
Thy royal sire, O chief, has sped
On the long path we all must tread.
The common lot of all is this,
And thou in vain art robbed of bliss.
For those—and only those—I weep
Who to the path of duty keep ;
For here they suffer ceaseless woe,
And dying to destruction go.
With pious care, each solemn day,
Will men their funeral offerings pay :
See, how the useful food they waste :
He who is dead no more can taste.
If one is fed, his strength renewed
Whene'er his brother takes his food,
Then offerings to the parted pay :
Scarce will they serve him on his way.
By crafty knaves these rules were framed,
And to enforce men's gifts proclaimed :
'Give, worship, lead a life austere,

---

[1] It was the custom of Indian women when mourning for their absent husbands to bind their hair in a long single braid.
Carey and Marshman translate, 'the one-tailed city.'

Keep lustral rites, quit pleasures here.'
There is no future life : be wise,
And do, O Prince, as I advise.
Enjoy, my lord, the present bliss,
And things unseen from thought dismiss.
Let this advice thy bosom move,
The counsel sage which all approve ;
To Bharat's earnest prayer incline,
And take the rule so justly thine.'

CANTO CIX.

— ⁓ —

THE PRAISES OF TRUTH.

———

By sage Jáváli thus addressed,
Ráma of truthful hearts the best,
With perfect skill and wisdom high
Thus to his speech made fit reply :
'Thy words that tempt to bliss are fair,
But virtue's garb they falsely wear.
For he from duty's path who strays
To wander in forbidden ways,
Allured by doctrine false and vain,
Praise from the good can never gain.
Their lives the true and boaster show,
Pure and impure, and high and low.
Else were no mark to judge between
Stainless and stained and high and mean,
They to whose lot fair signs may fall
Were but as they who lack them all,
And those to virtuous thoughts inclined
Were but as men of evil mind
If in the sacred name of right
I do this wrong in duty's spite ;
The path of virtue meanly quit,
And this polluting sin commit,
What man who marks the bounds between
Virtue and vice with insight keen,
Would rank me high in after time,
Stained with this soul-destroying crime ?
Whither could I, the sinner, turn,

How hope a seat in heaven to earn,
If 1 my plighted promise break,
And thus the righteous path forsake ?
This world of ours is ever led
To walk the ways which others tread,
And as their princes they behold,
The subjects too their lives will mould.
That truth and mercy still must be
Beloved of kings, is Heaven's decree.
Upheld by truth the monarch reigns,
And truth the very world sustains.
Truth evermore has been the love
Of holy saints and Gods above,'
And he whose lips are truthful here
Wins after death the highest sphere.
As from a serpent's deadly tooth,
We shrink from him who scorns the truth.
For holy truth is root and spring
Of justice and each holy thing,
A might that every power transcends,
Linked to high bliss that never ends.
Truth is all virtue's surest base,
Supreme in worth and first in place.
Oblations, gifts men offer here,
Vows, sacrifice, and rites austere,
And Holy Writ, on truth depend :
So men must still that truth defend.
Truth, only truth protects the land,
By truth unharmed our houses stand ;
Neglect of truth makes men distressed,
And truth in highest heaven is blessed.
Then how can I, rebellious, break
Commandments which my father spake—
I ever true and faithful found,

And by my word of honour bound?
My father's bridge of truth shall stand
Unharmed by my destructive hand:
Not folly, ignorance, or greed
My darkened soul shall thus mislead.
Have we not heard that God and shade
Turn from the hated offerings paid
By him whose false and fickle mind
No pledge can hold, no promise bind?
Truth is all duty: as the soul,
It quickens and supports the whole.
The good respect this duty: hence
Its sacred claims I reverence.
The Warrior's duty I despise
That seeks the wrong in virtue's guise:
Those claims I shrink from, which the base,
Cruel, and covetous embrace.
The heart conceives the guilty thought,
Then by the hand the sin is wrought,
And with the pair is leagued a third,
The tongue that speaks the lying word.
Fortune and land and name and fame
To man's best care have right and claim;
The good will aye to truth adhere,
And its high laws must men revere.
Base were the deed thy lips would teach,
Approved as best by subtle speech.
Shall I my plighted promise break,
That I these woods my home would make?
Shall I, as Bharat's words advise,
My father's solemn charge despise?
Firm stands the oath which then before
My father's face I soothly swore,
Which Queen Kaikeyí's anxious ear

Rejoiced with highest joy to hear.
Still in the wood will I remain,
With food prescribed my life sustain,
And please with fruit and roots and flowers
Ancestral shades and heavenly powers.
Here every sense contented, still
Heeding the bounds of good and ill,
My settled course will I pursue,
Firm in my faith and ever true.
Here in this wild and far retreat
Will I my noble task complete;
And Fire and Wind and Moon shall be
Partakers of its fruit with me.
A hundred offerings duly wrought
His rank o'er Gods for Indra bought,
And mighty saints their heaven secured
By torturing years on earth endured.'

 That scoffing plea the hero spurned,
  And thus he spake once more,
 Chiding, the while his bosom burned,
  Jáváli's impious lore :
 ' Justice, and courage ne'er dismayed,
  Pity for all distressed,
 Truth, loving honour duly paid
  To Bráhman, God, and guest—
 In these, the true and virtuous say,
  Should lives of men be passed :
 They form the right and happy way
  That leads to heaven at last.
 My father's thoughtless act I chide
  That gave thee honoured place,
 Whose soul, from virtue turned aside,
  Is faithless, dark, and base.

We rank the Buddhist with the thief,[1]
　　And all the impious crew
Who share his sinful disbelief,
　　And hate the right and true.
Hence never should wise kings who seek
　　To rule their people well,
Admit, before their face to speak,
　　The cursed infidel.
But twice-born men in days gone by,
　　Of other sort than thou,
Have wrought good deeds, whose glories high
　　Are fresh among us now:
This world they conquered, nor in vain
　　They strove to win the skies:
The twice-born hence pure lives maintain,
　　And fires of worship rise.
Those who in virtue's path delight,
　　And with the virtuous live,—
Whose flames of holy zeal are bright,
　　Whose hands are swift to give,
Who injure none, and good and mild
　　In every grace excel,
Whose lives by sin are undefiled,
　　We love and honour well.'
Thus Ráma spoke in righteous rage
　　Jáváli's speech to chide,
When thus again the virtuous sage
　　In truthful words replied:
'The atheist's lore I use no more,
　 Not mine his impious creed:
His words and doctrine I abhor,

---

[1] The verses in a different metre with which some cantos end are all to be regarded with suspicion. Schlegel regrets that he did not exclude them all from his edition. These lines are manifestly spurious. See *Additional Notes.*

Assumed at time of need.
E'en as I rose to speak with thee,
  The fit occasion came
That bade me use the atheist's plea
  To turn thee from thine aim.
The atheist creed I disavow,
  Unsay the words of sin,
And use the faithful's language now
  Thy favour, Prince, to win.'

CANTO CX.

THE SONS OF IKSHVÁKU.[1]

Then spake Vaśishṭha who perceived
That Ráma's soul was wroth and grieved:
'Well knows the sage Jáváli all
The changes that the world befall;
And but to lead thee to revoke
Thy purpose were the words he spoke.
Lord of the world, now hear from me
How first this world began to be.
First water was, and naught beside;
There earth was formed that stretches wide.
Then with the Gods from out the same
The Self-existent Brahmá came.
Then Brahmá[2] in a boar's disguise
Bade from the deep this earth arise;
Then, with his sons of tranquil soul,
He made the world and framed the whole.
From subtlest ether Brahmá rose:
No end, no loss, no change he knows.
A son had he, Maríchi styled,
And Kaśyap was Maríchi's child.
From him Vivasvat sprang: from him
Manu, whose fame shall ne'er be dim.
Manu, who life to mortals gave,
Begot Ikshváku good and brave:

---

[1] This genealogy is a repetition with slight variation of that given in Book I. CANTO LXX.

[2] In Gorresio's recension identified with Vishṇu. See Muir's *Sanskrit Texts, Vol. IV. pp.* 29, 30.

First of Ayodhyá's kings was he,
Pride of her famous dynasty.
From him the glorious Kukshi sprang,
Whose fame through all the regions rang.
Rival of Kukshi's ancient fame,
His heir the great Vikukshi came.
His son was Vána, lord of might,
His Anaraṇya, strong in fight.
No famine marred his blissful reign,
No drought destroyed the kindly grain;
Amid the sons of virtue chief,
His happy realm ne'er held a thief.
His son was Prithu, glorious name,
From him the wise Triśanku came:
Embodied to the skies he went
For love of truth preëminent.
He left a son renowned afar,
Known by the name of Dhundhumár.
His son succeeding bore the name
Of Yuvanáśva dear to fame.
He passed away. Him followed then
His son Mándhátá, king of men.
His son was blest in high emprise,
Susandhi, fortunate and wise.
Two noble sons had he, to wit
Dhruvasandhi and Prasenajit.
Bharat was Dhruvasandhi's son:
His glorious arm the conquest won.
Against his son King Asit, rose
In fierce array his royal foes,
Haihayas, Tálajanghas styled,
And Śaśivindhus fierce and wild.
Long time he strove, but forced to yield
Fled from his kingdom and the field.

The wives he left had both conceived—
So is the ancient tale believed:—
One, of her rival's hopes afraid,
Fell poison in the viands laid.
It chanced that Chyavan, Bhrigu's child,
Had wandered to the pathless wild
Where proud Himálaya's lovely height
Detained him with a strange delight.
Then came the other widowed queen
With lotus eyes and beauteous mien,
Longing a noble son to bear,
And wooed the saint with earnest prayer.
When thus Kálindí, fairest dame,
With reverent supplication came,
To her the holy sage replied:
'O royal lady, from thy side
A glorious son shall spring ere long,
Righteous and true and brave and strong;
He, scourge of foes and lofty-souled,
His ancient race shall still uphold.'
    Then round the sage the lady went,
And bade farewell, most reverent.
Back to her home she turned once more.
And there her promised son she bore.
Because her rival mixed the bane
To render her conception vain,
And her unripened fruit destroy,
Sagar she called her rescued boy. [1]
He, when he paid that solemn rite, [2]
Filled living creatures with affright:
Obedient to his high decree
His countless sons dug out the sea.

---

[1] From *sa* with, and *gára* poison.

[2] See Book I. CANTO XL.

Prince Asamanj was Sagar's child :
But him with cruel sin defiled
And loaded with the people's hate
His father banished from the state.
To Asamanj his consort bare
Bright Anśumán his valiant heir.
Anśumán's son, Dilípa famed,
Begot a son Bhagírath named.
From him renowned Kakutstha came :
Thou bearest still the lineal name.
Kakutstha's son was Raghu : thou
Art styled the son of Raghu now.
From him came Purushádak bold,
Fierce hero of gigantic mould :
Kalmáshapáda's name he bore,
Because his feet were spotted o'er.
Śankhan his son, to manhood grown,
Died sadly with his host o'erthrown,
But ere he perished sprang from him
Sudarśan, fair in face and limb.
From beautiful Sudarśan came
Prince Agnivarṇa; bright as flame.
His son was Śighraga, for speed
Unmatched; and Maru was his seed.
Praśuśruka was Maru's child :
His son was Ambarísha styled.
Nahush was Ambarísha's heir
With hand to strike and heart to dare.
His son was good Nábhág, from youth
Renowned for piety and truth.
From great Nábhág sprang children two,
Aja and Suvrat pure and true.
From Aja Daśaratha came,
Whose virtuous life was free from blame.

His eldest son art thou : his throne,
O famous Ráma, is thine own.
Accept the sway so justly thine,
And view the world with eyes benign.
For ever in Ikshváku's race
The eldest takes his father's place,
And while he lives no son beside
As lord and king is sanctified.
  The rule by Raghu's children kept
    Thou must not spurn to-day.
  This realm of peerless wealth accept,
    And like thy father sway.'

CANTO CXI.

COUNSEL TO BHARAT.

Thus said Vaśishṭha, and again
To Ráma spake in duteous strain:
' All men the light of life who see
With high respect should look on three:
High honour ne'er must be denied
To father, mother, holy guide.
First to their sires their birth they owe,
Nursed with maternal love they grow:
Their holy guides fair knowledge teach:
So men should love and honour each.
Thy sire and thou have learned of me,
The sacred guide of him and thee,
And if my word thou wilt obey
Thou still wilt keep the virtuous way.
See, with the chiefs of every guild
And all thy friends, this place is filled:
All these, as duty bids, protect;
So still the righteous path respect.
O, for thine aged mother feel,
Nor spurn the virtuous dame's appeal:
Obey, O Prince, thy mother dear,
And still to virtue's path adhere.
Yield thou to Bharat's fond request,
With earnest supplication pressed,
So wilt thou to thyself be true,
And faith and duty still pursue.'
   Thus by his saintly guide addressed

With pleas in sweetest tones expressed,
The lord of men in turn replied
To wise Vaśishṭha by his side:
'The fondest son's observance ne'er
Repays the sire and mother's care:
The constant love that food provides,
And dress, and every need besides:
Their pleasant words still soft and mild,
Their nurture of the helpless child:
The word which Daśaratha spake,
My king and sire, I ne'er will break.'

Then Bharat of the ample chest
The wise Sumantra thus addressed:
'Bring sacred grass, O charioteer,
And strew it on the level here.
For I will sit and watch his face
Until I win my brother's grace.
Like a robbed Bráhman will I lie,¹
Nor taste of food nor turn my eye,
In front of Ráma's leafy cot,
And till he yield will leave him not.'
When Bharat saw Sumantra's eye
Looked up to Ráma for reply.
The prince himself in eager haste
The sacred grass in order placed.
Him great and mighty Ráma, best
Of royal saints, in turn addressed:
'What, Bharat, have I done, that thou
Besiegest me,² a suppliant now?
Thus stretched, to force redress for wrongs
To men of Bráhman birth belongs,

---

¹ A practice which has frequently been described, under the name of *dherna*, by European travellers in India.
² Compare Milton's '*beseeching or besieging.*'

Not those upon whose kingly head
The consecrating drops are shed.
Up, lord of men! arise, and quit
This fearful vow for thee unfit.
Go, brother. seek Ayodhyá's town,
Fair city of supreme renown.'
  But Bharat, as his seat he took.
Cast all around an eager look:
'O people, join your prayers with mine,
And so his stubborn heart incline.'
  And all the people answered thus:
'Full well is Ráma known to us.
Right is the word he speaks, and he
Is faithful to his sire's decree:
Nor can we rashly venture now
To turn him from his purposed vow.'
  Then Ráma spoke: 'O Bharat, heed
Thy virtuous friends, and mark their rede.
Mark well what I and these advise,
And duty view with clearer eyes.
Thy hand on mine, O hero, place,
Touch water, and thy sin efface.'
  Then Bharat rose: his hand he dipped,
And purifying water sipped:
'Each citizen,' he cried, 'give ear,
Attend, each counsellor and peer.
My mother planned, by me untaught,
To win the sway I never sought:
Ne'er Raghu's son could I despise,
In duty's lore supremely wise.
Now if obedience to our sire
This dwelling in the woods require,
I, till the destined years be spent,
Will dwell alone in banishment.'

C c

The virtuous Ráma, wonder-stirred,
The faithful speech of Bharat heard,
And thus the hero's feelings found
Due utterance, as he gazed around:
  'Still to my father's word I hold,
Whate'er he bought, or pledged, or sold:
Ne'er shall his living promise be
Annulled by Bharat or by me.
Not thus my task will I evade,
My exile on another laid:
Most wise was Queen Kaikeyí's rede,
And just and good my father's deed.
Dear Bharat's patient soul I know,
How reverence due he loves to show;
In him, high-souled and faithful found,
Must each auspicious grace abound.
When from the woods I turn again
I with his aid shall nobly reign,
With one so good, of peerless worth,
A glorious lord of happy earth.
Her boon Kaikeyí sought and won:
I, as my father swore, have done:
And O, do thou, my brother dear,
The monarch's name from falsehood clear.'

CANTO CXII.

THE SANDALS.

High wonder mingled with delight
Took the great sages at the sight,
Thrilling their breasts who came to view
The meeting of the peerless two.
The saints and sages' holy train
Departed to their home again,
And high each holy voice was raised,
And thus the glorious brothers praised.
' High fate is his, the sire of two
Most virtuous sons, so brave and true :
With wonder and with joy intense
Our ears have heard their conference.
Then the great sages, longing all
To see the ten-necked tyrant[1] fall,
To Bharat, bravest of the brave,
Their salutary counsel gave :
' O thou of lofty lineage born,
Whom wisdom, conduct, fame adorn,
Thou for thy honoured father's sake
Shouldst Ráma's righteous counsel take.
All debts to Queen Kaikeyí paid,
Thy sire his home in heaven has made,
So virtuous Ráma we would see
From filial obligation free.'
Thus gave each royal sage advice,

---

[1] Ten-headed, ten-necked, ten-faced, are common epithets of Rávan the giant king of Lanká.

High saint, and bard of Paradise;
Then quickly vanishing from view
Each to his proper home withdrew.
Then Ráma's face his rapture showed,
And his full heart with joy o'erflowed,
While, as the sages parted thence,
He paid his humble reverence.

   Then Bharat shook in every limb
As suppliant thus he spoke to him:
'The duty of a king respect,
Held by our race in high respect:
And O, thy gracious ear incline
To heed my mother's prayer and mine.
The mighty realm to rule and guard
For me alone is task too hard
No power have I the love to gain
Of noble citizen, and swain
All those who know thee, warrior hand,
On thee their eager glances bend,
As labouring hinds who till the plain
Look fondly for the Lord of Rain.
O wisest Prince, thy realm secure,
And make its firm foundations sure.
Kakutstha's Son, thy mighty arm
Can keep the nation free from harm.'
He spoke, and fell in sorrow drowned
At Ráma's feet upon the ground,
And there the hero sued and sighed,
And 'Hear me, Raghu's son' he cried.

   Then Ráma raised him up, and pressed
His brother to his loving breast,
And sweetly as a wild swan cried
To Bharat dark and lotus-eyed:
'So just and true thy generous soul,

Thy hand may well this earth control:
But many a sage his aid will lend,
With counsellor, and peer, and friend:
With these advise: their counsel ask,
And so perform thy arduous task.
The moon his beauty may forgo,
The cold forsake the Hills of Snow,
And Ocean o'er his banks may sweep,
But I my father's word will keep
Now whether love of thee or greed
Thy mother led to plan the deed,
Forth from thy breast the memory throw,
And filial love and reverence show'

  Thus spake Kauśalyá's son: again
Bharat replied in humble strain
To him who matched the sun in might
And lovely as the young moon's light:
'Put, noble brother, I entreat,
These sandals on thy blessed feet:
These, lord of men, with gold-bedecked,
The realm and people will protect.'

  Then Ráma as his brother prayed,
Beneath his feet the sandals laid;
And these with fond affection gave
To Bharat's hand, the good and brave
Then Bharat bowed his reverent head
And thus again to Ráma said:
'Through fourteen seasons will I wear
The hermit's dress and matted hair:
With fruit and roots my life sustain,
And still beyond the realm remain,
Longing for thee to come again
The rule and all affairs of state
I to these shoes will delegate.

And if, O tamer of thy foes,
When fourteen years have reached their close,
I see thee not that day return,
The kindled fire my frame shall burn.'
　　Then Ráma to his bosom drew
Dear Bharat and Śatrughna too:
'Be, never wroth,' he cried, 'with her,
Kaikeyí's guardian minister:
This, glory of Ikshváku's line,
Is Sítá's earnest prayer and mine.'
He spoke, and as the big tears fell,
To his dear brother bade farewell.
Round Ráma, Bharat strong and bold
　　In humble reverence paced,
When the bright sandals wrought with gold
　　Above his brows were placed.
The royal elephant who led
　　The glorious pomp he found,
And on the monster's mighty head
　　Those sandals duly bound.
Then noble Ráma, born to swell
　　The glories of his race,
To all in order bade farewell
　　With love and tender grace—
To brothers, counsellors, and peers,—
　　Still firm, in duty proved,
Firm, as the Lord of Snow uprears
　　His mountains unremoved.
No queen, for choking sobs and sighs,
　　Could say her last adieu:
Then Ráma bowed, with flooded eyes,
　　And to his cot withdrew.

CANTO CXIII.

BHARAT'S RETURN.

Bearing the sandals on his head
Away triumphant Bharat sped,
 And clomb, Śatrughna by his side,
The car wherein he wont to ride.
Before the mighty army went
The lords for counsel eminent,
Vaśishṭha, Vámadeva next,
Jáváli, pure with prayer and text.
Then from that lovely river they
Turned eastward on their homeward way
With reverent steps from left to right
They circled Chitrakúṭa's height,
And viewed his peaks on every side
With stains of thousand metals dyed.
Then Bharat saw, not far away,
Where Bharadvája's dwelling lay,
And when the chieftain bold and sage
Had reached that holy hermitage,
Down from the car he sprang to greet
The saint, and bowed before his feet.
High rapture filled the hermit's breast,
Who thus the royal prince addressed :
'Say, Bharat, is thy duty done ?
Hast thou with Ráma met, my son ? '

 The chief whose soul to virtue clave
This answer to the hermit gave :
 'I prayed him with our holy guide :

But Raghu's son our prayer denied,
And long besought by both of us
He anwered Saint Vaśishṭha thus :
' True to my vow, I still will be
Observant of my sire's decree :
Till fourteen years complete their course
That promise shall remain in force.'
The saint in highest wisdom taught,
These solemn words with wisdom fraught,
To him in lore of language learned
Most eloquent himself returned :
' Obey my rede : let Bharat hold
This pair of sandals decked with gold :
They in Ayodhyá shall ensure
Our welfare, and our bliss secure.'
When Ráma heard the royal priest
He rose, and looking to the east
Consigned the sandals to my hand
That they for him might guard the land.
Then from the high-souled chief's abode
I turned upon my homeward road,
Dismissed by him, and now this pair
Of sandals to Ayodhyá bear.'

　　To him the hermit thus replied,
By Bharat's tidings gratified :
' No marvel thoughts so just and true,
Thou best of all who right pursue,
Should dwell in thee, O Prince of men,
As waters gather in the glen.
He is not dead : we mourn in vain :
Thy blessed father lives again,
Whose noble son we thus behold
Like Virtue's self in human mould.'
　　He ceased : before him Bharat fell

To clasp his feet, and said farewell:
His reverent steps around him bent,
And onward to Ayodhyá went.
His host of followers stretching far
With many an elephant and car,
Waggon and steed, a mighty train,
Traversed their homeward way again.
O'er holy Yamuná they sped,
Fair stream, with waves engarlanded,
And then once more the rivers' queen,
The blessed Gangá 's self was seen.
Then making o'er that flood his way,
Where crocodiles and monsters lay,
The king to Śringaverá drew
His host and royal retinue.
His onward way he thence pursued,
And soon renowned Ayodhyá viewed.
Then burnt by woe and sad of cheer
Bharat addressed the charioteer:
' Ah, see, Ayodhyá dark and sad,
Her glory gone, once bright and glad:
Of joy and beauty reft, forlorn,
In silent grief she seems to mourn.'

CANTO CXIV.

BHARAT'S DEPARTURE.

Deep, pleasant was the chariot's sound
As royal Bharat, far renowned,
Whirled by his mettled coursers fast
Within Ayodhyá's city passed.
There dark and drear was every home
Where cats and owls had space to roam.
As when the shades of midnight fall
With blackest gloom, and cover all:
As Rohiṇí, dear spouse of him
Whom Ráhu hates,[1] grows faint and dim,
When, as she shines on high alone,
The demon's shade is o'er her thrown:
As burnt by summer's heat a rill
Scarce trickling from her parent hill,
With dying fish in pools half dried,
And fainting birds upon her side:
As sacrificial flames arise
When holy oil their food supplies,
But when no more the fire is fed
Sink lustreless and cold and dead:
Like some brave host that filled the plain,
With harness rent and captains slain,
When warrior, elephant, and steed
Mingled in wild confusion bleed:
As when, all spent her store of worth,

---

[1] The spouse of Rohiṇí is the Moon: Ráhu is the demon who causes eclipses.

Rocks from her base the loosened earth:
Like a sad fallen star no more
Wearing the lovely light it wore:
So mournful in her lost estate
Was that sad town disconsolate.
Then car-borne Bharat, good and brave,
Thus spake to him the steeds who drave:
‘Why are Ayodhyá's streets so mute?
Where is the voice of lyre and lute?
Why sounds not, as of old, to-day
The music of the minstrel's lay?
Where are the wreaths they used to twine?
Where are the blossoms and the wine?
Where is the cool refreshing scent
Of sandal dust with aloe blent?
The elephant's impatient roar,
The din of cars, I hear no more:
No more the horse's pleasant neigh
Rings out to meet me on my way.
Ayodhyá's youths, since Ráma's flight,
Have lost their relish for delight:
Her men roam forth no more, nor care
Bright garlands round their necks to wear.
All grieve for banished Ráma: feast,
And revelry and song have ceased:
Like a black night when floods pour down,
So dark and gloomy is the town.
When will he come to make them gay
Like some auspicious holiday?
When will my brother, like a cloud
At summer's close, make glad the crowd?
  Then through the streets the hero rode,
And passed within his sire's abode,
Like some deserted lion's den,

Forsaken by the lord of men.
Then to the inner bowers he came,
Once happy home of many a dame,
　　Now gloomy, sad, and drear,
Dark as of old that sunless day
When wept the Gods in wild dismay :
　　There poured he many a tear.

---

[1] 'Once,' says the Commentator Tírtha, 'in the battle between the
Gods and demons the Gods were vanquished, and the sun was overthrown by Ráhu. At the request of the Gods Atri undertook the
management of the sun for a week.'

CANTO CXV.

NANDIGRÁM.[1]

Then when the pious chief had seen
Lodged in her home each widowed queen,
Still with his burning grief oppressed
His holy guides he thus addressed :
'I go to Nandigrám : adieu,
This day, my lords to all of you :
I go, my load of grief to bear,
Reft of the son of Raghu, there.
The king my sire, alas, is dead,
And Ráma to the forest fled ;
There will I wait till he, restored,
Shall rule the realm, its rightful lord.'
  They heard the high-souled prince's speech,
And thus with ready answer each
Of those great lords their chief addressed,
With Saint Vaśishtha and the rest :
'Good are the words which thou hast said,
By brotherly affection led,
Like thine own self, a faithful friend,
True to thy brother to the end :
A heart like thine must all approve,
Which naught from virtue's path can move.'
  Soon as the words he loved to hear
Fell upon Bharat's joyful ear,
Thus to the charioteer he spoke :
'My car with speed, Sumantra, yoke.'

---

[1] Now Nundgaon, in Oudh.

Then Bharat with delighted mien
Obeisance paid to every queen,
And with Satrughna by his side
Mounting the car away he hied.
With lords, and priests in long array
The brothers hastened on their way,
And the great pomp the Bráhmans led
With Saint Vaśishṭha at their head.
Then every face was eastward bent
As on to Nandigrám they went.
Behind the army followed, all
Unsummoned by their leaders' call,
And steeds and elephants and men
Streamed forth with every citizen.
As Bharat in his chariot rode
His heart with love fraternal glowed,
And with the sandals on his head
To Nandigrám he quickly sped.
Within the town he swiftly pressed,
Alighted, and his guides addressed:
'To me in trust my brother's hand
Consigned the lordship of the land,
When he these gold-wrought sandals gave
As emblems to protect and save.'
Then Bharat bowed, and from his head
The sacred pledge deposited,
And thus to all the people cried
Who ringed him round on every side:
'Haste, for these sandals quickly bring
The canopy that shades the king.
Pay ye to them all reverence meet
As to my elder brother's feet,
For they will right and law maintain
Until King Ráma come again.

My brother with a loving mind
These sandals to my charge consigned:
I till he come will guard with care
The sacred trust for Raghu's heir.
My watchful task will soon be done,
The pledge restored to Raghu's son;
Then shall I see, his wanderings o'er,
These sandals on his feet once more.
My brother I shall meet at last,
The burthen from my shoulders cast,
To Ráma's hand the realm restore
And serve my elder as before.
When Ráma takes again this pair
Of sandals kept with pious care,
And here his glorious reign begins,
I shall be cleansed from all my sins,
When the glad people's voices ring
With welcome to the new-made king,
Joy will be mine four-fold as great
As if supreme I ruled the state.'
　　Thus humbly spoke in sad lament
The chief in fame preëminent:
Thus, by his reverent lords obeyed,
At Nandigrám the kingdom swayed.
With hermit's dress and matted hair
He dwelt with all his army there.
The sandals of his brother's feet
Installed upon the royal seat,
He, all his powers to them referred,
Affairs of state administered.
　　In every care, in every task,
　　　When golden store was brought,
　　He first, as though their rede to ask,
　　　Those royal sandals sought.

CANTO CXVI.

THE HERMIT'S SPEECH.

When Bharat took his homeward road
Still Ráma in the wood abode:
But soon he marked the fear and care
That darkened all the hermits there.
For all who dwelt before the hill
Were sad with dread of coming ill:
Each holy brow was lined by thought,
And Ráma's side they often sought.
With gathering frowns the prince they eyed,
And then withdrew and talked aside.
 Then Raghu's son with anxious breast
The leader of the saints addressed:
'Can aught that I have done displease,
O reverend Sage, the devotees?
Why are their loving looks, O say,
Thus sadly changed or turned away?
Has Lakshman through his want of heed
Offended with unseemly deed?
Or is the gentle Sítá, she
Who loved to honour you and me—
Is she the cause of this offence,
Failing in lowly reverence?'
 One sage, o'er whom, exceeding old,
Had many a year of penance rolled,
Trembling in every aged limb
Thus for the rest replied to him:
'How could we, O beloved, blame

Thy lofty-souled Videhan dame,
Who in the good of all delights,
And more than all of anchorites ?
But yet through thee a numbing dread
Of fiends among our band has spread ;
Obstructed by the demons' art
The trembling hermits talk apart.
For Rávaṇ's brother, overbold,
Named Khara, of gigantic mould,
Vexes with fury fierce and fell
All those in Janasthán ¹ who dwell.
Resistless in his cruel deeds,
On flesh of men the monster feeds :
Sinful and arrogant is he,
And looks with special hate on thee.
Since thou, beloved son, hast made
Thy home within this holy shade,
The fiends have vexed with wilder rage
The dwellers of the hermitage.
In many a wild and dreadful form
Around the trembling saints they swarm,
With hideous shape and foul disguise
Their terrify our holy eyes.
They make our loathing souls endure
Insult and scorn and sights impure,
And flocking round the altars stay
The holy rites we love to pay.
In every spot throughout the grove
With evil thoughts the monsters rove,
Assailing with their secret might
Each unsuspecting anchorite.
Ladle and dish away they fling,
Our fires with floods extinguishing,

---

¹ A part of the great Daṇḍak forest.

And when the sacred flame should burn
They trample on each water-urn.
Now when they see their sacred wood
Plagued by this impious brotherhood,
The troubled saints away would roam
And seek in other shades a home :
Hence will we fly, O Ráma, ere
The cruel fiends our bodies tear.
Not far away a forest lies
Rich in the roots and fruit we prize,
To this will I and all repair
And join the holy hermits there :
Be wise, and with us thither flee
Before this Khara injure thee.
Mighty art thou, O Ráma, yet
Each day with peril is beset,
If with thy consort by thy side
Thou in this wood wilt still abide.'

  He ceased : the words the hero spake
The hermit's purpose failed to break :
To Raghu's son farewell he said,
And blessed the chief and comforted ;
Then with the rest the holy sage
Departed from the hermitage.

  So from the wood the saints withdrew,
And Ráma bidding all adieu
  In lowly reverence bent :
Instructed by their friendly speech,
Blest with the gracious love of each,
  To his pure home he went.
Nor would the son of Raghu stray
A moment from that grove away
  From which the saints had fled,
And many a hermit thither came

Attracted by his saintly fame
   And the pure life he led.

CANTO CXVII.

ANASÚYÁ.

But dwelling in that lonely spot
Left by the hermits pleased him not.
' I met the faithful Bharat here,
The townsmen, and my mother dear :
The painful memory lingers yet,
And stings me with a vain regret.
And here the host of Bharat camped,
And many a courser here has stamped,
And elephants with ponderous feet
Have trampled through the calm retreat.'
So forth to seek a home he hied,
His spouse and Lakshmaṇ by his side.
He came to Atri's pure retreat,
Paid reverence to his holy feet,
And from the saint such welcome won
As a fond father gives his son.
The noble prince with joy unfeigned
As a dear guest he entertained,
And cheered the glorious Lakshmaṇ too
And Sítá with observance due.
Then Anasúyá at the call
Of him who sought the good of all,
His blameless venerable spouse,
Delighting in her holy vows,
Came from her chamber to his side :
To her the virtuous hermit cried :
' Receive, I pray, with friendly grace

This dame of Maithil monarchs' race :
To Ráma next made known his wife,
The devotee of saintliest life :
'Ten thousand years this votaress bent
On sternest rites of penance spent ;
She when the clouds withheld their rain,
And drought ten years consumed the plain,
Caused grateful roots and fruit to grow
And ordered Gangá here to flow :
So from their cares the saints she freed,
Not let these checks their rites impede.
She wrought in Heaven's behalf, and made
Ten nights of one, the Gods to aid :[1]
Let holy Anasúyá be
An honoured mother, Prince, to thee.
Let thy Videhan spouse draw near
To her whom all that live revere,
Stricken in years, whose loving mind
Is slow to wrath and ever kind.'

He ceased : and Ráma gave assent,
And said, with eyes on Sítá bent :
'O Princess, thou hast heard with me
This counsel of the devotee :
Now that her touch thy soul may bless,
Approach the saintly votaress :
Come to the venerable dame,
Far known by Anasúyá's name :
The mighty things that she has done
High glory in the world have won.'

Thus spoke the son of Raghu : she
Approached the saintly devotee,
Who with her white locks, old and frail,

---

[1] When the saint Mándavya had doomed some saint's wife, who was
Anasúyá's friend to become a widow on the morrow.

Shook like a plantain in the gale.
To that true spouse she bowed her head,
And 'Lady, I am Sítá,' said :
Raised suppliant hands and prayed her tell
That all was prosperous and well.

The aged matron, when she saw
Fair Sítá true to duty's law,
Addressed her thus : 'High fate is thine
Whose thoughts to virtue still incline.
Thou, lady of the noble mind,
Hast kin and state and wealth resigned
To follow Ráma forced to tread
Where solitary woods are spread.
Those women gain high spheres above
Who still unchanged their husbands love,
Whether they dwell in town or wood,
Whether their hearts be ill or good.
Though wicked, poor, or led away
In love's forbidden paths to stray,
The noble matron still will deem
Her lord a deity supreme.
Regarding kin and friendship, I
Can see no better, holier tie,
And every penance-rite is dim
Beside the joy of serving him.
But dark is this to her whose mind
Promptings of idle fancy blind,
Who led by evil thoughts away
Makes him who should command obey.
Such women, O dear Maithil dame,
Their virtue lose and honest fame,
Enslaved by sin and folly, led
In these unholy paths to tread.
But they who good and true like thee

The present and the future see,
Like men by holy deeds will rise
To mansions in the blissful skies.
　So keep thee pure from taint of sin,
　　Still to thy lord be true,
　And fame and merit shalt thou win,
　　To thy devotion due.'

CANTO CXVIII.

ANASÚYÁ'S GIFTS.

Thus by the holy dame addressed
Who banished envy from her breast,
Her lowly reverence Sítá paid,
And softly thus her answer made :
'No marvel, best of dames, thy speech
The duties of a wife should teach :
Yet I, O lady, also know
Due reverence to my lord to show.
Were he the meanest of the base,
Unhonoured with a single grace,
My husband still I ne'er would leave,
But firm through all to him would cleave
Still rather to a lord like mine
Whose virtues high-exalted shine,
Compassionate, of lofty soul,
With every sense in due control,
True in his love, of righteous mind,
Like a dear sire and mother kind.
E'en as he ever loves to treat
Kauśalyá with observance meet,
Has his behaviour ever been
To every other honoured queen.
Nay, more, a sonlike reverence shows
The noble Ráma e'en to those
On whom the king his father set
His eyes one moment, to forget.
Deep in my heart the words are stored,

Said by the mother of my lord,
When from my home I turned away
In the lone fearful woods to stray.
The counsel of my mother deep
Impressed upon my soul I keep,
When by the fire I took my stand,
And Ráma clasped in his my hand.
And in my bosom cherished yet,
My friends' advice I ne'er forget :
Woman her holiest offering pays
When she her husband's will obeys.
Good Sávitrí her lord obeyed,
And a high saint in heaven was made,
And for the self-same virtue thou
Hast heaven in thy possession now.
And she with whom no dame could vie,
Now a bright Goddess in the sky,
Sweet Rohiṇí the Moon's dear Queen,
Without her lord is never seen :
And many a faithful wife beside
For her pure love is glorified.'
   Thus Sítá spake : soft rapture stole
Through Anasúyá's saintly soul :
Kisses on Sítá's head she pressed,
And thus the Maithil dame addressed :
' I by long rites and toils endured
Rich store of merit have secured :
From this my wealth will I bestow
A blessing ere I let thee go.
So right and wise and true each word
That from thy lips mine ears have heard,
I love thee : be my pleasing task
To grant the boon that thou shalt ask.'
   Then Sítá marvelled much, and while

Played o'er her lips a gentle smile,
'All has been done, O Saint,' she cried,
And naught remains to wish beside.
  She spake; the lady's meek reply
Swelled Anasúyá's rapture high :
'Sítá,' she said, 'my gift to-day
Thy sweet contentment shall repay.
Accept this precious robe to wear,
Of heavenly fabric, rich and rare,
These gems thy limbs to ornament,
This precious balsam sweet of scent.
O Maithil dame, this gift of mine
Shall make thy limbs with beauty shine,
And breathing o'er thy frame dispense
Its pure and lasting influence.
This balsam on thy fair limbs spread
New radiance on thy lord shall shed,
As Lakshmí's beauty lends a grace
To Vishṇu's own celestial face.'
  Then Sítá took the gift the dame
Bestowed on her in friendship's name,
The balsam, gems, and robe divine,
And garlands wreathed of bloomy twine;
Then sat her down, with reverence meet,
At saintly Anasúyá's feet.
The matron rich in rites and vows
Turned her to Ráma's Maithil spouse,
And questioned thus in turn to hear
A pleasant tale to charm her ear:
'Sítá, 'tis said that Raghu's son
Thy hand, mid gathered suitors, won.
I fain would hear thee, lady, tell
The story as it all befell :
Do thou repeat each thing that passed,

Reviewing all from first to last.'
   Thus spake the dame to Sítá : she
Replying to the devotee,
'Then, lady, thy attention lend,'
Rehearsed the story to the end :
'King Janak, just and brave and strong,
Who loves the right and hates the wrong,
Well skilled in what the law ordains
For Warriors, o'er Videha reigns.
Guiding one morn the plough, his hand
Marked out for rites the sacred land,
When, as the ploughshare cleft the earth,
Child of the king I leapt to birth.
Then as the ground he smoothed and cleared,
He saw me all with dust besmeared,
And on the new-found babe, amazed
The ruler of Videha gazed.
In childless love the monarch pressed
The welcome infant to his breast :
'My daughter,' thus he cried, 'is she :'
And as his child he cared for me.
Forth from the sky was heard o'erhead
As 'twere a human voice that said :
'Yea, even so : great King, this child
Henceforth thine own be justly styled.'
Videha's monarch, virtuous-souled,
Rejoiced o'er me with joy untold,
Delighting in his new-won prize,
The darling of his heart and eyes.
To his chief queen of saintly mind
The precious treasure he consigned,
And by her side she saw me grow,
Nursed with the love which mothers know.
Then as he saw the seasons fly,

And knew my marriage-time was nigh,
My sire was vexed with care, as sad
As one who mourns the wealth he had :
'Scorn on the maiden's sire must wait
From men of high and low estate :
The virgin's father all despise,
Though Indra's peer, who rules the skies.'
More near he saw, and still more near,
The scorn that filled his soul with fear,
On trouble's billowy ocean tossed,
Like one whose shattered bark is lost.
My father knowing how I came,
No daughter of a mortal dame,
In all the regions failed to see
A bridegroom meet to match with me.
Each way with anxious thought he scanned.
And thus at length the monarch planned :
'The Bride's Election will I hold,
With every rite prescribed of old.'
It pleased King Varun to bestow
Quiver and shafts and heavenly bow
Upon my father's sire who reigned,
When Daksha his great rite ordained.
Where was the man might bend or lift
With utmost toil that wondrous gift ?
Not e'en in dreams could mortal king
Strain the great bow or draw the string
Of this tremendous bow possessed,
My truthful father thus addressed
The lords of many a region, all
Assembled at the monarch's call :
'Whoe'er this bow can manage, he
The husband of my child shall be.'
The suitors viewed with hopeless eyes

That wondrous bow of mountain size,
Then to my sire they bade adieu,
And all with humbled hearts withdrew.
At length with Viśvámitra came
This son of Raghu, dear to fame ;
The royal sacrifice to view
Near to my father's home he drew,
His brother Lakshman by his side,
Ráma, in deeds heroic tried.
My sire with honour entertained
The saint in lore of duty trained,
Who thus in turn addressed the king :
' Ráma and Lakshman here who spring
From royal Daśaratha, long
To see thy bow so passing strong.'
Before the prince's eyes was laid
That marvel, as the Bráhman prayed.
One moment on the bow he gazed,
Quick to the notch the string he raised,
Then, in the wondering people's view,
The cord with mighty force he drew.
Then with an awful crash as loud
As thunderbolts' that cleave the cloud,
The bow beneath the matchless strain
Of arms heroic snapped in twain.
Thus, giving purest water, he,
My sire, to Ráma offered me.
The prince the offered gift declined
Till he should learn his father's mind ;
So horsemen swift Ayodhyá sought
And back her aged monarch brought.
Me then my sire to Ráma gave,
Self-ruled, the bravest of the brave.
And Urmilá, the next to me,

Graced with all gifts, most fair to see,
My sire with Raghu's house allied,
And gave her to be Lakshmaṇ's bride.
Thus from the princes of the land
Lord Ráma won my maiden hand,
And him exalted high above
Heroic chiefs I truly love.'

CANTO CXIX.

THE FOREST.

When Anasúyá, virtuous-souled,
Had heard the tale by Sítá told,
She kissed the lady's brow and laced
Her loving arms around her waist.
' With sweet-toned words distinct and clear
Thy pleasant tale has charmed mine ear,
How the great king thy father held
That Maiden's Choice unparalleled.
But now the sun has sunk from sight,
And left the world to holy Night.
Hark ! how the leafy thickets sound
With gathering birds that twitter round :
They sought their food by day, and all
Flock homeward when the shadows fall.
See, hither comes the hermit band,
Each with his pitcher in his hand :
Fresh from the bath, their locks are wet,
Their coats of bark are dripping yet.
Here saints their fires of worship tend,
And curling wreaths of smoke ascend :
Borne on the flames they mount above,
Dark as the brown wings of the dove.
The distant trees, though well-nigh bare,
Gloom thickened by the evening air,
And in the faint uncertain light
Shut the horizon from our sight.
The beasts that prowl in darkness rove

On every side about the grove,
And the tame deer, at ease reclined
Their shelter near the altars find.
The night o'er all the sky is spread,
With lunar stars engarlanded,
And risen in his robes of light
The moon is beautifully bright.
Now to thy lord I bid thee go :
Thy pleasant tale has charmed me so :
One thing alone I needs must pray,
Before me first thyself array :
Here in thy heavenly raiment shine,
And glad, dear love, these eyes of mine.'
    Then like a heavenly Goddess shone
Fair Sítá with that raiment on.
She bowed her to the matron's feet,
Then turned away her lord to meet.
The hero prince with joy surveyed
His Sítá in her robes arrayed,
As glorious to his arms she came
With love-gifts of the saintly dame.
She told him how the saint to show
Her fond affection would bestow
That garland of celestial twine,
Those ornaments and robes divine.
Then Ráma's heart, nor Lakshmaṇ's less,
Was filled with pride and happiness,
For honours high had Sítá gained,
Which mortal dames have scarce obtained.
There honoured by each pious sage
Who dwelt within the hermitage,
Beside his darling well content
That sacred night the hero spent.
    The princes, when the night had fled,

Farewell to all the hermits said,
Who gazed upon the distant shade,
Their lustral rites and offerings paid
The saints who made their dwelling there
In words like these addressed the pair:
'O Princes, monsters fierce and fell
Around that distant forest dwell:
On blood from human veins they feed,
And various forms assume at need,
With savage beasts of fearful power
That human flesh and blood devour.
Our holy saints they rend and tear
When met alone or unaware,
And eat them in their cruel joy:
These chase, O Ráma, or destroy.
By this one path our hermits go
To fetch the fruits that yonder grow:
By this O Prince, thy feet should stray
Through pathless forests far away'

    Thus by the reverent saints addressed,
And by their prayers auspicious blessed,
    He left the holy crowd:
His wife and brother by his side,
Within the mighty wood he hied.
So sinks the Day-God in his pride
    Beneath a bank of cloud.

ADDITIONAL NOTES.

ADDITIONAL NOTES.

PAGE 4.

Śaivya, a king whom earth obeyed,
Once to a hawk a promise made.

The following is a free version of this very ancient
story which occurs more than once in the *Mahábhárat :*

THE SUPPLIANT DOVE.

Chased by a hawk there came a dove
   With worn and weary wing,
And took her stand upon the hand
   Of Káśí's mighty king.
The monarch smoothed her ruffled plumes
   And laid her on his breast,
And cried, ' No fear shall vex thee here,
   Rest, pretty egg-born, rest !
Fair Káśí's realm is rich and wide,
   With golden harvests gay,
But all that's mine will I resign
   Ere I my guest betray'.
But panting for his half won spoil
   The hawk was close behind,
And with wild cry and eager eye
   Came swooping down the wind :
' This bird', he cried, ' my destined prize,
   'Tis not for thee to shield :
'Tis mine by right and toilsome flight.
   O'er hill and dale and field.
Hunger and thirst oppress me sore,
   And I am faint with toil :

Thou shouldst not stay a bird of prey
    Who claims his rightful spoil.
They say thou art a glorious king,
    And justice is thy care :
Then justly reign in thy domain,
    Nor rob the birds of air'.
Then cried the king : 'A cow or deer
    For thee shall straightway bleed,
Or let a ram or tender lamb
    Be slain, for thee to feed.
Mine oath forbids me to betray
    My little twice-born guest :
See how she clings with trembling wings
    To her protector's breast.'
' No flesh of lambs, the hawk replied,
    ' No blood of deer for me ;
The falcon loves to feed on doves,
    And such is Heaven's decree.
But if affection for the dove
    Thy pitying heart has stirred,
Let thine own flesh my maw refresh,
    Weighed down against the bird.'
He carved the flesh from off his side,
    And threw it in the scale,
While women's cries smote on the skies
    With loud lament and wail.
He hacked the flesh from side and arm,
    From chest and back and thigh,
But still above the little dove
    The monarch's scale stood high.
He heaped the scale with piles of flesh,
    With sinews, blood, and skin,
And when alone was left him bone
    He threw himself therein.

Then thundered voices through the air ;
    The sky grew black as night ;
And fever took the earth that shook
    To see that wondrous sight.
The blessed Gods, from every sphere,
    By Indra led, came nigh ;
While drum and flute and shell and lute
    Made music in the sky.
They rained immortal chaplets down,
    Which hands celestial twine,
And softly shed upon his head
    Pure Amrit, drink divine.
Then God and Seraph, Bard and Nymph
    Their heavenly voices raised,
And a glad throng with dance and song
    The glorious monarch praised.
They set him on a golden car
    That blazed with many a gem ;
Then swiftly through the air they flew,
    And bore him home with them.
Thus Kási's lord, by noble deed,
    Won heaven and deathless fame ;
And when the weak protection seek
    From thee, do thou the same.

                Scenes from the Ramayan, &c.

PAGE 12.

The twice-born chiefs, with zealous heed,
Made ready what the rite would need.

PAGE 7.

The ceremonies that attended the consecration of a king (*Abhikshepa, lit. Sprinkling over*) are fully described in Goldstücker's Dictionary, from which the following extract is made: 'The type of the inauguration ceremo-

ny as practised at the Epic period may probably be
recognized in the history of the inauguration of *Ráma*,
as told in the *Rámáyana*, and in that of the inauguration
of *Yudhishṭhira*, as told in the *Mahábhárata*. Neither
ceremony is described in these poems with the full detail
which is given of the vaidik rite in the *Aitareya-Bráh-
manam*; but the allusion that Ráma was inaugurated by
Vaśishṭha and the other Bráhmaṇas in the same manner
as Indra by the Vasus ...... and the observation which
is made in some passages that a certain rite of the inauguration was performed 'according to the sacred
rule'.........admit of the conclusion that the ceremony
was supposed to have taken place in comformity with
the vaidik injunction ...... As the inauguration of *Ráma*
was intended and the necessary preparations for it were
made when his father Daśaratha was still alive, but as
the ceremony itself, through the intrigues of his step mother *Kaikeyí*, did not take place then, but fourteen years
later, after the death of *Daśaratha*, an account of the
preparatory ceremonies is given in the *Ayodhyákáṇḍa*
(Book II) as well as in the *Yuddha-Káṇḍa* (Book VI.)
of the Rámáyaṇa, but an account of the complete ceremony in the latter book alone. According to the
Ayodhyákáṇḍa, on the day preceding the intended
inauguration *Ráma* and his wife *Sítá* held a fast, and in
the night they performed this preliminary rite: *Ráma*
having made his ablutions, approached the idol of
Náráyaṇa, took a cup of clarified butter, as the religious law prescribes, made a libation of it into the
kindled fire, and drank the remainder while wishing
what was agreeable to his heart. Then, with his mind
fixed on the divinity, he lay, silent and composed,
together with *Sítá*, on a bed of Kuśa-grass, which
was spread before the altar of Vishṇu, until the last

watch of the night, when he awoke and ordered the
palace to be prepared for the solemnity. At day-break
reminded of the time by the voices of the bards, he
performed the usual morning devotion and praised the
divinity. In the meantime the town Ayodhyá had
assumed a festive appearance and the inauguration
implements had been arranged .... golden water-
jars, an ornamented throne-seat, a chariot covered
with a splendid tiger-skin, water taken from the confluence of the Ganges and Jumna, as well as from
other sacred rivers, tanks, wells, lakes, and from all
oceans, honey, curd, clarified butter, fried grain,
Kuśa-grass, flowers, milk ; besides, eight beautiful
damsels, and a splendid furious elephant; golden and
silver jars, filled with water, covered with *Udumbara*
branches and various lotus flowers, besides a white
jewelled *chourie*, a white splendid parasol, a white bull,
a white horse, all manner of musical instruments and
bards...... In the preceding chapter. ... there are
mentioned *two* white *chouries* instead of one, and all
kinds of seeds, perfumes and jewels, a scimitar, a bow,
a litter, a golden vase, and a blazing fire, and
amongst the living implements of the pageant, instead
of the bards, gaudy courtesans, and besides the eight
damsels, professors of divinity, Bráhmaṇas, cows and
pure kinds of wild beasts and birds, the chiefs of
town and country-people and the citizens with their
train.'

PAGE 12.

Then with the royal chaplains they
Took each his place in long array.

'Now about the office of a Purohita (house-priest).
The gods do not eat the food offered by a king, who has
no house-priest (Purohita). Thence the king even when

(not) intending to bring a sacrifice, should appoint a Bráhman to the office of house-priest.' HAUG'S *Aitareya Bráhmaṇam. Vol. II. p. 528.*

PAGE 15.

There by the gate the Sáras screamed.

The Sáras or Indian Crane is a magnificent bird, easily domesticated and speedily constituting himself the watchman of his master's house and garden. Unfortunately he soon becomes a troublesome and even dangerous dependent, attacking strangers with his long bill and powerful wings, and warring especially upon 'small infantry' with unrelenting ferocity.

PAGE 53.

My mothers or my sire the king.

All the wives of the king his father are regarded and spoken of by Ráma as his mothers.

PAGE 70.

Such blessings as the Gods o'erjoyed
Poured forth when Vritra was destroyed.

'Mythology regards Vritra as a demon or Asur, the implacable enemy of India, but this is not the primitive idea contained in the name of Vritra. In the hymns of the Veda Vritra appears to be the thick dark cloud which Indra the God of the firmament attacks and disperses with his thunderbolt.'　GORRESIO.

'In that class of Rig-veda hymns which there is reason to look upon as the oldest portion of Vedic poetry, the character of Indra is that of a mighty ruler of the firmament, and his principal feat is that of conquering the demon *Vritra*, a symbolical personification of the cloud which obstructs the clearness of the sky, and withholds the fructifying rain from the earth. In his battles with Vritra he is therefore described as 'opening the receptacles of the waters,' as 'cleaving the cloud' with his 'far-whirling thunderbolt,' as 'casting the waters down to earth,' and 'restoring the sun to the sky.' He is in consequence 'the upholder of heaven, earth, and firmament,' and the god 'who has engendered the sun and the dawn.'

CHAMBERS'S CYCLOPÆDIA. *Indra.*

'Throughout these hymns two images stand out before us with overpowering distinctness   On one side is the bright god of the heaven, as beneficent as he is irresistible ; on the other the demon of night and of darkness, as false and treacherous as he is malignant... The latter (as his name Vritra, from var, to veil, indicates) is pre-eminently the thief who hides away the rain-clouds.........But the myth is yet in too early a state to allow of the definite designations which are brought before us in the conflicts of Zeus with Typhôn and his monstrous progeny, of Apollôn with the Pythôn, of Bellerophôn with Chimaira, of Oidipous with the Sphinx, of Hercules with Cacus, of Sigurd with the dragon Fafnir ; and thus not only is Vritra known by many names, but he is opposed sometimes by India, sometimes by Agni the fire-god, sometimes by Trita, Brihaspati, or other deities ; or rather these are all names of one and the same god :

πολλῶν ὀνομάτων μορφὴ μία.

Cox's *Mythology of the Aryan Nations.* *Vol. II. p.* 326.

PAGE 71.

And that prized herb whose sovereign power
Preserves from dark misfortune's hour.

'And yet more med'cinal is it than that Moly,
That Hermes once to wise Ulysses gave,

He called it Harmony, and gave it me,
And bade me keep it as of sovereign use
' Gainst all enchantment, mildew, blast, or damp,
Or ghastly furies' apparition.' *Comus.*

The *Moly* of Homer, which Dierbach considers to have been the *Mandrake*, is probably a corruption of the Sanskrit *Múla* a root.

PAGE 116.

True is the ancient saw the Neem
Can ne'er distil a honeyed stream.

The Neem tree, especially in the Rains, emits a strong unpleasant smell like that of onions. Its leaves however make an excellent cooling poultice, and the Extract of Neem is an admirable remedy for cutaneous disorders.

PAGE 178.

Who of Nishádá lineage came.

The following account of the origin of the Nishádas is taken from Wilson's *Vishnu Puràna*, Book 1. Chap. 15. ' Afterwards the Munis beheld a great dust arise, and they said to the people who were nigh : " What is this ?" And the people answered and said : " Now that the kingdom is without a king, the dishonest men have begun to seize the property of their neighbours. The great dust that you behold, excellent Munis, is raised by troops of clustering robbers, hastening to fall upon their prey". The sages, hearing this, consulted, and together rubbed the thigh of the king (Vena), who had left no offspring, to produce a son. From the thigh, thus rubbed, came forth a being of the complexion of a charred stake, with flattened features (like a negro), and of dwarfish stature. " What am I to do", cried he eagerly to the Munis.

" Sit down (nishída)," said they. And thence his name was Nisháda. His descendants, the inhabitants of the. Vindhyá mountain, great Muni, are still called Nishádas,, and are characterized by the exterior tokens of depravity.' Professor Wilson adds, in his note on the passage : ' The Matsya says that there were born outcast or barbarous races, Mlechchhas, as black as collyrium. The Bhágavata describes an individual of dwarfish stature, with short arms and legs, of a complexion as black as a crow, with projecting chin, broad flat nose, red eyes, and tawny hair, whose descendants were mountaineers and foresters. The Padma (Bhúmi Khanda) has a similar description ; adding to the dwarfish stature and black complexion, a wide mouth, large ears, and a protuberant belly. It also particularizes his posterity as Nishádas, Kirátas, Bhillas, and other barbarians and Mlechchhas, living in woods and on mountains. These passages intend, and do not much exaggerate, the uncouth appearance of the Gonds, Koles, Bhils, and other uncivilized tribes, scattered along the forests and mountains of central India from Behar to Khandesh, and who are, not improbably, the predecessors of the present occupants of the cultivated portions of the country. They are always very black, ill-shapen, and dwarfish, and have countenances of a very African character.'

Manu gives a different origin of the Nishádas as the offspring of a Bráhman father and a Súdra mother. See Muir's *Sanskrit Texts*, Vol. I. P. 481.

PAGE 195.

Beneath a fig-tree's mighty shade,
With countless pendent shoots displayed.

' So counselled he, and both together went
Into the thickest wood ; there soon they chose .

The fig-tee : not that kind for fruit renowned,
But such as at this day, to Indians known,
In Malabar or Deccan spreads her arms
Branching so broad and long, that in the ground
The bended twigs take root, and daughters grow
About the mother tree, a pillared shade
High overarched, and echoing walks between.'

Paradise Lost, Book IX.

Page 213.

Now, Lakshman, as our cot is made,
Must sacrifice be duly paid.

The rites performed in India on the completion of a
house are represented in modern Europe by the familiar
'house-warming.'

Page 243.

I longed with all my lawless will
Some elephant by night to kill.

One of the regal or military caste was forbidden to
kill an elephant except in battle.

Page 246.

Thy hand has made no Bráhman bleed.

'The punishment which the Code of Manu awards to
the slayer of a Brahman was to be branded in the forehead with the mark of a headless corpse, and entirely
banished from society; this being apparently commut-
able for a fine. The poem is therefore in accordance
with the Code regarding the peculiar guilt of killing
Brahmans; but in allowing a hermit who was not a
Dwija (twice-born) to go to heaven, the poem is far in
advance of the Code. The youth in the poem is allowed to read the Veda, and to accumulate merit by his
own as well as his father's pious acts; whereas the ex-
clusive Code reserves all such privileges to *Dwijas*, in-

vested with the sacred cord.' Mrs. SPEIR's *Life in Ancient India*, p. 107.

PAGE 264.

THE PRAISE OF KINGS.

'Compare this magnificent eulogium of kings and kingly government with what Samuel says of the king and his authority: And Samuel told all the words of the LORD unto the people that asked of him a king.

And he said, This will be the manner of the king that shall reign over you : He will take your sons, and appoint them for himself, for his chariots, and to be his horsemen ; and some shall run before his chariots.

And he will appoint him captains over thousands, and captains over fifties, and will set them to ear his ground, and to reap his harvest, and to make his instruments of war, and instruments of his chariots.

And he will take your daughters to be confectionaries, and to be cooks , and to be bakers.

And he will take your fields, and your vineyards, and your oliveyards, even the best of them, and give them to his servants.

And he will take the tenth of your seed, and of your vineyards, and give to his officers, and to his servants.

And he will take your menservants, and your maidservants, and your goodliest young men, and your asses, and put them to his work.

He will take the tenth of your sheep: and ye shall be his servants.

And ye shall cry out in that day because of your king which ye shall have chosen you.

I. Samuel. VIII.

In India kingly government was ancient and consecrated by tradition; whence to change it seemed disorderly and revolutionary: in Judæa theocracy was ancient and consecrated by tradition, and therefore the innovation which would substitute a king was represented as full of dangers.'

GORRESIO.

PAGE 271.

ŚÁLMALÍ.

According to the Bengal recension Śálmalí appears to have been another name of the Vipásá. Śálmalí may be an epithet signifying rich in Bombax heptaphyllon. The commentator makes another river out of the word.

PAGE 280.

BHARAT'S RETURN.

'Two routes from Ayodhvá to Rájagriha or Girivraja are described. That taken by the envoys appears to have been the shorter one, and we are not told why Bharat returned by a different road. The capital of the Kekayas lay to the west of the Vipásá. Between it and the Satadrú stretched the country of the Báhíkas. Upon the remaining portion of the road the two recensions differ. According to that of Bengal there follow towards the east the river Indamatí, then the town Ajakála belonging to the Bodhi, then Bhúlingá, then the river Śaradandá. According to the other instead of the first river comes the Ikshumatí ...... instead of the first town Abhikála, instead of the second Kulingá, then the second river. According to the direction of the route both the above-mentioned rivers must be tributaries of the Śatadrú ...... The road

then crossed the Yamuná (Jumna), led beyond that
river through the country of the Panchálas, and reached
the Ganges at Hástinapura, where the ferry was.
Thence it led over the Rámagangá and its eastern
tributaries, then over the Gomatí, and then in a
southern direction along the Málini, beyond which
it reached Ayodhyá In Bharat's journey the
following rivers are passed from west to east: *Kuṭi-
koshṭuká, Uttániká, Kuṭiká, Kapivaṭí, Gomatí* according to Schlegel, and *Hiranyavatí, Uttáriká, Kuṭilá,
Kapívatí, Gomatí* according to Goriesio As these rivers are to be looked for on the east of the Ganges, the
first must be the modern *Koh,* a small affluent of the
Rámagangá, over which the highway cannot have gone
as it bends too far to the north. The Uttániká or
Uttáriká must be the Rámagangá, the Kuṭiká or Kuṭilá its eastern tributary Kośilá, the Kapívatí the next
tributary which on the maps has different names, *Gurra*
or above Kailas, lower down *Bhaigu.* The Gomatí
(Goomtee) retains its old name. The Málini, mentioned
only in the envoys' journey, must have been the western
tributary of the Sarayú now called Chuká.' LASSEN'S
Indische Alterthumskunde., Vol. II. p. 524.

PAGE 296.

What worlds await thee, Queen, for this ?

'Indian belief divided the universe into several worlds
(lokáh). The three principal worlds were heaven, earth,
and hell But according to another division there were
seven : Bhúrloka or the earth, Bhuvarloka or the space
between the earth and the sun, the seat of the Munis,
Siddhas &c, Svarloka or the heaven of India between
the sun and the polar star, and the seventh Brahmaloka
or the world of Brahma. Spirits which reached the
last were exempt from being born again.' GORRESIO.

F F

PAGE 378.

When from a million herbs a blaze
Of their own luminous glory plays.

This mention of lambent flames emitted by herbs at night may be compared with Lucan's description of a similar phenomenon in the Druidical forest near Marseilles, *(Pharsalia, III.* 420*)*.

Non ardentis fulgere incendia silvae.

Seneca, speaking of Argolis, (Thyestes, Act IV), says :—

Tota solet
Micare flamma silva, et excelsae trabes
Ardent sine igni.

Thus also the bush at Horeb (Exod. II.) flamed, but was not consumed.

The Indian explanation of the phenomenon is, that the sun before he sets deposits his rays for the night with the deciduous plants.

See Journal of R. As. S. Bengal. Vol. II. p. 339.

PAGE 440.

We rank the Buddhist with the thief.

Schlegel says in his Preface : ' Lubrico vestigio insistit V. Cl. *Heerenius, prof. Gottingensis,* in libro suo de commerciis veterum populorum (OPP. Vol. HIST. XII, pag. 129,) dum putat, ex mentione sectatorum Buddhae secundo libro Ram eidos iniecta de tempore, quo totum carmen sit conditum, quicquam legitime concludi posse .... Sunt versus spurii, reiecti a Bengalis in sola commentatorum recensione leguntur. Buddhas quidem mille fere annis ante Christum natum. vixit : sed post multa demum secula, odio internecivo inter Brachmanos et Buddhae sectatores orto, his denique ex India pulsis, fingi

potuit iniquissima criminatio, eos animi immortalitatem
poenasque et praemia in vita futura negare. Praeterea
metrum, quo concinnati sunt hi versus, de quo metro
mox disseram, recentiorem actatem arguit.................
...... Poenitet me nunc mei consilii, quod non statim
ab initio,......eiecerim cuncta disticha diversis a sloco
vulgari metris composita. Metra sunt duo: pariter
ambo constant quatuor hemistichiis inter se acqualibus,
alterum undenarum syllabarum, alterum duodenarum,
hunc in modum :

$$\cup - \cup - \mid - \cup \cup - \mid \cup - \bar{\cup}$$
$$\cup - \cup - \mid - \cup \cup - \mid \cup - \cup \bar{\cup}$$

Cuius generis versus in primo et secundo Rameidos
libro nusquam nisi ad finem capitum apposita inveni-
untur, et huic loco unice sunt accommodata, quasi
peroratio, lyricis numeris assurgens, quo magis canorae
cadant clausulae : sicut musici in concentibus extre-
mis omnium vocum instrumentorumque ictu fortiore
aures percellere amant. Igitur disticha illa non ante
divisionem per capita illatam addi potuerunt : hanc
autem grammaticis deberi argumento est ipse recensio-
num dissensus, manifesto inde ortus, quod singuli edi-
tores in ea constituenda suo quisque iu licio usi sunt ;
praeterquam quol non credibile est, poetam artis suae
peritum narrationem continuam in membra tam minuta
dissecuisse. Porro discolor est dictio : magniloquentia
affectatur, sed nimis turgida illa atque effusa, nec sen-
tentiarum pondere satis suffulta. Denique nihil fere
novi affertur : amplificantur prius dicta, rarius aliquid
ex capite sequente anticipatur. Si quis appendices
hosce legendo transiliat, sentiet slocum ultimum cum
primo capitis proximi apte coagmentatum, nec sine
quadam inde aversum. Eiusmodi versus exhibet utrumque
recensio, sed modo haec modo illa plures paucioresve
numero, et lectio interdum maguopere variat'.

INDEX OF PRINCIPAL NAMES.

INDEX.